Endorsements for
Talmadge Farm

Leo Daughtry's story gives readers a cast of flawed characters that elicit sympathy, anger, love, and hate. A page turner.

— George Kolber
author of *Thrown Upon the World*,
and writer/producer of *Miranda's Victim*

In this generational drama set in the 1950s and 60s, the moral failings of a prominent businessman in North Carolina sow the seeds of his own destruction. At the heart of the novel is a thoughtful meditation on the inexorability of change, and what happens when justice results in a redistribution of success.

— *Kirkus Reviews*

Talmadge Farm is a classic. Through the lives of a farm owner's family and their sharecropping tenants, Leo Daughtry weaves a story of triumph and tragedy, of good and evil, and finally reconciliation. A true morality play.

— Gene Hoots
former tobacco executive and
author of *Going Down Tobacco Road*

TALMADGE
FARM

Leo Daughtry

Talmadge Farm

Copyright © 2024 by Leo Daughtry

ISBN: 978-1-970157-43-7

Story Merchant Books
400 S. Burnside Avenue #11B
Los Angeles, CA 90036
www.storymerchantbooks.com

Book Interior and E-book Design by Amit Dey
amitdey2528@gmail.com

To my parents, Namon and Catholeen, whose love
and belief in me nourished and sustained me.
They are the foundation of any achievements
I have accomplished in life.

"Let us not forget that the cultivation of the earth is the most important labor of man. When tillage begins, other arts will follow. The farmers, therefore, are the founders of civilization."

Daniel Webster

ONE

Dove hunting is religion in the South. Hard to know who feels more ecstasy—the men or the retrievers straining on their leashes.

Gordon Talmadge was especially eager for this year's hunt. As host, he relished entertaining the movers and shakers of eastern North Carolina. But this year he also wanted to show off his new Winchester 21, an American beauty he acquired on special order from a gun store in Raleigh. The custom engraving took an extra six months, but it was worth the wait.

He polished it one last time as the help bustled about Talmadge Farm, setting up tents and monitoring the hogs roasting over the pits. Even though it was still early, the air was thick with humidity. Claire joined him on the back porch, lighting a cigarette. "You're up early," she said to her husband. "Ivy's got things under control in the kitchen. Everything coming together out here?"

"I just came back from the field. I wanted to make sure Louis and Will put out enough sunflower seeds."

Claire laughed. "Isn't that illegal? And cheating? Shouldn't you give the doves a fighting chance?"

"Not on your life," he said with a wink. "Besides, when the game warden is your guest, you don't worry about the law. Remember last year? The rain threw off the doves' migration pattern, and we didn't get many birds. I aim to make sure it's a better year."

1

Claire took a long drag. She knew that whatever Gordon aimed for, he usually got.

At noon sharp, the hunters began to arrive. Gordon greeted each guest with a handshake and acquainted newcomers with old-timers. As the dogs barked in anticipation, the men preened over their shotguns, showing off L.C. Smiths handed down for generations and the occasional Parker heirloom. Gordon was proud he had the only Winchester, a true one-of-a-kind.

Once everyone arrived, Gordon led the half-mile procession towards the cornfield with Buster, his black Lab, and the other dogs following closely behind. Louis Sanders and Will Craddock, Talmadge Farm's sharecroppers, ferried guests who didn't want to walk back and forth in flat-bed pickup trucks.

As they arrived at the field, Gordon assigned positions around the perimeter. As usual, he took the prime spot in the southeast corner. He knew the birds' habit of alighting along the power line that ran down the eastern side of the field. He put his most important tobacco buyers on one side of him. On the other side, he put the mayor of Hobbsfield, Lew Dail, and his old friend Bill Barfield, a doctor from Raleigh who owned ten percent of the stock in Gordon's bank.

The Talmadge boys, Gordon Junior and David, staked out a spot down the hill under a pine tree. Gordon wandered over to check on them. "You two ready to get some birds?"

"Can't wait," said sixteen-year-old Junior. He practiced his aim, bringing Gordon's beloved L.C. Smith up to his eye. "This gun feels like it was made for my hands."

David swatted a mosquito and wiped the sweat off his glasses. At fourteen, this was his first dove hunt. He picked up the Beretta his father had given him and copied his brother's motions. "It's too heavy," he grumbled. "It'll backfire too hard."

"C'mon, son, man up," Gordon said. "Remember, let the birds come to you and aim three feet in front of them." Gordon patted his son on the back. "Do it just like we practiced, and you'll be fine."

As Gordon looked around to make sure all the hunters were in place, he took a moment to admire his property. Over the years, his family had amassed more than eighteen hundred acres. At the center was the Talmadge mansion—the crown jewel of Hobbsfield—built in 1880 by Gordon's grandfather, Proctor Talmadge. The brick house boasted stately columns, arched windows, and a wraparound front porch shaded by towering oaks. Vast woods held trees that were harvested and sold to furniture companies. Prized Polled Hereford cattle roamed the pastures on the northern end until they were sold to market. On the eastern side near the driveway, ninety acres were dedicated to tobacco.

"Boys, just think, someday all this will be yours. It's your legacy."

At one o'clock, silence descended over the field as the hunters lay in wait. At first, it seemed the birds, too, were paralyzed by the heat. But soon enough, the seed beckoned, and flights of doves began to make their way toward the field. The crack of shotguns pierced the sky followed by the ping of pellets raining on the nearby tractor shed. Whenever a dove plummeted to the ground, a hunter led his dog to the area, and the dog sniffed it out from the camouflage of the field, picked it up with a soft mouth, and reluctantly turned it over to his master.

Gordon was frustrated to miss his first few shots. Bill Barfield cackled. "I know you're proud of that new gun of yours, Gordon. But you can't shoot it worth a damn." Deep in concentration, Gordon ignored him until he began to understand the nuances of the gun. He connected with his next six shots, then fired off a double.

"Now she's working for me," he said. "Guns are like women, Bill. No two are the same. Give me enough time, and I can figure out how they like to be handled. Sorry you don't have the same luck, pal."

Claire tucked in a few loose strands of hair and dabbed on more face powder. She knew her makeup wouldn't stand a chance against the unrelenting humidity. She applied more hairspray to her chignon and walked over to the bed where she'd laid out the mint-green dress from Montaldo's she bought when she accompanied Gordon to a bank conference in Raleigh last month.

It had been a special evening. They'd had dinner with the Barfields and stayed overnight at the elegant Velvet Cloak Inn. Claire wished Gordon would take her to Raleigh more often, especially now that the boys were teenagers, but he always came up with an excuse about meetings or golf and how he'd be too busy to pay attention to her.

She briefly thought about what else might be keeping him busy in Raleigh. She often noticed a faint whiff of perfume—always a different scent—emanating from Gordon's clothing when he returned home. She'd almost asked him about it once but hadn't finished the question. She couldn't bear the idea of watching him fumble around for an answer.

The sound of shots in the distance interrupted her thoughts. The hunters would be making their way back to the house before long. She slipped into her dress, stepped into her heels, and went down to the kitchen to check on Ivy.

At five-thirty the bell rang calling the hunters to the barbecue. The men gathered their buckets together for the final count: one hundred thirty-eight birds total—nearly twice last year's take. Gordon congratulated everyone. "Don't forget, we'll put together a package of dove breasts for everybody to take home."

Gordon climbed into Will's truck for a ride back to the house. For the barbecue, large tents had been erected on the front lawn to accommodate two hundred guests. As the truck approached the house, Gordon could see guests milling about on the veranda, smoking cigarettes and enjoying iced tea, lemonade, and bourbon. "Faster, Will. I need to get changed."

Will mumbled an apology, but Gordon had already hopped out of the truck and up the front steps.

"Mr. Talmadge, you forgot your gun." Will picked up the Winchester, taking a moment to feel the smooth walnut in his hands.

Gordon stormed back to the truck and snatched it from him. "Give me that. I don't want it getting dirty."

Will scowled as he headed back to the cornfield. Sometimes he felt like blowing Mr. Talmadge's head off. As one of the two sharecroppers on Talmadge Farm, he was expected to work all day at the annual dove hunt and barbecue. But the son-of-a-bitch treated him no better than Louis Sanders, even though he was white and Louis was black and that alone should have set them apart.

As he passed his cabin, he saw Mary Grace come out the front door. He pulled up beside her.

"I thought you were in the kitchen helping Ivy and Ella?"

She tucked her brown hair behind her ears, and Will thought about how much his fourteen-year-old daughter looked like her mother—same clear green eyes, same smattering of freckles on her cheeks. "I ran home to check on Kitty before we serve dinner." Mary Grace had been looking after the barn cat for years, and she was about to have kittens.

"Any kittens yet?"

"Nope. Have you seen all the fancy people up at the house?"

Will chuckled. "Hell of a spectacle, that's for sure. Those outfits look uncomfortable to me."

She smiled, and Will realized what a rare sight it was to see his daughter smile. Two years ago, Ruby, his wife, came down with an infection following her third miscarriage. The doctors tried everything, but she never recovered.

Now it was just him and Mary Grace.

"At least we'll get shrimp tonight," Mary Grace said. "Assuming the guests don't eat them all."

"I'll put some aside for you."

After Gordon put his gun away safely in the hall closet, he hurried upstairs, dropping his clothes on the bathroom floor. Lathering up in the shower, he practiced his speech in his head. He dried off and put on a freshly pressed white shirt, khaki pants, and penny loafers. Giving himself the once over in the full-length mirror, he combed his dark hair. For a man of forty-three, he told himself, he looked pretty damn good. He splashed cologne on his neck and hurried out to the join the festivities.

He found Claire on the porch mingling with guests. She looked pretty, but he wished she'd lose the twenty pounds she'd put on since David was born. She used to be the most beautiful girl in Hobbsfield. If only she'd try a little harder. At least she still had a pretty face.

He squeezed her hand. "Hi, sweetheart. Need any help?" They both knew the question was rhetorical.

"Ivy's putting the food out now, and we'll be ready to eat at six thirty. How was the hunt?"

"It was great. Although David couldn't shoot a dove if his life depended on it."

"Just because you and Junior are good at something doesn't mean David will be, too."

"Nonsense. Any son of mine needs to learn to shoot."

When Claire gave the signal, guests began piling their plates with oysters and shrimp from Topsail Island, ham biscuits from nearby Pine Level, Brunswick stew, potato salad, baked beans, and hush puppies. Ivy kept a careful watch and replenished buffet items as needed.

Will manned the barbecue station, using two cleavers to chop the tender meat swimming in tangy vinegar sauce. Near the smokehouse, Louis and his teenage son, Jake, worked methodically to clean the doves and wrap them in butcher paper.

As the last rays of sunlight disappeared from the pink sky, Gordon popped a freshly shucked oyster into his mouth and moved towards the bar set up in the corner of the tent. Carrying a glass of Jack Daniel's, he greeted the men who had stayed behind from the hunt and kissed their wives' cheeks if he knew them well enough. When he reached Bill Barfield's table, he sat down.

"This might be the biggest crowd we've ever had," Gordon said. In addition to inviting all his best bank customers, he timed the event to the mid-point of the auction when all the tobacco buyers were in town.

Bill nodded. "Nothing like a Talmadge Farm barbecue."

"That's what I like to hear."

The lights flickered off and on, signaling to the crowd that they should migrate into the dance tent. As the moon rose and the first stars appeared, the sound of frogs and crickets coming from the nearby pond made music with the warm September breeze. The Big House was lit up like an opera house before the curtain went up.

Claire watched as Gordon took one last sip of his drink and walked up to the stage where the Emblems were poised to begin the entertainment. He tapped the microphone to get everyone's attention.

"Good evening. How are you folks doing tonight?" The crowd responded with cheers and whistles, making Gordon smile proudly.

"First of all, on behalf of Farmers and Merchants Bank, I'd like to welcome everyone to the tenth annual dove hunt and barbecue at Talmadge Farm. For those of you who didn't take part in the dove hunt, we bagged a record one hundred and thirty-eight birds. The hunters must have been a lot better this year, or the birds a lot stupider." The crowd laughed, and Gordon used the opportunity to take a sip of his drink.

"I'd like to give a special welcome to our tobacco buyers who are here this evening. From Liggett, Glenn Monk. From Lorillard, Pete Dunlap. My good buddy Steve Lawrence from R.J. Reynolds, who brought in a record twenty-four birds this afternoon. And Jimmy Woodard from American, who shot exactly two birds, one with his eyes closed, and one when his gun went off accidentally."

Claire knew Gordon was just getting started. She moved over to where Junior and David were standing at the edge of the crowd near the bar. Junior fidgeted with something in his hand, and Claire realized he was holding a bottle of vodka.

"Junior, what in the world?" She took a hard look at her son, noticing his glassy eyes.

He laughed loudly. "C'mon Mom, you know Dad won't care if we have one drink."

She took the bottle from his hand. "Looks like you've had more than one." She wished Gordon would rein in Junior's behavior. She turned her gaze toward David.

"I only had a taste. I swear. Stuff's terrible."

"Let that be a lesson to you. Now help your brother back up to the house. Your father won't want him making a scene."

On stage, Gordon had gone off topic. "Those folks in Washington need to stay the hell out of our business. It's bad enough they're trying to reduce price supports and quotas for tobacco. Now they're getting involved in our schools." A Negro bartender picked up a silver shaker and rattled the ice in subtle protest.

A few in the crowd applauded, either to indicate agreement or to get Gordon off the podium. It did the trick. "Once again, we're glad you're here. Now let's get on with the party." He directed the bandleader to start the music and then leaned into the microphone one last time. "Where's my beautiful bride?"

Claire waved and made her way to the edge of the stage.

"Let's show them how it's done," Gordon said.

The band struck up a lively rendition of "Sixty Minute Man," and Claire and Gordon danced the shag in perfect time to the music. Gordon had always been a good dancer ever since he and Claire had first started dating back at Jefferson County High School. It was one of the qualities she loved about him.

"Well, my dear, I did it again," he whispered in her ear. "This is easily the social event of the season."

Once the guests had moved to the dance tent, Will went into the kitchen to take his dinner break. Ivy pointed to the counter where she'd fixed him a plate. He wiped his hands on a dishrag and sat down at the kitchen table. Mary Grace and thirteen-year-old Ella Sanders were perched together, finishing their plates of barbecue and hushpuppies and saving the shrimp for last.

"I picked out the white satiny one with the belt for me," Ella said to Mary Grace. "And the yellow one with the big blue flowers for you. Did you see it? A red-headed lady's wearing it."

"Big blue flowers? Don't be ridiculous."

"I think it would look nice on you."

"I think so too," said Will. Mary Grace scowled at both of them.

Ivy looked up from the pile of dirty dishes she was scraping. "Ella, you supposed to be working out there, not staring at all them ladies' dresses."

Jake laughed. "That's her favorite part of the dove hunt."

"I picked out one for you too, Mama, the green one Miss Claire's wearing. It's the prettiest of all."

"Stop your foolishness, child. Finish up and go get me the rest of the plates."

As Ella walked outside to the dinner tent, the band struck up a tune. She hummed along, shimmying her hips and shuffling her feet like she'd seen the guests doing on the dance floor. She was so engrossed in the music she didn't notice Junior and David Talmadge coming toward the house.

"Look at you, Ella," Junior said. "All grown up and quite the little dancer."

As he passed her, he reached out and grabbed her hand. Startled, she pulled away, but he squeezed tighter and held on. "Come inside and dance with me," he said, jerking her towards him and running his hand down her back.

"Stop it, Junior," David said. "You're drunk."

As Junior hooted with laughter, Ella quickly pulled away, wiping her hand on her apron.

As the band started its second set, Will butchered the rest of the pig, carefully taking the meat off the bone, removing the fat, disposing of the carcass, and throwing the bones to Gordon's beloved dogs. Then he had to scrape down the grates, scrub the meat block, and hose down the whole area. At ten o'clock, he carried the dirty utensils to the kitchen.

Ivy took the knives from him and put them by the sink. "You go on home. I'm almost done here. I sent the kids a while ago."

Will gave her a grateful look and ducked out of the kitchen. Pulling up to the cabin, he could see the kerosene lamp shining through the window and knew Mary Grace was waiting up for him. Sure enough, she was sitting on the porch in Ruby's worn rocking chair that he had crafted out of pine boards when Mary Grace was born.

"You didn't need to wait up."

"I know."

Will sat down in the chair beside her and took a swig from the bottle of gin he'd swiped from the bar.

Mary Grace gave him a stern look.

"Just having a sip. I think I've earned it." He took out a cigarette and lit it. "Thanks for helping out today."

"Just doing what Mama would have done."

Will started to remind Mary Grace that she didn't need to shoulder the entire burden left behind by Ruby's death. But he knew her stubbornness ran as deep as his own.

Mary Grace stood up and kissed the top of his head. "Don't stay up too late."

Will took another swig and stared into the darkness as Ruby's rocking chair slowly came to a halt, the music of the party a faint cry in the distance.

TWO

September 1957

Slivers of sunlight shimmered through the chinks in the pine boards that made up the walls of the cabin. Ivy Sanders was already awake, enjoying the tranquility of the morning. Sundays were her glory days when she felt the chains of obligation loosen. On Sundays, she only had to answer to herself and the Lord above, and she could tend to the needs of her own family instead of tending to every whim of the Talmadges.

Ivy slipped out of the three-quarters bed and headed for the outhouse, careful not to wake Louis. It was just six o'clock, but the sun was working its way up, and she knew the coolness of the dawn would soon give way to the heat of Indian summer.

As she returned to the house, Louis was starting a fire in the wood stove that leaned precariously in the corner of the kitchen. She could hear Ella and Jake stirring in the room they shared.

"Good morning, my Queen of Sheba," Louis said, leaning down to give her a peck on the lips. "Looks like a perfect day to worship the Lord."

Ivy smiled. Louis said the same thing every Sunday.

————— x)C(x —————

12

After breakfast, Louis and Jake went outside to feed the chickens while Ivy sent Ella to collect some Queen Anne's lace from the meadow along the creek below the cabin. As Ivy packed ham biscuits for lunch, she caught a glimpse of her husband and son through the cloudy window. At fifteen, Jake was getting tall like his father. He resembled him, too, except that where Louis was solid muscle, Jake was skin and bones. She watched her son gently pick up each chicken to check its feet. Last year, one of the hens had come down with a bad case of bumblefoot, and Jake was determined to keep it from happening again.

Ivy noticed Ella making her way back toward the cabin, her arms full of white blossoms. She'd grown taller as well. But unlike her soft-spoken brother, Ella was lively, chattering all the time and entertaining them with made-up stories and songs. She loved poring through Miss Claire's fashion magazines, pointing out clothes, shoes, and pocketbooks she'd buy if she had money to spend.

When they were ready for church, Louis helped Ivy into their rusty Ford truck. Jake and Ella sat on a makeshift bench in the truck's bed, the only way all four of them could ride together. As they passed the Craddocks' cabin, they waved to Will, who was smoking on the porch.

Louis lit a cigarette and rested his elbow on the rim of the open window. Jake and Ella held tight to the edge of the wood slats as the truck bumped along the driveway and out onto the main road. "Did you hear Herbert Allen's done left farming for good?" asked Louis. "Every Sunday night he drives a truck full of produce from around here all the way up to some market in Philadelphia. Then he goes to New York and buys used tires."

"Used tires?" asked Ivy.

Louis explained that up north, drivers replaced the tires on their vehicles long before the tread wore out. "Down here we drive 'til there ain't a lick of tread left. But up there, they put new ones on when the old ones are still good. Herbert buys the used ones for a dollar apiece and brings them here to recap and sell."

The truck hit another bump. "I sure do hope the road he's driving on is smoother than this one," Ivy said. "Or he's gonna be using all those recapped tires for his own truck."

"I can't imagine making that trip. Ain't never been more than twenty miles out of Hobbsfield."

"Think we could give him some of our vegetables to take up there?" asked Ivy. "You know we got more tomatoes and peas than we can say grace over."

Louis shook his head. "Mr. Talmadge might not like it."

Ivy clenched her hands around the family Bible. Why did they need Mr. Talmadge's permission? He would hardly miss a few buckets of vegetables. Ivy glanced back again to make sure Jake and Ella hadn't bounced out of the truck.

About fifty cars and trucks were already parked on the lawn of Ebenezer Baptist Church for the Sunday service. Picnic tables dotted the grassy area underneath the oak trees, and a long table was laden with food covered by dish towels to keep the flies away. With a few minutes left before the service started, the Sanders had enough time to visit the cemetery on the church grounds.

Ivy opened a small iron gate and walked toward one of the tombstones, far enough from the road to make it a tranquil spot. Bending down, Ella placed the flowers she'd picked at the small headstone that read:

PAUL SANDERS
APRIL 12, 1938 – AUGUST 19, 1953

Had their son not fallen from the topmost rung of the tobacco barn, he would be nineteen years old. It happened four years ago, but tragedy had a way of compressing time. The pain never left, no matter how many farm seasons came and went.

Louis took off his newsboy cap, worrying it around in his powerful hands. Jake and Ella stood behind their parents as other mourners passed by to pay their respects to their own loved ones. All across the cemetery lay casualties of farm accidents, war, illness, childbirth, and, if they happened to be lucky, old age.

The church bell rang signaling the start of the service. Ivy said a final prayer for Paul. Walking inside the sanctuary, she took her spot in the choir up front while Louis, Jake, and Ella found seats in the back close to the door.

The opening hymn was the familiar gospel song "Go Down, Moses." The choirmaster waved his arms as the whole congregation swayed and joined emphatically in the refrain of "Let My People Go." Ivy could feel the spirit begin to move through her as her voice lifted up to the rafters.

Pastor Rice took the podium and welcomed the packed congregation. He asked them to turn their Bibles to Exodus, then traced the story of Moses overcoming his fears and leading his people on a journey to the promised land.

As he started his sermon, he began slowly. "My brothers and sisters, we need to ask ourselves, are we listening out for God's call? Moses was a shepherd. He was not a powerful man. He did not consider himself a man of greatness. He did not seek the spotlight. Yet God called out to him, and he answered that call."

The congregation responded with a thunderous "Amen."

Pastor Rice's voice grew louder as he continued. "And even though Moses never got there, even though he spent years wandering through the wilderness, he started his people on a path in the right direction. Brothers and sisters, are you moving in the right direction? Because God has promised us that if we follow Him, if we listen to Him, if we obey Him, we will be delivered. We will get to that promised land one day."

Pastor Rice wiped the sweat from his forehead as his voice rose to a crescendo. "And when we get to the promised land, there will be no debts to pay. No chains to shackle us. No burdens to carry. As God promised in the Book of Revelation, we will no longer have to eat the stale bread of captivity but can feast with our Savior at the Great Banquet that awaits us."

"Amen," roared the congregation.

As Pastor Rice began to pray, Ivy felt a familiar wave of deliverance wash over her. This was what she waited for all week long, this sense of peace. She knew in her soul that trusting in the Lord was the only way to get through this life.

The Sanders family shook hands with Pastor Rice as they filed out of the church and onto the lawn. Ivy hummed as they wandered over to the picnic area to join their friends, Sam and Cleo Bennett. The Bennetts' son, Bobby Lee, was like a brother to Jake and Ella.

"How was the dove hunt?" asked Sam.

"Mr. Talmadge was real pleased," Louis said. "There was doves a plenty for anyone with a decent aim. And I sure did enjoy my meal once I finally got to sit down and eat. Those oysters are mighty tasty."

As the men went to fix their plates, Ella ran up to Ivy. "We're gonna walk over to the creek beside the cemetery."

"Long as you stay with Jake and Bobby Lee," Ivy said.

Ella bounded off.

Ivy turned to Cleo. "I swear I'm worried to death about that girl. You know she's always liked attention. But now . . . I don't like the way boys are looking at her. And she don't even notice."

Cleo smiled. "She's already turning out to be a beauty, that one."

"That's what worries me."

After lunch, Louis stretched out in the shade of an oak and rested his eyes. Cleo and Ivy smiled at his snoring as they gathered up the tin cups and plates they'd brought from home. "I bet you're tired too," Cleo said. "You been working like a fool to get ready for the barbecue. At least the Talmadges give you the day off after."

"Trust me, I would've had to work if today wasn't the Lord's day," Ivy said. "I'm worn out."

Ivy and Cleo put the last of the food scraps in the trash can and shook out the picnic blanket. As they settled back down on the blanket, a breeze blew a patch of clouds in front of the sun, bringing a welcome respite to the lazy heat.

"Sam's planning to take Bobby Lee to visit the Army office in Raleigh," Cleo said. "You know that boy's been talking about being a soldier since he was ten years old."

Ivy wondered if Jake was tough enough to make it in the army. He was smart, one of the top students in his class, and she wanted more for him than a life spent toiling in the fields.

As the sky turned pink, the Sanders family collected their picnic basket and prepared to leave. Louis, invigorated from his nap, challenged Jake and Ella in a foot race to the truck, the three of them laughing the whole way.

Ivy knew work was waiting on them back at the cabin: peas to shell, clothes to darn, water to collect, wood to chop. But as they drove down the dusty road toward home, she held on to the sense of contentment that surfaced every Sunday. She knew it would slip away the minute she walked into the Big House come Monday morning.

THREE

February 1958

Mary Grace handed her father a plate of ham and eggs and sat down beside him at the table.

"Let's go into town next Saturday and get you some new shoes," he said as they hurried through their breakfast.

Looking down at her sock feet, Mary Grace was disappointed to realize her father had caught on to the fact that she'd been wearing Ella's old shoes because hers had gotten too tight. She'd been waiting until the last minute to put them on.

"We should get you a new dress, too."

"Mama's old dresses are fine. Just wish I could fit into her shoes. Are you sure we have enough for new shoes? I thought you were putting every bit of extra toward the hospital bill." The year her mama died, they'd had a bad harvest, and her daddy hadn't been able to pay the doctors who tried to save her.

"I've picked up an odd job here and there. I'll have enough by then." He swallowed the last of his coffee. "Leave those dishes for later — you'll miss the bus."

Mary Grace stacked the dishes by the sink and walked back to her room to put on her shoes. "Just make sure you get Mr. Talmadge's jobs done before you take on anybody else's."

"You sound like your mama."

Once Mary Grace left for school, Will began his trek deep into the woods of Talmadge Farm, far from the prying eyes of the sawmill workers, the cattlemen, and even Mr. Talmadge, who rarely walked all the way out to where his property met the Neuse River. He was supposed to be replacing some rotten wood in the barn—one of the endless jobs Mr. Talmadge made him do in the off-season—but that could wait.

As he walked past the empty farmland covered in frost, his mind drifted back to the long summer they'd spent in the tobacco fields. Pretty soon it would be time to start the process all over again. The spring planting and hoeing wasn't so bad, especially when the weather was just beginning to turn warm. But come late June, the humidity settled in just in time for topping, suckering, and worming. He looked at his cracked fingers. Pulling off the small leaves to keep them from "sucking" the nutrients from the bigger ones created a sticky goo that was hard to get off.

Topping—breaking off the top of the stalks when they got to a certain height—was worse because it created an even thicker film that was nearly impossible to wash off. Kerosene was the only way, but it left behind a terrible smell and made the skin split and blister. Priming—harvesting the bright green tobacco leaves from the bottom of the plant to the top—led to chronic backache because it required leaning over to reach for the lowest leaves on the stalk.

Then came barning—the process of tying tobacco leaves onto sticks in bundles or "hands" and hanging them from the rafters. Ruby'd had a special knack for tying hands and used to enjoy supervising the crew of women and children who helped out during barning.

Once the leaves were strung up, he and Louis fed the fire around the clock for five or six days to cure them. The final stage was sorting the leaves according to quality and packing them in sheets to sell at the warehouse. Problem was it was Mr. Talmadge's land, so he was the one who got to sell the sheets at auction.

Will was startled to hear the sound of whistling. He looked up to see Louis coming in his direction, smiling like he always did. Will groaned and tucked his bag behind the nearest tree.

"Fancy meeting you out here," Louis said. He was carrying his shotgun with several dead squirrels tied together on a rope hanging from his belt loop.

"Looks like you had a good morning. Leave anything for me?"

Louis laughed. "You gonna be hard pressed to get anything without your gun."

Will scowled. "My stuff's back there. Just walked up here to take a leak."

"I'll leave you to it, then." Will waited to retrieve his bag until the sound of Louis's whistling faded away. He hoped Louis didn't suspect anything, although his neighbor didn't spend too much time worrying about other people's business. That was more Ivy's style. Will knew she meant well—giving them leftovers, checking on Mary Grace—but sometimes Will wished she'd just leave him and Mary Grace the hell alone.

Not that he didn't wish he could do more for his daughter. He'd once had dreams of a better life. During World War II, he enlisted in the Army, expecting to be given training in a profession that would free him from the tobacco fields. Instead, he ended up as a line cook in the mess hall. When he came home there was nothing left to do but pick up a hoe and join his father in the fields. Once his father got killed, the land became his to sharecrop.

Will didn't fool himself. He knew the system was rigged against him. No matter how good a harvest he and Louis brought in, they had to settle for what was left after Mr. Talmadge took his cut. Before

Ruby died, she'd worked the winter months at the cigarette process-ing plant in Wilson to help make ends meet.

He needed to do something during the off season to pull his fam-ily out of debt, and he didn't have the patience to work for pocket change. He'd set up his moonshine still in a sheltered area next to an underground stream that supplied crystal-clear water. With a little practice and some coaching from one of Paul Plant's most trusted men, he quickly got the hang of it. Plus, he got to keep some of the liquor for himself. Every weekend, he hid the jugs in his truck bed and delivered them to Mr. Plant behind the general store on the road into town. He knew it was illegal, but he took great pains to be careful. The hardest part of the whole operation was when he had to work in the dark of night so no one would see the smoke from the still.

He knew Mary Grace wouldn't approve of the enterprise. And there'd be hell to pay if Mr. Talmadge found out. But if he played his cards right, he could make enough money to buy Mary Grace some new shoes and some clothes of her own. That was worth the risk for sure.

FOUR

Gordon set his golf clubs in the trunk of his brand new Ford Thunderbird. He'd kept the Cadillac for family outings but the new two-seater convertible was his to enjoy. It cost him four thousand dollars with all the extras, but he wrote it off as a business expense. After all, maintaining a certain image was part of being a successful banker.

He stepped on the accelerator as he pulled out onto the main road, eventually slowing to the speed limit as he approached town so he could appreciate the sign that greeted visitors: "Welcome to Hobbsfield, the town that tobacco built."

Like many towns in North Carolina, the courthouse held the prime position in Hobbsfield's town square. Across from the courthouse was Farmers and Merchants Bank, founded by Gordon's father, Stephen Talmadge, some fifty years ago. Gordon liked to joke that from his office window he could see the innocent and the guilty make their way up the courthouse steps and that he could tell the difference by the way they walked.

Gordon parked in front of the bank in his usual spot. Grabbing his briefcase from the front seat, he strolled into the bank. He nodded to the customers cashing checks at the counter and stopped at the desk of his secretary, Diana Wood. "I'll need you to have coffee ready in the conference room for my meeting." He turned to go but then looked back at her. "Is that a new dress?"

"Yes, it is, Mr. Talmadge," Diana said. "I'll get the coffee started."

Gordon thought how lucky he was to have hired Diana fresh out of high school after his former secretary, Margaret, retired. As much as he appreciated Margaret's efficient manner, Diana sure was easy on the eyes.

Ivy was rolling out a pie crust as Claire came into the kitchen. "Morning, Miss Claire. You're up early. Where you headed off to all dressed up?"

"I've got some errands in town, and then I'm meeting a friend for lunch." Ivy handed her a cup of coffee. "Is Ella not with you today?

"She's helping her daddy in the fields. They started topping and worming this week, and Louis can't find no extra farm hands. Although sometimes I ain't sure if Ella is much of a help."

Claire smiled sympathetically. "I know farming's not her favorite."

"Ain't that the truth. You should hear her carry on about pulling off the worms." Ivy chuckled loudly. "Louis promised her she could go to the movies on Saturday with Jake if she does a good job. Maybe that'll do the trick."

"I'm surprised Jake would take Ella with him," Claire said. "Junior won't let David anywhere near him and his friends."

"Jake don't mind. He likes having Ella around even if she is his baby sister." Ivy wiped her hands on a dish towel. "Can I fix you an egg? I know you like my sausages too; there's some links over there by the stove."

"Just grapefruit today. I'm trying to lose a few pounds before our trip to the beach."

Ivy gave her a stern look. "Miss Claire, you get lightheaded when you don't eat enough."

"I know. But you know how Gordon is."

Ivy pounded the dough with the back of her hand and kept her thoughts to herself.

When Diana buzzed the intercom, Gordon buttoned his jacket and strode into the conference room.

Jerry McMahon stood up and extended his hand. "Pleasure to meet you."

"I see Diana brought you coffee," Gordon said. Opening a silver box on the credenza, he offered him a cigar.

"Thank you, but I'll pass. Doctor says it's bad for my heart."

"Suit yourself." Gordon pulled out a cigarette and lit it with the gold monogrammed lighter that had belonged to his father.

Jerry opened his briefcase and spread out several brochures and reports. "Thank you for meeting with me this morning."

"Any friend of Governor Hewitt's is a friend of mine."

Jerry launched into his sales pitch, explaining that Governor Hewitt was contacting a handful of bank executives about supporting a coalition combining the research efforts of UNC Chapel Hill, Duke, and NC State.

He explained the governor's intentions to bring research and technology into North Carolina to diversify the state economy. "We can't put all our eggs in one basket. The future of tobacco isn't as bright as it once was. Between warnings from the medical community and increased competition from overseas suppliers, we're forecasting that tobacco will take a big hit. And if the secretary of agriculture has his way, he'll do away with tobacco price supports entirely. As it is, he cut tobacco quotas last year by twenty percent."

Gordon scowled as he took a long drag of his cigarette. "Don't I know it. But there are more ways to skin a cat. We have Thomas

Davenport in our corner, and the tobacco lobby is still one of the strongest in Washington."

"But the government continues to come under fire for buying up excess tobacco. It's costing them a pretty penny."

"D-d-d-dammit, the government would never just give up on us like that." Gordon was mortified to hear himself stutter and reflexively looked up at his father's portrait on the paneled wall. "Cigarettes are some of the most highly taxed goods in the country."

Jerry laughed. "Maybe so, but I'm not here to argue government policy. What I am here to talk about is the proposed Research Triangle Park and your potential involvement in it."

"I'm listening," Gordon managed to muster, but inside, he was seething. How dare this smug son-of-a-bitch come into his office talking about the demise of tobacco farming.

"Our first efforts at funding the development hit a roadblock, but now we've come up with an idea we think will be more attractive. We're hoping for your buy-in."

"Why me?"

"We want a diverse group of bankers behind this project, and you're running one of the most successful rural banks in the state."

Gordon nodded. Maybe this fellow wasn't so bad after all.

"Our plan is to create a nonprofit entity—Research Triangle Park Foundation—that will be the umbrella for a series of for-profit subsidiaries. They'll sell limited partnership interests to various institutional investors like yourself. It will be a win-win for everyone: the state, the universities, and the companies that will come to North Carolina. And having someone like yourself on board who's not only a banker but a tobacco farmer could really help our efforts."

Jerry slid the report across the mahogany table closer to Gordon. "All the financials and details are here. The ink has barely dried."

"Who else has signed on?"

Referring to a list, Jerry read out the names of prominent banks and insurance companies as well as the state pension fund.

Gordon was impressed with Jerry's confidence but hadn't forgotten his strong words about the tobacco industry. "I'll look over your proposal, but I'm not sure this makes sense for us. Our primary clients are the farmers and small businesses in Hobbsfield who need loans and lines of credit. I'm not sure I want to give money to an organization that's betting my industry will go under."

"It's the future of our state," replied Jerry. "And remember, this would be treated as an asset on your books, not a loan."

"I promise I'll look it over."

Gordon walked Jerry to the lobby and then went back into his office. From his desk, he watched the man get into an unremarkable car and ease his way down the street. A few minutes later, he flipped through the proposal. Truth be told, he felt ill-equipped to evaluate it. He probably should share it with his treasurer and the bank board. But after all, wasn't he the one in charge? He tossed it into the bottom drawer and looked over the phone messages Diana left on his desk.

As Claire drove away from the house, she noticed the hydrangeas in full bloom, their pink and purple blossoms rising to meet the morning sun. She planned to cut some later for the dining room. Passing the tobacco fields, she caught a glimpse of Ella and Mary Grace reaching up to remove the flowers from the tops of the stalks.

At the town square, she was lucky to find a parking space right on the square. Walking into Hudson Belk, she made a mental note of the list she'd left on her night table: swim trunks and a new pair of loafers for Junior, khaki pants for David, a couple of golf shirts for Gordon to take to the beach, and maybe some new sunglasses for herself.

As she browsed the men's department, she found the items she needed and looked at a new pair of overalls for Ivy's son Jake. Gordon preferred she not get too close to the families who lived on the farm, but she had grown up watching her father—the town pharmacist—quietly help people who couldn't afford their prescribed medication. Claire knew that for sharecroppers, some years were better than others, and she could see when the farm kids had outgrown their clothes.

She wandered into the girls' department, fingering the collars and full skirts of the brightly colored summer dresses. Not for the first time, Claire wished she had a daughter. She spotted a simple yellow and white checked cotton dress that would be nice on Ella, who was growing taller and prettier every day. She decided to get it for her and wait until next time to buy something for Jake.

On her way out, she stopped at the cosmetics counter. She sank down onto the stool as Barbara, her favorite salesperson, came over. "Hi, Mrs. Talmadge. Are you looking for some new makeup?"

"Maybe just a lipstick. There was a pretty dark pink in last month's *McCall's*."

Barbara studied Claire's face. "Here, let's try this one." Barbara pulled out the sample and dabbed some on Claire's lips. "We also have some new rouge colors you might like. And you have to see the eyeshadows we got in last week. They have a hint of shimmer. The pale green would be lovely with your blue eyes."

Claire closed her eyes and relaxed under Barbara's deft touch. "There, take a look." Claire looked into the mirror, pleased by her reflection.

"I'll take it all," she told Barbara with a smile.

Breezing out of Belk, packages in tow, Claire decided to make a quick detour on her way to the country club.

Claire entered the bank and was immediately struck by the chill of the air-conditioned lobby. She spotted Diana, Gordon's secretary, coming out of his office and noticed the tight fit of her lavender dress.

She missed Margaret, who had worked for Gordon's father and then for Gordon until her retirement two years ago. Gordon called it "putting her out to pasture," a cruel comment after her years of loyal service. That was when young, beautiful Diana came into the picture, ready to "take care" of Mr. Talmadge.

"Hi Mrs. Talmadge," Diana said. "I see you've been shopping today."

"I'm here to pay a quick visit to my husband." Claire looked past her into Gordon's office, where the door was open a crack.

"Mr. Talmadge is on a call, but I'm sure he'll be glad to see you when he's finished."

Claire reluctantly sat down in one of the chairs in the lobby, trying to keep the packages from spilling over. She could hear snippets of Gordon's conversation. "If people want credit, they can come to the bank and ask for a loan, and we'll give them cash." Gordon's voice was heated. "Why in God's name would we give out plastic cards?"

Claire glanced at her watch. She needed to leave to meet Rose at the club. Finally, she got up and walked into Gordon's office just as he hung up the phone. He looked up, frowned briefly, and then peered back down at his notes. "Hey there, darling, is there something wrong at the house? I've got a lot going on today. Apparently, nobody respects the way banks do business. Or tobacco farmers either for that matter."

Smiling, Claire sat down in the chair facing his desk and waited for him to look at her. "I'm on my way to meet Rose at the club. Remember? She's in town to visit her parents?"

Gordon seemed distracted. "What? Oh, right. Well, I'm playing golf with Neil Starling this afternoon, so I may see you out there. Have a good lunch."

Claire was stung by Gordon's dismissal. As she stood up to leave, he studied her face closely. There, Claire thought, he'd finally noticed her new look.

"You should visit the ladies' room on your way out," he said. "Looks like you've got glitter on your face."

Arriving at Jefferson County Country Club, Claire hurried past the large white columns and up the front steps to the ladies' room off the lobby. As she stared into the mirror, she noticed the bags under her eyes and the wrinkles around her mouth. She took a paper towel and dabbed at the shimmery eyeshadow. She wiped off the dark pink lipstick and reapplied her usual peach color. After a final look in the mirror, she went to the dining room.

Claire found Rose seated at a table overlooking the golf course. Apologizing for being late, she explained she had gotten carried away at the makeup counter at Belk. "The salesgirl got a hold of me and now I have a bag full of stuff I'll never use."

Rose laughed. "That's what they're paid to do, isn't it." She motioned to the drinks on the table. "I ordered us each a gin and tonic. The fact that I'm spending a day without the kids is a cause for celebration."

"How are the kids?" Claire asked as she took a sip of her drink. "And Charlie?"

Like Claire, Rose had married her high school sweetheart. The two had waited until Charlie finished law school to start a family, and now they lived in a big bungalow in Raleigh with their four children.

"They're running me ragged now that school's out. Lizzie's taken to making up plays for them to act out for us in the evenings. She makes her brothers participate whether they want to or not. The other day, they needed a tree for some scene, so Penn took Charlie's hand saw and hacked off part of our boxwood in the front yard and then brought it inside. I thought Charlie would kill him but honestly, all we could do was laugh."

"Well, I've gone on long enough," Rose said as they finished the shrimp cocktail. "Tell me what's going on with you."

Claire told Rose that Junior was attending summer school to make up for his bad grade in math during the year. "He's fit to be tied over it. I warned him about not taking his schoolwork seriously, but he doesn't listen to me. All he cares about is football, and Gordon sure doesn't mind that."

"Are you still playing the piano?" Rose asked. Claire's mother taught piano lessons, and Claire had been her most accomplished student.

"Not really." Claire finished the last bite of her club sandwich. "I tried to teach the boys when they were little. David actually plays pretty well, but Junior hated it."

The waiter stopped by to offer blueberry cobbler for dessert. Claire paused and then asked for two cobblers.

"Let's treat ourselves," she said to Rose. "Although I may regret it later. How do you stay so thin? I swear sometimes I just look at food and the pounds pile on." She made a mental note to have a light dinner.

Rose laughed. "Once I get Charlie and the kids fed, I'm lucky if there's anything left. And honestly Claire, you look great."

Claire frowned. "I'm not sure my husband would agree with you."

"Does Gordon really expect you to look like you did in high school? Good Lord, that was twenty-five years ago. And the last time I saw Gordon, he was losing his hair on top and had quite a belly."

Claire realized how good it felt to laugh. "Are you sure I can't convince you and Charlie to move back to Hobbsfield?"

After lunch, Gordon went back into his office and poured a vodka from the crystal decanter on the tea caddy. He pulled out a cigarette but realized he'd left his lighter in the conference room. As he went to retrieve it, he studied his father's portrait. Stephen Talmadge had been a brilliant man, graduating at the top of his class at Chapel Hill in just three years. Returning to Hobbsfield, he borrowed money from his father to found Farmers and Merchants Bank so that towns-people wouldn't have to travel to Wilson for their banking needs. His intelligence and serious nature engendered trust among his custom-ers, and in five years he was able to pay his father back what he owed him plus interest. During the Depression, he kept the business afloat by joining forces with other local banks.

Gordon turned his attention to his own portrait. Never a top stu-dent, he had always felt like a disappointment to his father, who didn't appreciate his athletic ability and wasn't amused by his natural charm. Gordon's stutter began at the age of eight when his father demanded to know why he hadn't done well on a spelling test. Throughout his childhood, Gordon struggled to live up to his father's high standards, knowing that he was expected to take over the reins of Farmers and Merchants someday. After college, when he joined his father at the bank, he assumed he'd have years to work alongside him and learn the ropes. But then nine months after his mother died of emphysema, his father dropped dead of a heart attack. Gordon, at age twenty-six, had to figure out how to run the bank on his own. Luckily for him, the booming wartime economy combined with his father's due diligence meant that Farmers and Merchants practically ran itself, and Gordon quickly began to appreciate the perks the role afforded him.

Back at his desk, Gordon swallowed the last of his drink and lit his cigarette. At one o'clock, Diana buzzed the intercom and told him Whit Bethune had arrived from Charlotte. Gordon tossed the sheet of paper he'd been doodling on into the trash can.

A former tobacco farmer, Whit Bethune invented a heating sys-tem for tobacco barns that was slowly replacing the old-fashioned wood-guzzling outdoor furnaces. Fueled by liquid gas or oil, the Gas-tobac burner had a thermostat that controlled the temperature dur-ing the flue-curing stage, eliminating the need for constant tending that the older system demanded. Recognizing the benefits, tobacco farmers all over the South were slowly converting to the new system. Gordon was planning to have one installed at the farm this fall once the auction was over.

Gordon decided to bring Whit back to his office rather than have the meeting in the conference room. He felt more in command sitting behind his desk away from the stern gaze of his father.

Whit settled into the leather chair across from Gordon and explained that he was looking for a line of credit to expand production of the Gastobac. "I've talked with some of the banks in Charlotte, but I'd like to see what you can do for me. Your daddy and mine go way back, and we trust one another, right?"

Gordon nodded. "How much are we talking about?"

Whit shifted into salesman mode. "Demand is through the roof. We can barely keep up with the orders so we're looking at ways to speed up manufacturing by buying supplies in bulk. We're also looking to diversify our product line. The technology can be used in poultry heating, home space heaters—the possibilities are endless."

There was that word again, Gordon thought. *Diversification.*

"Why would you bother finding other ways to use the technology if there's so much demand from tobacco farmers?" Gordon asked.

"It's good to hedge your bets," Whit said. "There may come a day when the feds do away with price supports."

"That's a long way off if I have anything to say about it." Gordon lit another cigarette and offered one to Whit. "How much are you looking for?"

Clearing his throat, Whit explained that he was seeking a two hundred thousand dollar line of credit. "We don't want to have to sell off a piece of the business, and we certainly don't want to take out a long-term loan. So, a line of credit is our most prudent option. We've already got orders from all the top farms in the state. We're just waiting for you to pull the trigger so we can ship one to you."

Gordon smiled vainly and tried not to look as impressed as he was. It would be a feather in his cap to land Whit as a client of the bank—something he could brag about to the board.

The two men negotiated a rate and finally settled on two points over prime. Whit opened his briefcase and handed Gordon a manila folder. "Here's a copy of our balance sheet, revenue and expense projections, and a letter from our accountant."

Gordon gave it a once-over. "We'll go over everything in detail, of course. But if there are no surprises, we have a deal."

Whit stumped out his cigarette and stood up to shake Gordon's hand. "Is that beauty sitting outside yours?"

"You mean my secretary, Diana?" Gordon laughed at his own joke. Not that he didn't fantasize daily about Diana, but he'd never do that to Claire; he only dabbled when he was out of town.

Whit slapped his leg. "You haven't changed a bit, Gordon. I was referring to the Thunderbird parked out front."

"It is. Do you want to take a spin? I have a few minutes to spare before my tee time."

"You bet."

Gordon grabbed his car keys and the two men strode through the bank. "See you tomorrow, Diana."

As Claire passed the fields on her way home, she saw Ivy working alongside Louis, Jake, and Ella. She waved at them but they didn't see her. Ivy must have finished up in the house. Claire had rather hoped Ivy would still be there when she got home. She parked the car and noticed the hydrangea blossoms had wilted in the afternoon sun.

Claire walked into the stillness of the house and put her keys in the basket by the door. Ivy had left a casserole ready to go in the oven and a pot of beans simmering on the stove. A fresh strawberry pie was cooling on the sideboard. Claire absentmindedly cut a sliver and ate it over the sink.

She moved into the living room and sat down at her beloved piano, where she played the opening bars of a Beethoven sonata that was one of her mother's favorites. As she played, her fingers began to take on a life of their own, expertly finding the notes as the sonata quickened and heightened. Claire lost herself in the music, aware of nothing but the intricacy of the piece, striking each chord with precision until she hit the finishing note with a flourish. She looked up triumphantly, flushed from the effort, and saw nothing but empty chairs around her.

FIVE

October 1958

M ary Grace hustled down the driveway just in time to glimpse the
  bus up ahead pulling away from the stop.

"Crickets," she yelled. She shouldn't have tried to get the wash on
the line this morning. It just seemed like since school started back, she
could never catch up on housework. Her dad used to pitch in more,
but these days he was always out hunting in the woods, sometimes
even in the middle of the night; he'd found someone willing to pay
good money for squirrel and rabbit pelts. And while the extra income
made things easier, she didn't like how her dad now spent many a
Friday night sipping moonshine from a mason jar and then lying in
bed all day Saturday complaining of a headache.

She'd have to see if Mrs. Baker would let her take the geometry
test during lunch, since she'd never make it to school on time now.
She kicked a rock into the grass and started down the muddy road in
the direction of Jefferson County High School.

She heard a car coming up behind her and moved over so it could
pass. The car drove past her and then slowed to a stop, and she realized it was the Talmadge boys. David Talmadge rolled down the window of the passenger seat. "Want a ride?"

Mary Grace hesitated. She usually kept her distance from them,
especially Junior, who ran with a fast crowd. But she thought of her

geometry test and, with a huff, got in the car. "Thanks. I lost track of time and missed the bus." As Junior sped down the road, Mary Grace noticed David's math book. "You ready for the test?"

"Not really. I didn't finish the homework. Can't seem to get the hang of it."

She leaned forward to get a closer look at David's notes. "The way I remember it is . . ." The car hit a bump and Mary Grace's head hit the ceiling.

"Here, let me climb in the back with you," David said. He got one leg up over the seat, but then Junior accelerated, and David sailed into the backseat, landing square in Mary Grace's lap.

Junior bellowed with laughter. "Nice one, little man."

Embarrassed, David adjusted his glasses and slid to the other side of the backseat. "Gosh, sorry. Are you okay?"

Mary Grace nodded. "I'm fine. Now as I was saying, the Pythagorean theorem is used to find the length of the side of a triangle." She paused. "You should get Jake to help you with this. He's good at math."

"David doesn't need that darkie helping him with anything," Junior said.

Mary Grace rolled her eyes. "I don't see what being colored has to do with learning math. Seems like you either know it or you don't. Maybe you can help him, Junior. What can you tell us about the Pythagorean theorem?"

"Shut up," Junior hissed.

Mary Grace glared at Junior before turning back to David's notebook. "Where were we?" As Junior pulled into the school parking lot, they heard the warning bell ring. "Here, why don't you just copy mine?" she said. "Might not help you for the test, but at least you'll have your homework done."

———————— x)(x ————————

Across town at Piney Grove—the Negro school near Ebenezer Baptist Church on the outskirts of Hobbsfield—Ella was bored, drawing a sketch in her notebook rather than taking notes.

When the final bell sounded, Ella moved through the drafty hallway with her friend, Annie Marie Holding. "Must have been quite a picture you drew," Annie Marie said.

"It was," Ella said. "I drew a picture of myself teaching the class. I was wearing a pink dress with a white belt and high heels. Next thing I knew, Mrs. Clemens was standing right beside me, watching me. I didn't even realize she was there."

Giggling, the girls pushed their way down the stairs and out into the crisp fall day. "I wish we could have classes in art like they've got at Jefferson County," said Ella as they climbed onto the bus. "They have music classes too, and a program they put on for the parents. Mama won't even let me sing in church anymore."

Annie Marie turned to look at her. "Why not?"

Ella shrugged. "I don't know."

"But you love to sing. *She* loves to sing. Didn't she name you after Ella Fitzgerald?"

"She did."

The bus came to a halt at Annie Marie's stop. "Bye Ella, see you tomorrow."

As Annie Marie climbed off the bus, Ella moved a few rows back to where her brother and Bobby Lee Bennett were sitting together, studying something intently. "What are y'all looking at?" she asked.

"Check it out." Bobby Lee handed her the brochure he'd gotten from the local Army recruitment office.

Ella studied the pictures of soldiers carrying guns. "Do you really want to join the Army?"

"Yes, I can't wait to get out of here. Maybe I'll even learn to fly one of those helicopters." He pointed to a picture in the brochure. "I'll fly it over Hobbsfield and wave at you two down in the fields."

"I sure hope I ain't still down in the fields," Jake said. "How was school today, little sister?"

"It was fine 'til I got caught drawing a picture during history class," Ella said.

Jake could read Ella's mind. "Don't worry, I won't tell Mama."

"She'd give it to me good if she found out." Ella and Jake were expected to work hard in school and get good marks, which was easy for Jake but harder for Ella.

They reached the stop for Talmadge Farm and said goodbye to Bobby Lee. "I swear I ain't never seen anybody more certain about the future than Bobby Lee," Jake said as they walked toward their cabin. "I wish I had a plan. But I can't see myself in the Army, marching around holding a gun." He pretended to march, knees high. Ella laughed.

"See, I look stupid," Jake said. "I wish I could go to college."

David climbed up the steps to the school bus and found an empty seat. During football season, he rode the bus home while Junior stayed after school for practice. David didn't mind. He often found more peace and quiet on a bus full of teenagers than in the car with his brother. He put his book bag down and settled into the next chapter of *Moby-Dick*.

"How'd you do on the geometry test?" He turned around and found Mary Grace in the seat behind him.

"It was awful," he said. "Especially the last section. It's my own fault. Or maybe I should say, it's Moby Dick's fault. I stayed up late reading."

She took the book from him. "I don't remember being assigned this book."

"We weren't. I'm reading it on my own. It's about a ship captain named Ahab who lost one of his legs when his boat was struck by a killer whale named Moby Dick. Ahab wants revenge on the whale and sets out to try and destroy it."

Mary Grace laughed out loud. "That's the stupidest thing I ever heard. A one-legged man trying to kill a whale? That could never happen."

David's face reddened. "It's hard to explain. The way Melville writes, it's like you're there, caught up in the journey, feeling Ahab's anger and despair."

"Seems to me like real life's got enough of that already," Mary Grace said. "I sure as heck don't need to go looking for it in a book. But then again, that sounds like what Miss Holmes tries to get us to talk about in English class."

"I love the way she discusses the books we read." David blushed again; he'd never admitted that to anyone. Luckily, the bus reached their stop soon after he finished talking.

"You know, maybe we should work out some kind of a deal," Mary Grace said as they approached her family's cabin. "I'll let you copy my geometry if you help me prepare for English class. That way I don't have to do the reading, and we can both stick to what we're good at."

David smiled. "It's a deal."

He watched as Mary Grace walked down the dirt path and up to the porch of the Craddocks' cabin. "Hey David," she called out. "Let me know if Ahab catches that whale."

SIX

August 1959

Ella stood in front of the small, cracked mirror in her bedroom, far enough away so that she could see herself from head to toe. Her family had just had one of their best tobacco seasons ever, and she'd been allowed to get a new outfit, a welcome change from shopping at the secondhand store like they usually did. She loved the way she looked in the pink blouse and gray swing skirt she'd picked out from the sale rack at Hudson Belk. The department store didn't permit her to try anything on, but she was a perfect size six so her mama didn't need to make any alterations.

She went to find Jake, who had promised to take her to the Saturday matinee at the Gem Theater. As usual, he was sitting at the table with a textbook. Jake was the only person she knew who liked doing homework. She didn't mind school so much—she loved seeing her friends and it was a welcome change from working in the fields—but she'd rather spend her free time studying Miss Claire's old *McCall's* magazines and listening to the latest rock 'n' roll tunes on their battery-powered radio than reading a history book.

"You ready to go?"

Jake looked up. "Do we have to? You don't even like cowboy movies." The Gem showed a Western every Saturday afternoon, reserving new releases for the evening showings.

"I know, but Mama won't let me go at night." Much to Ella's frustration, even though she'd turned fifteen last month, her mother wouldn't let her go into town at night on the weekends with her friends. "And it'll give me a chance to show off my new outfit." She twirled around, but Jake didn't react.

"Alright," he groaned. "Let me just finish one more math problem."

Squeezing into the front seat of the truck between Jake and her daddy, Ella could feel the scratchy crinoline against the back of her legs. She finished tying a scarf around her neck and adjusted the belt on her skirt.

When they got to the theater, there was already a line to see *Giant*, starring James Dean, Elizabeth Taylor, and Rock Hudson. Louis handed Jake a dollar bill. "I don't have any change for candy."

Ella kissed her daddy. "We don't need candy."

"What time's the movie over? Me and Will are sharpening the tractor disc blades this afternoon, but I can take a break to pick you up."

"Don't worry about us," Jake said. "We'll hitch a ride or walk. It'll still be light out."

Jake and Ella found two seats together upstairs in the colored section. They waved to Bobby Lee, who was sitting a few rows behind them with his older sister. Ella noticed Junior Talmadge downstairs in the center row surrounded by his football buddies. They looked to be passing a bottle of whiskey back and forth, laughing loudly in between sips.

Finally, the lights dimmed. Ella was impatient with the newsreel; events of the world seemed unrelated to her life on the farm. When the movie started, she was enchanted by the story, which was full of fistfights, romance, betrayal, and the hardscrabble life of the Rialto Ranch.

Nearly four hours later, when the lights came back up, Ella was disappointed, sad that it was over. "I could look at Rock Hudson all day."

Jake stood up and stretched his legs. "That was one long movie. Let's go. I need to finish my homework."

Walking home, they tried to hitch a ride, but no one stopped. Ella's feet began to hurt in her new white pumps, so she took them off, taking care not to step on a rock or a piece of broken bottle.

They were half a mile from the farm when they heard a vehicle slow down behind them. Junior Talmadge pulled up next to them and stopped the car. "What do we have here?" he slurred, clearly drunk. "Who gave you two permission to leave the farm?"

Ella felt Junior's eyes on her body and nervously fiddled with her scarf. Jake stepped in front of her. "We're just walking home."

Junior eyed Ella again. "Want a ride? Ella, you can sit up front with me." He patted the seat beside him.

"We'll walk," she answered, not making eye contact. She moved away from the car and continued down the road.

"Suit yourself." Junior spat on the ground at Jake's feet and stomped on the gas pedal, the tires spewing dust into the air. Ella brushed off her skirt and wiped the grit from her face.

"Dinner's ready," Claire called out from the bottom of the stairs. The Talmadges were eating early so Gordon could make it to his monthly poker game.

Junior stumbled into the high-backed chair at the dining room table across from David just as Ivy placed a steaming chicken pot pie on the trivet beside a dish of cooked carrots and a plate of biscuits. "I'm heading out, Miss Claire," Ivy said. "Just put the dishes in the sink and I'll take care of them in the morning."

"Have a good evening," Claire called out as she began spooning the food onto plates.

"How was your movie, Junior?"

As Junior gave a brief description of *Giant*, Claire studied him closely. His eyes were glassy and he appeared to be concentrating heavily on his words. She gave him a stern look, but he paid no attention. She really wished Gordon would speak to him about his drinking.

"I had a long conversation with Glenda this afternoon," Gordon said. "You know my sister loves to share her ideas about ways to increase the bank's revenue. What do women know about business, anyway?"

"What was she calling about?" Claire asked, trying to keep him on track.

"Some nonsense about car loans. Seems like a terrible idea to me. Everybody knows if you can't pay cash, you can't afford a car. Once you drive a car off the lot, it depreciates in value, and the loan is underwater, day one." Gordon reached for a second biscuit and Claire passed him the butter. "But on a different note, I'm looking into sponsoring the float for Miss North Carolina for the Mule Days Parade in October."

Junior's eyes lit up at the prospect of a beauty queen visiting Hobbsfield. "Maybe I could ride on the float with her. To represent the bank."

"How are you a representative of the bank?" David asked. "You don't work there."

"Our family owns it, stupid. Or maybe, as quarterback of the football team, I could represent Jefferson County High School."

David wasn't finished poking fun at his brother. "And isn't Miss North Carolina in college? Do you really think she'd be interested in you?"

"Shut up you little punk."

"Junior, mind your manners," Claire said.

"Too bad y'all didn't win the opening game," Gordon said to Junior. "Leading the Wildcats toward an undefeated season would be a good reason to put you on that float. But maybe I can work something out."

Junior bristled. Claire knew her son was still furious that his best receiver had dropped what he considered a perfect pass in the final minute of the first game of the season.

"May I be excused?" Junior stormed into the kitchen without waiting for an answer.

"What's gotten into him?" Gordon asked.

"He's still mad about the game," David offered.

"You win some, you lose some," Gordon said, wiping his mouth with his linen napkin. "Here's hoping I come out a winner tonight." He kissed the top of Claire's head and headed out the door.

"Good luck, Dad," David said. "Thanks for dinner, Mom."

As Claire began to carry the plates into the kitchen, she heard the familiar thud of a football being thrown against the side of the house. She hoped it would help Junior work out his aggression or at least sober him up. She hated to admit it, but her son was a sore loser.

Ivy was busy at the stove when Ella and Jake walked into the cabin. "Where have you two been? I almost sent your daddy out to find you."

"The movie went on forever, and then we had to walk home," Jake said, settling back down at the table to finish his homework. "What are you doing home so early?"

"The Talmadges ate an early supper—it's Mr. Gordon's poker night," Ivy said. "Jake, run up to the smokehouse and get a pork shoulder. I'm going to make a stew after supper for tomorrow's covered dish."

"I've got a chemistry test on Monday. I need to finish this math so I can study for it."

"You should've thought of that before you went off to the movies. You could've saved your daddy fifty cents, too."

Ella jumped to Jake's defense. "I talked him into it. I'll go get it. Just let me change my shoes first. I've got a blister on my heel."

Ivy stirred the rice in the iron pot and mixed up a batter for corn-bread. The cornbread was nearly ready when she realized Ella hadn't returned from the smokehouse. She looked out the window. "What in the world is keeping that girl?"

Jake looked up from his math homework, an uneasy feeling com-ing over him. He pictured the way Junior had looked at Ella. How drunk he'd been. Maybe he should have gone with her to the Big House. "I'll be right back," he said, hurrying out the door.

"Where you going, son?" Ivy called out, but he was already gone.

After stopping by the barn to pet the mule, Ella walked up the hill, thankful to be wearing socks over her sore feet. As she approached the smokehouse, Buster bounded off the porch, barking, and licked her hand.

She dug into her pocket and took out the key to unlock the pad-lock. Pulling open the heavy door, she stepped in but left it open a crack to let in some air and light. She'd always found the windowless room creepy, with hunks of hog saturated with a heavy coating of salt hanging from iron hooks. In the center sat a large cast iron pot that held the fire during the active smoking process. There was a pile of logs in the corner near the door. The smell of smoke permeated the stale air.

Ella spotted the shoulders hanging from a wire near the back corner. As she moved to get one down, the door closed behind her, plunging the smokehouse into darkness. Ella jumped, swallowing a scream, and slowly made her way back toward the door.

"What are you doing in here, Ella?"

A sliver of light came in through the slats, but Ella already knew the voice belonged to Junior Talmadge. "Getting a side of pork for Mama," she said. "Then I'll be out of your way." Ella could feel her hands begin to shake.

Moving closer, he gave her a menacing smile. "Let me help you," Junior said. With no warning, he grabbed her wrist and pushed himself against her. She could feel his hot breath on her face. "Then maybe you can help me."

As Ella tried to push him away, they got tangled up and fell to the dirt floor. She wanted to scream, but nothing came out. Pinned underneath his weight, Ella squirmed and kicked as Junior ripped her blouse open. He slid his hand underneath her skirt, and Ella bit him on the shoulder. He bit her back in retaliation, and she cried out in pain. "You little bitch," he whispered in her ear. "Trying to make me work for it?" Ella smelled the liquor on his breath and felt the weight of his legs pushing her thighs apart.

Suddenly, light flooded the smokehouse and Jake was there. Realizing what was happening, he grabbed a log from the wood pile and swung at Junior, hitting him in the shoulder. It bounced off him, but Ella was able to scramble out from under him. "You stupid mother fucker," Junior yelled. "I'm gonna kill you."

Junior jumped to his feet, shoved Jake against the wall, and punched him in the face. Ella knew Jake was no match for Junior. She struggled to her feet, grabbed the piece of firewood, and swung it at Junior, hitting him on top of the head. He put up his arms in defense but there was no stopping Ella. She exploded with anger, hitting him again and again until he fell to the ground in a heap. She continued to hit him until Jake grabbed her by the shoulders.

"Ella, stop. Give me that. Stop!" Jake wrestled the piece of firewood away from her. Buster was barking frantically in the doorway.

She turned to look at her brother. "Are you all right?" she asked, breathing heavily.

"Yeah. Are you?" Ella nodded.

They looked at Junior's crumpled body on the floor; a pool of blood was beginning to form around his head.

"We need to get out of here," Jake said. They raced down the path, slowing only when they caught sight of the kerosene lamp shining through the cabin window and their mama leaning against the stove.

SEVEN

August 1959

Claire was at the hospital bedside when Junior opened his eyes. The pain medication the doctor gave him in the emergency room had kept him sedated throughout the night.

"Hey there, sweetheart," Claire said, stroking his hand gently. "Gordon, look who's awake. Go find Eric."

A few minutes later, Dr. Eric Orlando gave Junior a thorough examination, checking his pupils for proper response to light and asking him questions to make sure he wasn't disoriented. "I think we're out of the woods," he said. "Looks like he's going to be okay."

Claire relaxed for the first time since she'd found him on the dirt floor of the smokehouse last night.

"Son, you've got a broken shoulder and a bad knot on your head," the doctor said, turning toward Junior. "And your face is pretty bruised up, but it looks worse than it is."

Junior reached up and felt the gauze wrapped around his hairline. "My head," he moaned.

Claire held a cup of water with a straw to Junior's swollen lips. He sat up to drink and then sank back into the pillows from the effort. Claire turned back toward the doctor. "So he's really going to be okay?" She needed to hear him say it again. On the ride to the hospital, in the ambulance, she thought she might lose her son.

Dr. Orlando beckoned Claire and Gordon to the hallway. "I don't want to upset him. He's lucky the shoulder doesn't need surgery, but he won't be back on the football field any time soon. He likely has a concussion, so he may have headaches, some dizzy spells, and his memory could be fuzzy for a while. But I've seen worse. Do you know what happened?"

"Someone attacked him on our property, and the bastard left him for dead." Gordon's voice was full of fury. "When I find out who did this, I'm gonna kill the son-of-a-bitch." He began pacing and lit a cigarette.

"Perhaps you should let Sheriff Owen handle it," Dr. Orlando said diplomatically.

"Will Junior remember what happened?" Claire asked.

"Hard to say. I've seen cases where the victim has no recollection and others where he can remember every detail. One thing's for sure, someone hit Junior good and hard."

They walked back into the hospital room and Dr. Orlando wrote a few notes on the chart at the foot of Junior's bed. "We'll keep him here another night." He started toward the door. "Say, Gordon, why don't you put out that cigarette? They're bad for you."

Gordon frowned, stumping out his cigarette in the ashtray by the bed. "I'm going to get another cup of coffee from the cafeteria. Claire, do you want anything?"

Claire shook her head. Now that they knew Junior was out of danger, she was worried they had a bigger problem on their hands.

When Junior woke up again a few hours later, he was much more alert. Claire finally asked him the question that had been troubling her. "Junior, why were you in the smokehouse last night?"

He didn't answer right away. "I think Buster was barking," he said slowly. "I went to check on him and the smokehouse door was open. I figured someone forgot to lock it. I started to close it and saw Ella Sanders in there. I asked if she needed help, and next thing I knew, her brother came in and hit me with something."

Gordon's eyes narrowed. "You mean to tell me Jake Sanders did this to you? You wait until I find that stupid little darky." He began pacing again.

"Gordon, hold on," Claire said, her mind racing. "Junior, are you telling us the whole truth?" Claire stared straight into her son's eyes.

He looked away and took a sip of water. "That's all I remember."

Claire sat down and opened her pocketbook. She dabbed on some peach lipstick and smoothed her blonde hair more than needed. She knew Junior wasn't telling the whole story. Jake Sanders was a skinny kid who'd never been violent in his life, and he was no match for her son, who was even brawnier than his father at the same age.

A nurse came in to give Junior his medication. "Goodness, what happened to you?" she asked. "That's some black eye you've got there."

"He had an accident at the farm," Claire said quickly.

As soon as the nurse left the room, Claire leaned in close to Junior. "If anyone asks you what happened, tell them you don't remember. Do you understand?"

"Yes, Mom," Junior responded, still not meeting her eyes. "Hey, did the doctor say when I can play football again? We have the game against the Clinton Dark Horses next week."

Claire hesitated. "We'll ask him about it later, son."

Gordon took his car keys out of his pocket. "I'm going home. There's a few things I need to take care of." His voice was steady but Claire could see the fury in his eyes and the way he gripped the keys through his white knuckles. She felt her heart begin to race.

"No." Claire spoke so sharply she startled them both. "I'm tired. You stay here with Junior, and I'll come back tonight."

"Claire . . ."

Claire ignored the warning in his voice and snatched the keys from his hand. She turned to Junior and kissed him on the cheek. "Get some rest, sweetheart. I'll be back later."

Gordon followed her into the hallway. "I will take care of this, Claire. One way or another."

"Promise me you won't call the sheriff. We need to gather all the facts here before we blow the whistle on Jake Sanders. Something about this doesn't make sense to me."

Gordon kissed Claire on the top of the head but didn't promise anything.

It was mid-morning by the time Ivy and Ella made their way to the Big House. Neither had slept a wink all night. Ivy was still wrapping her mind around what happened. Ella and Jake running home, frantic, describing how Junior attacked Ella, how Ella hit Junior over the head.

Once Louis had tended to Jake's bloody nose and she'd helped Ella out of her torn clothing, her fury had turned into dread as she realized the predicament they were in. It was obvious that Jake needed to get off the farm until they could figure out what to do. Mr. Gordon would never believe Junior was at fault. Or that Ella could have beaten up Junior. So they'd taken Jake to Pastor Rice's house where he could hide until they figured out what to do.

This was her worst nightmare come to pass. From the time she was a child, Ella had a natural beauty and openness to the world that everyone was attracted to. That beauty only intensified once she turned from a gangly teen into a full-fledged woman. Ivy just hadn't realized that danger would find her daughter on the farm, right under her nose. She should have known better.

"Listen, Ella, I know you don't want to go anywhere near the Big House today," Ivy said. "Believe me, I don't either. I'd like nothing more than all four of us to drive off this farm and never come back. But we need to carry on like normal until we get a chance to talk to Miss Claire. You need to tell her what happened."

Ella began crying. "She won't believe me."

Ivy knew Miss Claire had been troubled by the way Junior'd been carrying on lately, dipping into Mr. Gordon's liquor and coming home at all hours of the night. "You may be right, child, but it's our only hope."

Ivy had already lost one son; she didn't intend to lose another.

Ella climbed up the back stairs carrying the mop along with a pail of rags, a jug of white vinegar, and a bottle of Murphy's soap. She went back down to retrieve the Hoover, stopping on the landing as she lugged it up the steps.

She hesitated before opening the door to the master bedroom. Ella had never been in there before. The four-poster bed dominated the room. She pulled the sheets up tight and smoothed the bedspread into place, then arranged the silk-tasseled pillows. She picked up the pink dressing gown draped on the chaise lounge and hung it in the closet next to an array of dresses.

Ella paused over Miss Claire's wedding portrait, noticing how beautiful she looked in the satin gown, a single strand of pearls around her neck. She realized she'd never seen Miss Claire smile the way she did in the picture.

In the bathroom, Ella cleaned the tub and scrubbed the porcelain toilet. Moving to the sink, she shifted the pots of potions and creams around so she could wipe down the counter. As she picked up a bottle of aftershave lotion, she caught a whiff of the elixir inside. It was the stench of Junior. She was struck with a wave of nausea as she stared at her reflection in the mirror. The welts on her neck throbbed angrily. She pulled out her scarf and tied it around her neck in a frenzy, wondering if she'd ever forget the animal look in Junior's eyes as she lay pinned underneath him.

Feeling as if she might faint, she opened the bathroom window to let in some fresh air. She heard a car engine and saw Miss Claire pulling into the driveway.

Ivy was rolling out dough on the marble counter when Ella came downstairs with the news that Miss Claire was back from the hospital, and she was alone. Ivy tried to stay calm. "Good. Now's our chance. When she comes into the kitchen, look busy." She pointed to the stack of apples and told Ella to peel them.

While Ella sliced apples into a bowl, Ivy deftly placed the dough into two pie tins and fluted the edges, then put the pie crusts in the oven and set the timer.

The screen door opened.

"Afternoon, Miss Claire," Ivy said, struggling to keep her voice even. "Ella's helping me today. Will you all be having supper here tonight?"

"No," Claire said. "Junior's still in the hospital. That's where I've been since last night. They're keeping him for another night, but he's going to be okay."

Ivy said a silent prayer of thanks. At least they couldn't come after Jake for murder.

Claire sat down at the kitchen table. "He's got a broken shoulder, and his face is all bruised up. The doctor says he has a concussion, that his memory might be fuzzy for a while." She took a deep breath and looked at Ella. "Ella, I know something went on in the smokehouse last night; Junior said that he was trying to help you and that Jake hit him from behind. Can you tell me what happened?"

Ivy led Ella to the table, and they sat down on either side of Miss Claire.

"I'm the one," Ella said, "who hit Junior over the head. Jake was just trying to protect me."

"What do you mean, 'protect you?'" asked Claire.

Ella slowly recounted what happened in the smokehouse. She untied the scarf around her neck and showed Claire the welts where Junior had bitten her. Claire covered her mouth and gasped. Ella put her head down and quietly began to sob.

The timer went off like a siren. Out of habit, Ivy rose to take the pie crusts out of the oven, filled them with apples, put them back in, and reset the timer. She came back to the table and put her arm around her daughter.

"We shouldn't have left Junior there, but we were scared," Ella said. "The way Buster was carrying on, we knew somebody would find him before long."

"*I* found him," Claire said. "Lying in a pool of blood. Thank God he's okay." She lit a cigarette. "Where's Jake now?"

Ivy wiped her hands on her apron. "Jake's not here. We weren't sure it was safe for him to stay on the farm."

Ella put her head back down on the table. "I feel so bad," she whispered. "If it weren't for me, none of this would've happened."

Ivy lashed out before she could stop herself. "Ella this ain't your fault. Junior's been just like his daddy his whole life."

"That's enough, Ivy," Claire said sharply.

Ivy held her gaze until the timer rang again. She slowly got up and opened the oven, filling the kitchen with the smell of cinnamon and nutmeg. She put the pies on the counter, spread a cotton towel over them, and then closed the oven door with a hefty slam.

Claire took a long drag of her cigarette and stood up, holding the table for support. "I've got a headache," she said. "I'm going upstairs to lie down. Wrap up some of that pie for me to take back to Junior later. You can take the other one home to Louis and Jake." Claire swallowed her mistake.

"Miss Claire, you gonna talk to Mr. Gordon?" Ivy asked. "Tell him the truth of what happened?"

Claire nodded slowly. "I'll talk to him tonight, tell him it was an accident. A misunderstanding. He's plenty fired up at Jake, though, so I think it's smart for him to make himself scarce for a while. And Ella, Mr. Talmadge and I will talk to Junior about . . . his manners."

Ivy pursed her lips and turned away.

As exhausted as she was, Claire couldn't fall asleep. Her mind raced with images of the red welts on Ella's neck, of Junior bleeding on the dirt floor of the smokehouse, of Gordon pacing furiously in the hospital.

She felt tears come to her eyes. Why would Junior go after Ella Sanders? For heaven's sake, he could have his pick of any girl at Jefferson County High School. He was ruggedly handsome and captain of the football team, just like his father. She thought of what Ivy had said, that Junior was just like his father. For a fraction of a second, an image burst into her mind that was so appalling, so repulsive, that Claire shuddered. In the next second, she forced it from her mind.

Claire wiped her eyes and finally fell into a heavy, dreamless sleep.

"Manners?" cried Ella. "How can she call what Junior did to me 'bad manners?' He should be the one leaving the farm, not Jake. This is so unfair."

"I know, baby." Ivy enveloped her daughter in a hug. "It ain't fair. But you gonna have to put what happened out of your mind. There ain't no other choice. Do you think you can do that?" She took a step back and studied Ella's face.

"I'll try. But the way Junior was on top of me . . . he ripped my blouse open, Mama. I could hear him unzipping his pants. He was trying to . . ."

"I know what he was trying to do. But you fought back, baby. Don't you ever forget that. You fought back. And you and Jake put a stop to it."

"Where's Jake gonna go?"

"I don't know. We gonna have to trust that the Lord will provide."

Ivy dabbed the last of Ella's tears with a dish rag. "Now cut up that pie for me."

---————— x)(x ——————---

When Claire returned to the hospital later that afternoon, Gordon had nodded off in the chair, and Junior was sitting up in bed watching a television program.

Claire set down her purse along with the pie she'd brought. "Hi sweetheart. How are you feeling?"

"Better, except my head's starting to hurt again."

"You're probably due for your pain medicine. I brought you some apple pie."

"Thanks."

Gordon stirred, sitting up straighter in the chair and clearing his throat. "Our boy had a good afternoon. Ate some lunch and then slept for a while. Guess it was my turn for a nap." He stood up, stretching. "Since you're back, I think I'll head home and take a shower." He plucked the car keys from the top of her purse. "By the way, Sheriff Owen stopped by earlier."

Claire's heart sank. She followed her husband into the hallway.

"He heard we had an incident at the farm," Gordon continued. "I gave him the gist of what happened, and he wants Junior to come down to the station to give a statement as soon as he's released."

"Gordon . . ."

"I know what you're about to say, Claire. He cautioned me against taking matters into my own hands, said he'd handle it."

"But . . ."

"And I plan to let him handle it. But Jake Sanders better stay out of my sight until they haul him off to jail. He's got some nerve, coming after my son like that. No one hurts my family and gets away with it." He was working himself up all over again.

"Gordon," Claire said quietly. "Listen to me. This whole thing was *Junior's* fault. Not Jake's, and not Ella's. Our son attacked Ella in the smokehouse."

"Nonsense. You heard what Junior said. He was trying to help Ella . . ."

"Gordon, Junior is lying. I talked to Ella myself. Junior was trying to . . . have his way with her."

"And you believe that little hussy over our own son? She probably lured him in there, tried to seduce him."

"She is not a . . ." Claire lowered her voice to a whisper. ". . . hussy. She was nearly hysterical over it."

Gordon shook his head. "That still didn't give Jake the right to go after Junior."

"He was trying to protect his sister. When have you ever known Jake Sanders to cause a moment's trouble? He wouldn't hurt a fly."

Gordon frowned, and Claire thought she might be getting through to him.

Suddenly he put his arm around her shoulder. "Claire, honey, I think your hormones might be getting the better of you. Why don't you check on Junior and let the men handle this?"

Claire shrugged out of his embrace and struggled to keep her voice calm. "Stop it, Gordon. I won't look the other way on this. You need to call off the sheriff. Junior brought this on himself. It's time you quit worrying about how many touchdowns he makes and start worrying about what kind of man he's becoming."

Gordon looked around helplessly and ran his hand through his thinning hair. "You mean to tell me I'm supposed to let that punk off the hook? When he put my son in the hospital? Injured his throwing arm?"

"Yes," Claire hissed. "That's what I'm telling you."

Gordon glared at her and stormed down the hall toward the elevator. Claire watched him go, wondering if he would heed her advice. When she returned to Junior's room, he was wolfing down the apple pie and spilling crumbs all over the sheets. She sat down in the chair at his bedside. "Son, I need you to be honest with me."

"About what?" Junior was still watching his program. Claire marched over to the television set and switched it off. "Geez, Mom, what'd you do that for?"

"Because I want your full attention." Junior reluctantly turned his gaze in her direction. "What happened in the smokehouse with Ella?"

Junior sighed loudly. "I already told you. I tried to help Ella reach for a side of meat that was hanging up, and from nowhere, Jake came in and started clobbering me." He gingerly touched his bandaged head. "Would you go get the nurse? My head is throbbing."

EIGHT

August 1959

Jake swallowed hard as he heard the truck pull up to Pastor Rice's house. He'd been hoping he could return home, but his parents and Ella came by a little while ago and told him it wasn't safe for him to stay on the farm, that his best bet was to ride up to Philadelphia with Herbert Allen until things settled down. They'd shared a tearful hug, his mama reminding him that the Lord was with him. But after the events of the last few days, Jake wasn't sure he believed her.

Jake bid goodbye to Pastor Rice and squeezed himself into the bed of Mr. Allen's truck. He was surrounded by baskets of summer crops: tomatoes, beans, okra, watermelon, and peaches. He couldn't help feeling as if he, too, had been plucked from the earth, uprooted from everything he'd ever known.

As they headed out into the pitch black night, he closed his eyes and tried to sleep. But every time the truck bounced over a pothole, his nose ached from where Junior had punched him. He finally dozed off until the truck stopped and he heard the door open.

"We're almost to Richmond, son," Mr. Allen said. "I think we're in the clear now. How about you sit up front with me?" Jake settled into the passenger seat and opened one of the ham biscuits his mama packed him. Mr. Allen took out his tobacco pouch, filled his pipe, and puffed on it until the flame took hold. The aroma was sweet and soothing. "You want to tell me what happened, Jake? You don't look like you'd be a threat to nobody."

Jake softly relayed the story. "That's the truth, Mr. Allen. But the truth don't matter much." He tried to keep his voice steady. "And now I have to get off the farm."

Mr. Allen took a draw of his pipe. "Well, son, there's a lot to like about the city of Philadelphia. Especially for people like us. There's some church folks that can give you a place to sleep 'til you get on your feet. You're a smart boy, and brains can take you far in a big city."

Jake tried to let Mr. Allen's words reassure him, but he couldn't quiet the worry in his head. He tried not to think of his family. He wondered what Miss Thompson would say when he didn't show up at school. At seventeen, he'd never been anywhere, not even to Raleigh. Now he was all the way out of North Carolina and getting further away from home by the minute.

As the first light of dawn broke, the skyline of Philadelphia came into view. Jake was overwhelmed by the enormity of it. Mr. Allen pointed to his right. "That there is the Delaware River."

Jake nodded. "That's the river George Washington crossed during the Revolutionary War."

Mr. Allen chuckled. "You know your history."

"Yeah. But what I really like is math and science." As they drove further into the city, Jake told Mr. Allen about his interest in medicine. Although he'd never seen a black doctor in his life, Miss Thompson had heard about a colored man going to the medical school in Chapel Hill.

Mr. Allen took a final puff of his pipe before putting it away. "Dr. Jake Sanders. Can't wait to see the day."

"Sounds crazy, right? But Mama told me if I worked extra hard in school, I might be able to get out of Hobbsfield and do something

more with my life than suckering tobacco plants." His voice caught
in his throat. "I just never pictured getting out would look like this."

As they pulled up to Dock Street, Jake had never seen so many
vehicles and people moving about. Dock Street Produce Market
was the busiest of the city's outdoor markets. Stall after stall lined
the perimeter, selling all manner of produce to restaurant owners,
grocery store chains, and mom-and-pop stores. Jake could smell the
ripe scent of fresh fruits mixed with the stench of rotting vegetables
and garbage.

Mr. Allen eased the truck closer to where deliveries were processed. When it was their turn to check in, he introduced Jake to
Roger Shallcross, the produce market's manager. "Jake aims to stay in
Philadelphia for a while. I thought maybe he could help out around
here, in exchange for a dollar or a sandwich, just for a day or two 'til
he gets settled." Noticing all the tickets and ledgers Mr. Shallcross was
juggling, he added, "The boy's good at math."

Mr. Shallcross was a stocky man with a ruddy complexion, graying hair, and blue eyes. He gave Jake the once-over. "We can always
use help with the unloading, but you'll need to be quick on your feet.
As you can see, it's hectic. Why don't you start right here with Herbert's load?"

Jake began to unload the produce from Mr. Allen's truck, delivering it to the vendors Mr. Shallcross pointed out. When he finished,
Mr. Allen handed him his knapsack. "About three blocks over that
way is the Mother Bethel Church. Head over there when you finish
up here and they'll give you a bowl of soup. Don't stay here after
dark. It's dangerous."

Mr. Allen climbed into his truck. "I sure appreciate what you done
for me," Jake said. "Tell Mama and Daddy and Ella that I'm okay."

"Good luck son. I'll be coming back through next Monday morning." Jake watched Mr. Allen's truck as it pulled into the morning traffic. He gave a final wave as the truck moved out of sight.

Jake walked back to the delivery station. Like his daddy, he was a good worker who could always make himself useful. When the next truck pulled up, he waited until the driver checked in with Mr. Shallcross and then helped carry the loads to the correct stall. He'd never seen names like these before: Kovacevich, Klinghoffer, Giordano. He wondered what countries they came from.

After a while, Jake began to get the hang of the distribution system. Trucks would pull up, and Mr. Shallcross would count the inventory, grade it according to freshness, and put a ticket on it indicating which stall it should go to. He would call out the name of the vendor, and someone from that booth would come over and carry it back. Mr. Shallcross was right, it was hectic. A long line of trucks had formed, and the drivers had to wait for their shipment to get ticketed.

Eventually, there was a lull in the action. Mr. Shallcross handed Jake an empty crate and told him to pick up any stray produce that had fallen to the ground. "Once you're done with that, you can take a break. You can keep what you pick up."

Jake completed the task and then walked down the cobblestone street to a grassy area, grateful for the break. He looked into the crate. Some of what he had gathered was too rotten to eat. He fished out some bruised apples and an overripe tomato and then ate his last ham biscuit from home. He could see the Delaware River in the distance and the cargo ships stopping at factories along the banks, their smokestacks spewing black soot into the air.

When Jake returned to the market, he found Mr. Shallcross sitting at a makeshift desk in his office, muttering under his breath. Seeing Jake, Mr. Shallcross put his papers away. "The deliveries are done for the day." He handed Jake three dollars. "That's your pay. Put it somewhere safe."

Jake mustered whatever enthusiasm was left in his fatigued body. "Thank you, sir."

He took his knapsack and drifted aimlessly away from the market toward the river. He was overwhelmed by the sights and sounds of the city. The air was thick with exhaust. Buildings loomed above him, puffing out smoke like some giant version of Mr. Allen's pipe. Cars and trucks drove recklessly, honking at everything in their path. Jake stared at the river for a long while, realizing that if he stumbled into the muddy water, no one would even know he was gone.

NINE

September 1959

Gordon paced the lobby of the bank looking up and down the street for Leslie Evans. As the reigning Miss North Carolina, she was the Grand Marshal of the parade to kick off the Jefferson County Mule Days Festival. The bank was sponsoring her float, and Gordon made the executive decision that he would be riding alongside her. The parade was scheduled to start in an hour. "Dammit, she should be here by now," he mumbled.

"I'm sure they'll be here any minute," Claire said. "They probably just hit traffic on the way into town."

A few minutes later, Gordon spotted the tall brunette in crown and sash making her way down the sidewalk towards the bank. He put out his cigarette and hurried to meet her.

"You must be Leslie. You sure are a pretty thing. I'm Gordon Talmadge. And this is my wife, Claire."

"Nice to meet you." She explained they'd had trouble finding a parking place. "Let me introduce my father, Arthur Evans."

Gordon and Claire shook hands with Arthur, who was the same height as Gordon but was leaner. Claire thought the slight gray in his light brown hair made him look distinguished.

"I should have warned you about the parking," Gordon said. "We get quite a crowd in for the festival. In fact, it's the only thing bigger than the dove hunt and barbecue I host every year. Arthur, do you like to hunt? I can add you to next year's guest list."

Arthur shook his head. "I'm no good with a gun. Thank you for inviting us to stay with you tonight. We're looking forward to it."

"Will Mrs. Evans be joining us?" Claire asked.

"It's just Leslie and me," he said, sharing that his wife died of cancer some years ago. Claire could see a flicker of sadness in his deep-set brown eyes.

"Damn shame," Gordon said. "I'm sorry to hear that." He glanced at his watch. "Leslie, do you need to freshen up or anything? We need to get to the float. Arthur, you can watch the parade with Claire, and we'll meet up afterward and head over to the festival."

The Jefferson County High School marching band led the parade with a spirited version of "You're a Grand Old Flag." Following behind were antique cars, trucks covered with banners advertising local businesses, politicians waving flags, local beauty queens in convertibles, and, in the final slot, the Farmers and Merchants Bank float featuring Miss North Carolina. Gordon knew he might have gone a little overboard. For this year's float, he'd paid to have a replica of the bank built and placed on the float with room in front for him and Leslie.

Hundreds of people lined the street waving flags. As Louis pulled the float with the farm's new Deere diesel tractor, Gordon spotted Claire standing with Leslie's father along the parade route. He waved, but they were deep in conversation and didn't notice the float as it labored slowly down the street past the crowds. Gordon continued to wave until Claire looked up and pointed them out to Arthur.

The band wrapped up the first song and launched into "When the Saints Go Marching In." As they wound through the streets of downtown Hobbsfield, Gordon spotted Junior with his buddies in front of Claire's father's drug store. Gordon had planned for Junior to ride with them on the float, but after that business with Jake and Ella in the smokehouse, Claire had insisted Junior stay out of the spotlight.

No matter what Claire said, Gordon was convinced that Junior had meant no real harm to Ella, who'd probably led him into the smokehouse in the first place. Hell, he'd gotten handsy with Ivy back in the day when they were both teenagers. Those things happened all the time, and Ivy had certainly made no complaint.

Good thing that low-life brother of Ella's ran away when he did. If it weren't for Junior's broken shoulder, his son might have already gotten a football scholarship to State; instead, he was stuck on the sidelines waiting for his shoulder to heal. Gordon was still furious at Claire for insisting they drop the matter with the sheriff. Jake Sanders better not show his face in Hobbsfield ever again. "I'll kill that son-of-a-bitch."

"Mr. Talmadge, are you okay?" Leslie asked. Gordon hadn't realized he had spoken aloud.

"I'm fine." Gordon put the Talmadge smile back on his face and waved to the crowd.

Ella looked out the window as she sprinkled sugar over a pot of blackberries.

"Ella, watch what you're doing." Her mama was turning dough in a wooden bowl.

"Sorry." She angrily wiped the stray sugar off the counter and dusted her hands off over the sink. "Just making sure no one's coming up the drive."

"I told you, the whole family's at the parade. They won't be back for hours."

"I should be at the parade, too." Ella put the pot on the stove with a loud bang. "Not picking blackberries for the Talmadges' fancy dinner." She slapped the counter. "It's not fair," she yelled.

Ella knew her outbursts were upsetting to her parents, especially her father. But she couldn't go around acting like everything was the same when it wasn't. Jake was off in Philadelphia trying to find work in a city where he didn't know anyone. And Junior was watching the parade while she was stuck in the Big House cooking his dinner.

"Your brother loves blackberries." Ivy said, trying to change the subject.

Ella nodded. "He'd eat as many as he picked."

Ella knew her mother had been worried sick ever since Jake left town. Fortunately, Mr. Allen brought home a letter from Jake last week telling them that he was staying at a church and helping out at the big produce market.

Ivy pinched the dough into rolls and put them on a pan to rise. "Let's hope they sell blackberries at his market. He said he gets to eat the leftovers."

Ella wondered what Philadelphia looked like. Maybe if Jake found a job she could go up there and live with him and never have to see Junior Talmadge's hideous face again.

A car sputtered in the driveway and they both moved immediately toward the window, Ella quickly reaching into her pocket.

"That ain't Junior, baby. That's Will's truck pulling out."

Ella slapped the counter again. "Everywhere I go . . . I feel like he's about to sneak up behind me."

Ivy put an arm around Ella. "Give it time, baby, it'll get easier. And you know Miss Claire promised me they talked to Junior, told him to leave you alone."

"Since when does Junior listen to his parents?"

"Me and your daddy's keeping a close eye on things around here. We gonna keep you safe. Us and the Lord."

Ella wanted to believe her mama. But she'd taken to carrying a screwdriver in her pocket just in case. If Junior tried anything again, she'd plunge it into his eye.

--------- x)C x ---------

"Today was just about perfect, don't you think?" Gordon was beaming. Following the parade, Leslie had performed two songs as the opening act of the festival. Gordon had gotten a good plug in for the bank when he introduced her and then again as he stood with her afterward while she signed autographs. Now he and Claire were on their way back to the farm to host Leslie and Arthur for dinner. Gordon was driving with the window down so he could continue to wave at the pedestrians strolling through town.

Claire nodded. "Leslie was wonderful. You both were. In fact, I'm not sure who enjoyed being up there on that float more, you or her. Did you know that Arthur is involved in that project to bring the colleges together for a research park? My father's been talking about it."

"I think I'm going to call Randy Grant over at the *Times* and make sure he gives us a good write-up. It's not every day that Miss North Carolina visits our neck of the woods. I want to make sure he remembers that Farmers and Merchants brought her here."

Claire wondered if he'd heard a word she said. They drove up to the house and Buster ran over to greet them, licking Gordon's hand and then barking when Arthur's car pulled in behind them.

"Quite a place you've got here," Arthur said, lifting two small suitcases from the trunk of his car. "How many acres in all?"

"Eighteen hundred." Gordon led him to the front door. "I'll give you the cook's tour if you're up for it."

"Sure." Instead of following Gordon to the front door, Arthur walked around the porch taking in the flower beds. "Your roses are impressive. Are you a gardener, Gordon?"

Gordon laughed. "Not at all. I'll give full credit to Claire for the flowers. And to our gardener who helps with weeding and watering."

Claire walked over to join Arthur. "We used to have the roses in that corner over there, but when we moved them to this spot, they flourished. So I added in some additional shrubs and plants to take advantage of the different levels of sun and shade."

"As an amateur rose gardener myself, I recognize talent when I see it," Arthur said. He leaned closer to the blossoms. "Doesn't the Mr. Lincoln smell heavenly? I planted three of them in my garden just so I could enjoy the scent."

"They're my favorite," Claire said. "I make an arrangement for the house with them every week. I put some this morning in your guest room."

"Claire," Gordon interjected. "Why don't you show them to their rooms? I'm sure Leslie would like to rest, and I know Arthur is itching to take a tour of the farm."

The tall candles flickered in the light breeze as the swinging door to the kitchen opened and Ivy brought out the food. Claire sat at one end of the dinner table and Gordon at the other. Arthur sat to her right and next to him were Claire's parents, Bonnie and John Collins. Across from them, Leslie sat between Junior and David.

Even after all these years, Claire was still struck by the beauty of a perfectly set dining room table. The silverware sparkled in the soft light, and the blue and white Delft china atop the freshly ironed lace tablecloth perfectly matched the blue and white toile wallpaper.

"This roast beef is delicious," Arthur said. "Thank you so much for inviting us to dinner tonight."

"Glad to have you," Gordon replied. "And that beef is from cattle born and raised right here at the farm. You won't taste better anywhere in the world." He took a long sip of wine. "You were the belle of the ball today, Leslie. The *Hobbsfield Times* is going to do a story on your appearance. Of course, we all think you should have won the Miss America pageant. But you did North Carolina proud."

"Thank you," Leslie said. "It's an honor to represent North Carolina and travel around the state. Over the summer, I performed at the Fourth of July Festival in Wilmington, and in December, I'm going to sing at the Biltmore House. It'll be nice once the semester ends so I won't have schoolwork on top of all my appearances."

"Where are you in school, dear?" Bonnie Collins asked.

"Meredith College. I want to be a teacher. I love singing, and I hope to teach voice lessons someday."

"That's wonderful. I teach piano lessons out of our home. I think the ability to read music, to sing, or to play an instrument is almost as important as learning to read or write."

"I don't know if I'd go that far," Gordon said. "Music doesn't make anyone rich."

"I wouldn't say making money has to be the most important thing," Arthur said. "Catherine, my late wife, felt it was important for Leslie to have a variety of interests, including music and art."

Bonnie lifted her wine glass. "To the arts."

Gordon smirked at Junior. He raised his glass and took a long drink.

Claire noticed David listening intently to the conversation. He was probably impressed that someone was openly disagreeing with Gordon on some of his more fixed ideas.

"Don't forget about sports," Junior added. "They're important too. The thrill of victory. Going up against another team in a fight to the finish." He turned toward Leslie. "I'm hoping to play football in college like my dad did."

"I'm afraid I don't know much about football," Leslie said. "What are you planning to study?"

"Not sure yet," Junior said. "Maybe business. I'm in line to run the bank one day."

"I agree with you about sports, Junior," Gordon said. "In fact, for Christmas this year, I'm planning to give my employees four tickets each to the Dixie Classic basketball tournament."

As Ivy brought out a plate of rolls fresh from the oven, John Collins changed the subject. "What kind of work do you do, Arthur?"

"I'm on the civil engineering team for the new Research Triangle Park between Raleigh and Durham. We're about to break ground on the first phase."

Gordon poured himself another glass of wine. "Someone from the governor's inner circle came by last year to discuss it with me. He wanted the bank to be an early investor, but I thought the whole thing was premature. Maybe I should take another look at it now that they're further along."

John looked up sharply. "I don't remember your bringing this up at a board meeting. I would have pushed for it. It's a fantastic vision—a science and technology center right here in North Carolina that will attract the brightest minds in the country. We can't continue to rely on tobacco alone or farming in general for that matter. Diversification is the wave of the future."

Gordon turned red. Claire knew he didn't like being second-guessed, not by his father-in-law, not by anyone.

Bonnie spoke up. "John, I'm sure Gordon will involve the bank when the time is right."

"Ivy, how about bringing in the blackberry cobbler?" Claire called out to Ivy, who was clearing plates from the table.

A few days later, Claire was still thinking of the Evans' visit as she breathed in the scent of the new blooms on the Mr. Lincoln rose bush. What a wonderful evening it had been. Initially, she hadn't been excited when Gordon told her he'd invited Miss North Carolina and her chaperone to stay with them at the farm. As a member of the Hobbsfield Garden Club, she had a number of volunteer duties at the Mule Days Festival. Hosting company was a chore she could have done without.

But she couldn't have foreseen how delightful Arthur and Leslie Evans would turn out to be. Especially Arthur. He was refined, yet down to earth. After dessert, they had all gone into the living room for coffee, and her parents convinced Leslie to sing for them since they missed her performance at the festival. She selected a beautiful song, "Make Our Garden Grow," from Leonard Bernstein's operetta.

Claire had accompanied her on the piano, and Arthur offered to turn the pages of the music. Claire blushed thinking back on it. Every time he leaned in to turn the page, she felt a jolt of electricity. She was sure everyone in the room could see it, but when she looked up, all eyes were on Leslie. She wondered if she were imagining it, but when Arthur turned the final page, he leaned into her for a few seconds longer than necessary. As everyone applauded Leslie, he looked at her with longing in his eyes, then just as quickly backed away and clapped for his daughter. But in that second, Claire knew something passed between them.

Arthur was a perfect gentleman for the rest of the visit. He and David had a lively conversation about their favorite authors while Gordon and Junior tried to teach Leslie the basics of football. After one too many bourbons, Gordon nodded off in the wing chair, so Arthur walked her parents to their car. As the young people retired to bed, and Gordon snored softly nearby, Arthur talked to her about losing his wife and how hard it was to raise a daughter by himself. Claire had not had such a deep conversation with a man in a very long time.

At breakfast the next morning, Arthur and Gordon discussed the local banking economy and the details of the site construction for the Research Triangle Park. Claire entertained Leslie with the story of her reign as Queen of the Mule Days Festival when she was a teenager and described how she'd once dreamed of a career in music. When breakfast was over, they said their goodbyes, with Arthur inviting Claire and Gordon to visit them the next time they were in Raleigh.

Claire doubted she'd ever see Arthur Evans again. After all, she and Gordon didn't get to Raleigh too often, at least not together. She cut a few blossoms from the rose bush and brought them inside, hoping the scent would linger for a while.

TEN

Jake forced himself to wake up and get moving. Police sirens had kept him up most of the night. He wondered if he'd ever get used to the harsh noises of the city, so different from the soothing sound of frogs and crickets that lulled him to sleep at the farm.

He shook off his fatigue and hurried over to the market. He'd been in Philadelphia nearly two months now and still hadn't found a permanent job or a place to live. Most men were only allowed to stay at the Mother Bethel Church shelter for a month, but Sylvia, who ran the shelter, had taken pity on him and let him stay on in exchange for washing dishes and cleaning the bunk room. She even got him a job helping a janitor clean office buildings on the weekends. Every little bit helped.

He'd been sure he could get a factory position, but that idea had turned into a dead end. Several local plants had moved to the outlying towns in the past year, and the displaced workers—who had experience—snapped up any available jobs. He'd worked at the dock a handful of times unloading shipments from the barges until two thugs jumped him on his way home and robbed him of his pay.

At least Mr. Shallcross was still paying him to work at the market. The man never said much to him, but Jake sensed that he appreciated his work ethic. It helped that Jake had learned the system quickly; drivers bringing produce waited their turn for Mr. Shallcross to write up their tickets, and then Jake helped them deliver their goods to whichever vendor Mr. Shallcross specified.

But something had caught Jake's eye recently, and it was weighing heavily on his mind. When long lines formed, the drivers hopped out of their trucks, happy to stretch their legs and shoot the breeze while Mr. Shallcross wrote up their tickets. Last week, Jake had noticed a vendor grab a crate from an unattended truck and hurry it back to his booth when Mr. Shallcross wasn't looking. The pace of the deliveries was chaotic, and no one seemed to notice the blatant theft.

Yesterday he saw it happen again, a different vendor this time, taking crates off the trucks after they were ticketed. If those two vendors were doing this regularly, it meant the market wasn't getting its fair cut from the transaction. Jake didn't like the idea that vendors were taking advantage of Mr. Shallcross and the chaos of the market. But if he said something, would one of the thieves beat him up on his way back to Mother Bethel?

Jake arrived at the market just as Mr. Shallcross was processing the first delivery truck. Before he started working, Jake took a torn sheet of paper and a pencil from his knapsack and slid them in his pocket. Throughout the morning he quietly studied the vendors who were taking produce from unattended trucks.

By midday, when deliveries were done, he walked over to where Mr. Shallcross was working at his makeshift desk in his crowded office. He knocked softly, knowing Mr. Shallcross didn't like to be bothered. "Can I show you something before I leave?"

Mr. Shallcross barely glanced up from his ledger. "What is it?"

Jake explained what he'd noticed. "All in all, I counted thirty-eight crates that got pulled off trucks when you weren't looking. There may have been more that I didn't see. I wrote down the vendors who were doing it."

Mr. Shallcross motioned Jake to a nearby stool. "Let me see that." He looked over Jake's crumpled piece of paper and shook his head. "This would explain why the money I'm taking in comes up short. You've got a keen eye."

Jake noticed Mr. Shallcross looking at him closely. "Son, remind me again where you're from. South Carolina?"

"North Carolina."

"That's right. You came up here with Herbert Allen. What are your plans once we wrap up the season here? You know I won't be needing you in the winter months."

Jake paused. "I'm not sure. I've picked up an odd job here and there but nothing steady. Been meaning to ask if you know anyone who's hiring. I can do most any kind of work, and I catch on quick."

Mr. Shallcross pointed to Jake's inventory sheet. "I'd say so. And you're staying at a rooming house off Lombard Street?"

"No, sir, that didn't work out. I'm still at the shelter at Mother Bethel. But I've already been there longer than I should've. So again, if you know anyone hiring …"

"I'll think on it." He turned back to his report. "See you tomorrow."

The next day, Mr. Shallcross was waiting for him when he arrived at the market. "Morning, Jake. I want to talk to you."

Jake took off his cap and followed Mr. Shallcross into his office.

"I discussed your situation with my wife. We'd like to offer you a place to stay until you figure something out. We have a shed behind our house that should work just fine."

"Yes sir," he said, struggling to make his voice heard. "I'm mighty grateful."

"It's settled then. Bring your belongings with you tomorrow and you can ride home with me when we're done here."

Jake immediately thought of his mama. This seemed like one of those moments she always talked about, where the Lord answered a prayer you didn't know you were praying.

As Jake and Mr. Shallcross drove away from the crowds of Dock Street towards a more residential area, Jake marveled at the neighborhood. Beautiful old houses, one after another, on tree-lined streets surrounded a park where people sat on benches and blankets enjoying the sunshine of the late afternoon. Mr. Shallcross turned down a side street and into the driveway of a small and tidy brick house.

They walked up the steps and Kaye Shallcross met them at the front door. She was a plain woman, short like her husband, her gray hair pulled back into a neat bun. She greeted Jake with a warm smile and led him to the bathroom where he could wash up before supper.

Jake shut the bathroom door and picked up a white towel that was soft to the touch, nothing like the rough burlap of the towels they used at home. He fiddled with the knobs on the shower until he got warm water to come out. He flinched as the stream hit him square in the face but soon got the hang of standing to the side and letting the warmth drip down his shoulders. He inhaled the fragrance of Ivory soap as he lathered up.

Dressing quickly, he went into the parlor where he could hear the Shallcrosses talking in the kitchen over the music of a radio. The room was furnished with a colorful rag rug, a brown sofa marked by years of wear, and plain white curtains on the windows. The only adornment was a large wooden cross hanging on the wall.

Mrs. Shallcross eventually noticed him. "Good, you're ready. Let's eat while it's hot." Mr. Shallcross said grace, and then Mrs. Shallcross filled Jake's plate with beef stew. He took big bites, then dipped a white roll in gravy and finished it in two mouthfuls. He remembered his manners and tried to slow down. "This stew is delicious. Thank you for having me. I'm real grateful."

"I heard you were a big help to Roger yesterday," Mrs. Shallcross said. "He's been trying to figure out for a while now why his numbers weren't adding up the way they should." She smiled at her husband. "He assumes that everyone is as honest as he is. Would never have occurred to him that people he's been working with for years were stealing from him. At least until you came along. And for that, *we* are grateful. Now tell us a little bit about where you're from."

Jake told them about Hobbsfield. About his parents and Ella. About Talmadge Farm and the tobacco fields. About school and how much he liked learning. "My mama don't want me to end up working the fields for the rest of my life, so I came up here to find a different path." Jake was embarrassed to tell these kind people that he'd been forced to leave home.

ELEVEN

February 1960

Will sat on the porch of Lindsay's General Store smoking a cigarette. He'd just dropped off his weekly quart jars of moonshine to Paul Plant behind the filling station. He knew he should head straight back to the farm, but it was Friday, and he was flush with cash.

His buddy Glenn sat down beside him and asked him for a light. "Nice out, ain't it?"

Will nodded. "Long as you sit where the sun can hit you."

"How's business?"

"Alright, I guess. We just planted the seedbeds last week . . . getting the field ready now."

"I'm talking about your side business. Can't believe you ain't been busted yet." He gestured toward the filling station.

Will looked around to make sure nobody was listening. "I'm too careful for that. And it ain't easy, working in the cold all night, but it's worth it." He patted his wallet. "I get to spoil Mary Grace. Just wish I'd started it years ago. Would've been nice to spoil Ruby a little bit too."

Glenn chuckled. "She'd have beat you senseless if she knew what you were up to."

"You're probably right. But sharecropping ain't no way to make ends meet. And it keeps getting harder. Last summer, we barely found enough extra hands to get the harvest in on time."

"How come?"

Will shrugged his shoulders. "People are looking for work in town or leaving Hobbsfield altogether."

"You ever think about quitting?"

Will dug the toe of his boot into the gravel. "Where would I go? Long as my side business holds out, I'm staying put."

Glenn tossed his cigarette on the ground and stomped on it. "You got any product to sample? I sure could use a drink."

Will had been planning to save the jug in his truck for a rainy day. But it was Friday after all.

There was a note sitting on the table when Mary Grace got home from school. Before reading it she opened a window to let in some fresh air. The cabin felt stuffy and lifeless. Dishes from her father's breakfast were still sitting in the sink covered with a crust of eggs and gravy. She'd have to heat up some water or it would never come off.

She picked up the scrap of paper.

Mary Grace, I went to the store. Be back later. Love, Daddy

Mary Grace wondered if he'd really be back later or if she'd end up over at Ella's again, listening for the sound of his truck. She tossed the note in the garbage with the empty beer cans and went outside just as David Talmadge was driving past her cabin. He rolled down the window and waved.

She threw a hand up in greeting. He was probably meeting with friends in town before the dance tonight. She'd given half a thought to going herself—her dad would've been glad to buy her a new dress for the occasion. But in the end, she decided not to.

And anyway, she'd been taking pains to avoid David Talmadge lately, both at school and at the farm. She'd put a stop to their daily homework sessions after his creep of a brother attacked Ella. Mary Grace knew David was nothing like Junior, but it seemed disloyal to carry on like nothing happened.

She finished washing the dishes just as her father pulled up in his truck. When he came inside, he took out a small box from the pocket of his overalls.

"Look what I just bought at Lawson's Pawn Shop." Wearing a smile that lifted the corners of his scruffy mustache, he opened the box to reveal a gold locket. "It's for you, for your seventeenth birthday next week. Thought you could put a picture of your mama in there."

"It's beautiful." She could smell the booze on his breath but at least he wasn't drunk. "You sure we can afford it?" She looked at him skeptically.

"We can afford it," he said firmly. "It's real ten-karat gold."

"Thank you, Daddy." She started to take the locket out of the box.

"Hold on a minute." He smiled playfully. "You'll have to wait 'til next week. It's not your birthday yet."

She punched his arm and handed him a dish to dry.

TWELVE

Ella cut across the neat rows of tobacco stalks to the edge of the field and made her way to the Big House. The air was heavy with humidity, and she dabbed at her face with her scarf. Her mother met her at the door. Ella stopped abruptly at the doorframe and looked at her warily.

"He's not here," Ivy said. "Haven't seen him all day."

"Thank heavens. I got to get out of this heat for a minute."

"Did you wipe your feet? I don't want you tracking dirt all over the floor. I just mopped it and I got plenty more to do than go over what I've already done."

"Yes, Mama." She leaned on the counter and fanned her face. "It's hot as fire out there. I'm soaking wet. And look at my hands." She held them up so Ivy could see the purple resin on her fingers.

Ivy chuckled. "Girl, in all my life, I never seen anyone who hated farm work as much as you. Here, take a drink of water and rest a minute." She put a dish towel down on a kitchen chair so Ella wouldn't get it dirty. "And then I want you to take these jars of water down to the field. I'm sure you ain't the only one who's thirsty."

Ella sat down and greedily drank the water. "I wish priming didn't come during the hottest time of the year. My back's hurting something awful. It never used to be this bad."

"You're missing your brother, ain't you, baby?" Tears formed in her mother's eyes. "We all miss him."

Ella knew her mother was right. This farm season had been especially tough without Jake to help in the fields. He'd been gone almost a year, and they felt his absence every day. Even Bobby Lee Bennett, who used to pitch in every summer, had left for basic training in Fort Jackson. At least she still had Mary Grace.

"Remember baby, sometimes we got to use the strength God gave us," Ivy said. "Think about your daddy and Will. They've been working the fields so long neither one can stand up straight anymore. And remember, you'll be done in a few weeks."

"Yeah, and then I'll be back in school." Ella groaned. "And what's the point of school, anyway? Seems like all I'm cut out for is farm work. Or being a maid." She saw a wounded look pass over her mother's face. "I'm sorry, Mama," she added softly.

"Come on now, Ella. That ain't all you're cut out for."

"Why can't I be like Miss North Carolina and travel around singing for people?"

"Get that crazy idea out of your head," Ivy said, regretting once again having told Ella the details of Leslie Evans's visit to the Big House. "You know there ain't no such thing as a colored Miss North Carolina."

"Then maybe I'll be an actress like Lena Horne or Diahann Carroll." Ella reminded her mother that Diahann Carroll had lived in North Carolina before becoming a famous movie star.

"Stop wasting your time looking at those movie magazines," Ivy said. "That ain't real life. Right now, you need to set your mind to finishing high school. We'll worry about the rest later."

Ella wiped the sweat off her face with the towel her mother handed her. "I better get back to the field. Those boys Daddy hired will be wanting their water break."

"They're not giving you a hard time, are they?"

Ella gulped down the last of her water. "No, Mary Grace and I work clear on the opposite side from where they're working."

"Good. You better get on out there. I've got one more load of laundry to do, and I'll be along." Ivy walked into the laundry room as Ella picked up the crate full of water jars.

Suddenly, Junior walked into the kitchen. Ella froze, her heart pounding. He had the same look about him that Will did when he'd had too much moonshine. She thought of the screwdriver in her pocket but didn't have a free hand to reach it. She moved to set the crate down on the kitchen table, but he blocked her path.

"Ella," Junior said, appraising her with his eyes. "Aren't you looking as fresh as a daisy. Need any help with that?"

"Get away from her!" Ivy screamed. She marched into the kitchen and got between Junior and Ella, using a laundry basket to push him further away from her.

Junior burst out laughing and jingled the keys in his pocket. "Don't worry, I was just leaving. You ladies have a good evening." He walked out and let the door slam behind him. A few minutes later, they heard the tires squeal as he pulled out of the driveway.

Ivy finished folding the clothes, still quaking with anger. Thank God Junior would be leaving for college in a month. Maybe Ella would finally feel safe again in her own home. She pressed Mr. Gordon's shirt for tomorrow—starch on the collar and cuffs and a soft touch over the rest—and headed home. Normally, she'd help out in the fields until dark, but tonight she had a whole passel of field peas to shell.

As she passed the tobacco barn, she looked up to the heavens, like she did every time she walked by, and thought of Paul. Her oldest boy would have been twenty-two years old this year. Ivy wondered what he would look like as a grown man. Had he not been killed, he would have been able to help his daddy so that he could slow down. Or maybe he would have found a calling off the farm and made something more of himself.

She noticed the pathway through the woods needed tending. That was normally Will's job, but he was barely keeping up lately. At least this year's tobacco crop looked to be a strong one. The summer weather had been perfect—milder temperatures and not too much rain.

Ivy continued to her cabin, shooing the rooster away as he strutted in her direction. She went inside and took off her apron, hanging it on the nail behind the bedroom door. She noticed the letter propped up on the crate by the bed and picked it up.

Dear Mama, Daddy, and Ella,

Sorry my letters have been short lately, but I'm real busy with my jobs. I think I wrote last time about starting as a part-time stock boy at the Army Navy store. I also found a job in the evenings helping with deliveries for the lumber mill. The Shallcrosses don't want to take my money but I think I should give them something for room and board, especially since they let me move out of the shed and into the spare bedroom in their house. It's so comfortable, and believe it or not, they have hot and cold running water, and I've gotten in the habit of taking a shower. The best news of all is that Mrs. Shallcross is helping me get a scholarship into a special high school! I took the entrance exam last week, and I passed, except they're making me do 11th grade over again. She said she'd work with me this summer on English, Latin, and history. She is one smart lady. And God fearing too. I'm hoping I can get all As.

I've been helping Mr. Shallcross with the garden behind their house. He said they never got so many vegetables before. I showed him some of the tricks you use for growing healthy crops, Dad.

Thanks for sending the peach pie with Mr. Allen last week. The Shallcrosses said it was the best thing they ever tasted! Mr. Shallcross ate three pieces one after another. I know it must be getting close to harvest time at the farm, and I'm real sorry I'm not there to help. But like you keep saying Mama, I'm trying to make the most of the opportunity God gave me. I love you all and pray that I'll see you sometime soon.

Your devoted son and brother,

Jake

Ivy smiled and held the letter to her chest. She'd read it so many times she'd memorized every word. They'd been sending letters back and forth whenever Herbert Allen made a trip to Philadelphia. As much as she missed Jake, he seemed to be on a good path. Sometimes the Lord worked in mysterious ways. Ever since Paul's accident, she'd wanted something more than farm life for her second son and for Ella. And then God led Jake to the Shallcrosses.

She picked up the dishpan of field peas and carried it onto the porch, where she settled into the worn wicker rocking chair. As she split open the pods and scooped out the peas, she wondered what the Lord had in store for Ella. Ivy knew college was out of the question for her. They didn't have the money to send her to one of the schools for colored girls, and Ella didn't have the grades or motivation for a scholarship. Maybe Miss Claire could help them figure out a plan for her.

As twilight settled around the farm, a colony of bats flew high above her. She shuddered as the memory of that awful day came roaring back.

May 1932

Ivy hummed as she gathered up the sheets from the line behind the Big House. The sun had dried them completely, and all she had left to do was make the beds upstairs while her mama finished in the kitchen. It was her sixteenth birthday, and her mama had baked a vanilla cake in the Talmadges' oven for her. She'd smelled its sweet aroma all afternoon.

She bundled the warm sheets into a big pile and carried them upstairs. She started in the master bedroom. It was the prettiest room she'd ever seen, with blue floral wallpaper and a bed so high she had to use a stool to reach it. Next, she went into Glenda's room, taking time to admire the trinkets on her dressing table. Then she moved into Garner's room, carefully stepping around the toy soldiers he had lined up on the floor by the window. She carried the last set of sheets and pillowcases into Gordon's room.

Glancing out the window, she noticed a pair of bats diving over the cornfield. As she stretched across the bed to tuck the sheets in tight, she heard the door shut behind her. "Well, what do we have here?" It was Gordon. He was eighteen, all muscle, and played football at Jefferson County High School. She normally tried to stay out of his way.

Ivy went to stand up but Gordon shoved her back down on the unmade bed. She struggled to find her voice. "We . . . we . . . thought your family was gone all day." He smelled of booze and cigarettes and seemed to take up all the space in the room.

"I came back early because I have a date tonight," he said. Ivy tried to stand up again, but Gordon blocked her with his body, forcing her back down onto the bed. "Don't get up on my account. Is this what you do when we're gone—wallow around in my bed?" He loomed over her.

"I was just putting on your clean sheets. Let me finish up, and I'll get outta your way."

"I think you were waiting for me." Suddenly Gordon climbed on top of her, so heavy she couldn't breathe. "And here I am."

Ivy tried to scream but nothing came out. She struggled against him, but he held her down with one hand and yanked her dress up with the other. Her mind went blank, and she went limp, the weight of his body nearly crushing her.

As suddenly as it started, it was over.

Ivy felt a warm liquid streaming down her legs. Silent tears poured down her face as Gordon rolled off of her. Glancing over, he looked worried. "What'd you think was going to happen when I walk in my room and you're laid out in my bed waiting for me? You better not tell anybody about this or my family will kick your mama off the farm."

He stumbled to his feet, fastened his pants, and notched his belt buckle. "Now get out of here. I still have a date to get ready for." He looked down at the soiled bedding. "And take these sheets with you. They're filthy."

July 1960

Ivy heard an owl hooting in the distance and looked up from the bowl of peas. Tears were streaming down her face. Her heart ached for the young girl who hadn't known what to do that day, who hadn't even understood what was happening. She'd come back downstairs with the sheets and scrubbed at the stains in a frenzy. Her mother was so busy frosting the birthday cake she hadn't noticed. Later that evening, Ivy took one bite of that cake and got sick.

She never told a soul what happened.

Not long after that, her mother took ill with an infection that never got better. And so Ivy took her place as the maid at the Big House so she could help feed her five younger brothers and sisters. Luckily, Gordon was away at college most of the time, and she avoided him when he was home. He never put his hands on her again, but every time she saw him, she relived that harrowing day.

And then she met Louis, the farmer the Talmadges hired who moved into one of the cabins on the property. He was the kindest man she'd ever known. When he smiled, it felt like the warmth of the sun shining down on her. There was no way she could burden him with the ugliness between her and Gordon. It would break his tender heart. When they married, and he held her in his arms, she felt sheltered from everything bad in the world.

A few years later, Gordon married Miss Claire Collins and brought her to live on the farm. Ivy didn't think she could stand to see him every day, but what choice did she have? Fortunately, Miss Claire was generous and decent and easier to work for than the older Mrs. Talmadge. And Louis loved farming. So Ivy stayed on and learned to make pie so good no one ever asked for cake.

She buried the memory of that day way down deep. But every so often, it came hurling back at her, and she felt like that helpless sixteen-year-old girl lying motionless on the bed, unable to make a sound.

THIRTEEN

September 1960

Mary Grace stirred the beans on the stove to keep them from scorching and walked out onto the porch. Dinner had been ready for an hour, but still no sign of her father. Even though the tobacco sheets had been stored in the packhouse for a week now, he was probably busy with some last bit of something. Tomorrow was the big tobacco sale.

She finally caught sight of her father hurrying toward the cabin. Thunder rumbled in the distance, and it would be a matter of minutes before the rain followed.

"Come have something to eat," Mary Grace said as Will rushed in the door. She yelped when a bolt of lightning split a nearby tree then joined her father at the window as a thunderstorm descended upon the farm. Will cranked up the radio for the weather report, but all he could pick up was static.

They sat down at the table and tried to eat as rain pounded the roof. Abandoning their supper, they went back to the window, staring, as gale-force winds lifted up anything that wasn't nailed down, haphazardly snapping oak branches and causing longleaf pines to bow. Mary Grace struggled to stay calm as they felt the cabin walls shake. "I think we should move away from this window," she said.

———— x)(x ————

The newspaper would later report that four inches of rain fell in an hour and a half, with winds gusting up to seventy miles per hour. Will didn't need those details to know this was the worst storm he'd ever seen. He grabbed his poncho. "I'm gonna go check on the tobacco."

"You can't go out in that," Mary Grace said. "Wait 'til it's over."

Will slipped the poncho over his head and ran through the downpour to the packhouse, where the tobacco was neatly stacked, ready to be trucked to the warehouse.

When he arrived, he couldn't believe it. The storm had blown off part of the roof, and a whole side of the packhouse had been hit by the heavy rain. Sloshing through puddles of mud, Will picked up the leaves from the top sheets.

They felt like seaweed and disintegrated at his touch.

He figured nearly half of his and Louis's crop was ruined. Will crouched down in the mud, elbows on the ground, and let out a wail that echoed off the wooden walls and pushed its way into the roaring wind.

An hour later, the storm moved on. The sun pierced through the clouds as if it was just another September evening on Talmadge Farm.

Will spent most of the night pacing the cabin in a daze. He yearned for a few hours of sleep and a shot of whiskey. But after his last bender, Ivy made him pour out all the liquor he had stashed away in the bed of his truck. Finally, daylight peeked in through the cracked windowpane. Mary Grace silently handed him his breakfast and kissed him on the cheek before leaving for school.

Will met up with Louis to load the tobacco sheets onto the truck. The two men salvaged as much of the crop as they could, discarding the damaged leaves and making new sheets with any that weren't soaked through. In the end, his initial estimation was right; they'd lost about half of their yield in the storm.

As the truck bounced along the road avoiding the worst of the mud puddles, Louis turned on the radio. "Sixteen Tons" by Ernie Ford filled the silence. "Turn that shit off," Will said. "Don't we got enough troubles of our own without listening to his?"

Louis turned down the volume. "I know we done suffered a blow. Ain't nothing left to do but trust in the Lord."

Will didn't have the energy to debate the matter.

Approaching the Carolina Warehouse, they took their place behind the other trucks loaded with tobacco for sale. They saw Mr. Talmadge pull in behind them in his convertible Ford Thunderbird. "Goddamn, that car is shining like a bullet," Will said.

"Mr. Talmadge told me to wax it this morning before the sale so the buyers would be sure to take notice," Louis said.

"Didn't you just wax it before the dove hunt last week?"

"Yep. And I done it again this morning. With all that rain yesterday, there was leaves and dirt all over it. Now it looks brand new." Seeing the smile on Louis's face, Will shook his head in frustration. It galled him to see the way Louis took everything—good and bad—in stride.

When it was their turn, Will and Louis unloaded the tobacco sheets onto the forklift and rolled them into the warehouse that stretched almost as big as a football field. In row after row, farmers arranged their sheets into piles so the buyers could examine them up close.

The auction was the pinnacle event of the farm season. A high price for bright leaf was good for the whole economy. The farmers put on their Sunday finest, hoping to convince the tobacco buyers that their harvest was first-rate. Townspeople came out to watch the spectacle. Outside the auction house, there was a carnival atmosphere, with sock men selling their wares on the sidewalk and medicine men with carts hawking potions to cure any kind of ailment.

Inside the warehouse, the sales leader and the auctioneer presided over the action. Using a rapid-fire chant, the auctioneer moved quickly up the rows, stoking the bids to coax the highest price for each seller. As he chanted, the buyers used an elaborate system of nods, winks, and hand signals to place their bids. Following behind was the warehouse clerk, who calculated the value of the sale in his head and wrote it on a ticket.

When it was Gordon's turn to sell, he was pleased that the bidding brought a good price, especially since others seemed disappointed with their number. He motioned for Will and Louis to follow him to the parking lot. "Good news, boys, what we had to sell got top price. I knew we had a bumper crop this year. But those sheets that got wet didn't sell for shit, not to mention what's still sitting in the packhouse soaked through and ruined. Damn shame about that storm." Holding a stack of money, he counted out a wad of bills for each of them.

"I took off the top what each of you owed me for supplies and so forth," he continued. "So what you've got there is free and clear. At least where it involves me." He walked over to his car, got behind the driver's seat, and sped off.

Will looked at his measly handful of cash and thought of all the places he'd bought on credit: the general store, the doctor's office, the gas station, the encyclopedia salesman. They'd be expecting payment now that sale day was here. He heard a mosquito buzzing around his head. When he slapped it away, he saw blood on his hand.

Mary Grace tapped her pencil on her desk and looked at the clock for the hundredth time. She wondered how the sale was going. She still couldn't believe a storm wiped out part of her daddy's harvest the day before the sale. What dumb rotten luck her family had.

She was fed up with farming. All that worry over weather and worms. She wanted a future that didn't depend on Mother Nature, who had proven herself to be unreliable at best and downright cruel at worst. When the bell rang for lunch, she bypassed the cafeteria and went straight to the office.

"Can I help you with something?" asked Miss Parker, the principal's secretary.

"I'd like to talk to Mr. Simpson."

Without waiting for an answer, Mary Grace marched into his office. Mr. Simpson looked up, startled. "Hello there …"

"I'm Mary Grace Craddock."

"Of course. What can I do for you today, Mary Grace?"

Mary Grace sat down in the chair across from him. "I need a plan for my future, Mr. Simpson. I need to find a way to help my dad make money that doesn't involve working in the fields all day long for a tobacco crop that may or may not turn out to be any good. He lost a ton of money in yesterday's storm, and there's no way he can catch up. Creditors will be knocking at our door, and we have no way to pay them."

Mr. Simpson sat back in his chair. He wasn't used to students being this direct. "Well, you're an excellent student. Are you interested in college? Meredith College is close by, and it's a great school for girls who want to become teachers."

"Honestly, sir, we don't have the money to pay for college. And I don't want to waste four years sitting in a classroom listening to teachers babble on about nothing." She paused. "No offense, sir."

"What about secretarial school? There's a one-year program at the community college."

Mary Grace considered this for a moment. She thought of Mr. Talmadge and all the men who came to the dove hunt every year.

"No, sir. I don't think being an errand girl for some man who thinks he's more important than he is would be the right thing for me." She reddened slightly, catching sight of Miss Parker in the hall. "No offense, sir."

"Okay, then. What about nursing?" He waited for her reaction.

"Go on," she said impatiently.

"Well, the hospital is always hiring. You could train right now to be a nurse's aide; you don't even need to graduate for that. But you're smart. I recommend finishing high school and becoming a registered nurse. It pays pretty well, and the community college has a two-year nursing program. If you keep your grades up, they might give you a scholarship."

Mary Grace thought about this option. Gosh knows she'd had a lot of experience taking care of her mother through the years. And working for doctors didn't sound like such a bad idea. They seemed to be sensible people.

"Now *that*," Mary Grace looked right at Mr. Simpson, "is a good idea. A registered nurse. That's what I'm going to be."

Mary Grace left Mr. Simpson's office without looking back.

Will passed up the ride with Louis back to the farm after the auction. As he walked toward town, he stewed over his misfortune. It didn't seem right that Mr. Talmadge wouldn't make up for the loss. He sure as hell wouldn't miss the money, not with what he spent on parties and fancy cars. Not that it surprised Will. No, the years had taught him that sharecropping on Talmadge Farm was a no-win proposition. Too bad he had blown through all his moonshine money. The locket for Mary Grace. The new carburetor for his truck. The night he had one too many at Mabelle's Bar and bought so many rounds for his buddies that it took him a month to pay off the tab.

As he approached the town square, Will ducked into Mabelle's and tossed back a shot of whiskey, relishing the slow burn of the brown liquid through his body. He lit a cigarette and pictured the rain coming in through the packhouse, the tobacco sheets drowning in it. He ordered another shot and drank it down in one gulp. After sitting a while, he settled up with the bartender, using money he owed to somebody else. Mabelle's had stopped extending him credit.

He left the bar and headed down the street to Farmers and Merchants Bank. He didn't have an appointment, and his clothes were soaked in sweat, but he saw no point in waiting to say what he had to say. Plodding along in the heat, he felt like he was marching toward his own execution.

A statue of Brigadier General Lewis Addison Armistead astride his steed adorned the square. Although the general appeared headed for victory, history wrote that he was an early casualty of the Civil War. The American flag wafted in a lazy breeze right alongside the Confederate flag. Will gave a small salute to the general and opened the door to the bank.

He announced himself to Mr. Talmadge's cupcake of a secretary who sat guard outside his office. She pointed to a chair and picked up the telephone. "Mr. Will Craddock is here to see you, sir." She listened and then turned toward Will. "You're in luck. He's free. Go on in."

Will heard the heavy doors click shut behind him as he stepped into Mr. Talmadge's office. He sat down in the chair across from the oak desk.

"Will, let me guess why you're here," Mr. Talmadge's voice boomed. "You need a loan. Am I right?"

Will feathered the light stack of bills inside the pocket of his pants and then looked down at his dirt-encrusted shoes.

"Right as rain, sir," he replied.

"A poor analogy given the circumstances." Mr. Talmadge chuckled.

Will didn't understand the comment, but he nodded.

"Mr. Talmadge, that storm ruining my crop is gonna wipe me out." He then listed the litany of bills he owed and his concern for his daughter.

"Damn shame," Mr. Talmadge said. "But it seems to me it's more than just a storm that's led you here. And I'm not sure you're a good credit risk."

As he faced his transgressions, Will studied Mr. Talmadge's desk. A shiny silver letter opener glistened beside a matching inkwell and blotter. He wondered how sharp it was. And what it would feel like to plunge it into the flesh of Mr. Talmadge's heart.

Gordon lit a cigarette with his gold lighter and took a drag with enough force to fill his lungs. "Look Will, I'd like to help you. I really would. But giving you a loan might be putting good money after bad. How much do you need?"

Will had already calculated how much he was behind and the cost of what he needed to buy. "Would you consider four hundred dollars?"

Gordon whistled for effect. "I need to think about it. How about we continue this discussion on Friday?"

Friday was four days away. Will figured he could hold off his creditors until then. He nodded. "Much obliged to you, Mr. Talmadge."

Gordon stood up and offered Will a cigarette. Will tucked it behind his ear and backed up to leave, not turning around until he reached the door. He tried to read Mr. Talmadge's face to see if he could figure out which way he was leaning, but like the good poker player he was, Mr. Talmadge didn't give anything away.

That evening, to celebrate the end of auction season, Gordon took some of the tobacco buyers to the country club for steak, bourbon, and cigars. Afterward, he drove over the dark roads with the top down on the Thunderbird, feeling nostalgic as the evening breeze caressed his face. He thought about those beautiful fields of his, how the sun and the rain coaxed the seedlings skyward a little at a time, month by month, until they stood tall and proud, their lush green leaves ready for cropping. It really was a shame about that storm.

Turning into the farm, he caught a glimpse through the darkness of an oil lamp flickering in Will Craddock's window. Maybe it was the bourbon, but he felt a pang of guilt at Will's bad luck. Maybe he should loan him the four hundred dollars.

Claire was sitting at the piano when Gordon walked in the door. He kissed the top of her head and then poured a drink from the liquor trolley. "Want one?" he asked.

"No thanks." She walked around the piano to sit with him. Gordon took a gentlemanly sip of his whiskey and leaned back into the armchair.

"How was the auction?" Claire asked.

"Not our best, thanks to that storm. But we got a good price for what we had to sell." His expression sobered. "I want your opinion, Claire." He took another sip of his drink and told her that Will had come by the bank requesting a loan. "We've got enough underperforming loans as it is. But maybe we owe him something."

Claire mulled this over. "He has a vicious temper when he drinks too much. And he throws money away. Ivy tells me stories. But he's had a tough time for sure without Ruby. And there's Mary Grace to think about too. Maybe you should give him the loan."

Gordon looked into his empty glass as if the answer might be at the bottom. "Sometimes I think we should just get rid of our share-croppers and all the headaches they cause. It would mean more money for us."

"What are you talking about?"

"Some of the large-scale farms like ours have started using temporary workers who migrate up the coast, following the crops. They live in camps or cabins, and they're organized and paid by an overseer. I read about it in the *Farmer's Chronicle*. As with everything, there are pluses and minuses, but the arrangement is good for the bottom line."

Claire took a long drag of her cigarette. "Does that mean that Louis and Ivy and Will would have to leave the farm? This is practically the only home they've ever known."

"Whose problem is that?" Gordon said. "No one's forced them to stay here."

Claire shook her head. "I don't know, Gordon. Where would they go? What would I do without Ivy? I don't like the sound of this."

"Well, I plan to look into it. Talk to some of the other farmers. In the meantime, I'm going to tell Will he can forget about a loan from me."

FOURTEEN

October 1960

The late autumn wind blew fiercely off the Delaware River. Boats laden with supplies lumbered their way up the river to the factories bordering its banks. Jake had become familiar with this view and with the Ben Franklin Bridge in the distance, its girders gleaming in the early morning sun.

Business at Dock Street Market was slowing down as most of the outdoor merchants were closing up until early spring. The only vendors who stayed open through the winter were those who worked indoors selling refrigerated seafood or those who sold root vegetables brought up from southern states.

Jake was grateful for the lighter workload. It allowed him to get to school early and spend a few more minutes on the front steps looking over his homework. It was less than a fifteen-minute walk from the market to the school at the intersection of Broad and Vine Streets. On the way, Jake passed the Liberty Bell, City Hall with its soaring clock tower, and the boundary of the old Negro and Jewish communities where immigrants first settled at the turn of the century.

Arriving at school, Jake looked up at the imposing three-story building with its white marble tower topped in copper. Not for the first time, he wondered if he really belonged here. Still, he was thankful to be back in the classroom after a year's absence. His new school was associated with the parish where Mrs. Shallcross worked as the bishop's secretary. When she'd realized how important school was to Jake, and what a strong student he'd been, she'd helped him get a scholarship, although they were making him repeat eleventh grade. Turned out that being a top student at rural Piney Grove in Hobbsfield didn't amount to much at Roman Catholic High School in Philadelphia.

Sitting on the steps of the school's entrance, he held on to his Latin homework as a cold gust of wind blew. When the first bell rang, Jake tucked his white shirt into his gray flannel pants and straightened the maroon sweater that was part of the school uniform. But for the color of his skin, he looked just like any other boy walking through the heavy wooden doors to the chapel for morning prayers. The chapel's plain wooden lectern reminded him of the one at Ebenezer Baptist, although the delivery of the Bible readings was very different. Jake was still getting used to the way the priest gave them: more like a lecture than with a passion that stirred the soul.

After chapel, Jake went down the hall to his first class of the day, American literature. He hung his book bag on a hook and took his seat in the back of the class. Since the first day of school, he'd primarily kept to himself. Most of the boys in his class came from rich families, and it was just too hard to answer questions about where he'd come from and why he was in Philadelphia.

Father McCarthy walked up and down the rows, handing back their homework assignment from earlier in the week. They'd been given an excerpt—a word Jake had to look up—from *The Call of the Wild* by Jack London and asked to write an essay relating the dog's experience to something in their own life. Jake was disappointed to see his paper was marked with a red "C." Underneath was written, "See me after class."

Jake's mind raced while Father McCarthy asked a few students to read their essays aloud. He hoped he wasn't in trouble. When the bell rang, Jake retrieved his book bag and slowly approached Father McCarthy's desk.

"Thanks for stopping by, Jake. I wanted to tell you how much I enjoyed reading your essay about moving here from North Carolina. Although I hope Philadelphia's given you a more hospitable welcome than Buck received in Alaska."

"Thank you, sir."

"Would you be willing to read it to the class tomorrow?"

Jake hesitated. "I didn't do very well on the assignment. And I'm not sure anyone wants to hear about what it's like to work in a tobacco field."

"On the contrary, this year, we'll study writers who will us take us to places we've never been. You'll start to develop the tools to understand the feelings and motivations of people very different from you. I think your fellow students have a lot to gain from hearing your story."

Jake stood up straighter. "Okay, sir. When you put it like that, I don't think I can say no."

"Just keep working on your grammar, and you'll get that grade up in no time."

Jake was mulling over Father McCarthy's words as he walked down the hall and took his seat in biology. He looked around and realized his classmates were writing furiously in their notebooks. "Mr. Sanders, is there a reason you're not taking notes?" Father Garrity, along with the rest of the class, was staring at him.

"Um, no, sir."

"You'll have to speak louder than that if you expect me to hear you."

"No, sir." Jake could feel the blood rushing to his face.

"Maybe you have a perfect memory. Do you want to tell me what I just said?"

"I can't, sir."

"That's what I suspected. Do you get my point?"

"Yes, sir." Jake felt as if he wanted to drop into a hole in the floor. He bit his lip and took out his notebook and pencil.

"All right, now where was I? How do scientists test a hypothesis? By conducting a controlled experiment. Here's a basic example that even you, Mr. Sanders, will understand." He went on to describe an experiment in which half a group of potted seeds were watered and half were left dry and never sprouted. "In this experiment, we've proven the hypothesis that 'seeds need water to grow.'"

Father Garrity went on to explain the essential features of a controlled experiment. "Most of what I've said is explained in Chapter Two of your textbook. We'll have a short quiz tomorrow, so I suggest you study it tonight."

Jake wanted to redeem himself by telling Father Garrity that his daddy—who couldn't read or write—had been conducting controlled experiments with seeds and fertilizer for years in order to produce the highest quality tobacco in North Carolina. But he figured he'd had enough interactions with teachers for one day.

In the cafeteria, Jake picked up a tray with chipped beef and cottage cheese along with a carton of milk. So far, none of the students had invited him to have lunch, not even the one other colored boy in his grade who looked like he had a posse of friends. He took his usual seat at an empty table in the corner, pulled out his biology book, and opened it to Chapter Two.

It was raining when school let out. As Jake walked down the street to wait for Mrs. Shallcross, he reached inside his bag and took out the jacket Sylvia had given him at Mother Bethel. He was thankful to have it but wished he could exchange it for a Chesterfield coat like the other boys wore.

On the ride home, Mrs. Shallcross asked him about his day. He usually told her everything was fine, same as he did in the letters he sent home. But he was still burning with shame from being scolded by Father Garrity. So he recounted the day, holding nothing back. He expressed his fear that he wasn't smart enough to catch up with the class, that his teachers used words he didn't understand, and that he felt as if he didn't belong there. "And I have to read my essay to the whole class tomorrow, even though it's full of grammar mistakes."

"I guess we'll just have to show Father McCarthy that you're capable of doing better, won't we?"

"What do you mean?"

"I'll help you, Jake. I told the bishop I had a good feeling about you and your potential, and I still do. You may be behind right now, but you can catch up."

Jake suddenly realized she was right. He'd been the number one student in his class at Piney Grove, and there was no reason he couldn't catch up here, even if it meant working twice as hard as his classmates. And he certainly owed it to Mrs. Shallcross to do his best after everything she and her husband had done for him. "Yes, ma'am." He nodded. "I'm going to make you proud."

FIFTEEN

January 1961

Davidfollowed his buddy Wilbur Warren into study hall. He pulled out his algebra homework and looked at the first problem. "Hey, Wilbur, can you show me how to do this?"

"Again?" Wilbur asked. "Maybe you should stay after school and get the teacher to help you. Or maybe you could get Rhonda Lassiter to help you. You know she's got the hots for you. If you play your cards right, you could get into her pants."

David frowned at Wilbur's remark. It sounded like something Junior would say. "Never mind, I'll figure it out myself."

David didn't want to admit it, but he *did* need help. Just not from Rhonda Lassiter. Two years ago, he and Mary Grace had developed a perfect system. She'd helped him with math on the way home from school and let him check his test answers off her paper. Something about the straightforward way she explained things made sense to him. In turn, he summarized the books and poems that she didn't have time to read and helped her with her essays.

But after that business with Junior and Ella in the smokehouse, she had practically stopped talking to him. As if it was *his* fault his brother was a moron. She wouldn't even let him explain himself. And then, last year, she stopped coming to school. Ivy eventually told him that she had dropped out of school to become a nurse's aide at the hospital.

When he overheard his parents talking about not giving Will Craddock a loan, David realized the reason for Mary Grace dropping out of school. She'd probably never speak to him again—she must hate his entire family. Why would his father have refused Will a loan? From all appearances, it seemed as if four hundred dollars wouldn't make a significant dent in his father's bank account. It angered him to think that his father had not a bone of charity in his body or any appreciation for what Will did to keep the farm going.

David realized he'd been staring out the window. He looked at the algebra problem again and tried to concentrate.

Gordon bypassed the dining room and went straight to the liquor cart in the living room. He came in with a tall glass of bourbon and banged it on the table as he sat down to join Claire and David, who had nearly finished their dinner.

"What's the matter?" Claire asked.

Gordon took a long drink. "The board meeting is tomorrow and that idiot treasurer of ours, Millard Wellons, has put together a report that makes me look bad."

"Isn't that why you let the last treasurer go?" asked Claire.

Gordon ignored her question and speared a piece of pork chop with his fork. "Too many of the farmers tried the new Coker seed variety last season, and buyers didn't like the flavor of the leaves so they didn't get as good a price. They're calling me to extend their loan repayment period so they can make up what they lost."

"So you gave those farmers loans, and you refused Will Craddock even though his only mistake was packing his tobacco in the path of a storm?" David asked.

Gordon ignored him as well. Damn boy had been giving him a hard time lately with all his questions: Did you know they have to use a worn outhouse as their bathroom? Why can't you put electricity in the cabins? And running water? And a telephone? Hell, if David had his way, he'd just move the sharecroppers into the Talmadge mansion.

"The other bad news for farmers is that the feds are planning some changes in the allotment program," Gordon continued. "It hasn't been implemented as of yet, but pretty soon farmers will be able to transfer tobacco allotments from one farm to another within a county."

"I'm not sure I follow," said Claire.

Gordon took another sip of his drink. "Farms are going to go through a consolidation period, with the bigger players buying up the smaller ones."

"But you're one of the bigger players around here. Isn't this a good thing?"

Gordon pointed out that while it might be good for the farm, it would be bad for the bank. "A lot of our borrowers are small farmers. They can't afford to keep up with the latest advances: bulk barns, mechanical tractors, and the like. They'll be forced to sell. The buyers may not honor the loans that are on the books, and the small farms will simply declare bankruptcy. It's going to be a mess."

"Does my father know what a rough year it's been?" Claire asked. John Collins was on the board at Farmers and Merchants.

"I imagine he has an idea," said Gordon. "When farmers don't do well, the whole economy suffers. I'm sure he feels it at the pharmacy. He'll likely be sympathetic to my situation. It's Glenda I'm worried about. My sister better keep herself in line tomorrow at the board meeting. We Talmadges need to stick together."

He abruptly stood up. "I can't eat any more of this. It's cold. I'm going to have a smoke and turn in early."

———————— x✗x ————————

Gordon had installed a color television in his office at the bank in order to stay abreast of the news. The cabinet maker crafted doors so that when it wasn't in use it was hidden away. Gordon didn't want it sticking out amongst the antique furniture, Persian carpet, and paisley draperies that Claire had carefully chosen for him.

He turned on the set just as President John Kennedy took his oath of office. It was a cold day in the nation's capital, but the newly elected president stood at the podium without an overcoat as he delivered his address to the country. Gordon was a staunch supporter of the Democratic party and was delighted to have a president in office who had campaigned on the promise of maintaining parity of income for tobacco farmers and controls to bring supply in balance with demand. In fact, President Kennedy held up the tobacco program as a model for other farm commodities. This was music to Gordon's ears. Gordon was less excited about Kennedy's views on race relations, but ultimately, he valued his wallet over all else.

Diana popped her head into his office. "The conference room is ready, sir," she said. "I made copies of the financials for everyone. And I'll make a fresh pot of coffee just before ten o'clock."

"Thank you. Will you turn off the television, please?" The inauguration had provided a welcome distraction, but it was time to turn his attention to the quarterly board meeting. He opened a pack of filtered Winstons and took out a cigarette. He knew the filters were supposed to make them safer, but damn how he missed the raw taste of unfiltered tobacco.

From the window of his office, Gordon could see the board members arriving. Lillian, his younger brother's widow, came in first as usual. A natural worrier, she was so concerned about being late that she arrived well in advance of the meeting time. Seeing her always gave Gordon a pang of bitterness. He had adored his younger brother, Garner, who had idolized him. They had spent their childhood hunting, playing football, and trying to avoid the stern gaze of their father.

Gordon could remember like it was yesterday the phone call telling him Garner was dead, killed in an auto accident at Fort Bragg. He and Lillian had only been married a year.

John Collins arrived next. Claire's father had always been a tough one to read. Back in high school when he and Claire were dating, Mr. Collins had never been as impressed with Gordon's football accomplishments as Gordon thought he should be. Lately, Gordon felt a hint of disapproval from John that he couldn't quite put his finger on, which didn't make sense. Oh sure, he enjoyed the occasional dalliance now and then, but he was careful to keep his extracurricular activities away from Hobbsfield and his marriage. And hadn't he provided a hell of a life for Claire?

Next came Neil Starling, his golfing buddy, who owned nearly as many acres of farmland as he did, and Ruffin Grady, who ran the local insurance agency. Gordon smiled when he spotted Bill Barfield, his oldest friend, hurrying up the sidewalk looking disheveled and in need of a haircut. Bill worked so many hours at the hospital that he often failed to look after himself.

Gordon checked his watch. Typical. Five minutes until the meeting and no sign of Glenda. Finally, he saw Glenda's Chevrolet pull into a parking space. Of course, she would be right on time, not a minute early or a minute late. She was just like their father. Same shrewd eyes. Same frown of disapproval.

He stood up, wishing for all his life he could have a shot of bourbon. Instead, he marched into the conference room like a general into battle.

The conference table had been polished to a sheen, and the scent of furniture wax still hung in the air. The side table held a gleaming silver coffee urn surrounded by porcelain cups and saucers. Floor-to-ceiling velvet curtains flanked a portrait of Gordon flashing his

famous smile opposite the one of his father, Stephen Talmadge, looking down sternly.

As Diana served coffee, Gordon walked around the table and
greeted everyone, then took his seat at the head of the table. Glossing
over what he considered to be the most troublesome numbers in the
financials, he explained that revenues were still down, in large part
due to farmers experimenting with pesticides and new seed varieties.
"Some of my customers think that if a little pesticide is good, a lot
of pesticide is better. They don't bother to read the warning labels."

Forcing himself to sound upbeat, Gordon continued. "We've hit
a bump in the road for sure. But things will improve once harvest
season rolls around again. The farmers will recalibrate and get their
gold leaf back up to the highest standards."

Satisfied that the hard part was over, he looked around the table.

John Collins was the first one to speak. "Gordon, this is more than
a bump in the road. I had no idea so many loans were in default or
that revenues had gotten so low. If this continues, I don't see how you
can pay the dividends that—speaking for myself—we all count on."

Lillian looked pale. She put down her coffee cup and agreed with
John. "Gordon, forgive me, but I have to remind you that putting me
on the board was your father's way of making sure I was taken care
of when Garner died."

"I know," Gordon said. "But like I said, I think things will turn
around after the next tobacco season. And I'm planning to contact
some new corporate clients. Remember what a boon the Gastobac
loan turned out to be?" He mentioned his plan to approach some
local companies that were manufacturing bulk barns using technology developed at NC State. "These new barns will replace curing
barns and reduce labor costs by eliminating the need for hand tying
the leaves. I've got a call in to see if we can provide financing."

"Let's hope that works out," Glenda said. "But as things stand
now, Gordon, this is unacceptable." The room fell silent. "I've been
doing some research, and your spending is completely out of control."

She picked up a pencil and circled the expense related to promotion. "The bank cannot afford to keep underwriting your dove hunt every year. I don't see other banks doing that."

"Exactly," said Gordon. "Our father founded this bank to help local farmers. And putting on the dove hunt is one way we maintain the loyalty of our farmers and the tobacco buyers who pay those farmers year in and year out. We bring in a huge percentage of our revenue from those two sources alone."

"And how's that working for us right now, Gordon?" Glenda asked. She reminded him that he'd refused to jump on the bandwagon when credit cards and car loans were introduced by other banks. "You can't keep doing the 'same old, same old.' You need to adapt to the times."

Gordon shifted uncomfortably in his seat. "We're l-l-looking into some of those things. I'm not sure they're right for our client base." Hearing himself stutter, he felt his face turn red.

"Gordon, you seem to be missing the point," Glenda said. "We need to *expand* our client base and diversify our product line to compete with the banks that are encroaching on our territory."

Gordon looked around helplessly at Bill Barfield, who took the cue.

"Gordon knows the economy is changing. I'm sure he's prepared to do whatever it takes to get things back on track. And I'm sure he would be the first to agree that in light of the current numbers, he needs to cut back on marketing and promotion."

"That's not good enough," said Glenda, standing up and looking pointedly at Gordon. "You've got to get control of the expense side of the balance sheet *and* expand revenues. No more golf tournament sponsorships. No more fancy new cars. No more pageant queen floats. No more dove hunts."

Gordon turned to look at her, so furious he couldn't speak. She regarded him coolly. "And when is our next FDIC examination?"

The treasurer piped up. "It's in October, ma'am."

"Then I suggest you do a little more than 'look into' offering new ways to bring in business. Our reserves are well below what they should be. Do we all agree we'd like for Gordon to give a detailed report at our next meeting on how he plans to attract new customers and cut back on expenses?"

Everyone nodded. Suddenly, Bill perked up. "Say, Gordon, you should consider how the bank might get involved in that Research Triangle Park venture. They're about to launch the next phase. Might be a good opportunity."

Gordon sheepishly glanced at his father-in-law, who had advocated for it as a smart investment. "I'll look into it."

Bill held onto the dashboard as Gordon gunned the engine of his Thunderbird on the way to Jefferson County Country Club. They had a tradition of having lunch together after board meetings. Gordon was uncharacteristically quiet on the way over.

The host greeted them as they walked in the door. "Good afternoon, gentlemen. Mr. Talmadge, would you like your usual table?"

"Not today," Gordon said. "Do you have anything with some privacy? We have business to discuss."

"No problem, sir. The small banquet room is available."

When they sat down, Gordon unloaded. "Goddamn, Bill, that meeting was a train wreck. Can you believe my sister? All up on her high horse like that? My father founded that bank to help farmers, and that's what I've been doing all these years. It's not my fault that some farmers can't keep up with the times."

"Excuse me, sir?" the waiter said, looking hesitant to interrupt.

Gordon hadn't even heard him come in. "Boy, you need to make your presence known," he said impatiently.

"I'm sorry, sir. May I take your order?"

"I'll have a club sandwich. On the bank tab. And bring us both a stiff martini with an olive."

"I'll have the chicken salad," Bill said. "And bring me a Coke instead of a martini." He looked at Gordon. "I have to drive back to Raleigh this afternoon."

As the waiter left, Gordon lit another cigarette. "That's the third cigarette you've had since we left the bank," Bill said.

"And?"

"And they're not good for you. I know you don't want to hear this, Gordon, but the studies coming out on tar and nicotine are concerning, to say the least."

"What is it with everybody today?" Gordon shook his head impatiently. "Bill, I'll have you know that nearly half the people in this country smoke. Get over it."

The waiter, startling Gordon again, set down their drinks. "Are you a ghost?" Gordon barked, then took a long sip of his drink. "Bring me another martini when the food comes," he called out as the waiter ducked out of the room.

Bill raised an eyebrow but let it slide. "Listen, Gordon, I agree that Glenda was rough on you back there. You know she's always resented the fact that you get to run the bank. But she is a sharp cookie, and she brought up some fair points."

"Women don't have any place in the banking world. At least they shouldn't." He sat back in his chair. "If she and Lillian get together and lobby Neil or Ruffin, they could outvote me. I've got thirty percent of the stock and they each have fifteen."

"You can always count on my ten percent. But I do think you need to make serious cuts in your expense account and find some new ways to expand revenues. I know canceling the dove hunt is a big blow. Maybe you can pay for it out of your own pocket."

"Maybe."

When their lunch arrived, Bill tried to steer the conversation to safer topics, updating him on his family and mutual friends in Raleigh.

Gordon looked up and realized Bill seemed to be waiting for a response. "Gordon, did you not hear me? I asked how Claire and the boys are."

"What? Oh, I guess they're okay. Claire plays the piano all the time now. Frankly, it gets on my nerves. Can't a man come home and have a drink and a little peace and quiet? Maybe watch a television show?"

"Claire has always loved music," Bill said. "I think it's great she's playing again."

"Yeah, well, you're not the one who has to listen to it."

"How's Junior doing at East Carolina? I know his freshman football season didn't go so well. Sounds like he's still recovering from the shoulder injury."

"Don't remind me. And to 'add insult to injury'—if you don't mind my pun—his grades are way down. I hired a tutor for him, but he's on academic probation. We had a long talk with him over Christmas break." Claire was probably right, telling Gordon he'd indulged his older boy too much over the years.

"And what about David?"

"David's fine. Makes good grades. Always has his nose in a book. He's quite a chess player."

"I'll have to challenge him to a game sometime," Bill said. "Now how about we get you a cup of coffee?"

David yawned as he drove home from school. He wanted to get his homework done before Wilbur came over. He knew if he didn't finish it this afternoon, he'd never get it done. He'd been staying up late every night floating down the Mississippi with Huckleberry Finn.

Just before he reached the turn to Talmadge Farm, the car in front of him slowed and Mary Grace got out in her white nurse's uniform. David pulled up beside her and rolled down the window. "Hey, Mary Grace. Are you getting off work?"

She turned to look at him, her green eyes clear and steady. "Yes. Sarah Hinnant has been giving me a ride when our shifts line up."

"How are you doing? Everyone misses you at school." He blushed.

"I'm a nurse's aide. That means the nurses give me all the stuff they don't want to do themselves. About the only interesting part of my day is how full the bed pans are when I have to change them."

David paused, not sure how to respond. "Want a ride?"

"Why? So you can try to have your way with me? Like your no-good brother? I think I'll pass."

"Oh, come on, Mary Grace. That's not fair. I'm just offering 'cause we're going in the same direction."

It was Mary Grace's turn to pause. "It's a nice day. I don't mind walking. And let's get one thing straight: We are *not* going in the same direction."

David slowly drove past her, his hands trembling on the steering wheel. Why wouldn't she just get in the car? He wanted to tell her about the rumor at school that Mr. Buckley, the history teacher, was dating the new home economics teacher. And it wasn't a nice day, it was cold outside. But if she wanted to walk, then so be it. She could suit herself.

Stomping up the porch steps, David patted Buster and walked into the kitchen. Ivy was at the stove stirring a pot of soup. "There's some oatmeal cookies on the counter." Ivy enjoyed spoiling David, whose gentle nature reminded her of Jake.

David took a big bite of the warm cookie. "I saw Mary Grace coming home from the hospital. She didn't seem too happy to see me, not that she ever does anymore. Wouldn't get in the car with me for a ride up the driveway."

"Baby, that girl done been through it," Ivy said kindly. "Losing her mama. Cooking and cleaning and looking after Will. Dropping out of school and going to work. I try to help her when I can, but your mama keeps me running all day long."

David wiped off his glasses with his shirt, processing what Ivy said about Mary Grace. "Guess I should just leave her alone. Maybe she'll come around eventually."

He took two more cookies and sat down at the kitchen table, where he worked steadily on his homework for the next hour. He looked up when he heard Wilbur knocking at the porch door. After offering him a cookie, David led him into the living room where the chessboard was set up.

"I'll flip," Wilbur said, taking a penny from his pocket. "Heads, I'm white. Tails, I'm black." He flipped the coin in the air. "It's tails."

David took his seat and made his opening move.

They were both silent as they studied the board, concentrating on their moves.

"You're not playing your normal strategy," Wilbur said after David moved a pawn. "Trying something new?"

"Yep. Practicing for the tournament. By the way, would you give me Rhonda Lassiter's number before you leave? I'm going to ask her out."

"Trying something else new?"

David shrugged his shoulders. "Maybe."

Back at the office, Gordon browsed through his messages while doodling on the notepad in front of him. It still galled him to think about canceling the dove hunt. And he'd had his eye on another Cadillac.

The phone buzzed loudly, startling him. He'd told Diana to hold his calls for the rest of the day.

"Sorry to interrupt, sir, but Junior's on the phone," Diana said. "He says it's important."

"Put him through."

"Hey, Dad," Junior's voice was missing its usual swagger.

"What's going on, son?"

"Um, I don't really know how to tell you this. But I got into some trouble last weekend. I had to meet with the dean this afternoon. I thought it wouldn't be a big deal. But they're kicking me out."

"What do you mean, kicking you out? For the semester?"

"No, for good."

"I thought they were giving you the whole semester to get your grades up."

"It's not about my grades."

"Junior, what did you do?"

Junior explained that it wasn't his fault; he and his fraternity brothers got into a brawl with the guys from Kappa Sig after a night of heavy drinking.

"You got kicked out of school for a fraternity fight? Give me the name of that dean."

Junior waited a beat. "I guess you'll find all of this out when the school calls. It wasn't my first meeting with the dean. I got caught a couple times last semester in the girls' dorm after hours."

Gordon thought back to his own college escapades. "Can't the football coach make all this go away?"

"Dad, football's over for me. The coach told me at the end of the season not to expect any playing time next year. My shoulder's just never been the same since I broke it. I meant to tell you over Christmas break, but I didn't want to ruin your holiday, or Mom's."

"She doesn't give a damn about football, but she does care about you getting a decent education." Gordon felt a headache coming on. "So no more football?"

"I know, Dad. I'm sorry. What am I supposed to do now?"

Sensing the undercurrent of desperation in Junior's voice, Gordon tried to take a more fatherly tone. "Give me a minute to think about this, son. I'll call you back later."

Looking down at the legal pad on his desk, he noticed his doodles had turned into big black circles in ever-tightening circumferences. Damn that Jake Sanders; he better not ever show his face in Hobbsfield again. If it hadn't been for that fight in the smokehouse, Junior would be the star of the football team and surely wouldn't be in this mess.

He lit a cigarette and drew the smoke into his lungs to calm himself down. Pacing back and forth, he glanced out the window at General Armistead astride his horse and felt a surge of anger course though his body. Dammit, Junior was a Talmadge, and no college chancellor, dean, or coach was going to give his son the boot.

He stumped out his cigarette and instructed Diana to put him through to East Carolina's chancellor, Art Frailey. Forcing himself to smile so his voice would sound friendly, Gordon reminded Chancellor Frailey of the donation his family had made to the college last year. "Junior promised me he'll keep his nose clean from here on out. You won't regret giving him another chance. In fact, Claire and I were thinking of making a nice contribution to the sports program."

Gordon waited for his words to take effect. "Mr. Talmadge, unfortunately, Junior's not serious about his studies. He's more interested in socializing than getting a good education. I'm sorry, but my decision stands."

"What g-g-goddamn right do you have to embarrass me and my family?"

"I have an obligation to the students of this college to uphold our standards. If I let Junior back in, it will be a mockery of everything we stand for. I'm sorry, Mr. Talmadge." Gordon heard a click and then silence.

SIXTEEN

March 1961

Satisfied that Mary Grace was asleep, Will crept out from under the pile of patchwork quilts. Bracing against the cold air, he headed out into the night. Ever since Mr. Talmadge had denied his loan request, he'd doubled down on his moonshine operation.

In the full moon, Will could easily find his way down the worn path through the woods. Arriving at the still, Will built up the fire to get the water boiling, then added the corn meal and yeast. As he waited for the mash to heat up, he checked the tubing that would carry the steam from the mash into the box, where the cold water flowing through would condense it back into liquid whiskey.

He never heard them coming.

"Will Craddock, you're under arrest," a voice called out in the dark.

When Will looked up, Sheriff Owen and two officers with Alcohol Law Enforcement badges pinned to their uniforms were standing in front of him, their flashlights sweeping across Will's still and landing on their badges in a show of force.

As his heart pounded, he found his voice. "What the hell?" The deputy handcuffed him and turned him around while Sheriff Owen doused the flames of the still. "How'd you know I was out here?"

"One of our men got a tip."

Will quaked with anger on the march back through the woods. He wondered if Glenn had ratted on him; he'd put an end to giving out free samples since the auction. As they approached the driveway, he heard Buster barking and saw lights coming on in the Big House. He spotted Mary Grace shivering on the cabin porch, staring at him.

———————— x⟨⟨x ————————

Mary Grace spent the rest of the night worrying over the trouble her father was in. When morning finally came, she walked up the hill in the direction of the Big House. She knocked on the kitchen door hoping Ivy would answer. She was mortified when David came to the door.

He quickly opened it. "Is everything okay, Mary Grace? We saw the police cars last night."

She glared at him. "Everything's fine. I was hoping to have a word with your father."

"With Dad? Um, okay. He's in the living room. Follow me."

"I can find it myself . . ." But David was already leading her through the foyer past the staircase and into a large room with a grand piano in the corner. She unbuttoned her coat, feeling warmth all around her, a far cry from their drafty cabin where the wood stove put out too much heat in the front room and not enough for the back bedrooms. Gordon and Claire were sitting on the sofa.

"Dad, Mary Grace is here," David said. "She wants to talk to you."

Gordon looked up from his newspaper. "What can I do for you?" he asked coldly.

"Why don't you sit down, Mary Grace?" Claire said, not unkindly.

Mary Grace dusted off the back of her dress before perching on the edge of the nearest chair. She glared at David again, hoping he would leave the room; instead, he sat down in the chair next to hers, placing himself opposite his parents.

"I'm . . . I'm sorry my dad brought trouble out here." Mary Grace said. "And . . ."

"You and me both," Gordon said, snapping his newspaper shut. "I don't much like being awakened by Dan Owen in the middle of the night to find out that your father is running an illegal moonshine operation right under my nose. What a mess. You know this is not his first brush up with the law. But at least until now, he's kept his shenanigans off my property." Mary Grace looked at the floor, thinking of the three different times Will had spent a night in jail for drunken behavior.

Mary Grace forced herself to meet Gordon's eyes. "Sir, I know my dad brought this trouble on himself. But I'm hoping you can find a way to help him out, to help *us* out, on account of how hard he's worked for you all these years. Talk to the sheriff or something. With farm season coming up, we can't afford for him to miss work."

Gordon bristled. "He should've thought of that before he got mixed up in all of this. You better be glad I have connections at the newspaper. I'll have his head on a platter if this ends up in the *Times*. I don't need that kind of publicity."

Mary Grace looked down and explained that Will had likely started making moonshine after the storm had ruined his crop and they'd been unable to pay off their bills.

Mr. Talmadge frowned. "Don't you have family who can help with that?"

"No, sir. I work at the hospital, but it doesn't make much of a dent in what we owe."

"I thought you were in high school."

"Dropped out last fall to get a job."

"Dad, surely you can do something," David said. "Sheriff Owen is a friend of yours, right?" Mary Grace frowned. Why wouldn't he stay out of it?

A pregnant silence hung over the room.

Mr. Talmadge stood up. "I don't have time for this. I need to get to work. I'm not sure Will deserves it, but I'll make a call, see if we can work something out. But I don't care how many years he's worked here, if he gets in trouble again, I'm going to wash my hands of him."

"He won't, sir," Mary Grace said. "Thank you." She moved quickly towards the kitchen fumbling with the buttons on her coat.

"Mary Grace, wait." David followed her but she ran out the door without looking back.

SEVENTEEN

Ella reached in the upper kitchen cabinet for another pie plate. "Good thing you're helping me today," Ivy said. "Or else I'd be climbing up on a chair trying to get to that shelf." At seventeen, Ella towered over her mother.

"I'm glad there's something good about my being so tall," Ella said. "Most of the boys in my class come up to my chin. I feel like a giant next to them."

Ivy smiled. Ella seemed more like herself these days, and it was nice to have her daughter helping with the baking. Plus, Ella always enjoyed seeing how beautiful the Big House looked during the holidays.

Gordon and Claire had left that morning for a holiday party in Raleigh, so Ivy and Ella had the house to themselves. They turned up the kitchen radio and sang along to Christmas carols while they rolled out pie crusts and mixed up dough for gingerbread cookies.

"I'm glad to be done with school for two weeks," Ella said, putting a tray of cookie dough into the oven.

"And then just one more term, and me and your daddy are gonna have a *second* child graduate from high school." Ivy beamed with pride.

"Mama, don't go getting all worked up again. You know I won't be at the top of the class like Jake was."

"It don't matter, Ella, you're gonna graduate and that's what counts. And you got a plan for your future."

Ivy had asked Claire for advice on a path for Ella, and Claire had suggested a secretarial program at Jefferson County Community College that had recently opened to coloreds. When Ella discovered she'd get to wear dresses and sit in an air-conditioned office, she was sold. She'd even taken to practicing her telephone skills in her spare time.

Ella picked up an imaginary telephone. "Talmadge Farm Sweet Shop," she said in her fanciest voice. "May I help you?"

Ivy laughed and played along. "Um, yes, I need to order some pies for Christmas dinner."

"Well, ma'am, we've got the best pies in all of Jefferson County. What kind do you want?"

"Pecan. And pumpkin."

"Why yes, we can help you with that. Let me connect you to our order department. Hold please, and have a blessed day." She pushed an imaginary button to transfer the call and then hung up the phone.

Ivy chuckled. "Silly girl. You still got to finish high school first."

"I know." Ella sighed. "I wish I could start right after graduation and not have to work in the fields this summer."

"I know, baby. But your daddy needs you out there. It's getting harder to find decent workers. Kids nowadays ain't wanting to farm as much, they're looking for other things, kinda like you. And what with Jake gone, and Mary Grace working at the hospital, your daddy and Will need all the help they can get. And we need a good harvest this year so we can pay for that program of yours."

Ella was reaching into the oven to see if the cookies were done when Junior came into the kitchen with a slam of the door. Startled, Ella burned her finger on the pan. "Ouch," she said, jumping back and moving to the sink to put her finger in the cold running water.

"Excuse me." Junior's voice dripped with sarcasm. "Did you hurt yourself?"

Ivy gave him a look but held her tongue. Using a tea towel, she took the cookie pan out of the oven and set it on the stove.

Ella tried to keep her voice steady. "I'm fine."

"Glad to hear it." Junior reached over her, took three cookies from the pan and walked out the door. A minute later, they heard his car pull out with a loud screech.

"I swear I thought all our problems would be solved once he went away to college," Ivy said.

"I know," Ella said, sucking on her finger. "Now that he got himself kicked out of school, he seems worse than before. And he acts like I did something wrong. I mean, he came after me, right? What was I supposed to do, let him have his way with me?"

Ivy looked down, a hint of shame passing over her face.

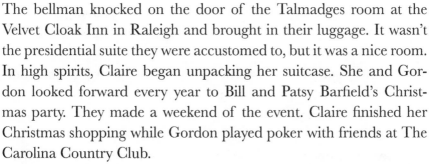

The bellman knocked on the door of the Talmadges room at the Velvet Cloak Inn in Raleigh and brought in their luggage. It wasn't the presidential suite they were accustomed to, but it was a nice room. In high spirits, Claire began unpacking her suitcase. She and Gordon looked forward every year to Bill and Patsy Barfield's Christmas party. They made a weekend of the event. Claire finished her Christmas shopping while Gordon played poker with friends at The Carolina Country Club.

Claire was especially grateful to get away this year. She pretended she was happy that Junior was home again, but in reality, life had been easier with her older son off at college. Since he'd been home, Junior had tried working at the bank but failed miserably. No one could cover up his mistakes, and Gordon had been heartbroken to admit Junior wasn't cut out for banking. He'd spent the summer working in the pro shop at the country club, where the golfers were more than happy to buy him drinks after his shift. Claire was constantly on edge. She tried to discuss her concerns with Gordon, but he insisted Junior would grow out of it eventually and settle down. Claire hoped he was right.

At least David was out from under his brother's shadow. He was having an outstanding first semester at Wake Forest University. He'd joined the chess club and signed up for two classes in the English literature program.

Claire put her suitcase in the closet and went to draw a bath.

"Want a drink, sweetie?" Gordon asked, interrupting Claire's thoughts. He pulled out a bottle of bourbon from his suitcase and waved it at her.

"I think I'll wait until we get to the party."

"Suit yourself." He switched on the television and settled on top of the damask bedspread. Within a few minutes, he dozed off.

As Claire undressed for her bath, she caught a glimpse of herself in the mirror. For once, she didn't criticize her reflection. This was the first time in a long while that she could fit into some of the expensive clothes hanging in the back of her closet. Worrying about Junior had caused her to lose her appetite; at least her son being kicked out of college had one positive outcome.

Stepping out of the tub, she put on her cotton bathrobe and applied her makeup. She walked out of the bathroom and picked up the dress she'd bought for the party. Gordon was snoring lightly on the bed.

"Gordon, honey, don't you think you should start getting ready?"

He sat up and rubbed his eyes. "I'm coming. I just need a quick shower."

Claire put on her pantyhose and unzipped the Montaldo's garment bag, smiling at the tag that read "Size 10." She hadn't been a size ten since before David was born. And she hadn't worn a red dress in ages. She stepped into the luxurious crepe de chine, reaching behind to fasten the zipper. She heard Gordon come out of the bathroom.

She completed the look with her double strand of pearls and diamond earrings that belonged to Gordon's mother. Touching up her

freshly curled hair, she stepped into her pumps and turned triumphantly toward her husband.

Gordon was sitting on the bed putting on his socks. He glanced
up at her.

"Would you hand me my shoes?" he asked. "They're in the
closet."

"Get them yourself, Gordon."

"What's gotten into you, Claire?"

"If you don't know, there's no point in explaining myself." She
looked at her watch.

"You'd better hurry or we'll be late.

A small fir tree sat propped up near the front door in the Sanders'
cabin. It was decorated with a popcorn garland and a few homemade
ornaments and topped with one of Ivy's most prized possessions, an
angel that Louis gave her on their first Christmas together. Three
presents lay at the foot of the tree, and four socks hung from the
mantle. Ivy continued putting up Jake's stocking, even though they
hadn't seen him in two years.

The wood stove provided cozy heat on the mild night, but outside, they could hear Buster barking, agitated by the raucous yelling
coming from the Big House. With his parents out of town, Junior was
throwing a party. Cars had been going up and down the driveway
all evening, and the festivities had spilled out onto the porch of the
Talmadge house. Ivy and Louis could hear the ruckus. An occasional
shot rang out. Apparently, Junior and his friends had pulled out his
father's shotguns for target practice.

"Do you hear that, Mama?" Ella stuck her head out of the bedroom where she and Mary Grace were listening to the radio.

Ivy stood up and eyed Louis nervously. "You think we should go
up there? Try to put an end to this?"

"No, baby, we got to stay outta their way. You know them boys been drinking all night. They ain't gonna listen to us." He put his arms around her. "Come on, now. Let's get back to the letter. I do believe the one you're reading might just be my favorite." He kissed her on the lips.

Ivy let him lead her back to her seat on the threadbare sofa. Reading one of Jake's letters had become a part of their evening ritual after Ivy finished her Bible passage. On special occasions, they read them all, starting with the first one he sent and ending with the most recent. Ivy picked up one they'd received a couple of months back. She cleared her throat and read the precious words out loud.

Dear Mama, Daddy, and Ella,

Sorry it's been a while since my last letter. I've been real busy with schoolwork. My roommate likes to cut up with his friends in our room, so I spend a lot of time in the library. He's a decent enough kid, but I know better than to waste time on foolishness. Plus you wouldn't believe the size of the library. I swear the whole Talmadge house would fit inside. It's got more books than you could imagine or that I could ever read, even if I lived to be one hundred.

My biology professor has taken a liking to me. I ask a lot of questions, and he seems to appreciate that. I help him clean up after lab sessions so that probably helps too. As usual, my hardest class is Latin. I'm sure English lit next semester will be hard too. But after my first year I can take more science classes.

I got a job working in the cafeteria in the evenings. I mostly just wash dishes and mop the floors, but I get a free meal during my shift and can take a plate of leftovers back to the dorm so the job goes a long way.

Mama, I know you will be glad to hear that there are a few other colored boys here, and we've gotten to be friends. They're mostly from up north. Ella, you asked in your letter if I was going steady with anyone.

The answer is no, because I don't have time for that. But you asking the question makes me wonder, Are you sweet on anyone?

The Shallcrosses invited me to stay with them for Thanksgiving. Of course, I'd rather be home with you, but it's nice to have somewhere to go. I hope one day you can meet them.

I love you and miss you. I'm glad we're sending letters through Pastor Rice now since Mr. Allen doesn't get up here much during the fall and winter months.

Your devoted son and brother,

Jake

Ivy put down the letter, her eyes misty. As usual, Louis was grinning from ear to ear. "I still can't believe it," he said. "Our boy's in college. I'd like to see that big fancy library."

Jake had graduated from high school last year, and the Shallcrosses helped him get a scholarship to nearby Villanova, a top Catholic university. It seemed that some of the colleges up north were interested in attracting Negroes, and Jake had the grades to earn a spot. Ivy didn't know what Catholic was, but Jake said they believed in Jesus, and the Shallcrosses were Catholic, so that was more than enough for her.

One of Jake's previous letters included a photograph of him with his high school diploma that Mrs. Shallcross had taken. Ivy kept it inside the crate next to her bed and took it out every night when she read his letters. She'd have liked to put it on the mantle beside the picture of Paul, but she was afraid Mr. Gordon might show up at the cabin and see it. As far as Mr. Gordon knew, Ivy and Louis had no idea where Jake was.

As Ivy was folding up the letter, something smacked against the side of the cabin. "What in the world?" She jumped to her feet as pelts continued to strike the cabin wall. Louis got up and cautiously approached the door. They heard muffled laughter and footsteps running away from the front porch. By the time Louis opened the door, the boys were halfway back to the Talmadge house, hollering and laughing in the darkness with Buster barking up a storm. Louis carried the lamp out onto the porch and saw broken eggs all over the side of the house.

"Hooligans," Louis said, shaking his head. "Sooner or later that boy gonna mess up so bad his daddy can't fix it."

"His daddy's best friends with the sheriff," Ivy cried. "There ain't nothing Junior can do that can't be fixed." As Louis got the mop and went to fill a bucket from the pump, Ivy put her hand on the Bible. "Lord, I know you got bigger things to worry about than my troubles. But please help me find a way to get Ella off this farm."

The Barfield house was glowing with soft white Christmas lights as Claire and Gordon walked up the sidewalk. Patsy Barfield spotted them as they entered the front door and rushed over. "Gordon, Claire, it's been ages." She hugged them and then tugged on her husband's elbow. "Bill, look who's here."

He turned around and greeted them warmly. "It's been way too long since we've seen you, Claire. I have to see this old coot at the bank board meetings."

Gordon gave him a scornful laugh. "And we know how much fun those have been lately."

"Claire, you look ravishing tonight," Bill said. "Gordon must be taking good care of you. I wish he'd do the same for himself."

"That dress is stunning on you," Patsy said. She turned back toward Gordon. "We missed the dove hunt this year. We were so disappointed you had to cancel it. I hope you got your renovation project finished."

Gordon and Claire exchanged a look. "Yes, well, we hated to call it off," said Gordon. "But Claire wanted to add more beds to the garden and we put in a grove of dogwood trees. You know how disruptive those things are with all the backhoes and dirt being carted in from the pastures." Claire squeezed Gordon's hand to signal that he had embellished his lie more than enough. "Which way is the bar?"

Claire let Gordon go ahead of her and took a glass of champagne from a waiter carrying a tray. She saw her high school friend Rose Wallace in the dining room by the buffet table and made her way over.

"Rosie! I was hoping you and Charlie would be here," Claire said.

"Yes, now that Lizzie is old enough to babysit, we're getting out more. Claire, what in the world have you been doing to yourself? You look amazing! Don't tell me Ivy has left you and Gordon for greener pastures?"

Claire laughed. "No. I could never do without Ivy. She basically runs the house. She's still turning out her pies, just not quite as often."

"That's right, you've got the boys off at college now. I can't imagine how quiet it must be. It's still chaos at my house."

Claire hesitated. "Not exactly. After Junior hurt his shoulder, he had to give up football. It broke his heart . . . and Gordon's too. And without football, well college just didn't really work out for him. He's trying to figure out his next move. David's finishing his first semester at Wake Forest. He comes home for Christmas on Monday."

"I can't believe David is old enough to be at college."

"He's doing really well; we're so proud of him. And would you believe he has a girlfriend? He's dating the loveliest girl from home who happened to end up at Salem College."

"How sweet."

Rose's husband, Charlie, came over and said hello to Claire. "I was just talking to Gordon," he said. "He's in the living room in the middle of a debate about the future of farming. Sounds like it was a tough year for farmers in Jefferson County with all the rain this past summer."

Charlie turned toward Rose. "Honey, I hate to do this, but we should get going. We promised Lizzie we'd be home at a reasonable hour."

Rose hugged Claire. "It's good to catch up with you. Let's have lunch in the new year. Hope you and Gordon and the boys have a wonderful holiday."

"Same to you. Merry Christmas."

Charlie took Rose's hand and led her towards the door as she called out goodbyes along the way. Claire watched them wistfully for a minute. It was obvious how much in love they were after all these years. She turned back toward the table and took a plate, foregoing the meatballs and cheeses for a few shrimp and some tomato cucumber salad. She took another glass of champagne, scooted around a few clusters of people talking, and looked for a place to sit down. She saw that Gordon was smoking cigars with a group of men in the crowded living room.

She wandered into the paneled den off the kitchen and sank into an empty wingback. Turning to greet the couple seated closest to her on the nearby couch, her eyes went wide.

It was Arthur Evans.

Claire nearly dropped her champagne glass. She hadn't seen him since the night that he and his daughter stayed at the farm during the Mule Days Festival two years ago.

"Claire, how nice to see you again. You look lovely."

"Arthur, what are you doing here? I'm sorry. I mean, it's just that I've never seen you here before in all the years we've been coming to Bill and Patsy's Christmas party." Claire struggled to gain her composure. "I didn't know you were part of their circle of friends."

"I've been working with Bill for the past year on a Research Triangle Park committee, and we play golf occasionally."

"Small world, isn't it? He and Patsy are dear friends of ours. Bill grew up in Jefferson County, and he and Gordon go way back."

The woman sitting beside Arthur stood up. "Arthur, I'm going to freshen up and then get a bite to eat. Meet me in the dining room?"

"I'll be there in a minute," he answered.

He smiled sheepishly at Claire. "Also, I've found from being a widower all these years, I often get invited to events so the hosts can introduce me to their unmarried lady friends."

"Oh, I didn't mean to interrupt. Are you with her? I mean, are the two of you on a date?"

"No, nothing like that. Just having the obligatory conversation. I'm glad you sat down. She and I were running out of things to talk about. People don't realize that when you've been alone as long as I have, you don't mind your own company. Not that I don't sometimes wish the right person would come along."

Claire blushed. She took a cigarette from her purse and Arthur leaned toward her to light it. She caught a whiff of his cologne, maybe something French. Claire mentioned his daughter Leslie and asked if she had graduated from Meredith College.

"You have a good memory. It was two years ago that we stayed with you at the farm. I still remember what a lovely evening that was."

"I enjoyed it as well. I don't often have the chance to play the piano for such an accomplished singer."

"Leslie's teaching music at Saint Mary's School and directing the children's choir at our church. It's nice to have her here in town." He ran his hand through his gray hair. "Speaking of music, do you have any interest in the symphony? Their Christmas concert last weekend was extraordinary."

"My parents took me a few times when I was young. Gordon is not a big fan of classical music. He'd rather go hunting or to a ballgame."

"Well, let me know if you ever want to come. I'm on the board, and I can get tickets for you. Say, how were your roses this year? I couldn't keep the black spot off mine with all the rain we had."

Claire settled into her chair and for the next hour, she and Arthur talked as if they had known each other all their lives. He asked about the boys and her parents and listened intently as she described her concerns about Junior. At one point he got her another glass of champagne. She tried to eat the food on her plate but found her stomach was tied up in knots. She looked up and realized Gordon was standing in the doorway staring at them. She wondered how long he'd been there.

"Claire." Gordon said sharply. "I've been looking for you. I think Bill and Patsy are ready for this shindig to wind down."

"Gordon, hello." Arthur stood up to shake Gordon's hand. "It's been a while." Gordon looked confused. "Arthur Evans. Haven't seen you since you were gracious enough to have us as guests at the farm a couple of years ago when my daughter performed at the festival in Hobbsfield. Seems Bill Barfield is a mutual friend of ours."

Gordon was trying to follow this. "Right, Miss North Carolina's father. I remember she was a real cutie. Our son, Gordon Junior, was smitten with her." He turned to Claire. "I'm going to find our coats. I'll meet you at the front door." He turned back to Arthur. "It's good to see you again. Give our best to your wife."

Claire was horrified. She stood up to apologize, but Arthur put his hand up. "Don't worry about it. He hasn't seen me in two years." He softly kissed her cheek. "I hope it won't be two years until I see you again. It's been wonderful."

Back at the Velvet Cloak, Claire put on her peignoir and slipped into bed. Still giddy from the champagne and the surprise encounter, she waited for Gordon to reach for her, part of the tacit agreement of their weekend getaway. For once, she was looking forward to it. Arthur Evans was all she could think about, and she might as well put that to good use.

———— x⟨C⟩x ————

Ivy bustled around the cabin, putting the roast chicken on the table beside the green beans, mashed potatoes, and gravy. "Louis, come carve this bird while I get the cornbread out of the oven."

It was two days before Christmas, and Ivy had invited the Bennetts to have Christmas dinner with them. The Sanders always celebrated early because Claire expected Ivy to work on Christmas Eve for the Talmadges' annual holiday drop-in and on Christmas Day for the family dinner.

Cleo and Sam Bennett and their son, Bobby Lee, arrived right on time. Cleo handed Ivy a homemade apple cake and gave her a big hug. Ivy stood on her tiptoes and embraced Bobby Lee. "We're sure glad you can be with us on your leave from Fort Bragg. I'm glad they let you off for Christmas."

"Thank you, Mrs. Sanders. It's good to see you."

Ivy couldn't put her finger on it exactly, but Bobby Lee seemed different. He used to be silly, always goofing around. Now he stood straighter and had an air of confidence about him.

Ella noticed it too. She followed him onto the porch. "Bobby Lee, look at you in your uniform, all official. You look like you're somebody important."

"It's high time you realized I'm somebody important," Bobby Lee said, eyes twinkling. "I'm a U.S. soldier in training for the Parachute Infantry Regiment of the 82nd Airborne Division at Fort Bragg, North Carolina. First ones in and last ones out in time of war. You should show me some respect."

Ella laughed. "Like that's ever gonna happen."

"Maybe someday. Hey, when did you get so tall? You're nearly as tall as I am."

"Look at my daddy. I guess it runs in the family. But you're not the only one who's important around here. I'm going to secretary school at Jefferson County Community College next fall."

Bobby Lee raised his eyebrows. "That is impressive. But what does a farm girl like you know about being a secretary?"

She gave him a shove. "Well, why don't you give me a call and find out." Ella picked up her imaginary telephone. "Sanders Christmas Shop, how can I help you?" Bobby Lee looked confused.

"Sanders Christmas Shop," Ella said, more insistently this time. "Is anyone on the line?" She looked at him impatiently.

"Um, this is Bobby Lee Bennett. I'd like to um, order a Christmas tree?"

"I'm sorry, sir, we don't sell Christmas trees here. But if you'd like a Christmas ornament or a Christmas pie, we can help you."

"Um, I'd like to buy a Christmas ornament?"

"Let me transfer you to that department, sir, although you're a bit late for the current holiday season. Have a blessed day." She pushed an imaginary button and hung up the phone.

Bobby Lee laughed. "You're hired. I don't think you even need the schooling part."

Cleo opened the door. "Dinner's ready."

They crowded around the pine table and held hands as Louis said grace. Ella wasn't sure, but Bobby Lee seemed to hold on to her hand after the prayer a second longer than he needed to. She looked over at him but he was already reaching for a piece of cornbread.

After dessert, the women washed the dishes while the men went outside for a smoke. Ivy stood at the door and beckoned for Bobby Lee to join her on the porch. She had something she wanted to discuss with him privately.

"How long until you get to come home on leave again?" she asked him.

"I think six months. And after that, who knows? If there's a conflict somewhere, my unit will probably get sent."

"You've got to do something for me, Bobby Lee. When you get back to Fort Bragg, I want you to find the nicest young man in the whole place. Someone about your age who's tall like you. Who's got good manners and comes from a God-fearing family. And then bring him home with you on your next leave."

Bobby Lee looked at her quizzically. "I don't understand."

"I need you to find Ella a husband."

His eyes widened. "I didn't know Ella was looking for a husband."

"She ain't. But she's old enough. And I've got to get that girl off this farm before something bad . . ."

"Before what?" he asked with a furrowed brow.

"Well, let's just say if she's gonna be a secretary in some office, it's gonna be better for her if she's hitched. You never know what kind of man she might have to work for."

Bobby Lee slowly nodded. "Okay, Mrs. Sanders. I'll do my best."

"Oh, and one more thing. Don't be telling Ella I asked you to do this. She wouldn't want me messing around in her business. But I'm her mama. It's my job to look out for her."

He hesitated for a second and then saluted her. "Yes ma'am."

The telephone rang, waking Claire from a sound sleep. She switched on the lamp, thinking for a minute they were still at the Velvet Cloak. But they'd gotten home yesterday. She glanced at the clock. It was past midnight.

"Gordon, answer the phone." She shook his shoulder. "Gordon, answer the phone." He grunted and reached for the receiver. Claire strained to listen but couldn't hear who was on the other end.

"I see," said Gordon, sitting up swiftly. "But he's okay?"

"What happened?" Claire asked, tugging on his sleeve.

"I see. And she was the only one with injuries?"

"Gordon, what happened?" Claire hissed.

"Thank you, we'll be there shortly."

"Junior crashed his car into a tree on Buffalo Road. He's okay . .
. just banged up. But one of the girls in the car—Kelly somebody—
was hurt badly. She's in surgery."

"Kelly McClure. I know her mother from the hospital auxiliary."
Claire felt like she might throw up. "Oh my God."

EIGHTEEN

Gordon heard a car in the driveway and peered out the bathroom window to see a stocky Negro man climbing out of a Lincoln. He was wearing a baseball cap and a heavy gold chain. Gordon flinched as the man flicked his cigarette butt into the rose bushes. Good thing Claire didn't see that, he thought. The man should show more respect.

Gordon finished shaving and wiped his face with a towel as the doorbell rang. Claire was sitting at the vanity putting on her makeup. He kissed the top of her head. "There's a man here to see me about some farm business. When I'm done, do you want to ride over to Wilson? We could check out a few antique stores, maybe eat an early dinner at The Grille Room?"

Claire studied him for a minute. "What's gotten into you?"

"Thought I should pay my bride some attention," he said, shrugging his shoulders. Truth was he was feeling more attracted to Claire these days now that she'd finally lost some weight. Plus, he hadn't much liked the way that Arthur Evans fellow was looking at her at the Barfields' Christmas party. And the way she was looking back at him.

"Well, honey, I wish you'd asked me sooner. I have a garden club meeting this afternoon. Peg has arranged for the chief landscape designer from the Biltmore Estate to give us a slide show." The doorbell rang again.

"Suit yourself."

———————— x)(x ————————

As Gordon went downstairs, he saw Ivy heading from the kitchen to the front door. "I'll get it, Ivy," he said. He didn't want Ivy curious about the stranger from Florida who might hold the key to big changes at Talmadge Farm.

Gordon opened the front door.

"Red Kincaid, sir," the man said, not bothering to remove his cap.

Gordon stuck out his hand. "Nice to meet you, Mr. Kincaid." Gordon winced as Red squeezed his hand in a vice-like grip.

"Call me Red."

"Would you like a glass of iced tea or something? You must be thirsty after your long drive. How far is it from Belle Glade?"

"Ten hours give or take depending on traffic. I stayed the night in Savannah with some kinfolk and it took me four hours from there."

Gordon had contacted Red through a farmer he knew outside of Raleigh who had taken advantage of his services.

"You ready to show me the property?" Red asked. "I've got other appointments today when I'm done here."

Gordon hastily put on his coat and stepped outside. Buster came out of the bushes to sniff Red's legs and then let out a low growl. Apologizing, Gordon instructed him to calm down.

"Handsome dog," observed Red.

"He's one in a long line of great hunting dogs," Gordon said, rubbing Buster's neck. "If you train them when they're young, they'll do just what you want them to do."

Red nodded. "I know what you mean."

"You got hunting dogs yourself?"

"No, German shepherds. They're watch dogs. It's what I need in my line of work."

"Trained to guard your property, huh?"

"You could say that."

The two men climbed into the farm truck and Gordon drove him out to the acreage designated for tobacco. "As you can see, the seed-beds are over there." He pointed to an area covered by staked plastic to protect the seedlings as they emerged. "In a few weeks, we'll trans-plant them to the twenty acres down there." He pointed to the area where Will and Louis were using the tractor to break up the topsoil. "Obviously, we rotate our planting field every year so we can burn away the undergrowth and put more ash in the soil."

Red nodded and spat out the window of the truck into the tall grass.

"And I'm sure you're familiar with the new policy allowing farm-ers to lease another farmer's quota and transfer it back to his own land. Next summer, I expect to have fifty acres of tobacco." Pointing to another field, Gordon explained that they'd also started planting sweet potatoes and snap peas to sell to the grocery chains. "We're hav-ing some difficulty getting shelf space, but we expect that to improve once customers get a taste of our produce."

"Tell me again, how many sharecroppers you got, Mr. Talmadge?"

"I've got two, and they're scrambling to find temporary workers during harvest. A lot of the locals who used to look for farm work in the summer are going elsewhere, taking jobs in factories around here or heading north. And don't get me started with the younger generation. They're not interested in farming. It's become an old man's game."

"So your sharecroppers have to hire out? They don't have enough kids to do the work?"

Gordon paused. "Well, of the few they have, one got himself killed up in the rafters of the tobacco barn, and one got into trouble and ran off. The other two are girls, so of course, they're not much help to begin with."

"It takes a lot of hands to harvest tobacco," Red noted. "I've got workers. That's it pure and simple."

"I'm listening."

"I got a big team of migrant laborers down in Belle Glade. We move up the coast from farm to farm starting in April all the way through November. We spend a certain number of weeks at each farm and do all the topping, suckering, and harvesting. You pay me, and I pay them. All you need to do is provide housing."

"One of those cabins back there could house a dozen workers. They don't need anything fancy. Just a running water pump, bunk beds, and an outhouse. I'll make sure they're properly fed. And you get to keep all the money from the tobacco you sell. No more splitting the proceeds with your sharecroppers. Once my gang has cured the last bit of gold leaf and gotten it ready for auction, I put them back on the bus and we move north to the next farm in line."

"Sounds like a pretty sweet deal," Gordon said.

Red Kincaid nodded and spat out the window again. "Besides putting bunk beds in your cabins, you'll also need to buy bulk barns. Our migrant workers aren't as skilled as your sharecroppers; they're not used to hand-tying and hanging tobacco sticks from the beams. Bulk barns allow you to do away with all that. Everything is cooked on shelves and the tobacco is taken to auction on pallets. It's a stream-lined operation, nothing like the way it's been done up until now. Farmers who want to get ahead are hiring contractors like me."

"I see," Gordon said, rubbing the bald spot on the back of his head. "So these workers of yours—are they experienced farmhands?"

Red scoffed at that. "They're not experienced in anything. They're lucky to have a job at all. Trust me, I'm doing them a favor. And I'll make sure they do the job right." Gordon's mind wandered back to Red's mention of German shepherds.

"They're not going to cause trouble, are they?"

"Not if they want to stay on my crew," Red answered. "Remember, they work for me. You won't have to get your hands dirty."

When they returned to the house, Gordon told Red he'd think it over and get back to him.

"I wouldn't wait long if I was you," Red said. "My calendar's filling up fast."

He nodded at Gordon one last time and hopped into his car. As he peeled out of the driveway, the sun hit the Florida license plate, blinding Gordon for a split second.

Feeling tired, Gordon sat down on the veranda and looked out over the acres of fields and trees. Was the farm ready for a change as big as this? He thought about Louis and Will and the dedicated work they'd put into the tobacco fields through the years.

Gordon thought of how his grandfather, Proctor Talmadge, owned slaves on Talmadge Farm, slaves who'd lived in the sharecropper cabins or in lean-tos out by the pines where they extracted the resin that his grandfather sold, making him rich enough to buy all this beautiful land.

Finally, he thought about Junior. He'd indulged his son for years, trying to build him up rather than make him feel inadequate, the way his own father had made him feel. But somewhere along the way, he'd miscalculated. And now Junior was drying out in a facility in Greensboro while he paid the medical bills of the unfortunate girl who nearly lost her leg in the accident.

It was time for a change.

NINETEEN

March 1962

Will finished the modest supper Mary Grace had left for him before she reported for her night shift at the hospital. He rinsed his plate at the water pump and then sat down on the porch to enjoy the last strands of pink daylight. He tried to ignore the pain in his mouth, but one of his teeth was coming loose and giving him a hell of an ache. Too bad he couldn't afford a visit to the dentist. He'd have to ask Louis to pull it out with a pair of pliers.

Thinking a beer would help lessen the pain, he got one and settled back into his seat, taking a long drink. He'd sworn off the hard stuff since he got busted, hadn't had a drop of liquor in almost a year. Figured he owed Mary Grace that much, especially since she'd convinced Mr. Talmadge to pull some strings after his arrest. He'd ended up with a suspended sentence, one year's probation, and a hefty fine he was still trying to pay off. He could barely look his daughter in the eye when the sentence was rendered.

Curiously, he noticed Mr. Talmadge walking down the driveway in his direction, Buster trotting along behind. Will hid the beer can behind his chair and stood up as straight as his stooped back would allow. "Evening."

As Gordon eased his large frame into Ruby's rocking chair, Will fought the urge to shove him out. To him, Mary Grace was the only person who had a right to sit there. Sometimes, alone at night, he'd sit on the porch and imagine Ruby beside him. Even after all these years, he missed her mightily.

"Will, I'm not going to mince words," Gordon said. "I'm making some changes around here. I'm expanding operations. Bought a tobacco poundage allotment from one of the other farmers in the county who's getting out of the business. That'll give me the right to plant more acres next year."

Will couldn't make sense of this. He and Louis could barely come up with enough workers to harvest the acres they had.

"I've ordered three bulk barns. They'll be delivered within the month. We're going to phase out the flue-cured barns altogether. No more tending the fire. No more risk of something blowing up. No more hand tying. Things are going to be a lot simpler."

"Guess I'll have to learn how to run a bulk barn, won't I?"

"And I'm bringing in a crew of migrant workers from Florida to help with the harvest. We just don't have enough laborers locally."

Will felt a sense of relief. Maybe this was good news.

"What I'm getting at," Gordon continued, "is that I need you to move out."

"Out of where?"

"Out of this cabin. Off this property."

"Wait, is this about moonshining? I told you I was all done ..."

"It's not about that. I'm bringing in a crew of a dozen workers in July and they'll need a place to live during harvest season."

Will tugged on his mustache. "You're kicking me and Louis off the farm?"

"Well, now, Louis is another story. He helps us around the house in addition to his farm duties. And Ivy has been here since before I met Claire. My wife counts on her to help run the house. For now, it's just you I need out."

Will clenched the arms of the chair he was sitting in until his hands hurt. "I've worked your land my whole life."

Gordon nodded. "Maybe I can help find somewhere for you and Mary Gail to live. Maybe talk to some folks about a job for you."

Will cradled his head in his hands, trying to shield his mind from the grim reality of what Mr. Talmadge was saying. "Don't bother. And for the record, my daughter is Mary *Grace*, the girl who once helped your son get a passing grade in math."

Gordon ignored this. "Tell you what, you and your daughter can stay through the end of June. I'll pay you to help with the barn installation and to build some bunk beds in here. But then you'll have to go."

Will watched, speechless, as Mr. Talmadge walked down the steps and whistled for Buster, who bounded off behind him. Will picked up his beer and chugged it down in one gulp. He resisted the urge to hurl the empty can at Mr. Talmadge's head.

Mary Grace tapped her foot as she waited impatiently at the end of the driveway. This was an important day, and she didn't want to be late. She found it unprofessional to show up late for work, but since her daddy needed the truck today, she had to pay Sarah Hinnant fifty cents for a ride. And it was anybody's guess if that dimwit would be on time. God knows she'd probably spend the money on lipstick.

She wiped at the angry tears in her eyes. She had come home from work yesterday morning to the news that Mr. Talmadge was making her and her daddy leave the farm.

For good or for bad, that shabby cabin with its thin walls, mismatched chairs, and cracked windowpanes was the only home she'd ever known. And how was she supposed to leave a place covered in her mother's fingerprints, from the homemade curtains she'd made out of leftover dress material to the scent of her that still lingered in the wardrobe?

Finally, Sarah's car came around the bend. Mary Grace rode silently to the hospital while Sarah nattered on about a new color of eyeshadow she'd bought. As they walked in the employee entrance, Sarah went into the nurse's break room while Mary Grace went upstairs to her supervisor's office.

She tapped lightly on the door and opened it. "Come in," Mrs. Hayes called out, barely glancing up from her typing. "Mary Grace, if you're here to ask for more shifts again, you know I gave you as many this month as I could."

"That's not why I'm here."

"Also, I have a new girl starting next week. I want you to train her, so I'll match her schedule with yours."

"Okay."

Mrs. Hayes turned to look at Mary Grace. "Was there something else?"

"Yes, ma'am. I wanted to talk to you about something. I've been here for a year and a half. And in that time, I feel like I've learned everything there is to know about the way this hospital works, and I've worked as hard as I could to be a good nurse's aide. I know some of the nurses don't like me, but that's usually because they're not doing their job properly, and I'm not afraid to point that out."

Mrs. Hayes raised her eyebrows.

Mary Grace went on to explain how she wanted to become a nurse herself but hadn't been able to save enough money for the program. "What I'm wondering is if there's any way the hospital could loan me the money, and then I could pay it back when I'm finished and working as a full-fledged nurse."

Mrs. Hayes took a moment to consider this proposition. "Mary Grace, I agree that you're one of the best aides we've ever had. It's why I have you train all the new girls. But the scholarships we offer are only for girls who've finished high school. And the hospital has never given a loan to our employees that I know of." She paused, thinking. "I wonder if Farmers and Merchants might be willing to give you a loan. I could go with you to discuss it with one of the loan officers.

Mary Grace could feel her face turning red. "I don't think that's an option, ma'am."

"I'll see what I can do about increasing your hours. I wish I could do more to help."

"I understand. Thank you for your time."

"How beautiful." Rhonda Lassiter's brown eyes widened as she took in the dogwood branches that Claire had forced into bloom and placed on the sideboard in the dining room. Claire learned the technique from the Biltmore Estate horticulturist and was experimenting with different plant species that grew in her garden. Next on her list were the yellow forsythias, which she thought might look lovely in the hallway against the black and white marble floor.

"Wow, Mom, you outdid yourself," David said. He was home for spring break from Wake Forest and had invited his girlfriend to join them for dinner.

"Son, you know your mother is the most talented gardener in the whole state," Gordon said, shaking the ice in his highball glass. "Consider yourself lucky to enjoy the fruits of her labors."

David looked at his mother. His father didn't usually notice his mother's gardening efforts. Or any of her efforts, for that matter.

Ivy put down a bowl of green beans and a plate of hot rolls beside the roast ham and candied yams. "Y'all have a good evening," she said softly. David noticed she'd been especially quiet since he'd been home.

"Rhonda, we're so glad you could join us," Claire said as they began serving their plates. She asked her about life at Salem College.

"It's going well, thank you. I love my history class this semester. The professor has a way of making it feel like whatever part of history we're studying is happening right now. I hope to be a teacher myself someday, or maybe a librarian."

Claire smiled. "If you want to be a librarian, you must be a book lover. There's a girl after my own heart. No wonder David enjoys your company. What are some of your favorites?"

"Gosh, it's hard to choose. *The Great Gatsby. Jane Eyre. Pride and Prejudice.*"

"She's the only person I know who reads more than I do," David said.

Gordon reached across the table for a hot roll and smeared it with butter. Sensing his father was impatient with the conversation, David asked him for news of the bank.

"Nothing to report there," Gordon said. "But I do have some new plans to modernize the farm."

David adjusted his glasses and squeezed Rhonda's hand under the table. He hoped his family was not overwhelming her.

". . . a team of migrant workers," Gordon was saying. "I'm planning to house them in one of the sharecropper cabins. We're going to put in bunk beds so a dozen or more can stay there."

David realized he'd missed part of what his father was saying. "Wait, Dad, what did you say?"

"Looks like my son is too smitten to pay attention to me." Gordon chuckled and winked at Rhonda. He repeated that he was bringing in a crew of migrant workers from Florida to do the bulk of the harvest work. "It'll be more profitable for me. I pay a one-time fee to the crew chief and then I get to keep all the profits from the tobacco sale."

"And these workers are going to stay in the sharecropper cabins?"

"Just the Craddocks'. Louis and Ivy are going to stay put for the time being. I gave Will notice last week, told him he has to be off the property by the end of June."

David paled. "Where will he and Mary Grace go?"

"I don't know, but that's not my problem." Trying to appease David, he told him that he'd agreed to pay Will to build several sets of bunk beds in his cabin and to help with the new bulk barn installation.

David began to clean his glasses and realized his hands were shaking. "So before you kick Will out of his own house, you're making him renovate it so the new workers can live there?" Rhonda was looking at him strangely, trying to place a calming hand on his white knuckles.

"I don't think I like your tone, son," Gordon said. "I've given him ample notice and offered to pay him up until he leaves, and I think that's more than fair. There's nothing in a sharecropper's contract that guarantees him a place for life. I have to do what's good for us."

"Anybody want more beans?" asked Claire.

David could only stare as his father went back to eating while his mother told them about a new flowering shrub she was putting in the garden. Just to throw some mud in his father's face, he couldn't resist asking him about Junior. "How's he doing at that facility you put him in, Dad? Has he sworn off the bottle?"

Gordon took a long sip of his drink. "He's doing just fine. Should be out in no time."

Not for the first time, David felt like being at home was its own brand of punishment.

David stopped his car in the driveway near the tobacco fields as the sun began to dip below the horizon. He got out and leaned against the fence, staring out at the empty furrows. He'd just dropped Rhonda off and didn't feel like going home. He couldn't believe his father's cruelty—kicking Will and Mary Grace off the farm. And his mother going on about beans and flowers. Did they not realize they were ruining people's lives? He wondered where the Craddocks would go.

At the sound of footsteps he turned around. Mary Grace was walking towards him.

"Hey," he said tentatively.

She gave him a withering look. "What are you doing out here?"

"Just . . . thinking, I guess . . . watching the sun go down. I'm on my way home. What are you doing?

"Going to the mailbox." She started to move past him.

"Mary Grace . . . I . . . I heard you're . . . moving soon."

She gave a scornful laugh. "I guess that's one way to put it. Another is that your father is throwing us out on our asses."

David blinked. "Where will you go?"

"Don't know yet. As far away from here as we can get if I have anything to say about it." She turned to walk away.

"I'm sorry he's making you leave."

"Oh, gee, thanks. Do you feel better now that you've said you're sorry? And what exactly is it you're sorry for? That my daddy can barely stand up straight from a lifetime of leaning over those stupid stalks?" She waved a hand in the direction of the fields. "That your father makes a fortune from those fields and doesn't do one ounce of the work? That a random summer storm blew in right before auction and ruined our season? That I had to drop out of school and get a job because your father—who owns a bank—wouldn't give my father a loan? And guess what, without a high school diploma, I can't qualify for a nursing scholarship, so I guess I'm stuck being a nurse's aide and cleaning bedpans for the rest of my life." Mary Grace was shouting now. "Are you sorry that you watched me beg your father for help when my dad got arrested?"

David felt stung. "Wait a second, I was trying to *help* you that day."

"Well I don't need your help. Or your pity. I don't need anything from any of you."

My God, she was impossible. "You know what? I'm tired of you acting like I'm the same as the rest of my family. I think it's awful that my father is making you leave the farm, and I told him so."

"How charitable of you."

"We used to be friends, Mary Grace. And then my idiot brother harasses Ella and suddenly *you* never speak to me again. It was awful what Junior did that day. But *Junior* did it, not me. He's a moron. Two months ago, he wrapped his car around a tree. I'm *nothing* like him, but you won't even talk to me long enough to figure that out. And we used to be friends."

"We were never friends, David. You were just bad at math."

TWENTY

May 1962

Will buttoned the shirt Mary Grace washed for him and tucked it into his dungarees. He rifled around in the top dresser drawer for a clean pair of socks. The only ones he found that weren't full of holes or gray from years of wear were a pair that Ruby had bought him years ago that he had never worn. He put them on. Maybe they'd bring him good luck.

He pulled the piece of paper out of his pocket and looked it over again. He'd copied it down from the board at the general store:

NOW HIRING. Smothers Ham. Looking for Experienced Truck Drivers. Full-Time Work. Interview at 323 Brightleaf Blvd. on Saturday, May 26. 10 a.m. - 3 p.m. No appointment necessary.

He dipped his fingers into a tub of pomade and smoothed down what was left of his gray hair. Taking out a pair of scissors, he peered into the cracked mirror and clipped a few strands that brushed his collar and then evened out his mustache. He laced up his pair of Sunday shoes that Mary Grace had polished for him and walked into the front room.

"Look at you," Mary Grace said. "You look exactly like a person I'd want to hire." She handed him a bowl of oatmeal and a cup of black coffee. "Let me just grab my sweater and I'll be ready." She hurried back over to the Sanders' cabin. She'd been staying there since her father had started building the bunk beds in their cabin.

As they headed in the truck toward the hospital, he drove faster than normal. He wanted to get there early so he'd be among the first men in line at Smothers Ham. Mary Grace gave him a kiss before climbing out of the truck. "Remember, look them in the eye and be polite. And don't leave until you've said everything you came to say. You'll do great, Daddy."

"Sure was nice of Miss Claire to let us use her car today," Louis said as he pulled onto the main road.

Ivy straightened the collar on her nicest Sunday dress. "She knows what a special day this is for Ella."

"And for Ella's mama," he added, patting her leg. "And don't Ella look pretty as a Georgia peach in Miss Claire's dress?" It was a dress Claire hadn't worn in years. Ivy had let down the hem as far as she could, but it was still a little short, barely grazing her knees.

"Ella, we sure are proud of you." Louis's eyes were bright with tears.

"Would you stop carrying on?" piped up Ella from the backseat. But she was just as excited as they were. She'd been practicing her graduation walk in Miss Claire's dress and heels ever since school let out two weeks ago.

"Those are happy tears, baby," Ivy said.

As they approached Ebenezer Baptist, where the graduation ceremony was being held, Ivy could see tables set up for punch and wreaths on the doors to the church. Louis eased the car carefully into a parking spot, and Ella immediately jumped out.

"Hold on a minute, Ella," Ivy said.

"But there's Annie Marie."

"She can wait. I've got a letter from Jake. He has something he wants to say to his sister, the high school graduate." She unfolded the letter and began to read aloud.

Dear Ella,

I hear Piney Grove is handing out diplomas to any old numbskull these days! Just kidding, little sister. I'm proud of you for making it all the way through high school. I remember how much you used to hate homework! Everybody always thought of me as the smart one in the family but sounds like you're pretty smart yourself. I know you will make a great secretary. Maybe you can move to Philadelphia when you finish your program. Living here has taught me that there's lots of opportunities in the world. Congratulations, little sister!

Love,

Jake

Ella smiled through her own happy tears as she got out of the car and gave her parents a long hug.

The Smothers Ham Company occupied a three-story red brick building near the railroad tracks on the east side of Hobbsfield. The sign above the building read: "Hams Made With Tradition."

Will took his place in the line of men and waited until he was told to take a seat and fill out an application. When he reached the question about having a criminal record or spending time in jail, he hesitated. Would they really bother to check up on him? He gambled that they wouldn't and answered NO. He turned in his application and sat back down, trying not to pull at his mustache.

When they called his name, he walked into an office where a man named Mr. Brown, the general manager, shook his hand. He asked Will to give him a short summary of his work history.

"I've been farming ever since I was a kid following my daddy in the fields. Common story you might say, but what makes me different is that I'm a good mechanic. Mr. Talmadge relies on me to fix the tractor, and I do all the work on my own truck."

"I see you were in the military during World War Two. We like to hire veterans."

"Yes, sir, I worked in the mess hall. Never did get to see combat. But I made sure the soldiers were well fed before they shipped out."

"Anything else you'd like to tell me about yourself, Mr. Craddock?"

"No, sir. Well, actually, yes, sir. I sure want this job. I know the roads around here like the back of my hand. I can drive daytime hours or all night long if you need me to. And you can rely on me Mr. . . ." Will realized he'd forgotten the man's name.

He pointed to the nameplate on the desk. "It's Mr. Brown. Thanks for coming in, Mr. Craddock. You'll be hearing from us in a few days."

Will stood up, surprised the interview was over so soon. He thought of what Mary Grace told him. He stuck out his hand and the man shook it. "Thank you for your time, Mr. Brown," Will said, looking him dead in the eyes. "I see you have a lot of other men here, but none of them will work as hard for you as I will."

"On your way out, tell my secretary to send in the next candidate."

Will did as he was told and then hurried down the steps. Back in the safety of his truck, he let out a whoop. "I'll be damned," he shouted. "I think that went all right."

Ivy dredged the last chicken thigh in buttermilk and flour and dropped it into the frying pan. The corn pudding and biscuits were already in the oven, and a pot of collard greens was steaming over a low flame. The table was covered by a freshly ironed gingham tablecloth and set with five mismatched plates and silverware she borrowed from the Talmadge's kitchen. Jelly jars for iced tea were set at each place. A vase of Queen Anne's lace picked from the hillside and candlesticks from the Big House completed the picture. An apple pie covered with a dish towel was cooling by the window.

Ella, still in her graduation dress, walked over to the table and rearranged the candlesticks. "If Mary Grace and Will aren't eating with us, who are the extra places for?"

"Girl, you ask too many questions. Help me peel these carrots. Here, put on an apron first so you don't mess up Miss Claire's dress."

Ella took a knife and started on the carrots, enjoying the sound of her mother humming. She waved to her daddy through the window as he came in from the fields and went around back to wash up. Ivy took the last piece of chicken out of the frying pan and laid it on a platter covered in butcher's paper. She poured off the grease and put the pan back on the stove, adding the carrots and a pinch of sugar.

"Ella, our company's gonna be here soon. Go on to your room and fix yourself up a little bit. Put on some of that lip gloss you had on earlier." She leaned over to straighten the gold cross necklace Claire had given Ella as a graduation present.

Ella looked up in surprise. Her mother never told her to fix herself up.

As she was putting the final touches on her makeup, she heard a knock at the door. When she opened it, she was confused to see Bobby Lee Bennett, dressed in his uniform. Beside him was a soldier dressed in an identical dark green uniform with gold buttons. "Bobby Lee?" She led them inside.

"Ella, this is Tommy Walker from my platoon," Bobby Lee said. "We've known each other since basic training. He's one of the smartest guys on the base. I've told him a lot about you."

Tommy removed his hat. "Pleased to meet you, Ella," he said. Ella noticed her mother watching closely.

"Pleased to meet you," she replied. She turned back to Bobby Lee. "Are your parents coming?"

"They . . . couldn't make it. It's just me and Tommy. Your mama heard I was home on leave and invited me and Tommy to your graduation dinner. Congratulations, by the way."

"Yes, congratulations on your graduation," Tommy said.

Ivy ushered them inside. "Now Bobby Lee, you come on over here and tell Louis and me how you've been getting along."

Tommy eyed Ella nervously. "So, congratulations on your graduation," Tommy said.

"Thank you," responded Ella patiently. "Are you from around here?"

"I'm from Laurinburg. It's not too far from Fort Bragg. Bobby Lee wanted to give me a taste of home, you might say."

"I see."

Tommy began talking, but Ella couldn't focus on what he was saying because she was distracted by the sight of Bobby Lee and her parents laughing together. Bobby Lee looked so solid and confident, and he seemed so at home helping her parents bring the food to the table. She felt lightheaded all of a sudden.

"Mama, is dinner ready?" she asked. Tommy stopped talking. She realized she hadn't heard a word he said.

Her mother ushered them to their seats, placing Ella between Bobby Lee and Tommy. After her father said grace, they began passing the food. "You boys must be glad for a home-cooked meal," noted Louis.

"Yes, sir," Bobby Lee said. "The food on the base ain't nothing like this. But then again, we're so hungry at the end of the day we'd eat shoe leather if they gave it to us."

Ella asked them about life on the base.

"We'll be finishing paratrooper school soon," Bobby Lee said. "Last month, we jumped off a tower, and now we're training to jump out of planes. Recruits who make it through become part of the 82nd Airborne Division. Nights, we're so tired I usually fall asleep before lights out."

"I can't believe you jump out of planes," Ella said. "What's it like?"

Bobby Lee's eyes lit up. "The second you jump out, everything seems still and calm, like you're the only living thing in the universe. You feel like you're floating. Then, all of a sudden, you have to take in everything around you: what you see, what you hear, where you're heading, when to pull your parachute. And then you plan your landing. But that first split second of the jump, man, it's something else."

"Wow," Ella said.

"Bobby Lee is turning into one of the stars of our platoon," Tommy said. "He'll probably make private first class soon. And we may have to jump out of planes for real with that situation heating up in Southeast Asia."

"What's happening there?" Ella asked.

"The brass isn't saying," Bobby Lee said, wiping his mouth. "But our motto is 'All the Way.' We have to be ready for anything at a moment's notice."

"Tommy, did you know Ella is starting secretary school in the fall?" asked Ivy.

Tommy nodded and swallowed a sip of tea. "Bobby Lee told me. Said you'd been practicing and you already sound like an honest-to-goodness secretary."

Ella turned to Bobby Lee. "You been telling tales on me?"

He smiled at her. "It wasn't a tale. I remember every word you said at Christmastime. 'Sanders' Christmas Shop.'"

Ella blushed and turned back to Tommy. "I start my program in August, and I finish up a year from now. And then who knows, I might take a job in Philadelphia."

"Philadelphia?" Bobby Lee said. "That's so far away."

"Not as far away as Asia," Ella said.

After dessert, Bobby Lee and Tommy stood up. "Thank you so much, Mr. and Mrs. Sanders, for your hospitality," Bobby Lee said. "Tommy and I sure hope to see you again, Ella. We'll be here a week before we have to go back to the base. How about joining us for a movie after church tomorrow?"

"That sounds nice," Ella said, holding the door open for them. As the two men put their hats back on, Ella caught Bobby Lee's hand and squeezed it. "And it was a nice surprise that you could be here tonight." She watched them walk down the steps and suddenly remembered her manners. "Pleased to meet you, Tommy."

"Louis, I think my plan done hit me in the backside," Ivy whispered as she got ready for bed. She was frustrated. She'd worked so hard to get Bobby Lee to bring Tommy to Hobbsfield and not let on to Ella that she was trying to fix them up. And Tommy seemed like a fine young man. But Ella hadn't given him the attention he deserved.

"What do you mean?" Louis asked. He worked to open the stubborn window so a little of the cool night air could find its way inside.

"Did you not see the way Ella and Bobby Lee were acting around each other? Flirting and carrying on?"

"But I thought Bobby Lee brought *Tommy* to meet Ella."

Ivy sighed as she climbed into bed. As much as she loved Louis, sometimes he couldn't see what was right in front of his face. "He did, but somewhere along the way, he got sweet on Ella himself. And I think she's sweet on him, too."

Louis considered this. "That ain't a bad thing, though, is it? We've been knowing the Bennett family a long time, and Bobby Lee was like a brother to Jake. He's always been looking out for Ella." The bed sounded its familiar creak as he stretched out his large frame into the space beside Ivy.

Ivy sighed again. "I guess not. It's just that her and Bobby Lee have known each other their whole lives, almost like cousins. I never once pictured them together. And I got it in my head that some nice soldier was gonna take Ella away from here."

Louis looked over at her. "Why you working so hard to send away the one child we got left at home?"

"I ain't, it's just that Jake having to run away to Philadelphia turned out to be the best thing that could've happened to him. Like a prayer I wasn't praying. It ain't that I *want* Ella to leave, but I guess I got it in my head that if she could get out of Hobbsfield, it might turn out to be the best thing for her, too."

Louis gave his wife a kiss on the lips. "My Queen of Sheba, maybe this is the Lord's way of answering *another* prayer you wasn't praying."

Ivy considered this for a long while. Finally, she leaned over and kissed him back. "Louis Sanders, you might just be the smartest person I know."

Ella tried on one outfit after another. Since last night, all she could think about was Bobby Lee. During church, he sat a few rows in front of her, and she felt helpless, staring at the back of his head while Pastor Rice's sermon droned on. Why had she never noticed how handsome Bobby Lee was? He was so familiar to her that she hadn't really given him a good, hard look until that dinner a few months back. And he seemed to have become even more good-looking since then with his high cheekbones, his lean physique, and his easy smile. She could feel her heart pounding in her chest just thinking about him.

Mary Grace watched Ella carefully apply makeup. "I don't see what all the fuss is about. You've known Bobby Lee your whole life."

"I know, but somehow he seems like a whole different person. Except he's still the same person. All in one person." She put her hands over her face. "I sound like a fool!"

"You're right about that," Mary Grace said. Ella burst out laughing.

When Ella saw the red truck pull up to the cabin, she stepped back inside so they wouldn't see her waiting. But when she went to answer the door, it was just Bobby Lee standing there.

"Where's Tommy?"

"He decided to go back to Laurinburg. I dropped him off at the bus station. I hope you're not disappointed it's just me."

Ella smiled and shook her head. "Just let me grab my pocketbook and I'll be ready."

Ivy stuck her head out the door. "Afternoon, Bobby Lee. Where's Tommy? I thought the two of you were going to take Ella to the movies." She raised her eyebrows.

"Well, ma'am, he decided to go home. After dinner, he said he felt like a third wheel." He lowered his voice to make sure Ella wouldn't hear him. "He thinks there's something between Ella and me. And I think he's right. I hope you're not disappointed."

"It's okay," Ivy said. "I was reminded last night that sometimes the Lord works in mysterious ways."

Ella came back with her pocketbook. "You kids have fun," Ivy said.

Bobby Lee opened the door of the truck for Ella. "We better hurry or we'll miss the start of the movie," she said.

"Don't worry, I already got our tickets. That's one of the things they teach us in the Army: planning ahead."

"I hear you, Army man. So does that mean you've got our date planned out all the way down to the last detail?"

He smiled at her. "You'll just have to wait and see."

As they climbed the stairs to the balcony of the Gem Theater, Ella had trouble concentrating on anything but Bobby Lee beside her. His

nearness felt comforting and exciting at the same time. When he put his arm around her, she felt her breath catch in her throat. She was sorry when the lights came up at the end of the movie. Enjoying the warmth of his body next to hers, she leaned into him for another minute until an usher shooed them out.

After the movie ended, he drove them to Hobbsfield Chicken & BBQ, one of the restaurants in the colored part of town.

"Bobby Lee, I think you need to relax," Ella said as they waited in line to order their food. "You're always standing up so straight."

He laughed. "That's the Army, Ella; they teach us to stand up straight like that."

"Why?"

"Just part of being disciplined, I guess. Wouldn't you rather be protected by someone who's standing up tall and proud than by someone who's like this?" He slouched low against the wall.

"I guess so. It's just I've spent the last three years trying to never stand up straight. My mama tells me that standing up straight calls too much attention to myself."

"Why would she say that?"

"I guess on account of I'm so tall. She doesn't want me being in the spotlight."

"It's hard for you *not* to be noticed, Ella, with how beautiful you are."

They reached the front of the line, placed their order, and then found a table in the back.

"Do you mind if I smoke?" Bobby Lee asked as he pulled a pack of cigarettes from his shirt pocket.

"No, it's okay."

"I need to ask you something."

"Sounds serious."

"It is, in a way. I'll only be here for another six days, and then I'm due back at the base. I was hoping I could see you every day."

"Well, you know I have to help my daddy in the fields."

"I can help, too, like I used to, and then when we're done, we can find something to do together—go to another movie or whatever."

"I like the sound of 'whatever.' What did you have in mind?"

They leaned back so the waitress could set down their plates.

"We could take a drive through the countryside, have a picnic dinner, sit by the pond on the farm, and watch the sunset." Bobby Lee held Ella's hand while painting a romantic picture of their wanderings. He added that he could call her every Sunday when he went back to the base.

"We don't have a telephone in our cabin."

"Why not? What if there's an emergency?"

"Mr. Talmadge won't spend the money. And my daddy can't afford to put one in. We've got my secretary course to pay for, and he's buying a burial plot at church on the installment plan. He's worried Mama won't have the money to bury him."

"That's no way to live, is it? Spending your days worrying about dying."

Ella shook her head. "No. But when we lost my older brother, Paul, he kind of shook hands with death."

"Well, if I can't call you, we can write letters then."

"Now that I can do," Ella said. "That's how we stay in touch with Jake."

"If you don't mind my asking, where is he? I don't think my parents ever knew why he left Hobbsfield or where he ended up."

Ella folded her arms around her waist. "I'll tell you the whole story someday, but let's just say he landed in a good place. Would you believe he's in college?"

"Really?"

"Yeah. A college up North. It's a Catholic school where he got a scholarship. Sounds like they're trying to get more colored folks to go there."

"One thing I like about Fort Bragg is how it mostly don't matter what color you are," Bobby Lee said. "I mean, there's a few white guys walking around calling us names, but as a whole, the military is a good place for coloreds. When you're training to go to war, you don't much care about the color of the soldier beside you as long as he has your back."

"Mama said Pastor Rice has been talking about folks trying to make it so colored people can go to white schools and restaurants and stuff," Ella said. "Can you imagine being able to eat at Nelson's?" Ella had always admired the fancy restaurant in downtown Hobbsfield with its chandeliers and candlelit tables. She and her mother peeked in every time they walked by on their way to the Five & Dime.

"Who knows, maybe someday I'll take you to Nelson's and order us a bottle of champagne."

Ella laughed. "Bobby Lee, you're crazy."

Later that night, as they pulled up in front of the cabin, Bobby Lee leaned over and kissed her gently. "Still think I'm crazy?" he whispered.

"Yeah," she said. "But I'm beginning to like crazy."

The next few days flew by. In the mornings, Bobby Lee came out to the fields to help Ella and Louis with the topping. In the evenings, they sat on the Sanders' front porch or walked down to the creek below the meadow. He told her stories about the men in his platoon and described what basic training was like. She sang her favorite Ella Fitzgerald songs for him.

On Thursday night, the Bennetts had them over for a fish stew. Ella saw her mother give Mrs. Bennett a long hug. "Would you have ever thought of these two together?" Ivy said. "And to think I tried to make Bobby Lee introduce Ella to someone else. Poor Tommy."

"Tommy's a nice boy," Cleo Bennett said. "He'll have his pick of girls. But I can't think of nobody better suited for Bobby Lee than your beautiful Ella."

On Friday, Bobby Lee brought Ella a small framed picture of himself in uniform. "I thought you could keep it by your bed," he said. "That way I can be close to you even when I'm not here."

Saturday came too soon. Bobby Lee drove out to the farm before heading back to Fort Bragg. He fidgeted nervously, but Ella was too upset to notice.

"What's wrong, Ella?" They were sitting on the steps of the front porch.

She smacked him on the shoulder. "I could kill you, Bobby Lee. Showing up here, surprising me at my graduation dinner, treating me so good, and then up and leaving right when I decide I like having you around. It doesn't seem fair."

"I know. I don't want to be away from you either. I been thinking about it all night." He took a deep breath. "Why don't we get married?"

"You mean it?"

"I mean it. We've only been together a week now, but it feels like the most natural thing in the world. Like we were always supposed to be together. When I'm not with you, all I can do is think about being together. I want you to be my wife, Ella. That is if you'll have me."

Ella's face brightened. "But how can we get married with you off at Fort Bragg?"

"We'll have to do it on my next leave in December. And then afterward, you could stay here and finish your secretary program. I know how much it means to you." He then suggested she could get a job on the base or in nearby Fayetteville. "I know it's not Philadelphia, but it is a growing city."

"Look at you, army man, planning it all out." Tears rolled down her face.

"Please don't cry."

"It's okay, these are happy tears. Yes, Bobby Lee Bennett, I will marry you!"

He kissed her softly on the lips. She put her arms around him and he kissed her again, more passionately this time. When they pulled away from each other, Ella was breathless.

"I better get going," he said. He touched a tear on her face. "Ella Sanders, I love you."

She gave him one last hug. "Know what?" he said, holding her close. "I was wrong about something. Parachuting from a plane ain't the best feeling in the world."

Every day, Will checked the mailbox as soon as he heard the mailman's truck stop. Finally he found a letter addressed to him in an official-looking envelope. As he carried it back to the house, the sun was setting behind the trees in the westernmost woods of the farm. Mary Grace had lit the kerosene lamp, and he could see her moving about the cabin, preparing dinner. In the distance, Louis and Ella were coming towards their cabin from the barn. Louis's laughter rang out through the twilight.

Will stopped for a minute, overcome. He had given most of his life to this place. He and Ruby had raised their daughter here. His blood, sweat, and tears had made those fields what they were today. Sure, the cabin wasn't much. Sure, Mr. Talmadge was a son-of-a-bitch. But this was his home. And as much as he hated to admit it, Louis and Ivy were like family, even if they were colored.

He looked down at the letter in his hand. He could practically hear Ruby whispering to him, "Will, it's time to move on." He wiped his eyes, knowing she was right. Maybe this letter would prove to be the fresh start he and Mary Grace needed.

Will sat down on the porch steps, tore open the envelope, and held the letter up to the last light of day.

Dear Mr. Craddock,

Thank you for your interest in working for Smothers Ham Company. Unfortunately, we cannot offer you a position at this time. We wish you the best of luck in the future.

Sincerely,
Walter Brown

Will read the letter twice, not believing what he was seeing. He put his head down and wondered what Ruby would say to him now. He tried to listen for her whisper, but it was nowhere to be found in the darkening sky. All that he heard was the wind rustling the leaves and a flock of birds flying overhead across the field.

TWENTY-ONE

June 1962

Mrs. Jennings, the owner of a rooming house close to the railroad tracks, lumbered in front of Will and Mary Grace as she led them down the long dark hallway. She stopped at a door in the back corner, inserted a key, and turned the knob. "This is the room that's available."

Will let Mary Grace go in first and then walked in behind her with his hands in his pockets. He eyed the tight quarters suspiciously as Mrs. Jennings flipped the wall switch to turn on the single lightbulb hanging from the ceiling. The first thing he noticed was the dingy gray walls with no windows. A small bed with a thin mattress sagged in one corner. A wardrobe took up all the room on one wall, and a chest of drawers sat on the opposite wall in between a stand with a washbasin on top and a chair with a tattered cushion.

Mrs. Jennings pushed her ample girth into the room. "I know it's small, but it's the only room I got right now. When a bigger room opens up, we can move you in there. In the meantime, we can bring in a pallet, and one of you could sleep on the floor."

"Kinda dark in here, ain't it?" Will asked. It reminded him of the jail cell where he'd spent lonely days and nights away from Mary Grace.

The woman shrugged her shoulders. "You could put a lamp over there. The bathroom's at the end of the hall. I'd suggest when your daughter's in there you stand guard outside the door."

Will's eyebrows rose. "What kind of people you got staying here?"

"Don't worry, there's no Negroes here. But there's a few men who like to dip into the sauce on the weekends, playing cards and the like. They're mostly harmless, but I'd still keep a watch on a pretty young thing like her."

Will felt the walls closing in on him. "I've seen enough," he said to Mary Grace. "I'll be outside."

He pushed past Mrs. Jennings and hurried down the hallway and out the front door. He sat down in the truck bed, lit a cigarette, and took a drag. He was craving whisky, but he'd once again promised Mary Grace he was done with the hard stuff. He aimed to mean it this time.

A few minutes later, Mary Grace stepped out of the boarding house and walked over to the truck. "You okay?"

"That room was so small I could barely breathe."

"I know, but we can make do. We can bring the lamp from home and the quilt and the curtains Mama made. And her rocking chair."

"Mary Grace, the room ain't got no windows. There's nowhere to hang curtains."

"We can hang them from the wall, then. Mama made them, and I think they should come with us. Besides, won't it be nice to have an indoor shower?"

Will scowled. He'd bet his life that the bathroom was every bit as small as the room they saw. "Yeah, while I stand guard."

"I bet Mrs. Jennings was just being careful. She introduced me to a couple of the boarders on my way out, and they seemed okay." She turned to look at him. "Listen, Daddy, you know we have to be off the farm in two days. This is the only option we've got. I told Mrs. Jennings we'd take it."

"What about that little house for rent off Beaman Street?"

"Too expensive. What you and me together have saved doesn't even cover the first month's rent. I know you're going to find a job any day now, but most landlords want you to already have a job before they'll give you a place to stay. And they won't count my work at the hospital."

Will couldn't bear it that Mary Grace was pitching in her own money towards a place for them to live. He knew she was trying to save up for nursing school.

"If you think this is what we should do, then we'll do it," he said. "I can sleep on the floor."

"It's just until we can figure out something better. You'll find a job any day now, and we can save more money and then look for a house to rent. And don't be silly. With your bad back, you wouldn't sleep a wink on the floor. You'd toss and moan all night, and then *I* wouldn't be able to sleep either. I'll sleep on the floor."

Will scowled again. She was right. If he lay down on the floor, he might not be able to get back up. He tried to picture the two of them in that tiny, airless cell, but for the life of him, he couldn't imagine it.

Mary Grace looked around the cabin, but she could barely recognize it as her home. The new platform bunk beds took up almost all the space in the bedrooms. Tools were strewn all around, and sawdust coated the floor. As she sat in the main room putting the last of her things into a big box, she could hear the sound of hammering coming from her dad's room. It was taking him every bit of time he had to finish the job.

She carried the box outside to the porch. It felt strange to be home this time of morning. She was usually either coming off a night shift and going straight to bed, or else she'd already left for her day shift.

She'd forgotten how beautiful the farm could be as the daylight climbed above the treetops and burned the morning dew off the leaves.

She walked next door to the Sanders' cabin. She'd been sharing a room with Ella ever since her dad started building the bunk beds, and most of her stuff had migrated over with her. She was surprised to find Ella in the kitchen.

"I thought you were working in the fields," she said, lugging the box back to Ella's room.

"I am, but I forgot my scarf."

Mary Grace smiled. She knew Ella would use any excuse to take a break from field work.

Ella eyed the box Mary Grace was holding. "You're packing up your stuff? No! First Bobby Lee has to go back to Fort Bragg, and now you're leaving too."

"Trust me, I don't want to go," Mary Grace replied. "And neither does my dad. But we don't have a choice. And besides, you'll soon be a proper married lady, and the only person you'll be wanting to share a room with is Bobby Lee."

Ella's eyes lit up. "Can't believe I'm getting married."

"I can't believe you are either."

"I've been practicing my vows. Want to hear?"

Mary Grace rolled her eyes. "No thanks. All that stuff about obeying your husband. I could never agree to that."

Will hammered the final nail on the bunk beds and stood back to examine his work. Building six sets of slabs had taken longer than he anticipated. Good thing Louis had pitched in or he might not have finished on time.

He'd waited to do the ones in his bedroom until last so he could sleep in his own bed as long as possible. Since he'd been on the couch for a week, his back was killing him.

He heard the cabin door open. "I've got everything packed up except for what I need tonight," Mary Grace said. "Ella has big plans for our last 'slumber party' together. And Ivy's making a special dinner tonight with all your favorites."

"That's nice," he said.

A moment later, they were startled by a loud knock at the door. Mary Grace opened it, and Gordon Talmadge's large frame filled the doorway.

"Good, you're here," he said, walking inside without waiting for an invitation. "I want to see if everything's ready for the crew."

He looked around at the tools, the dusty floors, and Will's and Mary Grace's belongings that were laid out in the main room. "What's all this mess?"

"I've only just now finished building the last of the bunks. And we're still getting our stuff packed up. We'll have everything cleaned up by the end of the day." He thought of Ivy's special dinner. "Noon tomorrow at the latest."

Gordon walked through the cabin and tested the sturdiness of the beds. "Well, at least you've done a good job on these bunk slabs." He came back into the main room. "But I'm not giving you your pay until you get all this shit cleaned up. Make sure you put those tools back in the shed. And I need you out of here by ten o'clock tomorrow morning. Not a minute later."

Will held Mr. Talmadge's gaze until he finally turned and walked away.

Gordon paced back and forth in his study, thinking about Red Kincaid. Truth be told, Gordon found the man intimidating. He remembered the steely look in Red's eyes and how you could see his muscles through the tight shirt he wore.

Claire walked by. "Gordon, what in the world? You'll wear a hole in the rug."

"Red Kincaid's showing up tomorrow afternoon with the work crew, and the cabin's not ready."

"I thought you were paying Will to take care of that."

"I am, but he says he only just finished the bunk slabs today. And it's a big mess over there."

"So he *did* finish the work?"

"Yeah, but there's clothes and boxes everywhere."

"Well, they are moving. They have to take everything they own with them. They're probably still packing."

"I told him I wasn't giving him his pay until everything was neat as a pin."

"Well, then, I'm sure he'll have it ready by tomorrow."

Gordon frowned. "He better."

Claire moved into the living room and the sounds of a Beethoven sonata drifted through the house.

Gordon recalled the threatening look Will gave him. He picked up the phone and dialed the sheriff's office. "Gordon Talmadge here. Can you put me through to Sheriff Owen?"

Dan's voice came on the line. "What can I do for you, Gordon?"

"I need a favor. I've given notice to one of my sharecroppers so we can make room for a migrant crew from Florida. He's supposed to be off the farm tomorrow by ten o'clock. Come to think of it, you know who I'm talking about. It's Will Craddock. The same fellow you busted for making moonshine on my property."

"I remember."

"Can you come out here in the morning in case Craddock pulls any funny business? He's always been a loose cannon."

"Sure, Gordon. I'll bring one of my deputies." He paused a beat. "You mentioned bringing in migrant workers. You need to be careful with that. Make sure they're registered and so forth."

"I'm sure the crew chief has everything in order."

"Just be careful. Meantime, I'll see you in the morning."

"Sure do appreciate it." Gordon hung up the phone, feeling somewhat relieved. Now if he could just get Claire to stop making all that racket.

Mary Grace noticed her father was especially quiet during their "going away" dinner. Louis, Ivy, and Ella did their best to make it a cheerful occasion, but her dad's mind seemed to be elsewhere.

After dinner, they went back over to their cabin to finish packing. Mary Grace had swept the floors, washed the windows, and thrown out the trash. The tools were lined up neatly on the porch ready to be returned in the morning. As her dad carried the last of his clothes out the front door, a small box fell from the bundle in his arms.

He opened it and peered inside. "Well, what do you know," he said.

"What is it, Daddy?"

"It's your mama's wedding ring. When she was sick in the hospital, she gave it to me to keep, in case she didn't make it. She wanted you to have it someday. I nearly forgot I had it." He took the plain gold band out of the box and studied it.

He handed the ring to Mary Grace, who held it up to the light. "It's beautiful."

Will looked at his daughter and handed her the ring. "Keep it. And when you get married, you can wear it as your wedding ring. Your mama would want that."

"Who knows if I'll ever get married?" scoffed Mary Grace. "Why don't you hold on to it for me?"

"No, sweetie, I want you to take it." He paused. "And I want you to know that I'm sorry I ain't been a better father to you. You were the best thing that ever happened to me."

He dropped the last of his clothes into the box. "I think that's everything. You go on back next door. I'm gonna ride up to the general store and get some aspirin for my back."

"Get some sleep tonight, Daddy. Remember, Sarah is picking me up in the morning for the early shift, and I'll meet you at the boarding house after work."

David finished his eggs and ate the last bite of bacon. He was getting ready to leave for work. Just like last summer, he was helping out at his grandfather's pharmacy, stocking shelves, manning the cash register, and delivering medicine. The job wasn't the most interesting, but it gave him a lot of downtime to crack open a book behind the register.

Claire walked into the kitchen dressed in her gardening clothes. "Morning, son," she said. "Do you have time to help me prune roses today?"

"Gotta be at the drugstore at ten. Myra's on vacation, so Grandpa needs me full days all week."

"I'll have to talk to that father of mine," Claire said. "Tell him to stop being such a slavedriver. Ivy, would you fix me some berries with a little cream, please?"

"Yes, ma'am."

David noticed his father outside on the front porch. "How come Dad's still here?"

His mother came over to where she could see Gordon pacing back and forth. "He's probably waiting for Sheriff Owen. Today's the day the Craddocks have to be off the farm."

"And he called the sheriff?"

"It's just a precaution, David. Your father was afraid Will might make trouble."

"I'm sure Mary Grace and her dad have no intention of staying where they're not wanted."

"I'm sure you're right, honey." She took another bite of berries and picked up the magazine she was reading.

A wave of sadness washed over David. Even though Mary Grace couldn't stand the sight of him, the farm wouldn't be the same without her.

As David drove away from the house, he passed the sheriff's car coming in. He noticed Will on the porch of the cabin and pulled up beside the yard. Maybe he'd say a quick goodbye to Mary Grace to make up for the terrible argument they'd had.

Will was sitting in the rocking chair cleaning a shotgun. "Good morning, Will," David said. "Dad told me you're moving off the farm today. Is Mary Grace inside? I was hoping to say goodbye."

Will didn't seem to register what David was saying. His eyes were bloodshot, and he was uttering nonsense. David noticed the nearly empty jar of moonshine at his feet. "I ain't gonna be able to breathe in that room," Will mumbled. "It's too small. Can't breathe. And it ain't right her sleeping on the floor. Ain't right."

"Are you okay?"

Will looked at David and finally realized who he was. "David Talmadge, the only one of your lot worth a damn. That father of yours is nothing but a son-of-a-bitch. He's lower than whale shit at the bottom of the ocean."

David laughed nervously. "He's not always my favorite person either, sir. Um, is Mary Grace inside?"

"No, she's at the hospital. Did you know she gives people baths and cleans up their shit all day long so we have enough money to live on? And that no good father of yours still kicked us out of the only home she's ever known?" Will held up the shotgun in his lap. "I figured he owed me this much."

David realized the gun Will was holding was his father's monogrammed Winchester. His stomach dropped.

He heard a vehicle coming down the driveway. When it came into view, he realized it was the sheriff's car. Will noticed it too. "Well, I'll be damned. Looks like your father's gonna have me hauled away like a criminal from my own home. Guess I should've figured as much."

David tried to stay calm. "Why don't you let me have that gun before my father sees you with it? You know how much he loves his Winchester."

"Do I ever," Will scoffed. "He prob'ly paid more for that gun than he gives me in a whole year. He made me build a special gun cabinet for it in the tool shed. Good thing I made myself an extra key."

The sheriff's car pulled up beside David's. Gordon stepped out of the backseat. "Will Craddock, what in God's name are you doing with my Winchester?"

"Gordon, get back in the car," Sheriff Owen said sharply. "Let us handle this." The deputy with Sheriff Owen stepped out of the car and kept a close eye on Will.

"But he's got my gun, Dan!" yelled Gordon. "My Winchester twenty-one."

Will suddenly stood up, knocking the chair to the ground and falling back against the cabin. He waved the gun unsteadily with one hand. "That's right, Mr. Talmadge. And I have half a mind to shoot you with it right through your stone-cold heart."

David hurried down the porch steps and across the yard toward his father, blocking his path. "Dad, get back in the car. He's not of a mind to see you right now."

"Get out of the way, David. That idiot's got my Winchester."

"Will Craddock, put down the gun." The sheriff's voice was amplified by the bullhorn in his hand.

David looked back and saw the deputy with his gun drawn, approaching the porch from the side and aiming straight at Will, who appeared confused by the commotion.

"Will, put the gun down before someone gets hurt," pleaded David.

His father pushed him aside and continued walking toward the porch. "Don't worry, that damn fool hasn't a clue how to fire my gun."

Will suddenly pointed the gun at Gordon. "I remember you always said aim a few feet in front of what you're trying to shoot."

And with that, he pulled the trigger. The gun blasted, and David fell to the ground, his leg on fire.

In the very next second, the deputy fired his pistol from the side of the cabin, and Will crumpled in a heap onto the worn floorboards of the porch.

TWENTY-TWO

July 1962

Claire studied herself in the mirror one last time before she went to check on David. She added a touch of rouge to her cheeks and looked for a belt so her dress wouldn't hang so loosely. How ironic that after all those years of trying to lose weight, it was chaos and tragedy that made the pounds melt away. She'd happily trade her shrinking waistline for a peaceful family life.

When she stopped by David's room, he was propped up in bed reading, his bandaged leg stretched out on top of the quilt. A tray with his breakfast dishes sat on the bedside table. His chess board was set up nearby. "Morning son," she said, squeezing his shoulder.

"Morning," he replied, glancing up briefly from his book.

"How's the leg?"

"The painkillers help." He smiled patiently. "Don't look so worried. The doctor says I'm going to be fine. I'm just bored."

"I know what the doctor said. But I'm your mother. You can't expect me not to worry." She fluffed the pillow behind his head. "I've got a few errands to run. Maybe I'll stop by the drugstore and ask your grandfather if he'll come play chess with you this weekend. Do you need more books from the library?"

"I'm good for now."

"Okay. Ivy's in the kitchen if you need anything."

As Claire carried the breakfast tray downstairs, she thought back to that horrible day. Hearing the ambulance siren in the driveway. She and Ivy running toward the cabins. David lying on the ground screaming while Will lay dead on the porch. If Will hadn't been so drunk, he probably would have killed Gordon or David or both of them.

Ivy took the tray from her as she walked into the kitchen. "Morning, Miss Claire. What can I get for you?"

"Just coffee, please. Peg and I are having lunch in town."

Ivy poured coffee into a mug and added a splash of milk and a pinch of sugar. She brought it to Claire and sat down beside her. "Miss Claire, I need to talk to you about something."

"Of course, what is it?"

"It's about Mary Grace," Ivy said. "She's always been strong of heart, that one. But losing both her parents, and her being an only child, it's real tough on her."

"That poor girl," Claire said. "I've been so worried about David I'd nearly forgotten about her. What was Will thinking? If he'd been taking care of his daughter instead of trying to get revenge on Gordon, none of this mess would have happened."

Ivy frowned. "That may be true, ma'am, but that ain't what I need to talk to you about." She took a deep breath. "I'm here to talk about the money Mr. Gordon owes Mary Grace."

"What money?"

"Mr. Gordon promised to pay Will for the work he did on the bunk beds for the migrant workers, and so far, he hasn't offered Mary Grace a penny. It ain't fair."

Claire reddened slightly and reached into her purse for a cigarette.

Ivy explained to Claire that Mary Grace had moved back into the Sanders' cabin. And that whatever money she'd saved from working at the hospital had gone to pay for her father's burial plot. "You know if Mr. Gordon had paid Will the day he finished the job, that money would belong to Mary Grace right now. It don't seem right that she can't have the money her daddy earned fair and square."

Claire took a long drag. "You make a good point, Ivy."

"It's the right thing to do. But I ain't finished just yet. See, I been praying over it, and the Lord done give me an idea."

"I'm listening," Claire said, not at all sure she wanted to hear the rest.

"You know Ella's getting ready to start secretary school next month?"

Claire nodded.

"Well, if Mary Grace had that money from Mr. Gordon, she could start nurse school at the same time. The girls could ride together, and she could stay on with us at least until she finished up."

Claire could feel the start of a headache coming on. "So Mary Grace would . . . *live* with you?"

Ivy looked at Claire pointedly. "We got Jake's bed just sitting there empty. She's been staying with us ever since her daddy started on the bunks. Seems only fitting she just stay on, now she done lost both her parents."

Claire put out her cigarette in the ashtray and swallowed the last of her coffee. "You've certainly given me a lot to think about, Ivy. And you make a good point about the work Will did. I'm just not sure Gordon will see it that way. He's still angry about what happened to David. So am I, for that matter. He may not be inclined to give money away on behalf of the man who shot his son."

"Well, maybe the Lord will help him find a way."

"Maybe so," Claire said. "I'll talk to him about it tonight. Guess that makes me an 'instrument of the Lord.'"

"That ain't never a bad thing, Miss Claire."

Claire stood up and walked toward the door.

"Oh, and Miss Claire, one more thing."

"Yes, Ivy?"

"Some of them workers who moved in next door look like they ain't had a decent meal in a while. I'm gonna make an extra pot of chicken soup for 'em. If that's all right with you."

Claire nodded and hurried out the door before Ivy could suggest anything else.

David woke to a knock on his bedroom door. Probably his mother, checking on him one last time before she left. "Come in," he said groggily.

The door opened and Mary Grace walked in. "Ivy told me where to find you," she said.

David tried to sit up and his glasses fell on the floor. Mary Grace picked them up wordlessly and slid them back on his face. He noticed the familiar smattering of freckles on her cheeks, but her eyes, normally a clear green, looked hollow.

"Thanks," he said, smoothing his hair and trying to make himself presentable. He realized he hadn't brushed his teeth yet. "I must have dozed off. The pain pills knock me out."

She studied the bottle beside the bed. "Yes, this will make you drowsy." Her eyes drifted to his bandaged leg.

They looked at each other as an awkward silence filled the room. Then they both spoke at the same time.

"Mary Grace, I'm sorry about your father . . ."

"David, I'm sorry my father . . ."

"Me first," David insisted. "I am so sorry about your father. I've been trying to imagine what you must be going through, losing your dad like that. I just keep thinking if I hadn't stopped at your cabin that morning, maybe it wouldn't have happened the way it did. Or if I had said the right words, your dad would have put the gun down. I keep replaying it over and over in my head trying to make it come out differently."

Mary Grace shook her head. "You can't undo what's already been done. I came here to tell you how sorry *I* am that my father shot at you. What was he thinking? Did you get into some sort of argument? Not that that's any excuse for picking up a gun."

"Argument? No, nothing like that. It seemed like, well, I guess he'd had a lot to drink, and he was talking to himself. And then my dad showed up in the sheriff's car. To tell you the truth, I think your dad was trying to shoot my dad but hit me instead."

Mary Grace stared at him wide-eyed.

"And I can't say I blame him for resenting my dad," David continued. "What with him making y'all move out." David began wiping his glasses. "I don't always understand why my father does the things he does."

"I know the feeling." Mary Grace sat down on the edge of the bed. "I thought we were going to be okay. I found us a temporary place at a boarding house, and my dad was looking for a job. But he was just so tired. Tired of suffering from bad luck and his own bad decisions. I hope he's found some peace. I don't know if I believe in Heaven, but if there is one, maybe he's been reunited with my mom."

Her eyes welled up with tears.

David handed her a tissue, wishing there was something he could do to ease her pain. "One thing I do remember about that morning is that your dad was talking about you when I saw him. He said you were the best thing in his life."

"Thanks for telling me that," she said, dabbing her cheeks.

"Where will you go now?"

"I'm not sure. Ivy said I can stay with them until I figure something out. I'd like to go to nursing school, but I'm not sure I'll ever get enough money saved."

Standing up to leave, Mary Grace adjusted the quilt on David's bed. "Where's your girlfriend? I expected her to be taking care of you."

"She spends a month every summer with her grandparents in Atlantic Beach. I'm planning to wait until she gets back to tell her about all of this. It's a lot to explain over the phone."

Mary Grace reached into her bag and handed David the worn copy of *Charlotte's Web* he had loaned her years ago. "I found this when we were packing."

"Did you ever read it?"

She shook her head. "Just the first few pages. You know I'm too busy to sit around reading books."

She examined his bandaged leg. "You need to make sure you change this dressing every day. And be on the lookout for redness or swelling. Let me know if you need any help with it. It's the least I can do."

"Say, Mary Grace, do you know how to play chess?"

She gave him a look. "What do you think?"

"If you want to help me, let me teach you to play chess. I'm bored out of my mind up here by myself."

"If you ask me, playing chess seems like a waste of time."

"Well, I didn't ask your opinion of chess. You offered to help me, and that's how you can help me."

An hour later, Mary Grace had learned the basic moves of each chess piece. She was a surprisingly quick study. David had forgotten how smart she was, but more importantly, he noticed her eyes had regained a hint of the brightness he remembered.

"I've got to get ready for work," she said. "Thanks for the chess lesson, I guess."

"You're welcome," David said. "Let's do it again tomorrow."

She rolled her eyes and walked toward the door. "We'll see. Hey David, one more thing about that morning at the cabin—what were you doing there in the first place?"

"Looking for you."

Gordon tried to concentrate as Millard Wellons, the bank treasurer, went over the monthly financial report.

"As you can see, we need to keep an eye on a number of loans in default."

"I'm aware," Gordon said. "Trouble is, all the farmers are in the same boat. It's a labor-intensive business, and the farmers who haven't converted to using labor contractors and installing bulk barns are struggling."

Gordon then mentioned a bright note—something his father-in-law lectured him about that he had just read in *Progressive Farmer*—to give Millard the impression that he was on top of things. "The scientists at State have finally gotten the formula right on the chemicals to control suckers, not to mention mechanical harvesters are coming down the pike. Can you imagine, using a machine to collect the leaves rather than stooping over all day doing it by hand? The initial capital outlay is not cheap, but the costs will be recaptured in a few years if the farmers can hang on, and in the meantime, we can extend a loan for the purchases."

"I wouldn't advise that, Mr. Talmadge," Millard said. "It will put the bank further in the hole. And what will we do with mechanical harvesters if we have to repossess them? They'll probably be worth about ten cents on the dollar in the resale market."

Looking at his list of questions for Gordon, Millard asked how he was progressing on generating business from the farm equipment manufacturers who had strong balance sheets and the wherewithal to pay back their loans.

Gordon couldn't bear to admit he hadn't gotten around to calling any of them. "I'm expecting to hear back from a couple of contacts any day now. I'll keep you posted."

Millard hesitated but decided to leave him in peace.

Gordon lit a cigarette and watched the smoke drift up toward the coffered ceiling. Truth be told, despite Millard giving him a list every month of potential businesses to approach, he hadn't landed any new corporate clients since last summer. He fished the latest list from underneath a stack of papers on his desk and studied it for a long while. He started to pick up the phone but instead decided to call it a day. He needed a stiff drink right about now.

He put out his cigarette in the crystal ashtray and picked up his briefcase. Maybe he'd take a look over the weekend at those trade journals he'd been carrying around, find some new ways to drum up business, offer a promotion or two. Then again, it was a holiday weekend. He put down the briefcase. The journals could wait.

As he walked toward his car, he admired the red, white, and blue banners decorating the town square. He'd have to remember to tell Claire how nice it all looked. She was in charge of the Town Beautification Committee this year for the Fourth of July celebration.

As Gordon got into his Cadillac, he saw Millard watching him from his office, probably judging him for leaving early. If Millard knew the half of what he'd been through the past few weeks, he might get off his back. Fortunately, Gordon had been able to keep the details of Will Craddock's death and David's injury out of the *Hobbsfield Times* thanks to his long-standing relationship with the publisher, who counted Farmers and Merchants as one of his top advertisers. He'd dodged a bullet on that one.

As he pulled up to the house, Gordon noticed the migrant workers spread out in the fields. They'd been there since sunrise and were hard at work when he left for the bank. It was a scorcher of a day, with temperatures above ninety degrees and nearly one hundred percent humidity due to last night's thunderstorm. He wondered if Red Kincaid was giving them enough water breaks in this heat. If any.

As he parked the car next to the back porch, he looked around for Buster. Gordon figured his beloved lab was keeping his distance from Red's German shepherd. Gordon didn't blame him. When the dog wasn't by Red's side, he kept him chained to his car near the migrant cabin as a reminder to the workers that they were within inches of his bite. Claire wasn't happy about having a dangerous dog around, but the tobacco was coming along nicely, and Gordon didn't want to interfere. Whatever it took to motivate the workers was fine with him.

Claire was at the piano as he entered the welcome coolness of the house. He had installed air conditioning a few years ago and now he was considering putting in a swimming pool next to the dogwood orchard. He made a mental note to call the local pool company for a bid. If he couldn't have his dove hunt, at least he could indulge himself with a swimming pool for his family and guests.

Claire looked up from the keyboard. "You're home early, sweetheart. The heat getting to you?"

"No. It was a slow day at the bank, right before the Fourth." Gordon poured himself a drink. He loosened his tie and sank down into the armchair. "How's David?"

She finished the last few bars of "Be Thou My Vision" and came around to sit on the sofa. "He's fine. I just checked on him, and he's napping. His biggest complaint is that he's bored."

"Maybe I should teach him to play poker," Gordon offered.

"Maybe so," Claire said. "Thank goodness he'll be healed up in time to go back to Wake Forest for the fall semester. I know he doesn't want to get behind in his classes."

"I still can't believe Will Craddock shot David," Gordon said. "Hard to believe the man lived right alongside us all these years in that cabin, and that's where he ends up dying. You can still see traces of his blood on the porch."

Claire thought about that. "Maybe we can get Louis to rebuild that section of the porch. That's a dreadful thing for Mary Grace to have to look at every day."

"Are you talking about the Craddock girl? Why is she still here?"

"She's living with Ivy and Louis."

"Why in the world would a white girl be living with darkies?"

Claire gave him a long look. She despised that word.

"She doesn't have anybody else, Gordon. They're the closest thing she's got to family. And she doesn't have any money, either. According to Ivy, she spent what little she had saved to bury her father."

"Well, I'm not sure we should allow it."

"I don't think you have much say in the matter unless you'd like her to move in with us?" Gordon chuckled at that idea.

Claire turned serious. "Ivy told me you never paid Will for the work he did on the cabin."

"Ivy needs to mind her own business," Gordon replied.

"That's not the point. Is she right?"

Gordon paused. "I was planning to pay him that morning and then let the sheriff escort him off the property. Saved myself some money, didn't I?" He got up to pour another drink.

Claire waited until her husband sat back down. "Gordon, you need to give that money to Mary Grace."

He held the highball glass up to the light, studying the amber color of the bourbon. "What are you talking about?"

"Now that her father's dead, that money rightfully belongs to her."

"Don't be ridiculous. The Craddock girl doesn't have the means or the know-how to come after me for that money. Especially since her father tried to gun down our son." He picked up the newspaper and turned to the sports page, considering the matter closed.

Claire snatched it out of his hand. "Gordon, it's high time you started listening to me. I tried for years to get you to rein Junior in, but you never listened." Claire knew she was off topic but couldn't stop herself. "Hell, you practically encouraged his bad behavior."

"Claire." Claire knew Gordon was admonishing her for cursing, but she was beyond caring about decorum.

"I think the problem is that Junior is just like you, and you never say 'no' to yourself, so by extension you couldn't say 'no' to him either. And look how that turned out. He nearly *killed* someone. And meanwhile, David, who works hard in school and is an upstanding young man, doesn't get so much as a second glance from you."

Gordon frowned. "That's not fair, Claire. I love both my sons. Didn't I learn to play chess? I should have taken a firmer hand with Junior, you're right about that. But everything changed for him with that goddamn shoulder injury. He was good enough to start at Chapel

Hill or State . . . but that business with the Sanders kids in the smoke-house ruined everything for him."

Claire shook her head. "Football was always going to come to an end eventually."

"I guess."

"Let's hope this facility Junior's in will help him turn things around."

"God knows I'm paying a pretty penny for it." He sipped his bourbon. "Claire, I love you. Everything I do is to protect our family, to preserve what we have, so that future generations of Talmadges can enjoy it as much as we have."

Claire realized this was perhaps the most honest conversation she and Gordon had ever had. Feeling a surge of tenderness, she leaned over and kissed Gordon on the cheek.

"Back to the Mary Grace issue . . ."

Gordon burst out laughing. "You're relentless tonight, woman."

"You need to give her that money." Claire put her hand on his leg. "You know it's the right thing to do."

Gordon took another sip of bourbon, enjoying the feeling of her hand on his leg. "You're right. I guess it wasn't her fault her daddy went off the deep end. I'll give her what I owed him. Hell, I'll even throw in some extra, make it easier for her to find a new place to live."

"That's the spirit. Doesn't it feel good to do the right thing?"

He smiled at her. "Not really. But I know what would feel good."

TWENTY-THREE

December 1962

Glory be, thought Ivy as she opened her eyes to the morning light drifting in through the window. She thought of the dozens of things she needed to do before they left for the church. As usual, the busier the day, the more important it was to remember the first thing on her list. She bowed her head and prayed.

Louis brought in a cup of coffee and gave her a kiss. "I got the water all ready for Ella's bath." He beamed at her. "Our little girl's getting married today."

Ivy felt peace like she'd never known. She thought back to the years of worrying about Ella, of watching her transform from a girl into a beautiful woman. But now Ella would have a husband to take care of her.

"She's got herself a good man," she said. "Just like I did. It's gonna be a great day." She looked toward the window. "How cold is it outside?"

"Not too bad. And once the sun gets overhead, it's gonna burn the chill right off. Looks like the Lord done give Ella a beautiful day for a wedding."

Ivy closed her eyes one last time. "And thank you, Lord, for this beautiful day. Amen."

─────────── x)(x ───────────

Ella's first thought when she woke up was that in a few hours, she would be Mrs. Bobby Lee Bennett. Finally, after all these months of waiting. Since becoming engaged, their courtship had been conducted almost entirely through letters. And while Ella adored reading Bobby Lee's sweet declarations of love, it hardly satisfied her desire to be in his arms. What a surprising turn of events that the goofy kid who teased her in grade school would become the man of her dreams.

For a while, she'd wondered if she'd ever be able to trust a man. But her mama kept insisting that when the right man came along, what happened with Junior Talmadge would fade into the deepest recesses of her mind. She said it with such conviction that Ella believed her, and then she fell in love with Bobby Lee and found it to be true.

Her parents wanted to bring Jake home for the wedding, but Miss Claire said it would be too risky, what with Junior home from rehab. Jake had been mightily disappointed; he'd broken down in tears when they'd given him the news during their weekly telephone call from Pastor Rice's house. The next week, he'd sent Ella five dollars so she and Bobby Lee could treat themselves to a nice meal while on their honeymoon in Durham, but his gift didn't make up for his absence on the most important day of her life.

Ella's thoughts were interrupted by Mary Grace wishing her a good morning. As usual, Mary Grace was awake early. Since starting nursing school, she spent all her free time studying.

"Can't you take a day off?" Ella asked. "It *is* my wedding day after all."

"I promise I won't bring my books with me to the wedding. How's the bride this morning?"

Ella sighed with pleasure. "I can't believe after today I'm going to be Mrs. Bennett. Sounds like I'm talking about Bobby Lee's mama. Guess we'll all have to get used to it. In fact, you being my maid of honor and all, I think you should start calling me by my formal name. Go ahead, give it a try."

Mary Grace ignored her request and went back to studying.

Ella was glad that Mary Grace had agreed to stand up with her at the wedding. She knew it was unusual, what with Mary Grace being a white girl and all, but honestly, there was no one she'd rather have beside her on her wedding day.

Ivy stuck her head in the door. "Ella, your daddy's got a hot bath ready for you. Hurry up and come on before the water cools off."

As Ella hopped out of bed and headed toward the door, Mary Grace pulled out a package wrapped in brown paper. "Ella, here, open this."

Ella untied the string to reveal a set of scented soap, hand lotion, and perfume. "Did you buy this for me?" She knew Mary Grace saved nearly every penny she earned for school.

"I did. It's my wedding present to you. Well, mostly to Bobby Lee. Pretty sure he doesn't want you smelling like field dirt on your honeymoon night."

Ella threw her arms around Mary Grace. "Thank you. I love it. And Bobby Lee will too. I can't wait for tonight. He's not going to know what hit him."

Claire fastened the clasp on her pearls and went to check on David. He'd gotten home from college yesterday and agreed to drive her to Ella's wedding since she had loaned her car to Ivy and Louis for the day. Good thing Gordon had taken Junior deer hunting in Greenville. He'd never understand why she wanted to go to this wedding.

It started with Ivy asking her opinion on a couple of decisions, and one thing led to another. In the end, Claire had booked her favorite florist to arrange the flowers, ordered a tiered cake, and paid for a seamstress to alter the dress Ella borrowed from Bobby Lee's sister. She even loaned Ella her stole to wear. She figured it was the least she could do to atone for the damage Junior had caused the

Sanders family. And then she got caught up in the excitement, having no daughter of her own to arrange such an occasion for.

"Are you ready?" she said, tapping on David's door.

"Coming," he called out.

"Don't you look dapper in that suit? Couldn't think of anyone I'd rather have as my date." Claire noticed that her younger son had filled out a bit, and the new glasses he wore made him look distinguished. His whole life he'd been compared to his handsome older brother, but he had turned into a fine-looking young man. She was pleased to see that his limp was barely noticeable.

"Do you think we'll be back by four? Wilbur's coming over to play chess."

"I think so," Claire said as they walked down the porch steps to David's car. "Ivy will be so glad to see you."

"I'm sure she's been looking forward to this day. I remember how happy she was when Ella got engaged."

"One of these days, it will be your turn. Speaking of, how's Rhonda? Did she have a good semester?"

"I guess so."

"Is something wrong, son?"

He hesitated. "That's the problem, Mom. There's nothing really 'wrong' between Rhonda and me. But at the same time, something feels not quite right."

Ivy stepped back to admire her handiwork. Crowded in the tiny room off the sanctuary of Ebenezer Baptist, she had coaxed Ella's long hair into waves and applied more makeup than she'd ever let her wear before. Her daughter looked radiant in the white satin dress with its sweetheart neckline and lace sleeves, and her eyes were shining with excitement.

Mary Grace wore a bright pink silk dress she had borrowed from a co-worker, although she refused to wear the matching hat. She had even humored Ivy by letting her pull her brown hair off her face and put some color on her cheeks. "But no lipstick," she insisted.

"You girls are as pretty as peaches in September," Ivy said. "Mary Grace, you're the spitting image of your mama, may God rest her soul. You look just like she did when your daddy first married her and brought her to the farm. I sure do wish they could see you now."

"Me too," Mary Grace said. "Can you imagine my dad all dressed up?"

Ivy laughed and put an arm around her. "He'd be itching to get out of his Sunday clothes and back in his overalls."

Cleo Bennett popped her head in the door. "It's almost time to start." She gasped when she saw Ella. "I've never seen a more beautiful bride."

Ivy carefully pinned the lace veil into Ella's hair and tugged at it to make sure it was secure. "Ella, I do declare, Miss North Carolina ain't got nothing on you."

Ella added a little more lipstick, adjusted her gold cross necklace, and picked up the bridal bouquet. She took one last look in the mirror and pronounced herself ready.

David glanced at his watch again. It was time to get this show on the road. His mom had said the wedding was at two o'clock, but the choir had performed one song after another and there was still no sign of the bride.

Finally, the choir stopped and the minister took his place at the front of the congregation with the groom and the best man, both dressed in army uniforms. The organist started the wedding march, and the wedding party walked slowly down the aisle.

Good, thought David. Maybe they would make it home for his chess game. He and his mother waved to Ivy who smiled broadly as she was escorted in by one of Bobby Lee's brothers. David thought of all the time he had spent with Ivy in the kitchen after school, eating the cookies they both knew she made just for him. It was good to see her this happy.

David was so focused on Ivy that when he looked back, he almost didn't recognize Mary Grace Craddock walking down the aisle, all dressed up in a flowing pink gown. Was this really the same girl he'd only ever seen in farm clothes or a hospital uniform? He couldn't take his eyes off of her.

"She looks beautiful, doesn't she," his mother whispered to him as Ella appeared at the back of the church.

"She sure does," he answered, his gaze locked on Mary Grace.

As the choir sang the hymn "Sweet Sweet Spirit," Ella and Louis walked slowly down the aisle toward Bobby Lee, who stood nervously beside Tommy Walker, his best man. When they reached the front of the church, Louis slipped into the pew beside Ivy while Bobby Lee took Ella's hand and squeezed it.

Ella paid close attention to Pastor Rice as he guided them through the opening prayer and read from the Scriptures. After the choir sang "Glory Be to God" and the congregation echoed "Amen," Pastor Rice asked for the wedding rings.

As Ella and Bobby Lee slipped the plain gold bands onto each other's fingers, Ella concentrated on repeating the words she'd been practicing for weeks. Her voice barely reached beyond the first row of pews, but Bobby Lee's rose all the way to the church rafters. After blessing the couple, Pastor Rice pronounced them man and wife. "You may now kiss the bride."

Bobby Lee turned toward her and gently kissed her as the congregation broke out in applause.

"Now everybody stand back while our bride and groom jump the broom," Pastor Rice said. "It's a custom that harkens back to when marriage between our people was not legally sanctioned. Let it remind us of how far we've come, and how far we still have to go."

Tommy placed a broom along the floor, and the congregation cheered as Ella and Bobby Lee, laughing and holding hands, leaped over it.

Claire dabbed at a few tears. The ceremony had made her nostalgic about her own wedding. Gordon had been so dashing in his tuxedo, and their spring wedding had been the social event of the season. She made up her mind to plan a trip for the two of them soon; they hadn't gotten away together in ages.

"Let's just say hello to Ivy and Ella," Claire said to David. "We don't have to stay for cake."

"You know what, Mom? Cake sounds good to me right now."

Mary Grace stood to the side while Ella posed for one picture after another. No doubt the bride was going to relish every moment of this day. As she watched Ella standing proudly between Louis and Ivy, she was overcome with gratefulness for all they had done to help her get through those long weeks after her father had been killed. Ivy had cried with her and prayed with her and held her so tight that she began to feel anchored to the earth again. Louis, never one to say much, made a desk for her out of old boards so she could have a place to study in the cabin.

And Ella. Mary Grace loved her like a sister. She was secretly happy that Ella would have to stay in Hobbsfield while she finished her secretarial program. Mary Grace couldn't imagine living on the farm without her.

"Mary Grace, come get a picture with us," Ella called out. Mary Grace walked over, although she wasn't sure she wanted to be photographed wearing this frilly pink thing. But at least she hadn't had to spend her own money on a dress. As thankful as she was that Mr. Talmadge had given her the money he'd owed her dad, she didn't plan on wasting a penny of it. He'd even offered to set up a savings account for her at Farmers and Merchants, but she'd declined his offer. Mr. Talmadge couldn't be trusted as far as you could throw him, as her father used to say.

When the photographer snapped the final picture, Ella and Bobby Lee went outside to cut the wedding cake. After watching the couple entwine their elbows and feed each other bits of cake, Mary Grace began helping Ivy and Bobby Lee's mother serve the guests.

"You got a piece for me?" asked a familiar voice.

Mary Grace turned around to find David Talmadge standing there.

"David. What are you doing here?"

"I got home from school yesterday. I'm my mom's date to the wedding. I've never been to a colored wedding before. The music was something, wasn't it? And Ella sure looked pretty."

Mary Grace nodded and asked him about his leg.

"I won't be running a marathon any time soon, but it's healing fine. I have a slight limp, but the doctors say that should go away if I keep doing my exercises."

"That's good to hear," she said. She brushed away a lock of hair that had fallen into her eye, handed him a piece of cake, and then turned back toward the table to continue helping out.

To her surprise, David touched her elbow. "Hey, is there somewhere we could go and talk?"

"Talk about what?"

"How about you come with me and find out?"

Mary Grace paused. She turned to Ivy. "I'll be back in a minute."

David led her to a bench near the entrance of the cemetery. "I've missed you," he said.

"David, I don't understand. What are we doing here?"

"I've missed you. I saw you up there at the front of the church, and I don't know, I realized something. I've missed you."

She stared at him. "You've said that three times now."

"I'll be home until the first week in January. Maybe we could see each other? Get a bite to eat in town? Or play chess?"

"I don't understand."

David blinked. "What I'm trying to tell you, Mary Grace, is that I like you. Standing up there in that dress like that . . ."

"Don't be an idiot, David. This," she said, holding up the outer layer of pink taffeta, "is not me."

"Geez, Mary Grace. Has anybody ever told you you're the most hard-headed person in the world? You refuse to read a single novel, and you don't like chess, which by the way, is the most outstanding game in existence, even though you could probably beat me if you practiced."

"I never said I didn't like chess."

He seemed at a loss for words and then grabbed her face and kissed her, hard at first, then tenderly. She was so taken aback she didn't respond until suddenly she found herself returning his kisses. She put her arms around him and it felt good and natural and true.

As their lips slowly parted, he looked her straight in the eyes. "So that's what I'm trying to tell you."

"You're saying we should date or something?"

He laughed. "Yes, that's exactly what I'm trying to say, although I don't seem to be doing a very good job of it. Don't you feel like there's something between us?"

She bristled. "David Talmadge, you have lost your mind. You have a girlfriend. Not to mention I'm pretty sure your parents wouldn't be too keen on the idea of us seeing each other. My daddy sharecropped for your father and then shot you. I barely have two pennies to rub together. And this dress that seems to have put a spell on you—it's borrowed." She got up from the bench and walked to the church without looking back.

David sat still for a moment. That hadn't gone quite as he envisioned it. But after a few minutes, he felt a renewed sense of optimism. After all, he was a clever chess player. He was home for an entire month, plenty of time to launch a solid offense. And she had kissed him back. Of that, he was sure. He ate his piece of cake in three big bites and headed back towards the church to offer Ella and her groom a hearty congratulations.

TWENTY-FOUR

April 1963

Gordon stepped off the hotel elevator and hurried over to the registration table. He straightened his tie and buttoned his suit jacket. He normally looked forward to the annual meeting of the North Carolina Bankers Association in Raleigh, but this year he felt a looming sense of dread as he approached the conference room.

Business at the bank had been up and down. Thankfully, a few of the corporate clients Millard Wellons suggested had panned out. And the 1962 tobacco harvest proved to be a strong one, which brought a measure of improvement to the bank's balance sheet. But due to the easing of federal regulations, the big players continued to buy out the small farmers, and that included many of the bank's customers.

True to his word, he'd cut back on his personal spending. He hadn't bought a car in two years, although he was itching to get his hands on a new Cadillac Coup de Ville convertible. He hadn't put in that swimming pool next to the dogwoods or hosted the dove hunt either. Gordon knew the board members had cut him some slack while David was recuperating. But he also knew their generosity wouldn't last forever.

It used to be that Farmers and Merchants practically ran itself, and Gordon could spend his time trading jokes with businessmen on the golf course or shaking hands at charity events. He missed those days. Keeping up appearances was one of his greatest talents. He used to treat this banking conference as a chance to smoke cigars with old friends and charm a lady or two.

Now he found himself studying the meeting schedule for any session that might lead him toward salvation.

Claire waved when she saw Rose Wallace's car at the entrance of the Velvet Cloak Inn. She climbed into the passenger seat and leaned over to hug her friend.

"I've missed you," Rose said. "It's been way too long."

"I know," Claire said, as they headed towards the restaurant Rose chose for lunch. "Gordon usually comes by himself to these bank things. But at the last minute, he invited me to tag along. So not only do I get to see you, but Patsy and Bill Barfield are having us over for dinner tonight."

"We missed you at their Christmas party."

Claire went silent for a moment. It was probably best they hadn't gone to the Barfields' party. She'd done a good job of keeping Arthur Evans from her thoughts. Besides, he'd probably found someone by now, might even be remarried. And her relationship with Gordon was better than it had been in years. She wondered if Arthur's attention at the party that night had reignited Gordon's desire for her. Or maybe it was Gordon's brush with death that made him reevaluate his priorities.

Rose asked Claire for news of the farm as they settled into the booth and looked over the menu.

"Ivy's daughter, Ella, got married in December. I ended up helping them with some of it. I have to admit, it was fun. I can't wait until it's Junior or David's turn to get married, although I guess in that case, I'll have to defer to the bride's mother."

"The farm would be the perfect setting for a wedding," Rose said. The two women mused about how the house could be decked inside and out with flowers, garlands wrapped around the winding staircase, a classical quartet playing for the service, and the Emblems closing out the evening with dance music.

After the waitress took their orders, Rose told Claire that her oldest, Lizzie, had won the leading role in the drama club's winter production. Penn had just made the varsity baseball team but hadn't gotten any playing time yet. Gray had a pet lizard that regularly got loose in the house. And Jennifer was a tomboy, always trying to convince her brothers to let her be a part of their backyard games.

"I swear I don't know what I'm going to do with that girl," Rose continued. "The other day she came to dinner wearing Penn's old football helmet. Said she forgot it was on her head! But enough about us. How are the boys?"

Claire was excited to tell Rose that Junior had gotten a job in Greensboro. One of Gordon's friends at Reynolds Tobacco had brought him on board as a "smokesperson" for their brand. The job involved driving around to local events and handing out free cigarettes to teenagers. It seemed to suit Junior well. And best of all, he was staying sober, which was a huge relief after Gordon had spent all that money on the rehab facility.

"He's dating a girl from Guilford College," Claire added. "I think she's one of those new age types. I believe they call them 'hippies.' He brought her to dinner at the house and she wore pants and said Ivy's pecan pie was 'groovy.'"

"Groovy?" Rose giggled. "At least she wasn't wearing a football helmet. I'm happy for Junior and for you. I know how much you worried about him. Sounds like he's finally settling down."

Claire sampled a tiny spoonful of tomato soup. "I don't know if I'd go that far. Gordon is paying for his apartment. But he says it's a fair tradeoff as long as Junior keeps his nose clean. I think Junior just needed to get out from under his father's shadow. The name 'Gordon Talmadge' is a lot to live up to in Hobbsfield."

"And what about David?"

Claire frowned. "I don't even know where to begin. He was dating the loveliest girl from home, Rhonda Lassiter. We were very fond of her. But he broke up with her over Christmas break."

"How come?"

"Because he claims to have feelings for Mary Grace Craddock. She's the daughter of Will and Ruby Craddock who worked for years as sharecroppers for Gordon."

"Wait, wasn't he the man killed in all that mess last summer? The one who shot David?"

"Yes."

"So you're saying that David has feelings for that madman's daughter?"

Claire took a sip of iced tea. "Yes. And would you believe she's still at the farm? She's living with Ivy's family while she goes to nursing school at the community college. I convinced Gordon to allow it because Ivy said Mary Grace didn't have any family who could take her in. If we'd had any idea David liked her, we never would have kept her right under his nose."

"Do you think she's trying to take advantage of him? He is a Talmadge, after all."

"That's the crazy part. She seems reluctant to get involved. David says she's stubborn, and proud, and it may take some time, but that he's never been more sure about anything in his life."

"Wow," Rose said. "He must really like her."

"Gordon is fit to be tied. We hope that being back at school will make David come to his senses and start seeing Rhonda again. She's such a lovely girl and a perfect match for David, as far as I'm concerned."

Rose seemed stuck on her previous thought. "What's Mary Grace like?"

"What do you mean?"

"What does he see in her?"

Claire paused, puzzled. She'd never considered this. "I don't know. I guess she's pretty enough, in a plain sort of way. She's petite, but she has a strong spirit like her mother did. She's a very hard worker. She used to help her father in the fields before she started at the hospital. She's still working part-time there, even while she's in school." Claire leaned back so the waitress could take her plate.

"Well, if this relationship works out, and I'm not saying it will, you could do worse than end up with a daughter-in-law who's pretty, strong, and hard working. In matters of love, the heart wants what it wants, and no amount of squawking from a mother will change that, will it?"

Claire tried to think of a reply, but nothing came to mind.

Gordon was grateful when the conference's morning session ended. He had listened to the speaker drone on about how to establish an audit committee to ensure compliance with state banking regulations. His stomach churned when the man mentioned the importance of adequate loan/loss reserves. He knew matters at Farmers and Merchants weren't where they needed to be on that front. No need to form a committee to point it out.

He'd intended to hit the lunch buffet before it got crowded but realized he didn't feel much like eating. Operating on the philosophy that somewhere it was time for a cocktail, he headed to the hotel bar and ordered a vodka and soda. He found a table in the back corner and took a long sip of his drink. He noticed a few other attendees had the same idea, including the regional vice president of Wachovia Bank, Clifford Jones.

"Hey there, Gordon."

Gordon stood up and shook his hand. "Cliff, how are you doing?"

"Can't complain. You look great. You've taken off a few pounds."

Gordon smiled and patted his stomach. "I had a few to spare."

"Mind if I join you?" Cliff sat down without waiting for an answer. "Park Anderson and I have a tee time lined up for tomorrow afternoon. We were hoping you could join us."

Gordon lit a cigarette. "I'll have to take a rain check. Claire and I are going back to Hobbsfield after the last session tomorrow."

"You brought your wife with you? That's a new one. She keeping you on a short leash these days?" Cliff chuckled.

Gordon could feel his chest tightening. He attempted to match Cliff's chuckle. "We're having dinner tonight with some old friends." Gordon took the last sip of his drink, hoping Cliff would get the hint and leave.

"Well, Gordon, I'd hoped we could have this conversation somewhere else, but I suppose I'll just get right to it." To Gordon's surprise, Cliff asked him about a potential merger between their banks. "We'd put you on the local board, and you'd still interface with all your customers who know you and trust you."

Gordon took another drag of his cigarette and then snuffed it out in the ashtray. He leaned in so Cliff would be sure to hear him. "Let's get one thing straight, Cliff. Farmers and Merchants Bank was founded by my father, Stephen Talmadge, to serve the people of Hobbsfield. He intended for it to stay in the family, and that's where I plan to keep it. We don't need outsiders coming in and trying to take over."

Cliff was unfazed. "Don't you owe it to your shareholders to let them know we're interested?"

"Put a number on the table and I'll notify them. But I can guarantee you they'll tell you the same thing I'm telling you now: take your money elsewhere."

Cliff stood up. "Good to see you, Gordon. I'll be in touch."

As Gordon watched him walk away, he wondered if word had gotten out that the bank was in trouble. He signaled the bartender to bring him another drink. A double this time.

—————— x❄x ——————

"Can you believe that son-of-a-bitch had the gall to look me in the eye and talk about taking over Farmers and Merchants?" Gordon barked as he and Bill sat in the Barfields' den sipping brandy while Claire helped Patsy clear the table. "'Merger,' my ass. We both know what he meant. It would just be window dressing. I'd be under the thumb of the new owners, and before you could say jackrabbit, I'd be replaced along with the rest of the board."

"Now Gordon, don't get all worked up about something that's not going to happen," Bill said. "Let him make the offer, and then tell him 'no thank you.' No sense making an enemy for no reason."

"He pissed me off. I think that's reason enough."

Bill smiled. "You never change, do you? Say, are you sleeping better these days? I know right after David got shot, you were having trouble sleeping."

"I'm sleeping just fine."

"Great. You look trim."

"Yeah, I guess all that dieting of Claire's wore off on me."

"How about your smoking? Have you cut back at all?"

Gordon made a show of looking around. "Dammit, Bill, seems to me like we're in your house, not a doctor's office."

"All right, I'll let it go. Just be aware that studies are coming out that confirm what the medical community has known for a long time: smoking is bad for your health."

Desperate to change the subject, Gordon shared with Bill some information he had picked up at the afternoon session about a federal program to fund hospital expansion under the Hill-Burton Act. "Jefferson Regional Hospital in Hobbsfield is planning to use it to build a new wing to house state-of-the-art radiology equipment. I was all set to apply to service the loan, but now I'm having second thoughts. In today's session, they said that hospitals that use Hill-Burton money will have to desegregate their beds. And provide a certain amount of free care to the poor."

"Desegregation is coming, Gordon," Bill said. "It's just a matter of time. If we don't do it voluntarily, it will be legislated. We already have a desegregated area at Rex Hospital here in Raleigh and at several other facilities where I have admitting privileges."

"My God, I can't imagine. Going to the hospital and seeing a Negro in the next bed." Gordon shook his head. "They're trying to force it in the schools, too."

"It's already happening. We've got a few Negro kids right here in Raleigh who've sued and been allowed to go to white schools. It's happening in Charlotte and Winston-Salem as well."

"Yeah, but no way it's going to stick. It's just a few uppities trying to make a stink. Those idiots in Washington can't come down here and tell us how to run things. As long as there's a hospital available to the Negroes, they ought to leave us alone."

"Perhaps if you visited a Negro hospital, you might not feel that way," Bill said diplomatically. "But back to the matter at hand, I think you should jump at the chance to help fund the hospital's new radiology wing. The loan could generate good revenue. Plus, it's remarkable how advances in X-ray technologies have improved our ability to diagnose. Could be good publicity for the bank."

As Bill went to the kitchen to check on dessert, his last words rang in Gordon's ears. Maybe Bill was right. Maybe he should apply to service a Hill-Burton loan. For the first time in months, Gordon felt lighter, more optimistic. Hell, maybe he could even skip tomorrow's conference sessions and take Claire shopping before they went home. There wasn't much on the agenda that piqued his interest. He'd found the answer he needed right here in Bill Barfield's den.

"It's always fun to see them," Claire said as they drove back to the hotel. "Can you believe Whit has decided to become a minister? I was sure he would go to medical school and become a surgeon like Bill."

"I know," Gordon said. "Guess he'll do his healing another way. Sure won't make as much money, though."

"Gordon, it's not always about the money."

"Blasphemy," he said, winking at her.

Gordon pulled the car into the hotel circle and gave the keys to the valet. He took Claire's hand as they headed inside. They could hear music coming from the ballroom. "Want to see if the banquet's still going on? Get a dance in?"

"You're feeling peppy, aren't you? I think I'd rather head upstairs. Maybe we can have a dance in the room."

"You don't have to ask twice," Gordon said, leading her to the elevator. It was comforting to feel connected to his wife again. Something about looking at the business end of a shotgun a few months ago made Gordon appreciate his marriage and everything he had.

"Gordon, something occurred to me when I was having lunch with Rose this afternoon." He unlocked the door to their room and held it open for her. "She was talking about her kids, and how Jennifer is a tomboy even though she's always dressed her in ruffles and bows."

Gordon made a show of locking the door behind them and began to nuzzle her neck. She pulled away from him. "Wait a minute, Gordon, I'm trying to make a point here."

"What point is that?" he asked, continuing his efforts.

She held him at arm's length. "Hear me out. Rose said they eventually stopped trying to turn Jennifer into something she's not, and they signed her up for tennis lessons."

"Claire, for the life of me, I can't figure out why we're talking about Jennifer Wallace right now."

"We need to stop trying to control everyone and everything around us. I'm tired of being at war with the families who work for us. First it was Jake. Then Will. Now Mary Grace. It's exhausting."

"Right," Gordon said, still trying to follow her train of thought.

Claire cut to the chase. "If David really likes Mary Grace Craddock, we should try to get to know her and accept David's interest in her. I'm beginning to think that parents don't always know what's right for their children."

Gordon was in no mood to argue; he had other things on his mind. "You're right. Let's have her over for dinner sometime. Now Claire." He offered his hand. "May I have this dance?"

Claire laughed and fell into his arms.

Energized by the banking conference and his romantic weekend with Claire, Gordon got to work on the application for the Hill-Burton loan for the hospital. Millard Wellons calculated the long-term revenues from servicing the loan and declared it a win-win for the bank. Within a few weeks—and after several calls by Gordon to his contacts in Washington, D.C.—Farmers and Merchants Bank was designated the government's choice.

Two months later, Gordon was thrilled to see his picture on the front page of the *Hobbsfield Times*. Randy Grant wrote an enthusiastic article about the planned radiology wing that included a mention of Farmers and Merchants' role. Gordon was pictured holding the shovel at the groundbreaking ceremony along with the president of Jefferson Regional and the mayor of Hobbsfield. First thing tomorrow, he'd ask Diana to have the article framed and hung in his office.

As he went to find Claire to show her the article, Gordon recalled his conversation with Bill Barfield. He should call him right away to thank him for encouraging him to make this strategic move. He'd have something to crow about at the next board meeting.

Gordon still held out hope that desegregation would turn out to be a passing phase. But just in case, if he ever found himself in the hospital, he'd be sure to request a private room. You just couldn't be too careful.

TWENTY-FIVE

July 1963

Mary Grace put down her textbook when she heard the sound of a truck pulling up to the cabin. Looking out the window, she was glad to see it was Ella rather than that horrible man, Mr. Kincaid, who managed the migrant workers.

"Welcome back, Mrs. Bennett," Mary Grace said as Ella walked in, placed her suitcase on the floor, and sat beside her on the couch. "How was your trip to Fort Bragg?"

"Good. Too good. It was so hard to leave Bobby Lee. We were like a real married couple, just for the weekend. He showed me around the base and the town of Fayetteville. It's nice, lots of pretty houses and plenty of businesses looking for office help. But then I had to come back here. I don't even know when I'll see him again."

The original plan had been for Ella to join Bobby Lee at Fort Bragg last month when she finished secretarial school. But now that he expected to be deployed soon, Ella was staying on in Hobbsfield until he came back from his tour. She had just been hired by the county clerk's office and was set to begin working next week.

"It's good you'll have your new job to focus on," Mary Grace said. "It'll help take your mind off Bobby Lee."

"Speaking of men, did you play any chess while I was gone?" asked Ella, her eyes dancing.

Mary Grace gave her a look. "You know I didn't. David won't be home from summer school for a few more days. And would you believe he said in his last letter that he wants me to have dinner with him and his parents the day he gets home?"

"You mean at the Big House? Like a fancy dinner in the dining room?"

"I guess so." Mary Grace made a face. "I'm not sure I can stand to be in the same room as Mr. Talmadge for a whole night. Plus, I'm sure I'll say something embarrassing, and that will be the end of it all."

Mary Grace still found the whole thing incredible, that she and David Talmadge were a couple. She mostly had Ivy to thank for it. After David kissed her at Ella's wedding, she'd fumed about it. But when she told Ivy what happened, Ivy had cackled with laughter. "Child, that boy's had a soft spot for you since he was fourteen years old. Guess he finally got up the nerve to do something about it!"

Mary Grace hadn't bought it. But David came to the cabin the next day, bringing his chess board and flowers he picked from his mother's garden. He apologized for catching her off guard with the kiss and invited her to continue their chess lessons. Somehow they ended up kissing all afternoon. He'd broken up with Rhonda and taken Mary Grace out for a hamburger in town a few times when she didn't have to work. Somewhere along the way, she'd become a solid chess player.

Then he'd gone back to college, and Mary Grace was sure he'd forget about her. Instead, he wrote her letters so sweet she was almost embarrassed for him. She even wrote him back a few times, but she preferred to keep it short and simple, using postcards she bought at the hospital gift shop. No sense going on and on.

Every morning, Mary Grace woke up convinced that it would never work out. There were just too many differences between them. And yet every night, right before she fell asleep, the tiniest bit of hope crept into her mind, that David Talmadge might still be there tomorrow.

Ivy stepped out onto the porch and locked the door to the Talmadge kitchen, feeling the moist heat hit her all at once. Mr. Gordon was taking Miss Claire to the country club for drinks and dinner, so she was free to leave early. She had even gotten a few things prepared for the big dinner for Mary Grace and David tomorrow night.

She dabbed at her face as she headed down the path toward home. It must be over a hundred degrees in the sun. She paused for a minute, watching the migrant workers in the tobacco field.

She'd like to go back inside and bring them some jars of water and cold watermelon slices, but last week when she did that, Mr. Kincaid told her to mind her own business. As if she had any choice—she couldn't help but notice what was going on right under her nose. She'd heard him yelling at the workers for taking too many breaks and watched him turn his dog on two men who tried to sneak into town. She saw him doling out four loaves of bread, two packs of bologna, and a bag of beans each day to feed twelve men and boys. Scotty, one of the younger boys on the crew, once whispered to Ivy that Mr. Kincaid paid them two dollars a day or less, deducting any supplies that he bought for them at the general store, keeping meticulous records of every penny he spent.

She and Louis did what little they could. Louis had built two outhouses so there would be enough facilities for everyone. Ivy began making more food than the Talmadges could possibly eat and giving the leftovers to Scotty to share among the workers. Ivy had even talked to Claire about the way Mr. Kincaid treated the workers, but so far, nothing had changed.

Standing on the porch of what had been Will Craddock's cabin, Red Kincaid distributed the week's pay to each of the workers living there. When he called out "Number nine," no one stepped forward.

"Where's nine?" Red barked.

One of the other men spoke up. "That's Clyde Ellis. He's in his bed. He don't feel good."

"What's the matter with him?"

"Pa's throwing up blood," said a boy who looked no more than seventeen. "He needs to see a doctor."

"What's your name, boy?"

"Trevor Ellis."

"Well, Trevor, that ain't going to happen any time soon unless your pa's got thirty dollars for the doctor and another ten for me to drive him there."

Red stormed into the cabin. The smell of sweat made him gag as he followed the sound of moaning to the bunk room in back. Poking Clyde Ellis with his boot, Red told him to turn over so he could get a good look at him. "You don't look that sick to me. I'd better see you in line tomorrow morning or you're out of here. Understand?" The man nodded but lay motionless on the soiled mattress.

The following evening, David led Mary Grace into the kitchen, where Ivy was minding several pots on the stove. "Sure smells good in here," David said. His glasses steamed up as he leaned over to see what was cooking.

"Get over here, boy, and give me a hug," Ivy said, embracing him. "How long's it been since I seen you? Three, four months now? How was summer school?"

"Over now, thank goodness."

Ivy put her arm around Mary Grace. "Don't be nervous, baby. You look real pretty. Your makeup looks good. And I like your hair like that." Mary Grace wore her hair in a high ponytail wrapped by a ribbon that matched her yellow piqué dress.

"Thanks," she said. "Ella made me sit still in a chair for an hour. At least I got some studying in while she worked on me." Mary Grace smoothed her dress.

David put his hands on her shoulders and looked into her eyes. "You're going to be fine. Now let's go into the living room. My grandparents are already here."

"Mr. and Mrs. Collins, they real sweet folks," Ivy said. "Like David said, you gonna be fine. Just be yourself."

Mary Grace tried to stay calm. "That's what I'm worried about."

While Claire and her mother perched on the piano bench looking through pieces of music, Gordon sat patiently as his father-in-law prattled on about how the savings and loan industry was structuring home mortgages to make it easier for borrowers. Gordon had hoped he would notice the article on the hospital groundbreaking ceremony that he shamelessly displayed on the coffee table, but he seemed oblivious.

"Our tobacco crop is coming along beautifully," Gordon said, trying to change the subject. "They're bringing in the bottom leaves as we speak."

"I saw those workers of yours out in the field," John said. "Where did you say they came from?"

"They're from Florida," Gordon answered. "And they're not mine. They work their way up the coast and only stay here until the harvest is in. Using them is saving me a boatload of money."

"Cheaper doesn't necessarily mean better," John noted.

The nerve, thought Gordon, trying to suppress his irritation. His father-in-law should stick to what he knew: pharmacy prescriptions and running a soda fountain for teenagers.

Claire and her mother moved over to join them. "Gordon, that reminds me," Claire said. "Ivy said the crew chief—that Mr. Kincaid—seems to have some . . . questionable practices. Working the men for hours on end and not paying them a living wage."

Gordon had had enough. "Claire, tell Ivy to keep her nose out of it. I hired Red Kincaid to do a job, and I'm going to let him do that job as he sees fit. Is it too much to ask, to let a man do his goddamn job without everybody looking over his shoulder all the time?"

Silence hung over the room as they all stared at him. Gordon realized he might have gone too far. Then David walked into the living room with the Craddock girl. Gordon had never been so happy to see anyone in his life. "David, Mary Gail, come on in and join us."

"Dad, it's Mary *Grace*," David said.

"Gordon, it's Mary *Grace*," Claire said.

"Mary Grace it is," Gordon replied as he stood up to greet them.

David glanced at his mother. She gave him a helpless look.

Mary Grace relaxed just a little as they moved from the living room to the dining room. Taking her place between David and his grandfather, she remembered to sit up straight like Ella told her.

As they settled into their seats, Ivy began bringing the food to the table in fancy bowls and platters. Roasted pork with cranberry sauce. Stewed peas and carrots. Mashed potatoes. Creamed corn. Mary Grace knew Ivy had fixed that just for her. Okra and tomatoes. A plate of buttered rolls *and* a plate of biscuits.

After watching Ivy make several trips to and from the kitchen, Mary Grace started to get up and help her. But Ivy frowned and shook her head, so she sat back down.

"Ivy, what a feast," Bonnie Collins said. "You've got enough food here for a dozen people."

"Well, ma'am, whenever Miss Claire and Mr. Gordon have special guests, I like for them to eat well." Mary Grace felt Ivy touch her shoulder as she headed back toward the kitchen.

"Claire tells me you work at the hospital," Bonnie said as they began filling their plates.

"Yes ma'am," Mary Grace said.

"Mary Grace just found out that the hospital is giving her a scholarship to finish out her nursing program," David said, putting his arm around her. "It's the first time they've done that for anyone without a high school dip. . . for anyone in her circumstance."

"I'm not surprised," John said. "You have quite a stellar reputation from what I hear. Your supervisor, Barbara Hayes, is a friend of mine. She says you're the hardest working aide she's ever had. They must have big plans for you once you get your degree."

"Thank you, sir," Mary Grace said. "My mama used to say, 'Without labor, nothing prospers.' If we all work hard to do our jobs—and by that I mean the aides, the nurses, the doctors—then the patients can focus on healing and getting their strength back. It's nice to see people get better and know you played a part in it."

Mary Grace felt her face turn red. She hadn't meant to go on and on.

"I remember Ivy saying what good care you took of your mother when she was sick," Claire said.

Mary Grace looked straight at Gordon. "I was twelve years old when my mother died. I realize now that if we could have paid for proper medical care before she got so sick, she might still be around today. My dad and I did what we could, but it wasn't nearly enough."

Trying to turn the conversation to brighter topics, Gordon described the hospital expansion program that Farmers and Merchants was helping finance. "Once the new wing is finished, Jefferson Regional will take in charity patients free of charge."

Mary Grace looked at Gordon again, this time in a kinder way. "I think it's great that your bank is helping bring this program to Jefferson Regional."

Gordon nodded. "Let's hope the rest of Hobbsfield agrees with you." He turned to his father-in-law. "John, you read the article in the paper, didn't you? I'm proud of it. Shows the bank is a good corporate citizen."

"Let's just hope you can turn all that goodwill into profits."

David reached for Mary Grace's hand as they walked out the front door of the Big House.

"So how was it?" David asked. "I could tell you were nervous."

"I don't think I embarrassed myself too badly," she said. "And I loved your grandparents. But I have to ask, does your family eat like that every night? I've never seen so much food on a table before."

David laughed. "No! Even on special occasions, we don't usually have that much food. Ivy got carried away."

"You know Ivy was the one who convinced me you weren't just going through a temporary bout of insanity when you kissed me at the wedding."

"Remind me to thank her for that." David tried to pull her in for a kiss, but she gently pushed him away.

"Your grandparents will be leaving soon. I don't want them to see us making out."

"Especially since you just demolished my grandfather at chess."

"I know! I never should have agreed to it." Mr. Collins liked to play chess with David, but David had gotten too advanced to make it a fair competition. So David had suggested his grandfather play Mary Grace, who proceeded to beat him twice in a row as Gordon snickered in the background.

"I think your dad was more excited than I was when I won," she laughed.

"Probably so. He likes a winner."

"Well, as I told them both, you're a good teacher."

When they reached the front porch of the Sanders' cabin, David fidgeted with his glasses. "There's something I need to tell you."

So this was it, thought Mary Grace. The dinner had probably made him see that she'd never fit into his world. "You know what, I'll save you the trouble," she said. "You've finally realized I'm not right for you, haven't you?"

He looked up in surprise and then laughed. "Wait, you thought I was breaking up with you?" He shook his head. "I love you. That's what I wanted to say. I've always loved you. I didn't know it until I was away from you at summer school. I could barely get through my classes. All I could think of was you." David paused for a moment and smiled at Mary Grace. "Now before you mess this up any further, I'm leaving. But I'll be back tomorrow as soon as you get home from school. And the day after that. And the day after that if you'll have me."

He turned around and took the three rickety porch steps in a single jump, whistling as he walked back up the path.

"You really are insane, David Talmadge," she yelled out after him. "You know that, right?"

When she finally finished in the kitchen, Ivy picked up the big basket of leftovers she prepared and headed out the porch door. She was proud of Mary Grace. She seemed to handle everything just fine at the dinner table, except when she forgot she was a guest and tried to clear the dishes from the table.

"Ivy!" Ivy looked around but didn't see anyone. "Ivy, over here." She looked off the path towards the woods and saw Scotty hiding behind a tree.

"Scotty, I was just coming to find you. I got a whole host of food to give you." She walked toward him and held up the basket. Suddenly she saw the boy's stricken face. "What's wrong?"

"It's my pa," he whispered. "He's real sick, been throwing up blood. My brother, Trevor, tried to get Mr. Kincaid to take him to the hospital, but he said we had to pay him ten dollars for a ride and we ain't got it to spare. I was wondering if maybe Mr. Sanders could drive my daddy to the hospital in his truck? He and Trevor are trying to walk there, but I don't think they're gonna make it."

Ivy was torn. Louis was at the sawmill on the other side of the farm. He probably wouldn't want her taking a risk like this. For sure Miss Claire and Mr. Gordon wouldn't want her getting involved. But at the end of the day, she answered to the Lord.

"I'll drive you to my pastor's house," she offered. "He'll know what to do."

They hurried toward the cabin and got in Louis's truck. Ivy pulled slowly onto the main road as they looked for Clyde and Trevor. Scotty spotted them as they tried to duck down into a ditch. He rolled down the window. "Trevor, it's me. Ivy's gonna give us a ride."

Clyde was burning up with fever. He was shivering and pouring sweat and coughing into a rag that was covered in blood. After helping to settle him in the back of the truck, Ivy sped down the road, praying she'd get Clyde to safety before it was too late.

TWENTY-SIX

January 1964

As Jake crossed the quad on the first day of spring semester, he paused to admire St. Thomas of Villanova Church, which stood at the helm of campus. Its stone facade looked especially beautiful nestled in a blanket of snow.

Founded in 1842, Villanova University was named for Thomas Garcia, a Spanish friar of the Order of Saint Augustine who was an accomplished preacher and educator. Not normally a fan of history, Jake had soaked up every detail of the life of St. Thomas. His devotion to the poor. His commitment to understanding and finding solutions for the fundamental causes of poverty. The endless examples of his austerity. These were values Jake aspired to as he thought about his future.

Halfway through his junior year, Jake remained deeply grateful for the opportunity to be a student at this esteemed university. So far, he had earned high marks in all his classes, and he hoped to continue the trend in the higher-level science classes he was taking this semester.

Walking into biochemistry, Jake took off his coat and slid into an empty seat just as the professor stood up to begin his lecture. He was curious to see a colored girl sitting two rows in front of him. He'd never had a girl in his class before, much less a colored one. All of the colored students he knew were boys—most of them athletes, including Jake's roommate, Jimmy Davis, who ran on Villanova's track team. Most students assumed Jake ran track also. He didn't bother to correct them. Jake had found that white students at Villanova, while tolerant of Negroes, didn't go out of their way to get to know them or include them.

"Good morning, I'm Professor Armstrong." Jake began taking notes as the professor gave them an overview of the course. "Before we get started, did anyone see the news over the weekend? Anything noteworthy happen that relates to our subject matter?"

A number of students shifted uncomfortably in their seats, trying to avoid the professor's gaze. Jake hadn't realized there was anything in the news that wasn't related to President Kennedy's assassination or Lyndon Johnson taking over the office. Throughout the Christmas holiday, the Shallcrosses had been deeply mourning the death of America's first Catholic president.

The girl in front of Jake raised her hand.

"Yes?" The professor nodded at her.

"I assume you're talking about the Surgeon's General's Report?"

"Exactly, Miss . . .?"

"Felicia Downing."

"Exactly, Miss Downing. Can anyone tell me what the report said?" He looked around the room.

Felicia waited a beat and continued. "The report said that smoking is a direct cause of lung cancer and is linked to heart disease, bronchitis, and other diseases."

"That's right. Thank you, Miss Downing. I suggest the rest of you read the report before our next class. And if you're one of the millions of Americans who smoke, I suggest you read it twice."

Jake thought about what a stir the report must have caused back in North Carolina, where almost everyone he knew smoked as readily as they breathed.

———————— x)C(x ————————

After class, Jake took his time gathering his books so he could walk out behind Felicia. "Congratulations," he said to her.

She turned back to look at him. "Are you talking to me?"

He forced himself to speak louder. "Yes. Congratulations on making a good impression. I've found that professors remember students who make an impression on the first day. Especially students like us. I'm Jake Sanders, by the way."

"Felicia Downing."

"I'm surprised I haven't met you before now."

She explained that she was in the nursing program. "We're all day students, so I commute back and forth. My dad is making me take this class even though it's not part of nursing. He's a doctor, and he thinks the nursing program is not challenging enough for me."

"Wow, your dad is a doctor?"

"He went to medical school at Howard University. He has a practice near Black Bottom." Black Bottom was a colored neighborhood in west Philadelphia.

"Is that where you live?" he asked.

"We used to. We moved to Ardmore seven years ago. It's outside the city just a couple of train stops from here. What about you?"

Jake hesitated. He never knew how much of his past to share. "I'm from North Carolina. I moved to Philadelphia a few years ago."

"North Carolina, huh? Did your family want a better life up North? I'm guessing your dad found a better job up here than he was able to get in the South?"

"Something like that." Jake was struck by how self-assured Felicia seemed. "Say, do you want to be lab partners? I find I'm usually the last one picked around here for any group project. I would imagine it might be the same for the only girl in the class."

"Especially when that girl is a Negro, right? That depends—are you committed to doing well? Because my parents have high expectations of me. I don't plan to let them down."

"Same here," Jake said.

"Okay, then, it's a deal." Jake could tell she was getting ready to walk away.

"I've got some time until my next class," he said quickly. "Do you want to have lunch?"

Felicia checked her watch. "It's a little early for lunch, don't you think?"

"How about coffee?"

As one cup of coffee turned into two, Jake realized he'd never met anyone like Felicia. She was intelligent and confident and beautiful, and for the first time in his life, Jake Sanders was smitten.

A few weeks later, Professor Armstrong stopped Jake on his way out. "I'm impressed with your performance in my class. I'd like to offer you a position in my lab in the afternoons. We're studying tumors, trying to gain a better understanding of how cancer cells stimulate blood vessel growth. You mentioned once that you're interested in medicine, and I think it would be a good experience for you."

"Forgive me, sir, for asking, but is it a paid position?"

"No, but it's valuable experience, and I guarantee you'll learn a lot. It will look good on your application to medical school."

"I'd love to, sir. Trouble is, I work in the cafeteria three nights a week starting at four-thirty. And I really need that money." As generous as the Shallcrosses had been to him, Jake tried to earn all his own spending money and some extra to give them when he went back for holidays. At first, Mr. Shallcross wouldn't accept Jake's money, but Jake had finally worn him down. It made Jake feel better to give the couple something in return for all they'd done for him.

"Tell you what, how about you leave the lab early on the days of your cafeteria job and stay later on the days when you're not working?"

Jake nodded. "I can make that work, sir. Thank you for the opportunity."

"Very well. You can start on Monday."

Felicia heard the whole exchange as she waited for Jake in the hallway. "Congratulations. Looks like I'm not the only one who made a good impression."

"Thank you. I wonder why he didn't offer it to you also."

"He's probably never had a girl in his lab before," she scoffed. "Besides, I don't want to sit behind a microscope all afternoon."

"There's only one problem with it," Jake said as they headed for their usual table in the cafeteria.

"What's that? As far as I can tell, you've hit the jackpot."

"Not quite." He paused a moment to summon the courage. "It's less time I get to spend with you."

In March, Felicia invited Jake to dinner at her parents' house. Jake dressed carefully, selecting the dark pants and white shirt he normally wore only for Mass with the Shallcrosses. Jimmy whistled as Jake combed his hair. "I may be going out on a limb here, but I think you like this girl."

"She's amazing," Jake said softly.

"Well if you really like her, you should bring her mom a present. Flowers or something. That's what my mother always tells me when I meet a girl's parents."

Jake thanked him for the tip. He knew nothing about dating, especially dating someone as special as Felicia. "I do like her. I've never met anyone smarter. She's two years younger than me, but she has opinions on everything. And she likes to debate things that are happening in the world. Apparently, that's what she and her parents do for fun."

"Guess everyone has their own idea of fun," Jimmy said. "But you're so quiet. You don't like to argue."

"Maybe that's why she likes me. Because I let her do the talking." Jake took his coat out of the small closet they shared. "I can't wait to meet her dad. He's a doctor, and I want to learn everything I can from him about what medical school was like for him and how his practice works."

"Maybe you should bring him a present, also," Jimmy noted.

On his way to the train station, Jake spent more than he meant to on a bouquet of yellow roses for Felicia's mother. The florist told him that yellow was a symbol of friendship, which Jake thought would be a perfect choice for the occasion.

Arriving at the Downings' house, he was impressed by its size. He'd never seen a house this large owned by coloreds. He wiped his sweaty palms on his pants and knocked on the front door. When it opened, he was relieved to see Felicia, who greeted him with a hug. "You look handsome, Jake. Come on in."

Jake handed the flowers to Mrs. Downing and shook the hand of Dr. Downing, whose imposing voice made him appear much larger than he was.

"We've been hearing a lot about this lab partner of Felicia's," Dr. Downing said. "Figured it was time we made your acquaintance."

"It's nice to meet you both," Jake said. "I've enjoyed getting to know your daughter." They moved into the living room to sit down.

"Felicia tells us you're from North Carolina," Mrs. Downing said.

"Yes, ma'am," Jake said.

"What part?" Dr. Downing asked. "I visited Charlotte once. One of my classmates was from there."

"The eastern part, sir."

"Speak up, son. I can barely hear you."

"The eastern part," Jake repeated. "Near the coast."

"And how long have you been in Philadelphia?"

"About five years. I graduated from Roman Catholic High School before I came to Villanova."

"I'm guessing your father moved your family to Philadelphia for the opportunities that the city offers. We have our own struggles here, but it's nothing compared to what folks in the South have to deal with."

"Right."

"So what does your father do now?"

"He works in the farming industry." Jake could feel his hands start to sweat. "Um, what I mean to say is that he works with farmers at the Food Distribution Center."

Jake was shocked to hear the lie come out of his mouth. But once he started, he couldn't seem to stop. "When we first moved here, he worked at Dock Street Produce Market, but then a few years ago it moved to a new location in south Philadelphia near the Walt Whitman Bridge. He oversees distribution for the produce and seafood terminals."

"Yes, I remember when they demolished the Dock Street Market. How does your father like the new facility?"

Jake remembered how Mr. Shallcross described it. "He says it's much bigger and a lot nicer. It's got covered loading docks, indoor spaces for the vendors, and refrigeration units for the produce and seafood so there's a lot less waste and rot. They're planning to build a hotel and a truck stop nearby for the people who make the deliveries."

"What about your mom?" asked Mrs. Downing.

"My mom works as a church secretary. And I have one sister. She got married a year ago."

"Well, maybe your parents can join us the next time you're here."

"Maybe so."

Jake was relieved when a timer went off in the kitchen and Mrs. Downing signaled them to the table. As they sat down to a dinner of baked salmon and roasted potatoes, the enormity of Jake's lies began to hit him. He had denied the existence of his family, substituting the Shallcrosses in place of his own parents.

As the Downings carried on a lively conversation about all sorts of issues—Dr. Martin Luther King, Jr., and last summer's March on

Washington; President Johnson's efforts to push through a bill that would provide federal protection to minorities; the rising popularity of a British band called the Beatles—Jake tried to contribute. He had planned to ask Dr. Downing about becoming a doctor, but his heart had gone out of it. He felt deeply ashamed for lying about who he was. He could feel Felicia looking at him, but he couldn't meet her gaze.

After dinner, he thanked Dr. and Mrs. Downing for their hospitality and said he needed to get back to the dorm to study. Felicia followed him out onto the front steps. "You were awfully quiet at dinner," she said. "Even for you. I hope it wasn't too much. I know my parents can be a lot."

"Your parents were great," Jake said. "I've just got a headache."

"See you tomorrow?" Felicia said. She looked up at Jake expectantly, and he knew she wanted him to kiss her.

"See you tomorrow," he said. He quickly turned away from her and walked in the direction of the train station without looking back.

Jake broke it off with Felicia the very next day. A part of him still wanted to tell her the truth, that he was the son of a sharecropper and a maid. That his family had so little standing in their town that he'd had to run away because no one would have believed his story. That he'd been no better than homeless when he arrived in Philadelphia until the Shallcrosses took him in. That he was worried he wasn't good enough for her. But he couldn't bear to admit he'd been ashamed of who he really was.

It was probably for the best that they not see one another again outside the classroom or the lab. He couldn't imagine his parents meeting the Downings and watching his daddy try to talk to Dr. Downing about current events. Felicia eventually requested a new lab partner, and as hard as it was for Jake to watch her work with someone else, he felt a sense of relief.

TWENTY-SEVEN

May 1964

Gordon sat back in his leather chair feeling immensely satisfied with himself. He'd been rereading the article in the *Hobbsfield Times* all morning long: "Hospital Celebrates Grand Opening of New Radiology Wing."

Yes, that Randy Grant was an outstanding reporter. Gordon's favorite part of the article was his own quote. "'Farmers and Merchants Bank has been taking care of the citizens of Hobbsfield for fifty years,' said Gordon Talmadge, bank president. 'We're pleased to help finance the new radiology wing and do our part to make sure that everyone who needs hospital services gets them whether they can afford them or not.'"

The article featured a host of pictures, including one of him and Claire being given a tour of the new wing by Jefferson Regional's top surgeon. He thought he looked especially distinguished in his custom linen suit and the cufflinks Claire had given him for his fiftieth birthday.

They'd even had a notable moment with Mary Grace at the opening. She'd just finished nursing school and was being trained to work in the new wing. Gordon looked at the picture of her team and was pleased to see she was prettier than he remembered.

He couldn't wait to get this article framed and put up in the bank lobby with the others. They might even have to take down the portrait of his father in the conference room to make space.

Days like this reminded him of what he liked about banking. He knew the balance sheet still had room for improvement. But maybe the board would cut him some slack with all the good publicity he'd brought in lately. He might even be able to reinstate the dove hunt.

He buzzed Diana. "Can you get me Red Kincaid from Belle Glade on the phone?" Gordon needed to check in with him about this summer's migrant crew. He knew a few of last year's workers had run off in the middle of the summer, and Louis had been stuck rounding up extra hands to get the harvest in on time. Some of the crop had stayed out in the field too long, affecting the grade. Gordon couldn't let that happen again.

Diana buzzed him back after several minutes. "No answer, Mr. Talmadge. Shall I try again in a little while?"

"Yes. Keep trying until you get him."

Ella was always the first to arrive at the County Clerk's office each morning. She'd grown up hearing her daddy say how important it was to make yourself useful, and now she understood what he meant. In the nine months she'd been there, she'd become a vital part of the office.

She enjoyed the hustle and bustle of customers coming in and helping them obtain marriage licenses, building permits, birth certificates, and death certificates. She considered it a privilege to play a small role in other people's major life events. Not to mention getting to wear fashionable dresses, nylons, and high heels. Working also served as a welcome distraction to the sobering fact that Bobby Lee was overseas in Vietnam.

"Good morning, Ella," Mr. Crocker called out as he walked down the hall to his office.

When Ella brought him his coffee, he pointed to a stack of papers on his desk. "Ruth's going to be out today. You'll need to answer the phone. And would you mind filing these documents?" Ruth Joyner, Ella's co-worker, had worked at the clerk's office for thirty years but had recently developed a sore throat.

"I'll get started right now."

The morning passed quickly. At noon, Ella took her lunch break. Instead of bringing her usual sandwich from home, she treated herself to a hamburger and vanilla milkshake from Collins Drug Store. Mr. Collins, Miss Claire's father, greeted her warmly and asked after Bobby Lee. Now that coloreds were allowed at the soda fountain, the drug store was busier than ever, and she had to wait a few minutes before being served.

On her way back to work, she noticed a car with a Georgia license plate pull into a parking space in front of the courthouse. Ella was surprised to see Pastor Rice get out of the front seat flanked by two men dressed in business suits and carrying briefcases. They passed right in front of her, but Pastor Rice was engrossed in conversation and didn't notice her. Ella watched the three men open the heavy carved wood door of the courthouse and disappear inside. She wondered what they were doing. Pastor Rice had a reputation for stirring the civil rights pot from the pulpit, but she'd never seen him at the courthouse before.

That evening, Ivy came home to find Ella at the table working on a long letter to Bobby Lee. "Baby, you sure have a lot to say. Looks like you're writing a book, not a letter."

Mary Grace was holding a towel and a bar of soap ready to go out back for a bath. "You should do what I do. I just write postcards to David at Wake Forest—short and sweet."

Ivy went to the stove and began heating up some country ham and collards for supper. "How was work today, baby?"

Ella looked up from her writing. "Ruth was out sick so I got to answer the phones. I wish I could do it more often."

Ivy laughed and reminded Ella how she used to practice answering the telephone. "You drove us all crazy, but I guess it paid off."

"Also, I got a hamburger at the drug store on my lunch break," Ella continued. "Mr. Collins himself came over to say hello."

Ivy smiled. "Miss Claire's daddy is a good man."

"Yes," Ella agreed. "He's mighty nice."

Louis walked in. "You ladies talking 'bout me?"

"No, we're talking 'bout Mr. Collins," Ivy laughed. "But I suppose you're a good man too." She laughed and leaned in to receive his kiss.

"Ella, I found a letter for you in the mailbox," Louis said, waving an envelope. "Looks like it might be from Bobby Lee."

Ella hopped up, grabbed the letter from him, and ripped it open. A few minutes later, she squealed.

"He's coming home! They're finishing their tour, and he says he'll be back sometime next month."

Mary Grace rushed in the door wearing fresh clothes, her hair wet. "What's wrong?"

"Bobby Lee's coming home," Ella said.

Supper that night was a festive occasion, with Ella making elaborate plans for Bobby Lee's return. "I've got to get a 'welcome-home' outfit. Maybe you can come with me to the store," she said to Mary Grace. "And I can help you pick out one for when David comes home from college."

Mary Grace raised her eyebrows. "Maybe so. Although he's staying for summer school again so it'll be a while before I need a 'welcome-home' outfit."

"How was work today, ladies?" Louis asked as he took another piece of cornbread.

"This morning a man came in who had been in a bad tractor accident," Mary Grace said. "We used the new X-ray machine to look at his leg. The doctor said he's never been able to see so clearly which bones were broken and which ones weren't. Isn't that amazing?"

Louis nodded. "What about you Ella?"

"I processed a marriage license for a couple from out in the country," Ella said. "Real sweet folks. I even told the lady about a dress I saw last week in the thrift shop. Thought she might like it for her wedding dress."

Ivy frowned. "Ella, that ain't your job, telling people about dresses."

"I know, but it just popped into my head, and the lady seemed real glad I told her." She took another bite of ham. "Oh, and I saw Pastor Rice at the courthouse today. He was with two men I've never seen before in fancy suits. And you know who they were talking about?"

"Who?" Ivy asked.

"Mr. Gordon."

"Ella, what have I told you about listening in and gossiping?"

"That it's the devil's work."

"That's right." Ivy finished the last of her cornbread and took a long drink of water. "What were they saying?"

Gordon slid out from behind the wheel of his new Cadillac convertible. He'd finally given in, justifying the expense by telling himself that he deserved it for his fiftieth birthday. Strolling into the bank, he checked to make sure the newspaper article was properly framed on the lobby wall. As he passed Diana's desk, she handed him a stack of messages. He sat down in his office and flipped through them. Still no word from Red Kincaid. Where was that son-of-a-bitch? He needed to line up at least two dozen workers before the growing season got underway.

He hadn't made it past the front page of the *Times* when Diana opened the door without knocking. He looked up, startled at the breach of protocol. "Sir, there's a man here to see you. Says it's urgent that he give you a package."

"I'm busy," Gordon replied. "Ask him to leave it with you."

"He insists on giving it to you himself."

"All right. Send him in, I guess."

A man wearing a crumpled suit walked into his office. "Gordon Talmadge?"

"The one and only," Gordon said, extending his palm for a handshake.

"This is for you," the man said, placing a large envelope in his outstretched hand before walking out without another word.

"What the hell," Gordon said. The envelope was from an out-fit called the Southern Farmworkers Legal Aid Society. He'd never heard of it. He opened it and pulled out the document inside.

He skimmed the first few pages and then stopped when he saw his name in bold. "What the bloody hell?" he shouted.

Diana hurried in. "Sir, is everything all right?"

"Close the d-d-door." Gordon felt the color drain from his face.

He was being sued for one million dollars.

Seems a Clyde Ellis, one of last summer's migrant workers, had gotten sick and was blaming his illness on the living conditions at Talmadge Farm.

He'd never heard of Clyde Ellis. How in God's name could he be sued? Time to get this straightened out. He buzzed Diana. "Get me Red Kincaid."

A few minutes later she buzzed him back. "I got a busy signal, sir."

Gordon paused, his thoughts flying in all directions. "Get me Sheriff Owen." He rapped his knuckles on the desk impatiently.

"Sir, I have Sheriff Owen on the line. I'll put him through."

"Morning, Gordon. What can I do for you?"

Gordon tried to keep his voice lighthearted. "I'm hoping you can help me sort something out, Dan. Seems one of the migrant workers we had at the farm last summer got sick, and now the son-of-a-bitch is trying to sue me. For a million dollars."

Dan whistled and Gordon felt his chest tighten. "A million dollars—that's a lot of money."

"I run a bank, Dan. I'm aware."

"I'm not sure how I can help."

"Can't you arrest this fellow? For bringing about such a ridiculous suit? After all, the crew chief was the one responsible for the workers. Not me."

"Is the crew chief named in the suit?"

Gordon studied the papers. "Yes, it names us both. They're from an outfit called the Southern Farmworkers Legal Aid Society. I had nothing to do with the man getting sick. Red Kincaid's the one they want."

"Those crew chiefs can be shady, Gordon. I told you as much when you first mentioned this whole idea. Did he have all the proper registration for his workers?"

"I don't know. I hired him to do a job. And I let him do that job as he saw fit."

"Well, let's hope he tells the same story. In the meantime, you should talk to a lawyer. There's not much I can do."

"Do me a favor, Dan. Keep this between you and me until I get it sorted out."

"I won't say a word, my friend. But you know that lawsuits become a matter of public record once they're filed with the court."

Gordon hung up the phone and lit a cigarette. As the soothing nicotine filled his lungs, he calmed down. He reminded himself that he was a Talmadge and no one was going to ruin his good name. Especially not low-life migrant workers from Florida with nothing in their pockets but holes.

He buzzed Diana. "Can you try Red Kincaid again?"

A few minutes later, she buzzed him back. "Um, Mr. Talmadge? I tried, but it's now saying that number has been disconnected."

———————— x✖x ————————

Gordon whistled as he walked down the sidewalk, trying to summon a casual attitude he didn't quite feel. He walked into Hinnant &
James law firm and sat down in one of the leather chairs. He tapped
his fingers on the arm of the chair as the secretary chatted on the
telephone. The Oriental rug and mahogany furniture in the waiting
room gave off the same air of authority and old money as the decor
in his own office. Yes, his friend Yates Hinnant was a very successful
lawyer. Had even spent time on the bench. He would surely tell him
there was no merit to this suit.

"May I help you?" It took a moment for Gordon to realize the
secretary was speaking to him.

"I need to see Yates. Tell him Gordon Talmadge is here. I don't
have an appointment, but we're old friends, and I need a favor."

A few minutes later, Yates came out to greet him. His time on the
bench and in private practice had turned his hair a shiny gray, and
his broad smile suggested a congeniality that would put any jury at
ease. "Gordon, good to see you, buddy," he said. They shook hands.
"What brings you by?"

"Can we talk in your office?"

"I hope you're here to tell me you're planning to host the dove
hunt again this fall," Yates said as he ushered Gordon back to his
office.

Gordon tried to smile. "No more dove hunts for us, Yates. A lot
of the old timers are no longer around. And the buyers from overseas
don't seem to be interested in shooting birds and eating the best barbecue in North Carolina. No, I'm here about another matter."

Gordon handed him the envelope. Yates put on his reading
glasses and carefully studied the summons. When he came to the last
page he looked up. "I think you've got yourself a problem here."

"How is that possible? I had nothing to do with those workers.
The only thing I did was hire the labor contractor, Red Kincaid. He
made it clear to me that he would be responsible for managing his
crew."

"Did you sign a contract with him?"

"No," Gordon said. "We shook hands on it, and I took him at his word."

"Do you know if the workers were properly registered and if he kept records of his payments to them?"

"How could I be expected to know that?" Gordon bellowed. "As I said, Red Kincaid was in charge of the workers. Can't you just call the Southern Farm people and tell them that?"

"I'm afraid it's not that simple. The Southern Farmworkers Legal Aid Society has been gaining traction throughout the South in recent years. They bring in top lawyers to work pro bono for people like these Ellis folks who can't afford representation. I have a suspicion they're on the lookout for a big fish to fry."

"Well, the fish they're looking for is Red Kincaid. Not that someone like him has that kind of money."

Yates nodded slowly. "Exactly. The first thing we need to do is get ahold of this Kincaid fellow. Figure out what kind of spin he's going to put on this. See if he's hired a lawyer yet. Do you have a number for him?"

"I did, but my secretary says it's been disconnected. I've been trying to reach him for the past few days."

Yates looked at his watch. "Gordon, I have an appointment in a few minutes. Let me hang on to this and do some digging. I'll get back to you in a day or two."

"I appreciate your help. The sooner we get this cleared up, the better. No one needs to be the wiser."

As Gordon headed back to the bank, he realized he hadn't eaten lunch. But this lawsuit had made him lose his appetite anyway. He walked through the lobby and went straight to his office.

He sat down at his desk, trying to remember what he'd been planning to do today. He pictured the migrant workers out in the fields in the scorching heat and the crowded bunk areas of the Craddock cabin. Maybe those weren't the greatest working conditions. But didn't Red Kincaid say most of those people were barely employable to begin with? That they were lucky to have a job at all?

Diana buzzed him. "Mr. Talmadge? Randy Grant from the *Times* is on the phone. Says he needs a quote from you about an article he's writing?"

Gordon smiled. Randy was probably writing a follow-up on the new hospital wing. Something to turn this day around. "Put him through."

TWENTY-EIGHT

Mary Grace shivered as she knocked at the Talmadges' kitchen door. She waved as Ivy hurried out of the laundry room to open it.

"Child, how many times have I told you, you ain't gotta knock? Just come on in. It's freezing out there."

"I know. I'm sorry. I don't know if it will ever feel right to just walk into this house. I wanted to check on the patient before I leave for work."

"Go on up. Here, let me take your coat first. Miss Claire ain't up there. She done left already."

Mary Grace tiptoed through the dining room and up the grand staircase. When she got to the bedroom door, she knocked softly and entered. "Mr. Talmadge? It's me. How are you feeling today?"

Gordon, propped up in bed with pillows, waved her over. "Better, thank you."

"You look good. Your color's back. Take some deep breaths for me."

Gordon was recovering from a case of pneumonia that hit him over Thanksgiving. Claire thought he had the flu, but Mary Grace realized he was in bad shape and insisted he go to the hospital. He was admitted immediately and treated with a course of antibiotics. The doctors kept him in the hospital through mid-December and then sent him home to recuperate. Christmas came and went without much fanfare.

Mary Grace studied him as he took a few deep breaths. "You sound good. The doctor said you can return to normal activities when you feel up to it, and I think you're ready. Just don't do anything strenuous, and try to avoid stressful situations."

He gave her a wry smile. "There's nothing waiting for me except stressful situations."

"Well, maybe a few more days of rest won't hurt. I'm heading to the hospital now, but I'll be around tonight. Let me know if you need anything."

"Thank you, my dear. If I haven't said it before, you're a damn good nurse. You may have saved this old man's life. My son's a lucky fellow to have you."

She smiled. "You've said it, sir. But thank you for saying it again."

As Mary Grace stood up, she noticed cigarette butts in the ash-tray on the bedside table. "Mr. Talmadge, you know what the doctor told you about smoking. It's not good for your lungs, especially for someone who's had pneumonia. I think I'll take these with me and then you won't be tempted." She picked up the pack of Camels and put them in her pocket.

"I take it back, Mary Grace, my son's not lucky at all. Pretty sure he wants you to leave us all alone."

The ringing of the phone startled Gordon from his television pro-gram. While laid up in bed, he'd started watching *As the World Turns*. He knew it was a bunch of horse shit, but he fancied that he looked a lot like the leading man—strong jaw, high cheekbones, and shiny black hair. And watching those ladies sashay around in their tight dresses wasn't a bad way to pass the time.

There was a knock, and Ivy poked her head in. "Mr. Gordon, a Mr. Hinnant is on the phone for you. Says it's important."

Gordon sat up in bed. "Okay, I'll get it. Will you turn off the television for me?" He took a sip of water and picked up the phone. "Yates."

"Gordon, how are you feeling, buddy?"

"Like I'm back in the land of the living. I'm planning to go back to work next week." No more *As the World Turns*, he thought wistfully.

"We were worried about you for a while there. And what a tough time to get sick, during the holidays." He paused. "I'm going to cut to the chase here, Gordon. I know this is the last thing you want to deal with, but I've postponed it as long as I can. The mediation date is set for next Friday at the courthouse in Raleigh, and I need you to be ready."

"Got it. Have they assigned a mediator?"

"Clarence Newby."

"Excellent." Gordon had heard a rumor last year that the retired judge was considering a run for state Senate. "Maybe I'll call him up and offer to support his campaign. Grease the wheels a little."

Yates warned Gordon against this, pointing out that Judge Newby had a reputation for being fair-minded and was familiar with the ins and outs of the farming industry. "We were lucky to get him. Don't do anything to jeopardize that. And remember, he doesn't issue a judgment—his role is to help us reach a mutually agreeable settlement with the Ellis fellow."

"Understood."

"How about you come by my office Tuesday after lunch? I know you were up to speed on our defense before you got sick, but it won't hurt to review everything again."

"Sounds like a plan. See you on Tuesday."

Gordon took a deep breath, realizing how nice it felt to do so. It was a terrible thing, not being able to catch your breath. When he'd first gotten sick, he wasn't sure he was going to make it. Luckily, he'd had good people taking care of him. Bill Barfield had come straight from Raleigh to his private room at Jefferson Regional and worked with his doctors to make sure he was getting the best treatment. Once he came home, Claire was tireless, getting him everything he needed before he even realized he needed it. And Mary Grace had checked on him almost every day, although her bedside manner could use some fine-tuning.

While he was sick, he'd entertained the irrational thought that somehow the lawsuit would go away. But now, here he was, almost fully recovered and still stuck in this mess.

Damn that Red Kincaid. In their interviews, Clyde and Trevor Ellis described in detail how the crew chief had forced them to work twelve-hour days in the heat; how he failed to provide enough food or proper equipment to do their jobs; how they suffered from skin rashes because they had no protection from the nicotine leaching out of the leaves; how pesticides were sprayed right after the rain making them more toxic; and how they were not allowed to leave when Clyde Ellis became ill. Apparently, the man had almost died from tuberculosis, and a number of the other workers had contracted it as well from the cramped living conditions provided by Talmadge Farm.

The Southern Farmworkers Legal Aid Society said the workers had basically been treated no better than slaves. But Gordon kept returning to the same refrain: how was he to have known? It's not as if he was down at the cabin checking on the sleeping conditions or monitoring their hours in the fields. That's what he'd hired Kincaid for.

And now the man had up and disappeared. Yates had sent an investigator down to Florida, but Kincaid was nowhere to be found. Yates figured once he caught wind of the lawsuit he'd hightailed it up north somewhere.

Gordon still didn't understand quite how the Southern Aid people had ended up in Hobbsfield. But once they'd latched on to the Ellis family, they'd practically put roots down. As Yates said, they were looking for a big fish to fry, and he was the biggest fish in the county.

The worst part of all was that article in the *Times*. What an embarrassment. Gordon had always considered Randy Grant a friend, but not any longer. Right there on the front page, Randy had outlined the details of the suit and even interviewed Clyde Ellis about the living conditions at Talmadge Farm. Gordon had called him immediately to demand a retraction, but Randy said he was just doing his job. Gordon immediately canceled his subscription, as well as the advertising contract for the bank, but the damage had been done. The whole town knew about the lawsuit. Made Gordon look like the village idiot.

Once he got over the initial shock, he'd been looking forward to a public trial where he'd be vindicated, earning sympathy for having been dragged through the mud and respect for the dignified manner in which he endured it.

But Yates insisted that Gordon's "I didn't know" defense wouldn't hold water. And that a jury could well be sympathetic to a pitiful family's story of mistreatment and award them a multi-million-dollar settlement. And that the press might very well skewer him. So they'd agreed to try mediation, where the terms of the settlement would be kept confidential and out of the press.

Thinking of it all, Gordon reached for a cigarette but realized Mary Grace had taken them. He sighed and got up to see if *As the World Turns* was still on.

Claire walked into the kitchen hoping to catch Ivy before she left, but the house was quiet. A large pot of soup filled with chunks of chicken, carrots, onions, celery, and spices was simmering on the stove. The smell made her mouth water.

She took off her bright red winter coat, hung it in the hall closet, and went upstairs. "I'm home," she said as she walked into the bedroom. "How are you feeling, sweetheart? You look a lot better than when I left this morning."

Gordon had just showered and was sitting up in bed watching the news. He smiled at her as she kissed him on the cheek. "Good. Even better now that you're here. How was your visit with David?"

"Give me just a minute to freshen up," she said, closing the bathroom door. She put on some fresh lipstick and came out of the bathroom, turning off the television and settling in beside him on the bed. "I wondered what reason David could possibly have for asking his mother to visit him at college, especially since we just saw him over Christmas. And guess what? He wanted me to help him pick out an engagement ring for Mary Grace. He's planning to ask her to marry him next month."

"Really?"

"Yes, on Valentine's Day. He wants to come home and surprise her with the ring."

"Well, I'll be damned." Gordon smiled. "Good for David. I have to admit, that girl has really grown on me. But do you think she even wants a Valentine's proposal and a big ring? She doesn't seem the type for a fuss."

Claire laughed. "I know. We agreed she would probably roll her eyes and tell David he was ridiculous for spending so much money on a piece of jewelry. But he can't help it. He wants to surprise her."

"It never occurred to me that David would get married before Junior," Gordon said.

"I know. But at least Junior's in a good place now. He has a steady job, and he's still dating Olivia, so maybe that should be enough for us."

"Probably so," Gordon agreed. "My dear, I think we're becoming wise in our old age."

She swatted him. "Speak for yourself. I'm not old."

"I hate to ruin the moment, but I had a call today from Yates." Gordon explained that the mediation was back on and scheduled for the following Friday.

"Oh Gordon, I was hoping with you being sick it would all just go away."

"Me too. But Clarence Newby has been appointed mediator. I'm hoping he'll be sympathetic to the situation I was in. Help us work something out where I agree to pay a reasonable settlement. And then we can put this whole mess behind us."

"Let's hope so. I'm ready to focus on planning a wedding that will be the talk of the town. Are you hungry? Ivy's got chicken soup on the stove for us, and it smells wonderful."

Thinking about the lawsuit, Claire felt a twinge of unease. She'd had a bad feeling about Red Kincaid from the very beginning. But she pushed the worry away and tried to hold fast to Gordon's optimism, whether it was warranted or not.

Gordon woke before dawn and wished he could stay within the comfort of the blankets a little longer. But the day of reckoning was here. Claire sat up as he slipped out of bed. "You don't have to come with me," he told her. "You'll just be sitting around the courthouse for most of the day."

"I know I don't have to," she said. "But I want to. For moral support."

Gordon turned on the shower and stood under the hot spray, hoping the heat would loosen the tension in his back. He dressed carefully, selecting his favorite suit and red tie. As he picked up his gold lighter from the dresser, he studied it for a moment, thinking of his father. What would Stephen Talmadge say to him right now? Knowing his father's critical nature, he'd probably take the Ellis fellow's side and castigate Gordon for being too stupid to protect himself.

Walking into the kitchen, he heard Buster barking furiously. Ivy brought him bacon, eggs, and strong black coffee. "What's got Buster all riled up?" he asked her.

"He's mad because Louis put him in his pen. Ronnie Sims is here—he's brought the two hogs you ordered. It's finally cold enough. He and Louis are gutting them and setting them up to drain. They'll butcher and smoke them tomorrow."

"That's right," Gordon said. "Maybe this year we'll give some of the less desirable cuts to the outreach committee at the Methodist church to dole out to people who need it."

"That's a mighty fine idea, Mr. Gordon."

"My father always said, 'To whom much is given, much is expected.'"

Ivy nodded. "From the book of Luke."

Gordon was impressed. He'd never spent a whole lot of time studying the Bible. He blew on his hot coffee. "Hopefully by the time Ronnie comes back tomorrow, this whole lawsuit will be over and done with."

As Ivy walked back toward the stove, Gordon could have sworn he heard her say "Galatians 6:7." He'd have to remember to look that passage up later. It probably had something to do with letting the innocent go free.

As Gordon and Claire walked to the car, a movement near the barbecue spit caught Gordon's eye. It was the two one-hundred-eighty-pound hogs hanging upside down, their blood dripping into the galvanized tub below. For a moment he thought his breakfast might come up.

He hurried into the Cadillac, turned the key in the ignition, and waited for the heater to warm the car. As they headed toward Highway 70, Claire talked excitedly about her ideas for David's wedding. Gordon finally switched on the radio, hoping she would take the hint that he was too nervous for idle chatter. As they neared Raleigh, he wondered if he should have ignored Yates's advice and called up

Clarence Newby. He could have offered him a hefty contribution for his Senate run. Gordon's mind hopscotched to the notion that maybe he should consider a Senate run himself in a couple of years. That could be the next chapter of his life. After all, he had the credentials necessary to win a seat: successful farmer, bank president, leading-man handsomeness, not to mention the Talmadge name. And wouldn't Claire make a great senator's wife?

These thoughts lightened his step as they walked into the lobby of the courthouse in Raleigh. Yates was already there jotting down some notes. "Nice to see you, Claire. I don't know how long this is going to take. We'll be using the conference rooms down the hall. You can wait here, or there are some shops and a cafe just down the street if you want to stretch your legs or get a bite to eat." He turned to Gordon. "I think we're all here now. Just waiting on Clarence to call for us."

Gordon and Claire sat down next to him. "Yates, is that the opposing team over there?" Gordon motioned toward a group standing on the other side of the lobby.

"I believe so," Yates said, barely looking up from his notes.

Gordon studied them for a moment, picking out the one who must surely be Clyde Ellis. He didn't look like the sorry Negro he remembered when he pictured the migrant crew from two years ago. This man looked downright presentable. Somebody must have cleaned him up and gotten him some decent clothes. Gordon felt his optimism begin to slip away.

Claire leaned in close. "You see that Negro man with them?" She pointed to the man standing near Clyde Ellis.

"Yes, what about him?"

"I've seen him before somewhere."

"Claire, how would you know him?"

She sat back, concentrating. "I remember now. He's the one who led the ceremony at Ella's wedding. He's the minister of Ivy's church, Ebenezer Baptist."

Gordon was confused. "Why would he be here? And how would he know migrant workers from Florida?"

"I don't know."

Yates interrupted them. "There's Clarence. Looks like he's ready for us."

Claire kissed Gordon on the cheek. "Good luck. I'll be waiting for you when it's over."

Claire spent the morning finishing *Gift from the Sea*, the novel she'd brought. Then she walked down the street, browsing in the shops and eating a sandwich at a quaint cafe busy with customers who looked like they didn't have a care in the world. Returning to the cold bench in the lobby, she waited for another hour, only catching a brief glimpse of Gordon as he came out of the men's room. He rushed out looking disheveled, which she interpreted as a bad sign.

So she went back to the shops and bought a blouse she'd seen in the window. She didn't need it, but it gave her something to keep her busy. Returning to the courthouse a second time, there was still no sign of them. It was almost four o'clock. She sat back down on the bench and smoked a cigarette. Then she walked down the long hall to the empty ladies' room and touched up her makeup in the mirror. Returning to her seat, she pulled out her book and opened it to the first page. She'd just have to read it again.

At four thirty, Gordon and Yates came out of the conference room. She stood up to greet them but Gordon stormed by her and out of the building.

Claire turned to Yates. "What happened?"

"I think Gordon needs a few minutes to calm down. I'll let him fill you in on the details. I still think we came out better than if we'd tried it in front of a jury. And at least this way, it won't be back in the newspapers. I know that was important to Gordon."

"Thank you, Yates." She hurried outside to find Gordon.

———— x)C x ————

It was nearly dark when Claire eased the car back onto Highway 70. She'd wanted to go straight home, but Gordon insisted they go to a bar where he downed two shots of bourbon in straight succession. She ordered food so he'd have something in his stomach to absorb the alcohol. Finally, he told her what happened.

"Five hundred thousand dollars, Claire. That's what I agreed to pay those Ellis people. As if I have that much cash just floating around in my pocket. I'm going to have to borrow against the farm to come up with a sum of money like that. It's outrageous!" Claire tried to keep Gordon calm, but he was too caught up in his own hysteria to listen to her.

"For a while, I thought it was going well. Yates did a fine job of explaining how I hired Red Kincaid as my contractor and that no money was ever exchanged between me and the crew. We offered fifty thousand to cover the hospital bills and help the Ellis family get a new start."

"But they wouldn't take it?" Claire asked.

"We were in two different rooms. I guess when Newby presented our offer, their lawyers started bringing up how the living conditions were so bad that Ellis contracted tuberculosis and would have died if he hadn't gotten to a hospital when he did. They went on about lost wages and fair labor and how ultimately I'm responsible for what goes on at my farm. They asked for seven hundred fifty thousand. We went back and forth until they came down to half a million and wouldn't budge. Newby said we needed to either agree to their offer or take it to court and let a jury decide."

Claire winced as Gordon signaled the waiter to bring another drink. She considered calling Bill Barfield but then thought better of it. Gordon wouldn't want his friend to know the situation had gone so badly.

Eventually, she convinced him they needed to go home. She was relieved when the motion of the car put her husband right to sleep. As she took the exit for Hobbsfield and drove down the winding road towards the farm, Gordon woke up, all out of fire and complaining of a splitting headache.

"I'm sorry about all this Claire," he said. "I should have listened to you in the first place and none of this would have happened. You had a bad feeling about Kincaid from day one. And you were against letting Will go."

She patted his hand and tried to sound stronger than she felt. "We'll be all right. At least it's over."

Claire parked the Cadillac next to the back porch. As they walked toward the house, the sickly sweet metallic odor of blood from the slaughtering of the hogs hit them all at once. Gordon leaned over and threw up in Claire's rose beds.

Ivy hummed the morning hymn as she mashed sweet potatoes and stirred creamed corn on the stove. Even though it was Sunday, she'd been called back to the Big House to make a celebratory dinner for David and Mary Grace, who had gotten engaged last night.

In church, Ivy had felt overcome with the holy spirit. So many good things were happening. Ella was pregnant. David had proposed to Mary Grace.

And now Mr. Gordon's lawsuit was over.

She had spent many a sleepless night worrying over it. How could she have known that driving a sick man to Pastor Rice's house two years ago would lead to Mr. Talmadge being sued? All she'd known at the time was that Pastor Rice had taken Clyde Ellis to the Negro hospital one county over, and that he'd arranged for Trevor and Scotty to stay with a family who lived nearby.

When she'd tried to follow up, Pastor Rice told her not to worry about the Ellis family. And since there was no one she trusted more, Ivy heeded his advice. But then last spring, Mr. Gordon got hit with the lawsuit, and Ella brought home the newspaper article that listed Clyde Ellis as the one making the claim.

Ivy knew that somehow, Pastor Rice, with his big ideas about justice and his connections to important people, had gotten Clyde hooked up with those lawyers bringing the suit. And ever since, she'd been petrified that Mr. Talmadge would find out about her role in it and send them packing. As much as she'd love to get off this farm, the farm was all she'd ever known. And where would they go? She knew from watching Will and Mary Grace that it wasn't easy to find an affordable place to live in Hobbsfield.

But now the lawsuit was over, and her burden was lifted. She'd overheard Mr. Gordon say he had agreed to pay half a million dollars to Clyde Ellis. She wondered what the Ellises would do with that much money. They could buy a palace if they wanted to!

Ivy knew the Lord wouldn't approve, but she had to admit she'd secretly enjoyed watching Mr. Talmadge squirm and holler over the lawsuit. Carrying on about how he hadn't known what was going on. All he'd had to do was open his eyes and see what was right there in front of him, but he was too busy acting like the only rooster in a coop full of chickens.

Ivy hummed louder as she leaned over to check the ham she was serving for tonight's dinner. Just like the Bible says in Galatians 6:7, she thought to herself, you reap what you sow.

TWENTY-NINE

May 1965

"We couldn't have asked for a more perfect day for David's graduation," Claire said to Gordon. She looked back one last time at the stately brick chapel overlooking the wide expanse of lush green lawn. "And there's no more beautiful campus than Wake Forest, especially with the magnolia trees in bloom."

"I agree. It's nice to get out of Hobbsfield, even if it's just for the afternoon."

Claire was glad to see Gordon in a good mood. It had been a harsh winter, but spring had arrived right on schedule. In the fields, the tobacco plants were sprouting with promise, and in the garden, tulips and roses in all shades of the rainbow were bursting with color. Gordon's friend from First Southern had come through with a loan for the Ellis settlement, and they could finally move on to happier occasions.

"How about David getting that award from the English department?" Gordon waited for his turn to pull out of the parking lot. "I didn't realize we had a scholar on our hands."

"I'm so proud of him. And how lucky are we that he's taken a position to teach back home in Jefferson County?"

"We have Mary Grace to thank for that," Gordon noted. "She loves that job of hers as much as she loves David. It's nice she was able to take the day off to come with us today. Although I have to admit, I'm glad she's riding home with him. Not much of a talker, is she?"

"No, not usually. Although these days, she's had plenty to say, mostly about what she *doesn't* want at the wedding."

Gordon burst out laughing. "She's her own woman, that one. I still can't believe she made David return the ring he picked out for her."

"Only because she plans to wear the wedding band that belonged to her mother. I guess it's one of the few things she's sentimental about. *I* can't believe the big day is only three weeks away. At least she agreed to have a wedding at the farm rather than just going down to the courthouse."

"I know, but why does she insist on making it such a simple affair, cake and punch only? My garden club is helping me do the flowers, and I can't even offer them a cheese wafer or a deviled egg in return."

"You've got to remember, she's the daughter of sharecroppers. She doesn't know much about being part of high society."

"But I could teach her. And I could plan the most spectacular wedding Hobbsfield has ever seen."

"I agree. I know you wanted to do a big dinner and dance for the reception, put on a show like we used to with the dove hunt. But at least we'll have the people there who matter. The local politicians. The country club set. The town business owners. It'll be the perfect opportunity to show Hobbsfield that the Talmadge family is better than ever. I just can't believe our own maid is going to be enjoying herself as a guest in our home."

"We've been over this. Ivy and Louis and Ella are like family to Mary Grace. And as for Ivy, I don't think she's any more comfortable with the idea than you are. But Mary Grace was clear. She will not have Ivy working in the kitchen on her wedding day."

Claire hurried to change the subject before Gordon got riled up. "Can't wait to see you all dressed up standing beside our son. You're so trim people won't know which one of you is the groom and which is the best man."

"That's easy. Who else but me could hold the title of 'best man?'"

—————— x ⟩⟨ x ——————

Gordon nodded at the customers in the lobby at Farmers and Merchants as he strolled into his office. Diana was at her desk sipping coffee. "How was the graduation?"

"Wonderful. David won an award for being one of the top students in the class. He's a bright boy, that one."

"Just like his father."

Gordon smiled. He'd always liked Diana. He took off his suit jacket, hung it in the closet, and sat down.

He then read the message on his desk and shook his head. Another farmer in arrears was going to have to sell. Damn shame, he thought.

Glancing at the loan packet from First Southern Bank, he flinched. Gordon couldn't believe he'd had to grovel for a loan like a piece of white trash. Good thing his old buddy Ernie Massengill from First Southern had come through. He knew it was a sizable amount of money, but for shit's sake, the appraisal on the farm backed it up. He didn't relish paying it all back, but he'd picked up a handful of allotments from smaller farms in recent years, and with a strong harvest or two, he'd be on his way to better days in no time.

Gordon tossed the loan packet into his desk drawer. He'd sign the paperwork later. Time to put his focus back on drumming up new business for Farmers and Merchants.

He heard a knock on the door and looked up as Diana came rushing in, a worried look on her face.

"What's wrong?"

"There are six gentlemen in the lobby. They're from the State Banking Commission. I told them they could make an appointment, but they said they need to make copies of all our bank records, including those in your office, right now."

Gordon paled and found himself unable to speak.

"Mr. Talmadge, are you okay? What should I do?"

He found his voice. "There's nothing we can d-d-do but let them have what they want." He shook his head. "I never should have gotten involved with that Hill-Burton transaction. The minute you start doing business with the feds, you're a sitting duck."

"They said you could wait in the conference room." She hesitated. "Has the bank done something wrong, Mr. Talmadge?"

"Close the door behind you on your way out," Gordon barked. Diana reddened and hurried out.

Gordon stood up to leave and at the last minute, reached into his desk drawer to retrieve the loan packet from First Southern. Opening his office door, he nearly collided with one of the auditors. "Is everything in here unlocked? Sir, you can't take any documents out of the office."

"This is personal property. It's unrelated to the bank."

"I'll be the judge of that," the man said, grabbing the folder out of his hands.

Gordon stumbled into the conference room in a daze, taking a seat at the head of the table. It was the only place he could avoid the disapproving gaze of his father's portrait hanging behind him.

"Finish up," Gordon growled, jerking impatiently. "Only a moron would use this many pins to take in a pair of pants." The tailor looked up in alarm and stepped back from where Gordon stood in his sock feet having his tuxedo pants taken in.

"Gordon, what's gotten into you?" Claire looked at him, astonished. He hadn't had the courage to tell her about the bank audit, not while she was caught up in the excitement of David's wedding. He was expecting a call from the auditors any day now. No need to mention anything until he knew the extent of the problem he was facing.

He mumbled an apology to the tailor and went to the dressing room to put his pants back on.

During lunch at the club, he put on a better show for Claire while she updated him on who was planning to attend the wedding and how the new house was coming along. David and Mary Grace had found a small bungalow a few blocks from Claire's parents' house, and Claire was helping them buy furniture and choose paint colors.

Eventually, they finished their lunch and Gordon returned to the safety of his office, where he could worry in peace. He knew the auditors would figure out that the bank's loan/loss reserves were woefully inadequate. He'd been meaning to move some money in there from the farm account, but he'd been strapped for cash for a while now between Junior's alcohol treatment facility, the medical bills from that McClure girl, plus the lawsuit. And now it was too late. The auditors had frozen all the bank's assets until they had finished their examination.

Diana buzzed him as he was lighting a cigarette. "Sir, I have Carl Woodard on the phone. He's the commissioner of banks for North Carolina."

"I know who he is," snapped Gordon. "Put him through."

Gordon took a long drag and picked up the phone. "Gordon Talmadge here."

"Mr. Talmadge. I'll get right to the point. As I'm sure you're aware, you've got a lot of underperforming loans. After reviewing your records, we've discovered that your bank's loan/loss reserve is deficient by two hundred thousand dollars."

Gordon scrambled for words. "That can't be right."

"I assure you it's an accurate assessment. I'm giving you notice that Farmers and Merchants is officially on probation. If you cannot rectify the situation within thirty days, we will revoke your charter and shut down operations. The bank will be in receivership and up for sale to the highest bidder."

Gordon took in a mouthful of smoke and erupted into a coughing fit. "You know that Farmers and Merchants has been a sacred institution in Hobbsfield for fifty years under my family's stewardship."

"I'm aware of your rich history in this community. That's the only reason I'm not holding you criminally liable for not disclosing the bank's financial condition to its stockholders. But I can't overlook the fact that you have breached your fiduciary responsibility to the board. You, along with your stockholders, will be receiving an official notice from my office within five business days. I suggest you convene the board immediately and inform them yourself."

Gordon slammed down the phone. Pacing around the office, he popped two aspirin and washed them down with three hefty fingers of scotch. He lit another cigarette and sat behind his desk waiting for the pressure in his head to let up. A clap of thunder pierced the silence, jangling his nerves. He looked outside and noticed the darkening sky of a thunderstorm.

After putting on his coat, he grabbed an umbrella from the closet. "I'm leaving early," he said to Diana, slamming his office door behind him. "I need you to put together an emergency board meeting as soon as possible." He walked out before she could ask any questions.

Halfway home, it started to pour. As the windshield wipers whipped back and forth like daggers, his headache returned with a vengeance and he felt dizzy. He gripped the steering wheel and wondered for a moment if a deliberate accident might solve all his problems.

Gordon picked at his breakfast while Claire showed him sample bridal bouquets. "I've narrowed it down to these two. Mary Grace told me to decide, and I'm thinking the white roses. But is it too simple? Maybe this one with wildflowers would be better? Or do you think it will overpower Mary Grace? She's so petite. Maybe I should start over and do one that's a mix of the two. What do you think? Gordon, are you listening to me?"

He snapped back to attention. "Yes, Claire, I agree."

"Agree with what?"

"That it's pretty."

"Honestly, Gordon, I wish you'd pay attention. The wedding's on Saturday. You should have taken this week off. I could use your help."

"I'm sorry, Claire. Too much going on at the bank." He knew he should tell her about the audit, but she had already moved into the kitchen to get Ivy's opinion on the bouquets. Wouldn't it be great if his life were as simple as choosing one bunch of flowers over another?

The emergency meeting was set to start at eleven. As the board members arrived, Gordon poured a scotch to steady his nerves, downing most of it before the meeting began. Entering the conference room, he skipped the usual pleasantries and went straight to his seat at the head of the table. "I know you're all wondering why you're here today."

Bill Barfield tried to lighten the mood. "Yeah, Gordon, don't you have a wedding at your house this weekend? Can't believe Claire let you out of her sight."

Gordon ignored him and forged ahead. "Last week, we were audited by the state banking commission. They discovered that our loan/loss reserves are deficient. They've given us thirty days to correct the situation. I've been thinking about the best way to handle this . . ."

"Hold on," Glenda interrupted loudly. "Did you say we were audited? And we're in noncompliance?"

"Yes, that's what I said."

Glenda folded her arms and glared at him. "How much is the deficiency?"

"Two hundred thousand dollars," Gordon muttered, trying to keep his voice even.

"Did you say *two hundred thousand dollars*?" Glenda raised her voice in disbelief. The room was silent.

"This is troubling news to say the least," Bill said. He turned to the treasurer. "Millard, were you aware of this?"

"We've been watching the reserves for some time, Dr. Barfield, but we hadn't yet come up with a prescription for how to correct the situation. However, I think Mr. Talmadge has identified a solution." He was relieved to turn the baton back over to Gordon. Millard didn't like sitting in the hot seat, especially when he had warned his boss time and time again that they needed to address the problem head-on and not simply stuff it in a bottom drawer.

Gordon fiddled with his red silk tie. "If we all come together and chip in a portion of our dividends from the past year, we can shore up our reserves and get things back on track."

Glenda laughed. "Don't be ridiculous. I can't speak for anyone else, but I've already spent that money. You are the one who has grossly mismanaged the bank, and you alone are responsible for fixing it. Our only mistake was not ousting you a long time ago."

John Collins raised an important point. "Each of us as a member of the board has the obligation of oversight. It may not just be Gordon's problem—we could all be liable for this situation. It might be wise for us as a group to hire an attorney and get some advice."

Bill cut him off. "Let's give Gordon a chance to rectify the situation on his own before we go hiring lawyers and spending money we don't have."

Gordon's sister-in-law, Lillian, spoke up. "I hate to say it, Gordon, but Glenda's right. You need to come up with the money to fix this."

The other board members nodded in agreement. Gordon tried to laugh but it didn't carry. "I'm afraid I'm a little short on cash at the moment."

"For God's sake, Gordon, you own Talmadge Farm, eighteen hundred acres of prime farmland that yielded a bumper crop last year." Glenda was practically shouting. "If you're short on cash, take out a loan against the farm."

The room became deathly quiet. Gordon thought about the First Southern loan packet he still needed to sign. There was no way Ernie Massengill would give him an additional two hundred thousand. Hell, without his bank salary, Ernie might not give him anything at all. He could feel all eyes staring at him, including his father's on the wall.

"Th-th-that's not an option," he said quietly.

On Friday, Gordon drove into work in a fury, outraged that the tent company's truck had blocked his car in the driveway for the better part of an hour. Not that he was looking forward to being in the office, but it was better than the wedding hysteria happening at the farm. A hush went through the lobby when he entered the bank. Storming past Diana, he went straight to his office.

He knew the employees were wondering about the board meeting. He didn't have the heart to tell them he'd been ousted just yet, not with the damn wedding to get through. He'd tell them first thing Monday morning. He idly flipped through the messages Diana had left on his desk. Guess there was no need to call any of these folks back.

He opened his newspaper just as Diana buzzed him. "Mr. Talmadge, I have Ernie Massengill from First Southern on the line."

Gordon felt an irrational flicker of hope. "Put him through."

"Are you calling to tell me you've changed your mind, Ernie? Your board reconsidered and approved an extra two hundred thousand?"

Ernie chuckled. "You're a banker, Gordon, you know better than that. Half a million was a stretch to begin with." He cleared his throat. "No, this is actually a courtesy call. I wanted you to hear the news straight from me. When the board learned ..." He cleared his throat again. "I'll spare you the particulars. First Southern is putting together a bid to acquire Farmers and Merchants. We've been in contact with your sister, and all signs indicate that your board will agree to the acquisition."

Gordon slammed his fist on his desk and stood up. "How dare you," he shouted. "How dare you talk to that bitch behind my back. You're a dirty traitor." Ernie tried to protest but Gordon wasn't finished. "I came to you for help, and this is how you repay me?"

"I think once you've had a chance to calm down, Gordon, you'll see that this was a business transaction, nothing more, nothing less. You know better than anybody that no bank worth its salt would offer a personal loan of seven hundred fifty thousand dollars to someone with questionable ability to pay it back, even with the farm as collateral. If you take a step back, I think you'll agree that having us assume your loans will be beneficial to your customers."

Gordon sank back down in this chair, feeling spent. "What am I going to do, Ernie?"

"Have you considered selling the farm? Or even a piece of it? We've been in contact with a developer from Raleigh who's eager to get his hands on some acreage in this part of the state. Willing to pay top dollar for it, too."

"No way in hell, Ernie."

Gordon hung up and looked at his watch. Claire had insisted he be home by three thirty; the minister was coming at five to lead them through a rehearsal for the wedding. He buzzed Diana. "Hold my calls. No exceptions."

Reaching into his briefcase, he pulled out the farm ledger he'd brought from home. He spent the next two hours gulping down scotch and poring over the numbers. At two thirty, he poured one final drink and buzzed Diana again. "Get Ernie Massengill back for me."

When he got Ernie on the line, Gordon didn't mince words. "Give me his number, Ernie. The developer from Raleigh who wants to buy the farm."

As Mary Grace and Ella walked toward the Big House for the wedding rehearsal, Mary Grace checked to make sure her mother's ring was still in her pocket.

"Look at that," Ella gushed as they caught sight of the wedding tent. Claire's garden club had created an elaborate arch covered in greenery and flowers to serve as the backdrop for the vows. Two dozen flower arrangements in glass jars were staged on the side porch ready to be placed throughout the house the next morning. A five-tier wedding cake complete with a miniature bride and groom on top was sitting on a silver cake stand in the laundry room covered loosely with waxed paper.

"We should have just gone to the courthouse," Mary Grace said, covering her face with her hands.

Ella laughed. "Too late now. But we've still got time to practice your walk down the aisle."

"I think I can handle walking. It's the rest of it I'm worried about. All those people staring at me. Trying to make small talk with the Talmadges' fancy friends."

"Mary Grace, you hold your head high and smile. You're as good as any one of those people putting their butts in the seats. You'll say vows, eat cake, and then you and David can drive off to your honeymoon. That's where the real fun is anyway."

David had arranged for a three-night stay in a hotel in Wrightsville Beach that overlooked the ocean. "I hope you're right. And I'm excited to finally see the ocean."

"Girl, what have I been telling you?"

Mary Grace blushed. "That the only thing I'll be looking at on my honeymoon is the ceiling of our hotel room."

Ella nodded. "That's right. Just be careful you don't end up like this at the end of it." Ella patted her growing stomach. "I sure wish Bobby Lee could be here for the wedding."

"Me too. Let's just hope he's back from Vietnam before the baby gets here."

Buster ambled over to greet them. Mary Grace reached down and idly rubbed his head. "You know Junior's coming in tomorrow morning."

"Yep. Mama told me."

"David said he's bringing his girlfriend to the wedding."

"Good for him," Ella said sarcastically. "He better not come anywhere near me."

"I'm sure he won't. David really does think he's changed since the accident. He's sober now. Hasn't had a drink in over two years. But I guess we'll see for ourselves tomorrow."

"You'll have to let me know. I, for one, will be focusing all my attention on the bride."

They walked up the steps and into the kitchen where Ivy was busy preparing all of Mary Grace and David's favorites. Much like the wedding plans, Mary Grace's idea for a simple dinner on the eve of the wedding had gone unheeded, this time by Ivy.

"Baby girl, you're making me stay out of this kitchen for the wedding tomorrow, but for tonight's dinner, you can't keep me out. You and David are like my own children, and tonight, you're gonna eat like kings."

"Thank you, Ivy, everything was delicious." Mary Grace tried to stifle a yawn as Ivy and Ella collected the plates from their dinner.

The rehearsal had taken longer than it should have because Mr. Talmadge, who'd been stumbling around drunk all night, kept interrupting the minister and forgetting which pocket the rings were in. But at least now dinner was over and she was one step closer to getting this whole thing behind her.

"Keep your seats, everyone," Claire said. "Ivy made blueberry pie, David's favorite."

"I'm going to take a smoke break before dessert," Gordon said.

"Make it quick," Claire said, frowning.

Gordon came back a few minutes later holding a glass in one hand and a bottle of bourbon in the other. He waved the bottle around. "Anybody else want one?"

"Sit down, Gordon," Claire said tersely. Mary Grace saw Claire exchange a look with her mother.

"Suit yourself," he shrugged.

As Ivy served pie, Mary Grace watched Gordon finish his drink at an alarming pace. As he poured another, she realized he was drinking as fast as her father did when he was on a bender. She tried to get David's attention but he was explaining a complicated chess strategy to his grandfather.

Glenda—who had been invited despite Gordon's protests—took a few bites of pie and put her fork down. "Gordon, it's customary for the best man to give a toast at the wedding. Have you worked out what you're going to say?"

"As a matter of fact, I have," Gordon said loudly. "I'm going to tell Mary Grace how honored we are to have her join our family. And I'm going to tell her how sorry I am that *you* are part of that family."

Glenda and Lillian gasped.

John Collins couldn't contain himself. "Gordon, that was rude. I think you owe Glenda an apology."

Gordon, his eyes glassy, turned his attention to his father-in-law. "Please. I've been wanting to tell her off for years. And speaking of apologies, I think you owe me one, John. When all hell's breaking loose at the bank, you haven't lifted a finger to defend me. Haven't you been enjoying the fruits of my labor all these years? Collecting your quarterly dividends. Coming over here every weekend and eating at my table. Haven't I been a good provider for Claire? Hell, I've even been faithful to her in recent years."

Claire went ashen.

"Gordon, this is hardly the appropriate place for this conversation." Mr. Collins said firmly. "All the bourbon you've been guzzling tonight is making you say things you'll regret. How about we call it a night? Let the bride and groom get some rest. And as for you, you should take a few aspirin and sleep it off."

"But I haven't finished my toast," Gordon protested.

"That's enough, Gordon!" Claire spoke in a sharp voice Mary Grace had never heard before.

"Oh, to hell with all of you," Gordon said. He stood up and walked unsteadily out the French doors leading to the porch. A few minutes later there was a loud crash. They looked out the window to see that Gordon had knocked over the table holding the flower arrangements. Broken glass and flowers were strewn about everywhere.

"Oh my God," Claire wailed. "The flowers."

The next hour was a blur. Glenda and Lillian left in a huff to go back to their hotel. Claire's parents offered to help clean up the mess, but Claire insisted they go home. Mary Grace, David, and Ella helped Claire salvage what they could of the arrangements. Ivy found vases from the house to replace the broken ones.

"Mom, why don't you turn in?" David suggested to his mother. "We're almost finished here."

"Thank you, son, I will. I'm exhausted." She turned to David and Mary Grace. "I'm sorry Gordon made such a scene at your dinner. My father just told me that the bank is in some sort of trouble. That must be why Gordon's been so rattled lately. But that's no excuse for his behavior."

"It's okay, Mom," David said. "Do you think he can pull it together for tomorrow? We've got all those people coming."

"If anybody can pull it together for a social occasion, it's your father."

As Claire went upstairs, David and Mary Grace hastily swept up the last of the flowers and checked for any stray broken glass. "I think we got it all," Mary Grace said.

"Are you still planning to show up tomorrow?" asked David. "After tonight, I wouldn't blame you if you didn't want to join this crazy family of mine."

"I'll show up. How else will I get to see the ocean?"

Suddenly, they heard a loud mumble followed by a string of cursing.

"Dad?" They walked around to the opposite side of the porch and there was Gordon, sprawled out on the settee. David groaned. "I thought you had gone to bed. What are you doing out here?"

Gordon sat up and rubbed his eyes. "It's all gone to hell. Five hundred thousand. Two hundred thousand. People think I grow money out here on the tobacco stalks. They can shove it up their asses, those damn Southern Farm lawyers. And the goddamn bank commissioners. I ought to shoot that son-of-a-bitch Ernie with my Winchester. David, get me my Winchester."

"Dad, you're drunk."

"Let me handle this one, David," Mary Grace said. "Really, you go on inside. Check on your mom. I'll see you tomorrow." She eased him towards the door.

"Are you sure?"

"Yes. I may not know how to glide down the aisle in heels or make small talk with rich people, but drunk fathers, that I can handle."

Mary Grace went into the kitchen where Ivy was on her way out. "You need to get on home, child," Ivy said sternly. "Tomorrow's your big day."

"I'm coming in a few minutes. Can you do me a favor? Make a pot of coffee. And is there some BC Powder somewhere?"

As Ivy brewed coffee, Mary Grace found what she needed from the kitchen and went back out on the porch. "Mr. Talmadge, here, let me help you sit up." He grumbled in protest and she used all her strength to pull him to a sitting position. "I've got two raw eggs in this glass, and I want you to drink them in one swallow."

He tried to push the glass away. "That's disgusting."

"I'm telling you, it'll help you feel better. It's what I used to give my daddy when he drank too much."

Gordon hesitated and then drank it in one gulp. Mary Grace went back to the kitchen and returned with a cup of coffee. She handed him the mug and poured the BC Powder into a thermos of water. "Once you finish the coffee, we'll start on the water."

Mr. Talmadge reluctantly drank most of the coffee and some of the water and then dozed off. Every few minutes, Mary Grace would rouse him and make him drink more water. She continued with this for the better part of an hour, tiptoeing inside several times to refill the thermos.

Finally, he sat up straight, looking more awake and almost sober. "Mary Grace, I've got to use the bathroom." He stood up and stumbled against the side table.

"If you go inside, you'll wake everybody up. Just go off the side of the porch."

He looked at her strangely, then walked around to the edge of the porch out of her view and relieved himself. He sat down on the front steps and she came over and sat beside him.

"Feel any better? You know David's counting on you to be his best man tomorrow."

"I feel more like a punching bag these days than anybody's best man," Gordon scoffed. "I'm going to have to sell the farm."

"What?"

He nodded. "I'm going to have to sell the farm. Maybe not the whole thing, but a substantial portion. I've spent my whole life trying to protect this place . . . it's my legacy . . . something to pass down to my sons and grandchildren . . . and I messed it all up. I ruined everything. I knew the bank was in trouble; I just didn't want to admit there was a problem. And I won't be able to keep this bank audit out of the paper. The whole town will be laughing at me."

"Mr. Talmadge, I don't know anything about banking. But you can't spend your time fretting over what people might think or say. You have to put your head down and focus on fixing the trouble at hand."

They sat in silence for a few minutes as an owl circled in the moonlight looking for prey. "I'm sorry I turned your daddy down for a loan all those years ago," Gordon said. "And sent the two of you packing. I think I can see how he ended up sitting on his front porch mad enough to shoot somebody. Maybe things would have turned out differently for you and him if I'd given him that loan."

Mary Grace turned to look at him, but he continued to stare into the night. "I appreciate your saying that. Maybe things *would* have turned out differently. But with or without that loan, my daddy had his demons, and there's no sense worrying about what might have been."

Gordon took a deep breath. "I think it's time for us to turn in. We've got a wedding tomorrow, and the bride and the best man need to be ready." Mary Grace stood up to help him. "Don't worry, I can make it inside without waking up the whole house."

"Good night, Mr. Talmadge." She watched as he shuffled toward the door, looking as fragile as the glass vases that had shattered into pieces.

THIRTY

October 1965

The first thing Ella noticed when she walked into the County Clerk's office was how disorganized it looked. The stack of papers to be filed was overflowing, and deeds were scattered across the counter. Three customers waited in the lobby while Sherry, the girl who'd been hired to take Ella's place, struggled to help an elderly woman fill out paperwork.

"Mr. Crocker said for you to go straight back to his office," Sherry called out. "Congratulations on the baby."

"Thank you." Ella still found it hard to believe that she was the mother of a two-month-old, especially since Bobby Lee hadn't been there to share the experience with her. Luckily, Pauline was an easy baby, especially with Ivy and Louis doting on her the way they did. Ella loved being a mother but sometimes found herself bored by the monotony of her days and the endless cycle of feedings, naps, and diapers. She longed for the office and the string of customers to chat with.

As she passed the break room, she noticed the coffee pot was empty and fought the urge to make a new pot. She tapped lightly on Mr. Crocker's open door.

"Ella, come in," he said. "Sit down. Looks like motherhood is agreeing with you."

Ella crossed her ankles and folded her hands in her lap. It felt good to have on heels and a nice dress again. "Thank you, sir."

"And you had a little girl, right?"

"Yes. Pauline. She's named after my older brother, Paul. He was killed in an accident at the farm."

"Happens all the time. No one realizes how dangerous farming really is—the cutters, the fertilizers, the fires, and so on." He realized he was getting off-topic. "Well, congratulations on little Pauline. You're probably wondering why I asked you to come by."

"Yes, sir."

Mr. Crocker rolled his chair away from his desk, opened the window a crack, and then lit his pipe. A moment later he picked up a letter from the jumble of papers on his desk.

"Ruth Joyner has handed in notice of her retirement, effective immediately. If I'm being frank, her work has not been up to par in quite some time. I've realized over these past few months without you how vital you were to the operation of this office. You had clearly taken on some of Ruth's responsibilities, which she was none too happy to resume when you left. And Sherry, who graduated from the same secretarial program you attended, has not lived up to your standards."

He took a puff from his pipe and blew the smoke toward the window in a show of courtesy. "Ella, we need you. I know you just had a baby, and that you're planning to move to Fort Bragg when your husband comes back from Vietnam. But that might not be for a while with the way this war is going. What I'm getting at is: Will you come back to work for us? At least for the time being? It would be a new position that more accurately reflects your responsibilities: Office Manager."

Ella's mind was racing. She asked if there was a raise to go along with the new title.

"We're dealing with a budgetary crunch at the moment, but I think I can offer an extra ten dollars a week over your previous salary."

"Does that mean I'll be making the same amount that Ruth made?"

"Not quite, but remember, she worked here for thirty years."

"But like you said, I've been picking up her slack for a long time."

He stared at her for a moment and sighed. "All right, let's make it twelve dollars more a week."

"It's just that, sir, I'll have to figure out an arrangement for Pauline." No sense in letting on to Mr. Crocker just how eager her mother and Bobby Lee's mother would be to help with Pauline. "And I'm saving up to help my parents buy a house."

"Fifteen more a week. That's the best I can do."

"Thank you, sir."

"So we have ourselves a deal?"

"Just one more thing . . ."

"What's that?"

"I'll need some extra time off around Christmas. My husband is coming home on a two-week leave, and I want to spend as much time with him as possible."

"It's a deal."

Gordon sat with his back to the dining room windows, pushing a mound of scrambled eggs around his plate. "Not hungry?" Claire asked.

"Not really. I didn't sleep well last night. I'll take another cup of coffee, though."

Claire called for Ivy and asked her to bring in more coffee. Hearing tires rumble over the driveway, she stood up and went to the window. "Are you expecting someone, Gordon?"

"Must be the surveyors. They're marking the new road and the footprints of the buildings. Construction is supposed to start in the spring."

"I still can't believe it. Your family's legacy is being converted into an industrial park."

Claire felt tears coming and hurried upstairs. She was still trying to accept the circumstances they found themselves in. When Gordon's friend at First Southern found out about the bank audit, he refused to give him the loan. He'd apologized profusely and then turned around a few weeks later and acquired the bank. To come up with the money for the settlement, Gordon had been forced to sell the farm to an investment group out of Raleigh that was planning to develop a "business center," housing companies that didn't want to pay the steep rents in Raleigh or Durham. The town council issued an entitlement within a matter of weeks, appreciating the impact the new venture would have on the economy of Hobbsfield and the entire county.

Gordon followed Claire upstairs and found her at the window watching the surveyors, a lit cigarette in her hand. He put his arms around her waist and kissed the back of her neck. "I'm sorry, Claire. I didn't mean for any of this to happen."

She shrugged out of his embrace and gave him a withering look. "Any of what? Looking the other way while people were living like animals on our property? Ignoring our son's behavior until he almost killed someone? Ruining the farm—not to mention our good name—because you can't stay on top of things at the bank? Humiliating me in front of my parents? And God only knows what you did before I came into the picture."

"Come on, Claire," Gordon said softly. "That's not fair. And how many times have I apologized for the rehearsal dinner? I was drunk out of my mind." He gave her a pleading look. "All we've got left is each other, Claire. I know I've made mistakes. Terrible mistakes. But I love you, and I'm going to spend every breath in my body trying to make it up to you."

He put his arms around her again, and this time, she allowed him to do so.

"At least we get to stay in the house," he said. It was the one part of the deal Gordon had insisted on.

"I know," she said. "But nothing around us will be the same. Guess we should tell Louis and Ivy they'll need to find another place to live."

The telephone rang and Claire went to answer it. "It's Diana from the bank," she said, covering the receiver with her hand. "Do you have a meeting with Russell Stokes today? Diana says you were supposed to review a few accounts with him."

"Tell her something's come up. I'll come by next week. I don't feel like it today."

"Why don't you lie down for a bit? I've got to leave for my Hospital Auxiliary meeting."

Gordon rested his head on the pillows. Touching his forehead, he wondered if he was running a fever. He could hear Buster barking ferociously, warning the surveyors that they had no business being at Talmadge Farm. Ivy yelled at him to calm down, but he ignored her commands.

Gordon's parking space in front of the bank was occupied by a 1965 Oldsmobile, likely belonging to Russell Stokes, the bank's new president. Workmen on a ladder were installing the new "First Southern Bank" sign. The old Farmers and Merchants block letters lay unceremoniously on the ground in a heap.

He knocked on the back door, and Diana let him in. He was relieved he didn't have to go through the main lobby where he might run into former customers and have to engage in awkward conversation at best or avoidance at worst.

"Wait here, Mr. Talmadge," Diana said. "I'll see if Mr. Stokes is ready for you."

A few minutes later Diana gestured for Gordon to go into his former office. Russell shook his hand and motioned for him to sit down.

Gordon realized he hadn't sat on this side of the desk since his father had been bank president. Other than a new gallery of family photographs, nothing in the office had changed. There hadn't been time to remove the furnishings that Claire had chosen.

Gordon spent the next hour sharing with Russell the personal histories of the bank's high-profile clients and telling off-the-record stories that might help leverage the bank's relationship with them.

"I appreciate your help today, Gordon," Russell said.

Gordon nodded, suddenly overcome with emotion. "Some of my customers have been with me for over thirty years. I want to be sure they're taken care of. It's what my father would have wanted."

Sensing that Gordon was struggling to maintain his composure, Russell changed the subject. "I hear the developer is about to start moving dirt around at the farm." He pointed out the positive impact the project would have on the bank, bringing in corporate accounts and personal home loans. "All that vacant farmland near you will eventually be turned into housing developments."

"Traffic in and out of town is going to pick up," Gordon said. "I've already spoken to the city planners about putting up a traffic light at the north edge of town—it will be the first."

"There goes the neighborhood."

Gordon gave a small chuckle. "The price of change."

Diana knocked on the door and stuck her head in. "Mr. Stokes, your eleven o'clock is here."

As Gordon pulled out of the employee lot, he noticed the workmen had finished installing the new bank sign. Waiting at the stop sign for traffic to clear, he watched them hurl the old lettering from Farmers and Merchants into the back of their truck, probably headed for the town dump.

THIRTY-ONE

June 1966

Claire cut another bloom from the Queen Elizabeth and stepped back to study her inventory. Just a few more, and she'd have enough for the arrangement she wanted to bring to Mary Grace and David. Good thing she'd made her way to the garden early. In an hour, all the construction noise would start again, and she wouldn't be able to hear herself think.

From the porch steps, she looked out at the vanishing forest line. She hadn't realized how much the trees contributed to the sense of peacefulness the farm held. Gordon had insisted that the excavation for the industrial park begin at the far edges of the farm to keep the disruption to a minimum. But week by week, the bulldozers and chainsaws marched closer to the house, mowing down everything in their path.

Probably for the best that Gordon couldn't get out much these days. When the work first started, he drove to the construction site every morning and reviewed the day's plan with the project manager. "Keeping an eye on things" was what he called it.

It took a while for him to realize he no longer owned the land, no longer had a say, and that the project manager was just humoring him. But then he'd had another bout of pneumonia a few months back, not as severe as last year, but bad enough to curtail his activities.

There were days when he hardly had the energy to get out of bed, much less walk through the overturned grass and mud. And all of this chaos took a toll on his mood. He had a particularly difficult day when he saw the cornfield—the site of so many dove hunts—being leveled, and an equally rough day when the flue-cured barns were demolished.

Claire walked back inside and placed the stems on a towel in the laundry room. As she rummaged around in the cabinet looking for the tall crystal vase, she heard Ivy come in. She hurried to the kitchen.

"How's our sweet girl today?" she asked Ivy, taking a smiling Pauline from her arms. Ella's baby was ten months old and growing every day.

Ivy laughed. "We had ourselves a morning. Baby girl poured her peaches over her head thinking she was the funniest thing ever. Got it all over her mama too, so Ella had to change her clothes while we took Pauline out back and washed her off. She's sassy, this one."

"Are you sassy?" Claire cooed to Pauline, who looked back at her with Ella's wide brown eyes. "I don't believe it, not for a minute."

"She gonna help Granny make a peach pie today."

"Oh, good," Claire said. "Maybe peach pie and ice cream will cheer Gordon up." When Gordon had negotiated a way for them to stay in the house, they'd considered it a win at the time. But the constant racket of construction they lived with made it a hollow victory.

As if on cue, a crack ricocheted through the house indicating that another tree that had stood proud and tall in Talmadge soil for decades had come crashing down. Pauline wailed in protest.

Ivy smiled as she watched Claire carry Pauline into the living room. Funny how Claire and even Mr. Gordon had taken to Pauline the way they had. Things had been so unsettled for so long, she guessed Pauline helped them take their mind off their troubles.

As Ivy started the pie crusts, she thought about how far Mr. Gordon had fallen. Now watching the way he was with Pauline—turned out there was good somewhere in him after all. Not that she'd ever forget what he did to her all those years ago. But having troubles of his own seemed to have softened his heart.

Even Junior had surprised her. At Christmas, he'd looked her in the eye and asked her to give the present he was holding to Ella for the baby. Said he wished them all the best. Ivy knew it was as close to an apology as they'd ever get from Junior. Ivy suspected that the girlfriend he'd run off and married last fall was a good influence, even if she did wear those short skirts and mannish pants.

Ivy jumped as a boom rang through the house. She looked out the window at the construction machinery on the western side of the property. Mr. Gordon had insisted that the developer postpone the demolition of their cabin to give them time to find a new place to live, but so far, their search had been fruitless. They'd spent most of their meager savings to buy Herbert Allen's workshop where he used to recap used tires. Louis was planning to open a repair shop for cars and farm machinery.

As Ivy rolled out the crusts, she thought about Bobby Lee. When her son-in-law was home at Christmas, he carried an edginess about him that hadn't been there before his second deployment. But spending time with Ella and the baby had helped. He barely put Pauline down the whole time he was home, and it had been a tearful goodbye for all of them when he returned to the base to head back to Vietnam with his unit.

"She's going to be walking and talking soon," Claire said as she carried Pauline back to the kitchen and put her in the playpen. "She pulled up on the piano bench and babbled along to the music." Claire gathered some wooden spoons and a small tin bowl and handed them to Pauline.

"I know." Ivy took the pot simmering with peaches and sugar from the stove and poured it into the pie pans. "She's gonna be a talker like Ella. May the Lord give us patience."

"I wonder if our grandbaby will be a talker. David barely said a word until he was three."

Ivy chuckled. "I remember. I think he was just biding his time 'til he figured out what he wanted to say." Ivy put the pies in the oven and set the kitchen timer. "I thought I'd send a pie along with the vegetable soup. Mary Grace always did love peaches, and maybe she'll feel up to eating today."

Since becoming pregnant, Mary Grace had suffered terrible morning sickness yet insisted on going to work every day at the hospital, where she had risen up the ranks to become a nursing supervisor. She could barely keep anything down and was tinier than ever. Claire had been going by their house almost every afternoon with a food basket Ivy specially prepared for them.

"Let's hope so. David is beside himself with worry." Ivy knew they were all thinking about Mary Grace's poor mama and the babies she'd lost. She wasn't sure Miss Claire and Mr. Gordon could stand it if something happened to this baby.

Back at the cabin, Ivy put the supper dishes in the kitchen sink and changed her clothes. Pastor Rice had called her this afternoon at the Talmadges' house—something he'd never done before—to tell her about a house in Hobbsfield's colored section that was coming up for sale. It was owned by the Stafford family, long-time members of Ebenezer Baptist, who were moving to Wilmington next month. Pastor Rice said it was perfect for the Sanders—all on one floor with three bedrooms, enough land for a vegetable garden, and just a short distance from the shop where Louis planned to set up his machinery business.

"I ain't sure I want to see it," Louis said to Ivy. "You know they're asking more than we're wanting to pay. And why are we not meeting Pastor Rice at the Staffords' house?"

"I don't know, but he told me we should come by his house first," Ivy replied. "Come on, Ella, we need to go."

They walked outside and crowded into the cab of Louis's truck, Ella holding Pauline firmly on her lap.

Pastor Rice met them in his driveway as they climbed out of the truck. "Come inside and say hello to the missus, and then we'll ride out to the house. I think you'll like it. It checks off all the boxes."

"Except for the price," Louis mumbled.

They shuffled into Pastor Rice's tidy kitchen. They could hear voices in the next room.

"You got company?" Louis asked.

"In a manner of speaking."

Ivy walked into the den expecting to see one of the church ladies with Pastor Rice's wife. Instead, a thin man sat there, sipping a glass of iced tea. It took her a moment to recognize him.

"Jake," she whispered.

Time seemed to stop in the moments it took her to run across the room and grab him. She collapsed beside him and put her arms around him. "My baby's home!"

"Pastor Rice sure did pull one over on us." Louis laughed as they drove back home. Ivy, with Pauline on her lap, kept turning around to make sure Jake was still there. He and Ella were riding in the back of the truck together just like they used to.

"Can you believe how grown up he is?" Ivy's heart was bursting with joy. "And can you believe he's gonna be a doctor?" Jake told them that after spending an extra year at Villanova working in his professor's lab, he had been awarded a scholarship to Bowman Gray

School of Medicine in Winston-Salem where he would be one of its first black medical students. "We ain't seen that boy in seven years, and now he's gonna be just two hours away from us."

Picking up on the joyful tone in her grandmother's voice, Pauline babbled excitedly in reply. "That's right, Pauline. Uncle Jake is home!"

Jake walked slowly around the cabin. It was smaller than he remembered, but the smells—tobacco and cinnamon and cape jasmine and creek water—were exactly the same. He noticed the photographs of his graduation from high school and Villanova resting on the mantle over the fireplace.

Louis carried Jake's bag to Ella's bedroom. "Son, you're gonna have to fight for a place in that room. Ella and Pauline done taken over every inch of space." Jake peeked in, noticing Ella had put together a makeshift makeup stand beside the crib that was covered in lipsticks and eye shadows.

"I'll sleep on the couch," Jake said. "You sure it's all right for me to stay here until my program starts next month? Pastor Rice said I could stay with them if I needed to."

"I'm sure." Ivy was not letting Jake out of her sight until he left for medical school, and she knew that Mr. Gordon had more pressing matters to deal with than Jake. She sometimes wondered if he even remembered why Jake left in the first place.

Jake looked out the cracked windowpane. "I can't believe they're demolishing the farmland. It's unreal."

Ivy put her arm around Jake. "I'm glad you made it home before our cabin is gone. We only got a couple more months 'til they tear it down." She moved into the kitchen. "Are you hungry? I can heat you up a ham biscuit or some peach pie."

"Peach pie, please. I've missed your pie."

Ivy couldn't remember a night when she'd felt happier. When Ella came back from rocking Pauline to sleep, they stayed up talking for hours, sharing all the little details they hadn't been able to fit in their letters and phone calls.

It was getting late by the time they ran out of stories. Ivy yawned and Louis patted her on the knee. "Guess we'll have to go back tomorrow to look at the Stafford house," he said. "Although I still think it's outta our reach."

"We'll worry about that tomorrow," Ivy said. "And if that one don't work out, another house will come along. The Lord will provide." She stood up. "Jake, let me get you a quilt."

"Wait a minute, Mama. I've got one more thing to tell you." Ivy leaned closer so she could hear him; she'd forgotten how soft-spoken Jake was. "You know how I've been working every chance I got since I've been with the Shallcrosses? I wanted to pay them some rent money for letting me live at their house and be a part of their family for so long."

Ivy and Louis nodded. "Well, I spent the night with them one last time before I left to come home. And Mr. Shallcross told me that he had invested all the money I gave him, every dime of it, and he said my money had grown over the years and he wanted me to have it. He gave me a check for three thousand dollars."

Ivy felt tears coming again. "Glory be. How will we ever repay that family? They've done so much for you already. And now this? You gonna be all set up for your future. Now let's get you settled so you can get some sleep."

Jake laughed softly. "Mama, I still haven't finished. Pastor Rice and I were talking about the Stafford house. With the money Ella has saved, plus my three thousand dollars, you'll have enough for the down payment. You can buy the house."

They all stared at him until Ella let out a scream. "I'm going to write a letter to Bobby Lee right now. I know it's late, but I'm too excited to sleep." She hugged her brother.

"Hang on, Ella." Ivy spoke more sharply than she'd meant to. "There's one thing we've got to do before we do anything else." She grabbed her children's' hands as she bowed her head, and Louis began to lead them in prayer.

———————— x)(x ————————

Ella got to the office a few minutes late. She'd had a hard time getting out of bed after all the excitement of Jake's return. She unlocked the door, turned on the lights, and walked down the hall to the break room to start the coffee. As she settled into her daily routine of answering the phone and helping customers with applications, the idea that Jake was back kept popping into her head like a firecracker in the night sky.

A miracle is what it was. And her parents were going to have their own house. Another miracle. Ella was proud that she had saved enough to contribute to the down payment.

"I'm taking my lunch break now," she said to Sherry. "Can I bring you a sandwich from the drug store?"

"No, I brought my lunch from home today. You're awfully chipper. Did you get a letter from Bobby Lee?"

"No, but I'm expecting one any day." Ella waved the envelope in her hand. "And I'm sending one off to him right now. I've got the most unbelievable news."

As she walked to the post office, Ella wondered what Bobby Lee was doing right this minute. Was he playing cards with Tommy at the barracks? Was he studying her picture? Was he hiking through jungles in shoes that were falling apart? Was he parachuting out of a helicopter? She tried to keep her worry at bay and not let her imagination run wild. This war seemed to have no end in sight, and even while students demonstrated against it, more recruits were sent over every day.

At least she finally had some good news to share with Bobby Lee. She pictured him reading about Jake coming home, the smile on his face when he read that she and her brother were together again and able to help buy her parents a house of their own. As she slid the letter into the outgoing mailbox, she pictured the reunion she and Bobby Lee would have the next time he came home. She had the perfect outfit planned. By that time, she expected that Pauline would be chatting up a storm, having mastered "Dada" and other important words.

The office was busy all afternoon which helped the time pass until Ella turned out the lights and flipped the "Open" sign in the window to "Closed." Driving home, she wondered which of Jake's favorites her mama had made for supper: chicken livers or pork chops. There'd be more peach pie for sure.

Pulling up to the cabin, she noticed a car parked in front. As she got closer, she realized it was the Bennetts' car. They probably came by to see Pauline. As she parked the truck and hopped out, her mama and Mrs. Bennett came out to meet her. Her mama wore an expression Ella couldn't read.

"Ella, it's Bobby Lee," Ivy said. "He was doing some kind of rescue mission and there was an explosion. Baby, he's in real bad shape."

Jake could sense the nerves underneath Ella's nonstop chatter. They were on their way to the Womack Army Community Hospital in Fayetteville. Three weeks ago, surgeons at the Air Force base in the Philippines had performed a complicated operation on Bobby Lee to reposition the leg bones that had pierced through his skin and remove the shrapnel lodged inside the bone. Once stable, he was flown to a San Francisco hospital for a brief stay before making his final journey to North Carolina to start rehabilitation.

Through a series of phone calls, Bobby Lee's parents had finally pieced together what happened. Bobby Lee's platoon had been sent to a battle site to retrieve three infantrymen wounded in an attack by the Viet Cong. While they were ferrying the men back to the helicopter, the Viet Cong began launching mortars at the rescue operation. Five of Bobby Lee's platoon members, including his friend Tommy from Laurinburg, had been killed. Somehow, despite explosions happening all around him, Bobby Lee managed to save all three wounded soldiers before being hit by a final round of mortar and collapsing in the helicopter.

The Army told Bobby Lee's parents that their son had been presented with a Purple Heart, given to soldiers wounded in battle, as well as a Distinguished Service Cross, a medal awarded for valor. They also said that Bobby Lee's injuries were too severe for him to return to military service. His Army career was over.

When Jake and Ella reached the hospital in Fayetteville, a nurse escorted them down the long hallway to Bobby Lee's room. Ella's high-heeled shoes clicked against the linoleum floor. The nurse stopped at one of the doorways. "This is your husband's room."

Ella opened the door and saw Bobby Lee lying in the bed by the window, a curtain half drawn around his bed. His face had not changed, but his legs were covered with thick casts and raised above the bedsheets by pulleys. Bobby Lee lifted his head off the pillow and smiled weakly. Ella's eyes filled with tears as she leaned down to kiss him. He reached up and pulled her towards him in a long embrace. Jake sat down in a chair by the door just out of sight.

Ella settled in next to Bobby Lee, and they held hands for a long while without saying anything. Ella tried to gauge her husband's mood, but his eyes looked vacant. Ella finally broke the silence, asking him if he was in a lot of pain.

"It comes and goes." Bobby Lee's expression hardened. "Did you hear what happened?"

She stroked his hand. "Yes. The Army's been keeping your parents informed. They told us how you saved three men practically by yourself. They said you're a hero."

"Hero. What a load of shit."

Ella realized she'd never heard Bobby Lee swear before. "No, Bobby Lee, they said it was an act of bravery and selflessness. That's why they gave you those awards."

"Who cares about awards?" Bobby Lee was practically yelling. "My men were counting on me. *Tommy* was counting on me. And now they're all dead." He shook his head. "And the Army thinks I'm damaged goods. I'll never get back over there and get revenge on those gooks for what they did to my men. My *friends.*"

A heavy silence hung over the room. Jake wondered if he should intervene. He wasn't sure Ella was equipped to deal with this.

Ella pulled Bobby Lee's face toward hers. "Look at me, mister. If not for the grace of God, you'd be lying right there in the grave beside them." Bobby Lee turned away but Ella wasn't finished. "And since God had the grace to let you live, you need to start focusing on getting better so you can come home to Pauline and me."

"Don't really have a choice, do I?"

Ella held Bobby Lee's hand for a long while until he dozed off, sleepy from the pain medication. When the nurse came back and announced visiting hours were over, Ella stood up and motioned for Jake to come in. She gently woke Bobby Lee. "I have to go now, baby. But before I leave, there's someone here who wants to say hello to you."

"Hey, buddy," Jake said softly. "Long time, no see."

Bobby Lee was groggy. "Jake Sanders? Is that you? I thought for a minute Ella'd gone and replaced me."

"It's me. Back from the dead."

"Guess that makes two of us."

———— x❳C x ————

Ella pushed Pauline's stroller into the ladies' room and touched up her makeup. She had taken extra care with her outfit, choosing a bright yellow dress with a wide collar and matching belt to go along with her new strappy heels. Bobby Lee had been at the rehabilitation hospital for eight weeks, and she liked to look her best for her weekly Sunday visit.

When the doctors removed Bobby Lee's casts, his legs had atrophied so much that they looked like they belonged on a different body. Angry scars ran from his thighs to his ankles. It took effort for him to wiggle his toes, and the doctor prescribed twice-daily sessions with physical therapists so he could learn to walk again.

Ella had offered to move to Fort Bragg to be closer to him, but Bobby Lee insisted she stay in Hobbsfield because it was best for Pauline, and they needed her income. Ella suspected the real reason was that he hated for her to watch him struggle. At first, he could barely stand up on his own. He was impatient with his slow progress and lashed out at everyone around him. But gradually he gained more strength, and now he could move around fairly well using his walker. His state of mind was slower to improve.

It was an especially hard day when Tommy Walker's family drove from Laurinburg to visit. Bobby Lee struggled with his emotions as he recounted the rescue operation and apologized for not saving their son. Mr. and Mrs. Walker insisted that Tommy wouldn't want Bobby Lee to blame himself and that they were praying for his full recovery. It had been a moment of healing, and they had ended the day fondly recalling Ella's graduation dinner and how Bobby Lee foiled his own plan to introduce Ella to Tommy.

Ella knocked on the door lightly and pushed the stroller into the room. Bobby Lee was sitting up in bed. He smiled as Pauline called out "Dada."

"I could hear you ladies coming all the way up the hall," he said, tilting his head to receive Ella's kiss.

"Lucky for me, Pauline napped in the truck most of the way here. But she's good and awake now. Where's Amos?" She motioned to the empty bed.

"He got discharged." Bobby Lee's roommate had suffered injuries so severe that the doctors had amputated his left leg. "His family took him home this morning."

"That's good, right?"

"I guess. He still has pains all during the night where his leg used to be. They say that's what happens when you lose a limb."

"Thank God that didn't happen to you."

"I know. Never thought I'd say it, but I'm lucky my injuries weren't worse."

"How were your therapy sessions this week?"

"Pretty good. An Army staffer came by on Friday to talk about my discharge benefits." Bobby Lee explained that his rank of master sergeant, combined with the injuries he sustained, entitled him to a hefty pension. "Maybe I'll use the GI bill to take a class at the community college."

"Baby, that's wonderful news." Ella smiled as she bounced Pauline on her lap. "So when are they letting you out of here?"

"In three weeks, if all goes according to plan."

"I can't wait." Ella hadn't felt this optimistic in a while. It was the first time Bobby Lee had talked about his future with any kind of positivity.

Pauline whined, struggling to get down from Ella's lap. "I swear, she won't keep still a minute."

"Let's take her down the hall," Bobby Lee said. The last time Ella had brought Pauline they took her to one of the empty therapy rooms with mats on the floor so that Pauline could move about and play freely.

"Good idea." Ella put Pauline in the stroller and placed Bobby Lee's walker beside the bed.

"Nope. Don't need that anymore." Bobby Lee swung his legs down onto the floor, pushed the walker aside, and reached for a cane that was leaning against the wall. He stood up, inched the cane forward, and slowly walked toward the door.

Ella let out a scream of delight. "Baby girl, look at your daddy. He's walking."

"Can't go very fast," Bobby Lee acknowledged. "And my balance is still shaky."

"Sounds like me in these heels," Ella laughed. She squeezed his hand. "We'll take it one step at a time."

THIRTY-TWO

December 1966

Mary Grace switched the radio to another station. David laughed. "I don't think you're going to find one that's not playing Christmas music."

Exasperated, Mary Grace turned it off. "I guess you're right. But they play it all day long at work, and I'm sick of hearing the same songs over and over."

He kissed her hand. "Where's your holiday spirit?"

She patted her stomach. "I think the baby sucked it all out of me."

"Well, maybe you'll find some holiday spirit in Old Salem. I can't wait to show you around."

They were on their way to spend the night in Winston-Salem and visit Old Salem, which David described as a historic Moravian village. He had planned the trip as something fun for them to do before the baby came. Mary Grace hoped she'd be able to enjoy it.

She was ashamed to admit it, but she was having trouble getting excited about the baby. Her pregnancy had been difficult. She'd never been so sick in her life as she was in the first few months when soup and crackers were all she could keep down. Strong odors sent her running to the bathroom. David had to give up coffee because she couldn't stand the smell of it.

Finally, when she was about six months along, she began to feel better. But now she was just plain uncomfortable. And huge. My goodness, she didn't know a person her size could grow so large. She'd had a front-row seat to Ella's pregnancy, and Ella had never looked this big. Then again, Ella was a good eight inches taller than she was.

She'd also had a front-row seat to Ella's baby. And it wasn't that she didn't like Pauline; she just couldn't understand all the fuss. Everybody cooing in Pauline's face when she was clearly too young to respond in any meaningful way. Bragging about Pauline talking when all she was doing was making nonsense sounds. Even Mr. and Mrs. Talmadge lost their minds when they were around Pauline, grinning over her like she'd done something incredible when all she was doing was sleeping. *Sleeping.*

And all day long, the questions and comments never ended. "When are you due?" "Have you picked out a name?" "You got twins in there?" And Mary Grace's personal favorite: "Look at the size of the bun in that oven." And the *touching.* Patients and co-workers alike felt entitled to pat her like she was some kind of pet. It was horrible.

Mary Grace knew she should feel grateful to be bringing a new life into the world. Goodness knows David was so excited he could hardly stand it. But all she was really looking forward to was going back to work once she got the damn thing out.

Ivy dried the breakfast dishes and packed them away in the last remaining box in the cabin while Ella and Louis carried the dresser from the bedroom out to the truck. Pauline toddled from one room to the next, confused as to where the furniture had gone. "Pauly chair?"

"Pauline, your highchair is going to our *new* house, along with your toys and your crib, and all the rest of your stuff," Ivy explained.

Pauline tilted her head. "Pauly chair?"

Bobby Lee laughed. "I guess she ain't going to understand until we get to the new house." He leaned on his cane.

Ivy knew it was hard for Bobby Lee, having to watch Ella help Louis move the furniture while he minded the baby. But he'd come a long way toward accepting his life outside the Army. His original plan was to take a class at the community college until he puttered around Louis's new repair shop and discovered he had both a knack and a love for fixing things.

Ivy knew they had the Lord to thank for all of it. For sparing Bobby Lee's life on the battlefield. For healing his legs enough so he still felt like a man. For helping Louis's repair shop become a success. Her husband was busier than he could say grace over helping people fix their vehicles and farm equipment. Seems he had learned a thing or two working on all those fancy cars Mr. Gordon brought in over the years.

Ella picked up Pauline and swung her around. She turned to Bobby Lee. "You ready?"

"I'm ready." He made his way onto the porch.

"I'm gonna check one more time to make sure everything's tied down good," Louis said.

Ivy watched as her daughter's family piled into Bobby Lee's truck and pulled slowly down the driveway, mattresses and furniture bouncing in the back. As she turned around and walked through the empty rooms of the cabin, she could feel the memories of their life buried in these walls.

She pictured her older son Paul crawling around in the front room, stacking blocks that Louis had made from scrap wood. Jake sitting at the table, poring over that old, tattered biology book he loved so much. Ella standing in front of the fireplace, singing for them and curtsying while they clapped. All three kids wading in the stream and chasing each other through the meadow. The five of them sitting on the porch, shelling peas, laughing.

Then she pictured Paul lying unconscious on the floor of the tobacco barn, his body twisted at an odd angle. Jake hidden away in Herbert Allen's truck like a criminal. Ella putting a screwdriver in her pocket every time she walked to the Big House.

She pictured Louis toiling in the fields in the scorching summer heat, scrubbing the tar off his fingers and struggling to get out of bed each morning. All the while knowing that not one ounce of the soil he tilled nor the harvest he produced would ever belong to him. Louis had endured the indignities of a lifetime of sharecropping with grace and humility, but Ivy was thankful he'd never spend another day in a tobacco field as long as he lived.

Finally, Ivy pictured the face of Gordon Talmadge, both the teenage bully he'd been all those years ago and the weak man he'd become.

Louis walked back in. "You ready? We might have to set that last box on the seat in between us. The back of the truck is plumb full." He noticed Ivy's tears. "Hey there now, what is it?" He put his arms around her.

She returned his embrace and wiped the tears away. "It's nothing." She smiled at him and kissed his cheek. "Let's go. This ain't our home anymore."

Claire poured herself a cup of coffee and watched her scrambled eggs go cold while she waited for the toast to brown. Oh well, she thought, there were worse things than cold eggs. Eventually, the toaster spit out the bread, and she carried her plate over to the kitchen table, getting back up once to get the jam and a second time for a knife. Soon enough, Gordon would wake up, and she'd have to start this whole process over. He was sleeping later and later these days. Not much motivated him to get up at a reasonable hour anymore.

Claire spread jam on her toast and took a few bites of breakfast. She got up for a third time. She suddenly didn't feel like sitting for a minute longer. Without the familiar presence of Ivy bustling about, the kitchen seemed bigger somehow, colder. Claire had tried to get Ivy to reconsider, to stay on working for them at least three days a week. In her mind, it was a perfect setup. She could bring Pauline with her along with David and Mary Grace's baby once it arrived. But Ivy remained firm. Her days of working at the Big House were over.

Claire wasn't sure which was worse—losing Ivy or her daughter-in-law asking Ivy to take care of her new baby once she went back to work. After all, *Claire* was the child's grandmother, for goodness sake. Why not ask her? But Mary Grace insisted it would be easier to leave the baby with Ivy, who kept Pauline while Ella worked.

Maybe it was just as well, with Gordon's health being what it was. He'd never gotten his strength back after that second bout of pneumonia. And he was so thin. Bill Barfield had offered to set him up with a specialist after the holidays, but she knew they were all wondering if the demise of Gordon's reputation was at the root of his health problems.

She wondered for the hundredth time if staying in the house had been the right decision. Maybe they should have "retired" to Raleigh. After all, they had friends there. They could have bought a modest house, and Gordon could have dabbled in charity work and played golf with Bill. But Gordon refused. Come hell or high water, he was not leaving Talmadge Farm.

So they continued to live in Hobbsfield, where it seemed like half of their friends now avoided them. Claire knew Gordon had been especially wounded when his friend Neil Starling had put together a dove hunt at his estate over Labor Day and neglected to invite him.

Claire walked aimlessly around the house, sipping her coffee. Maybe Christmas would brighten Gordon's spirits. She idly touched the tiny tree sitting atop the table in the foyer that David had set up for them. She thought of the giant fir trees that used to adorn the foyer and the living room. Every inch of the house covered in greenery. Ivy humming Christmas carols while she baked pies in the kitchen.

Now their background music was the sound of construction as the farm gave way to the steel and concrete structures going up around them for the business park, which would bring a string of cars along the road and new customers to pump up the Hobbsfield economy. All that was good, Claire thought, but what about the farmland, the forest, the pastures, the long-distance sound of the train winding past the Neuse River? The *Times* predicted that in a year or two, the population would exceed fourteen thousand people, many of whom would have no recollection of the old Hobbsfield, "the town that tobacco built."

"Morning sweetheart," Gordon said. Claire looked up, grateful to see him coming down the stairs in his bathrobe. She was tired of being alone.

"Morning. How about a cup of coffee?"

"That sounds nice. And would you bring me a cigarette so I don't have to look at that damn warning label on the pack? It really gets my goat, the feds scaring people who are just trying to enjoy a smoke." He moved into the living room and sat down on the sofa.

Claire brought him his coffee and a cigarette and sat down beside him. "I hope Mary Grace and David will have a nice time in Winston-Salem. The Brookstown Inn is charming, especially this time of year."

"I hope so too. Lord knows, those two need a getaway. They've had an awful year, what with Mary Grace's pregnancy making her so sick. And then there's David teaching at that goddamn school."

"Now Gordon, don't get worked up. You know David views it as a privilege to teach at Jefferson County's first integrated high school."

"I know he does," Gordon grumbled. "I wonder if we have Wake Forest to thank for that, filling his head with all that progressive shit."

Claire deftly changed the subject. She couldn't have this conversation again. "I wonder if the baby will be a boy or a girl."

"I personally am hoping it's a girl so the first Talmadge grandchild will have a normal name."

Mary Grace had given sole naming rights to David, who had decided to name the baby after his favorite literary characters. The baby would be "Charlotte" if a girl, and "Huck"—short for "Huckleberry"—if a boy.

"I keep thinking Mary Grace will intervene with a better name for a boy," Claire said. She was secretly worried about Mary Grace's lack of interest in the baby. The girl didn't seem to have any opinion about the name, or the color of the nursery, or preparing the layette, or any of the normal things a first-time mother should care about.

"Mary Grace has always been hard to predict." Gordon took his last sip of coffee. They looked up as the sound of hammers penetrated the silence. "So Louis and Ivy are leaving today, huh? I can't believe they want to walk away from all this tranquility." He chuckled as the pounding continued.

"Yes, I saw their truck pull out a little while ago. They want to get settled in the new house in time for Christmas. I keep expecting Ivy to walk through that kitchen door any second."

"I have to admit, I'm proud of Louis for setting up his own business," Gordon said. "I've been telling my friends—the ones who still talk to me—that they should take their cars to his garage."

"That's nice," Claire noted. "Ivy said she would try to help me find someone to take her place. But she hasn't given me any names yet. Maybe she'll get around to it after the holidays."

"Too bad you couldn't convince her to stay on. We'll never find anyone who's as good a cook as she is. I sure am going to miss her chicken and dumplings. And her cornbread. And her apple pie."

"I know she's a good cook, Gordon, but she's more than that. She's like family to me."

Gordon looked at her sharply. "What a strange thing to say, Claire. Are your hormones getting the better of you today?" Claire cut her eyes over at him but he softened the blow with his signature wink.

She shook her head and reached for his hand. "You never change, do you, Gordon?"

He smiled. "Never have. Never will." He glanced out the window. "All that racket outside is making my head hurt. How about you play something for us on the piano until it's time for *As the World Turns*."

David took Mary Grace's hand as they walked down the staircase to the hotel restaurant. This trip had been a good idea, after all. He'd had his doubts, not sure if Mary Grace would like Old Salem or if she would think the whole idea of people dressed in period costume pretending to be from the eighteenth century was silly. But the charm of it seemed to rub off on her.

He was pleased that she was wearing the dress his mother had bought her. The pregnancy—once she finally got over those first few months—had brought out a fullness in her face and a brightness to her eyes that he found beautiful. Of course, he knew better than to tell her this.

As he might have predicted, Mary Grace had handled pregnancy differently than anyone he'd ever heard of. His calm, stoic wife, normally unfazed by any challenge, had been undone by the tiny life growing inside of her. Her litany of complaints over the past eight months was as varied as it was extensive.

Ivy and his mother were concerned. But he suspected that Mary Grace's impatience was less about physical discomfort and more about hiding the fact that she was terrified something might go wrong.

They walked across the wood-planked floor of the inn's lobby to the entrance of the restaurant. "David Talmadge, party of two," David said to the host. A waiter led them to a table in the corner by the window where they could see Christmas lights twinkling across the street.

"This has been a really nice day." Mary Grace opened the menu. "Thank you for bringing me here. I know I haven't exactly been a joy to live with lately."

"I'm not sure what you're talking about." David's eyes were dancing. "You've been spreading cheer to all who know you."

"Shut up." She smacked his hand with her menu and then went back to studying it. "I don't know what to get." She touched her stomach. "This baby is pressing down so hard that my stomach no longer knows what it wants. In fact, I think I need to visit the ladies' room. Another of the many joys of being pregnant: going to the bathroom thirty-eight times a day." She stood up.

"And there she goes, spreading more cheer." David watched his wife make her way gingerly toward the lobby, probably glaring at the people smiling at her large belly. Yes, this had been a good idea. He couldn't wait for her to see that he'd smuggled the chess board into his suitcase as a surprise. He knew nothing would make her happier than spending the evening in their room doggedly trying to capture each other's king. She'd gotten remarkably good, relying on nothing but her own instincts. He'd been studying a new book of strategy just to stay one step ahead of her.

"Mr. Talmadge?" The waiter said, tapping him on the shoulder. "It's your wife. She says the baby's coming. She told us to bring your car around to the front."

"The baby's coming?" David jumped up so fast that the glasses on the table fell over. He tried to right them but knocked the silverware off in the process. He began to reach down to pick it up.

"Go on, sir. We'll take care of that." The waiter gently pushed him in the direction of the lobby.

Everything became a blur as they climbed into the car. David drove the five miles to the hospital in a panic, desperate for someone other than himself to be in charge of the situation. He knew he could get there faster if Mary Grace would just stop talking. But she kept going on about how her water had broken, and how that meant the baby was on its way, and maybe that was a contraction she'd been having earlier.

"CAN YOU BE QUIET SO I DON'T CRASH THE DAMN CAR?" David shouted. Mary Grace looked at him in alarm. David was mortified. Not only could he not get them to the hospital fast enough but he had yelled at his wife when she was about to have a baby.

Before he could start his apology, Mary Grace took his hand. "David, take a deep breath. It's going to be okay."

Now David was pacing up and down the hall of the waiting area. Hours had passed since they'd taken Mary Grace to the birthing area. The nurse came out every so often to tell him everything was fine, that the baby was taking its own sweet time. He sat down in a chair, remembering that he hadn't eaten any dinner. He thought about the chess board back in the hotel room. Guess the baby had other ideas for tonight's activity.

David felt a tap on his shoulder. He jumped, thinking for a minute it was the waiter again. He must have dozed off. He looked up at the nurse, who was waiting patiently for him to become coherent, and tried to shake off the cobwebs in his brain.

"Congratulations," she smiled. "You're a father."

He took off his glasses. "Really? Is Mary Grace okay?"

"Mama and baby are both doing fine. Mary Grace is still a little loopy. We gave her some laughing gas for the pain towards the end."

"Can I see her? I mean them. Can I see them?"

"Yes. She's been asking for you."

David felt a pang of love so strong for his wife that his knees almost buckled. He opened the door to her hospital room cautiously. He'd somehow expected her to look beaten down and exhausted, but she looked radiant. "Hey there," she said. "Get over here and meet your son."

A son. For the second time in as many minutes, David felt his knees start to buckle. He put a steadying hand on the end of the bed and moved closer. There, lying in her arms, was the tiniest human he'd ever seen.

"David, look at him. Isn't he beautiful? He's a few weeks early, so he's smaller than normal. Otherwise, he's perfect. The doctor checked him out from head to toe. Look at his tiny little fingers. Do you want to hold him?"

David felt the panic that had gripped him earlier return. He took a deep breath and sat down on the edge of the bed. "I think he looks really safe right where he is." He watched as his son scrunched up his face as if to cry and then relaxed again, settling back into the warmth of his mother's arms.

"Hello there, little Huck." David touched the baby's finger and then his cheek.

"It's Billy."

"Billy?"

"Yes. His name is Billy."

David wiped his glasses. "But I thought you said . . ."

"I know what I said," she told him. "But when they handed him to me, I took one look at him, and . . . and . . . I don't know how to put it into words. I felt some sort of flash, like lightning. Ivy would probably say it was a message from God. Anyway, at that moment, I realized it was worth it. The whole horrible pregnancy. The nausea. The weight gain. The *touching*. It was all worth it." She looked down. "And at that moment, I realized he was 'William Gordon Talmadge.'" She tucked the baby in close. "William for my father. Gordon for your father. We'll call him Billy for short."

David wasn't sure whether Mary Grace had experienced a profound vision or was just high from the drugs, but it didn't really matter. He kissed her tenderly. "William Gordon it is." He moved in to get a closer look at Billy. "I think I'm ready now." He held out his arms to take his son.

THIRTY-THREE

December 1966

The next morning, Gordon tried to keep up with Claire as she hurried into the hospital. He knew he couldn't ask her to slow down. She'd been exasperated with him all morning. David had called before the sun was up with the news that the baby had arrived while he and Mary Grace were on their trip. Gordon had taken the call but hadn't been alert enough to ask if it was a boy or a girl. Claire had spent the two-hour drive to Winston-Salem alternating wildly between excitement that the baby was here and frustration that they didn't know if it was Charlotte or Huck.

Gordon stopped for a minute to catch his breath and then trotted along behind her towards the hospital lobby. He'd obviously been staying indoors too much; he was out of shape, and this cold air was making him cough. When he made it inside, Claire was already at the front desk asking for Mary Grace Talmadge's room number.

Gordon leaned on the desk, breathing hard. Feeling a coughing fit coming on, he reached for his handkerchief. The woman working the desk winced as his coughing turned violent. Claire looked at him in alarm.

"Gordon?"

He looked down at his handkerchief and realized there was blood on it. He looked at her helplessly and then collapsed on the cold linoleum floor.

When Gordon woke up, he was in a hospital bed. Confused, he looked around. He thought he smelled Claire's perfume. His head was aching. He reached up and felt a bandage on his forehead. He started to get out of bed and realized he was wearing a hospital gown.

A doctor pulled back the curtain and walked in. "I see you're awake, Mr. Talmadge. I'm Dr. Janis."

"What happened? Where's my wife?"

"You're in the emergency room. You fell in the lobby and hit your head, requiring four stitches. Your wife was with you earlier, but she went to the maternity ward a little while ago to visit your daughter-in-law. Congratulations on the new grandbaby."

Now he remembered. They were in Winston-Salem at the hospital to see Mary Grace. "Thank you. If you'll send someone to help me get dressed, I'd like to meet the little bugger myself."

"Hold your horses. Your wife said that before you fell you were coughing up blood."

Gordon nodded. "That's happened once or twice lately. Figured I might be coming down with pneumonia again."

"We'd like to get a chest X-ray and run some tests. We'll keep you overnight while we sort it out."

For the next several hours, Gordon was poked and prodded and X-rayed by so many different people he couldn't keep up with it all. Claire and David came and went, at some point telling him he had a grandson named Billy. It had a nice ring to it. He wondered what happened to Huck.

Later that afternoon, they finally moved him to a room on the fifth floor. He could see the exhaustion on Claire's face and knew it mirrored his own. They'd been up since six. "Sweetie, why don't you go on back to the hotel with David? He said he got you a room for the night. That way, you can get a good night's sleep, and he can bring you back tomorrow. I'm in capable hands here."

Claire leaned in to kiss him on the cheek. "I'll be back first thing in the morning." As she was walking towards the door, she stopped and turned around. "I love you, Gordon."

"I love you too, Claire."

Mary Grace knocked softly on the door and pushed it open. Gordon was propped up in bed, looking weary. "How are you feeling, Grandpa? I've got someone here who wants to meet you."

He looked over. "Mary Grace." He smiled at her fondly. "Don't tell me they've handed you your discharge papers already?"

"No. I just convinced them to let me take Billy on a little walk. It's easier to bend the rules when you're a nurse."

Mr. Talmadge let out a small laugh. "Lucky for you. I get in trouble every time I try to bend the rules."

"I'm sorry you had a fall. That's quite a bruise you have there. How are you feeling?"

"Never better." He tried to smile but it looked more like a grimace.

She walked over and sat on the edge of the bed so he could see the baby.

"Well, would you look at that? In all my life, I've never seen a baby so tiny." He reached down to stroke Billy's head. "He's perfect. Absolutely perfect. But then again, we always knew he would be."

"I guess you heard we came up with a new name?"

Gordon nodded. "Billy Talmadge. It's got a nice ring to it."

"It's Billy for short. William Gordon Talmadge is his full name."

Gordon started to speak but his voice caught in his throat. "You . . . named him after me?"

"Yes. And after my father. Huck is a ridiculous name for a child."

Gordon laughed. "That's what I thought all along." He reached down and took the baby's tiny hand. "William Gordon Talmadge, I'm pleased to make your acquaintance. Although God help you, being named after two stubborn old coots like me and Will Craddock."

The next morning, Gordon was feeling better. He had slept well, at least until a gaggle of doctors in training had come by to practice taking his vital signs like he was some sort of guinea pig. Damn, but he was ready to get out of this room.

Claire paced the floor while they waited for the doctor to come in. Gordon knew how impatient she was to get back to little Billy. "Claire, why don't you go on ahead? I'll wait for the doctor. Hopefully, he'll let me out of here, and then I'll come find you on the maternity floor."

She smiled at him gratefully. "I'll tell Mary Grace and David you'll be there soon."

Gordon had just dozed off again when there was a knock on the door. A heavyset man with graying hair walked into the room and shook Gordon's hand. "Hello, Mr. Talmadge. I'm John Peak. I'm a pulmonologist. A lung specialist."

"I'm familiar with the term. And call me Gordon. I hope you're here to tell me I can go home. I'm guessing this is pneumonia, which I've had before. Plus I've got a brand new grandson I'm dying to see. His name is Gordon too."

"Congratulations." Dr. Peak sat down in the chair by the bed. "Gordon, do you have family with you? Would you like them to be here while I go over your test results?"

"I think I'm capable of hearing them by myself."

"Gordon, I won't mince words. You have advanced lung cancer."

"Come again?"

"You have lung cancer." He pulled an X-ray image from his folder and held it up to the light. "As you can see here, you have a series of tumors on both lungs, indicating it's very advanced . . ."

The audacity of this fellow, thought Gordon. *Cancer?* Sure, he'd been feeling a little puny lately, hadn't had much energy, but that was mostly due to all the stress he'd been under. He put up his hand. "I think I'll just stop you right there."

"I know this may come as a shock. But as I was saying . . ."

Gordon raised his voice. "I believe I said I'm not interested in what else you have to say."

Dr. Peak paused. "All right. I'll give you some time to absorb all of this. How about if I come back this afternoon? Maybe your wife can join us?"

Gordon leaned over until he was right in the doctor's face. "I want you to get the hell out of this room and don't ever come back."

Dr. Peak stood up and moved towards the door. He tried one more time. "If you like, I can send a chaplain by ..."

"GET OUT."

Dr. Peak hurried out the door as Gordon picked up his coffee cup and threw it as hard as he could, realizing too late that it was made of Styrofoam. He watched as it landed without a sound, its contents forming a puddle on the floor.

At lunchtime, Claire showed up with David in tow. They were both elated by Billy's newest accomplishment: a burp. David told his father how he had changed his first diaper and Claire described how Mary Grace kept correcting the nurses on the proper way to do things.

"I swear, Gordon, I don't know who's more impatient to get out of here, you or Mary Grace. Did the doctor ever make it by? Are they releasing you this afternoon?"

Gordon hesitated. "Yeah, he came by. Wants me to stay another day or so while they run more tests."

"Well, what did he say? What are they testing you for? Is it something serious?"

Gordon hesitated again. No sense spoiling their excitement. "Nah, he didn't act like it was anything serious. In fact, I don't even think the idiot knew what he was talking about."

"Okay. We're going to get a bite to eat in the cafeteria. Want us to bring you something?"

"Don't worry about me. You all eat and then go see what Billy's doing. I'm sure he's showing up all the other babies in the nursery. And tell Mary Grace I'd love to see him again if she can sneak him back down here after visitors' hours."

Claire kissed him on the cheek. "I'll check on you later."

Gordon tried for a while to work on a crossword puzzle David had given him, but he couldn't get his mind to focus. Was it really true he had cancer?

He was relieved to find *As the World Turns* on the hospital television, but he had trouble concentrating. He thought about those tumors the doctor had pointed out. How hard it was for him to take a deep breath. What if the doctor was right?

He dozed off again until something startled him awake. He opened his eyes, but it had gotten dark outside. When he switched on the lamp he discovered a Negro standing by the door.

He sat up with a start. "Listen, boy. If you mean to rob me, I'll blow your head off."

The fellow watched him, saying nothing.

As Gordon's eyes adjusted, he realized the "boy" was actually a man wearing a hospital badge. "Oh, I'm sorry. I didn't realize you were part of the custodial crew." He gave a small laugh, trying to put the man at ease. "Clumsy me, I spilled my coffee."

The man continued to study him. Finally, he spoke, so softly Gordon could barely hear him. "No, sir, I'm not part of the custodial crew. I'm a medical student. Do you not remember me? I was in here this morning taking your blood pressure."

Gordon thought back to the group of students learning to take vital signs. Come to think of it, one of them *had* been Negro. Funny he hadn't taken more notice of that. What was the world coming to? Who in their right mind would see a Negro doctor?

"I remember now. Did you come to take my blood pressure again? For extra practice?" Gordon didn't like the way this fellow was looking at him.

"No, sir. I came to see if you remembered me."

"Well, we've already covered that. So you can be on your way."

The man stepped closer. "No, sir. I came to see if you remembered me."

Gordon reached for the button to call the nurse. Badge or no badge, this son-of-a-bitch was a lunatic.

The man covered his hand so he couldn't push the button. "What the hell?" Gordon said, pulling his hand away.

"I came to see if you remembered me from Talmadge Farm."

For the first time, Gordon studied the man's face and saw Louis Sanders' eyes looking back at him.

"Jake Sanders?"

Jake had pictured this moment for years. He thought of the things he wanted to say to Mr. Talmadge. That he was a bully. That he was a bigot. Before Philadelphia, Jake had grown up thinking all white men were like Mr. Talmadge, brandishing power in any direction they chose, never mind who got hurt in the process. Thank goodness he'd met Mr. Shallcross, who taught him that skin color had nothing to do with character, that the measure of a man was how he treated others.

Jake remembered leaving the farm in the dead of night tucked in the back of Mr. Allen's truck, terrified that Mr. Talmadge and the sheriff would hunt him down. In Jake's mind, Mr. Talmadge had always been big and strong and threatening, someone to be feared.

But this man in bed covered up with a sheet looked old and tired and frail. And afraid.

Jake stepped back. "Don't worry, I'm not going to hurt you. You're too pathetic for that."

"Why you son-of-a-bitch. I ought to . . . ."

"Ought to what?" Jake countered. "Shoot me? Call the law on me? I'm a grown man, Mr. Talmadge. I'm pretty sure the Hobbsfield sheriff's office won't be too worried about me coming back to North Carolina. If they'd even take your call. I understand you're not the big man in town you once were."

Gordon scowled at him. "You beat the daylights out of my boy and left him for dead. Pretty much ruined his football career."

Jake waited a beat. "I wish I could say that's what really happened. But it was actually my little sister who beat up Junior."

"What are you talking about?"

"That day at the smokehouse? I went to find Ella, and Junior was on top of her, pulling her dress up."

Gordon shrugged his shoulders. "She probably lured him in there. She always was too pretty for her own good."

Jake shook his head, furious. "She was screaming for him to stop. I knocked him off her and he came after me. She picked up a piece of firewood and clobbered him over the head."

"So how come you're the one who ran away?"

"Because we knew Junior would never admit to getting beaten up by a girl. And as bad as it would have been if I'd gotten in trouble for it, it would have been worse for Ella. So I left. I gave up my life. My family. *Everything.*"

Gordon considered this. "Well, you seem to have landed in a pretty good spot for someone like you."

"Someone like me?" Jake's voice was full of contempt. "You don't know anything about me."

As Jake turned to leave, Gordon began to cough uncontrollably. Jake watched as the old man struggled to reach for a handkerchief on the bedside table that lay just beyond his grasp. Jake hesitated but then handed it to him. Mr. Talmadge's coughs eventually subsided into wheezes until he lay spent from the exertion. Jake noticed there were drops of blood on the handkerchief.

"What kind of doctor you planning to be anyway?" Mr. Talmadge asked, still breathing hard.

"An oncologist. I spent some time after college studying tumor cells."

"What a coincidence. They tell me I've got cancer."

Jake gave him a hard look. "What kind?"

"Lung cancer. Apparently, it's pretty advanced. You got any special treatment up your sleeve for that?"

"I'm no expert, but I don't think there are many treatments for lung cancer once it's past a certain stage. I'd say stop smoking cigarettes, but it may be too late to change anything."

Gordon nodded. "So this may be it for me, huh?"

"Possibly. But you need to ask your actual doctor these questions."

Mr. Talmadge gave a small chuckle. "I'm not sure he's coming back. I may have scared him off."

They were interrupted when an aide came in and dropped off a tray.

Mr. Talmadge sat up straighter in the bed, his voice stronger. "Well, Jake, this has been a hell of a day." He extended his hand. "Think we can let bygones be bygones?"

"Don't hold your breath." Jake left the room without looking back.

THIRTY-FOUR

May 1967

Damn shame not to be able to breathe. Gordon felt the pinch of a needle.

"There, that should make him more comfortable." He recognized Mary Grace's voice. "I'm sorry he had a bad night."

Gordon tried to tell Mary Grace to stop pinching him, that it wasn't funny, but he couldn't get the words out. Was that Red Kincaid over there in the corner behind the chaise lounge? He should tell Claire he'd finally found that scumbag. But where was she?

"Hey sweetheart, come on now, one breath at a time, nice and slow, you can do it." There she was. Good. His wife was the most beautiful woman in the world. But she looked worried. And she'd gotten far too thin. He should tell her to eat more. But she was too far away to hear him. If she'd come back, he'd tell her. Better yet, he should tell Ivy to make a buttermilk pie, Claire's favorite. But where was Ivy?

"Boys, let's move him outside onto the porch. It might be easier for him to breathe in the fresh air." There was Claire, his beautiful wife. What was it he wanted to tell her?

He felt his head bob as the boys lifted him from his bed and carried him down the stairs and out to the porch like a rag doll. They put him in a rocking chair, and he felt Claire wrap a blanket around his shoulders. Who were these boys? Wait, he knew them. They used to live in this house. What were their names again?

Gordon felt Claire holding his hand and could sense Buster at his feet. He tried to enjoy the warmth of the sun, except it hurt to take a breath. Hurt a lot. Damn shame not to be able to breathe.

"David? Mary Grace? I think he's stopped breathing. MARY GRACE." Gordon could hear Claire yelling urgently and noticed a flurry of faces but couldn't keep them in focus.

As Gordon took his last breath, he noticed the tobacco was ripe for the picking. Ah yes, it must be time for the dove hunt. He turned toward the bright sunlight and looked out at the acres of fields and forests below. Talmadge Farm. What a magnificent place his grandfather had built here. Gordon vowed not to ever let anything happen to it. There was his grandfather now. And his younger brother, Garner. How wonderful that they came to the hunt. This would be his best one yet.

Gordon led them to the prime position by the oak tree in the southeast corner of the cornfield. He looked up to see a lone dove flying high above. He picked up his Winchester, aimed three feet in front, and got off the perfect shot. He turned to his brother with a satisfied smile. "Bird down."

THIRTY-FIVE

May 1967

Claire stood in the shade outside Hobbsfield United Methodist Church until everyone settled into their seats. When the funeral director gave the signal, she slowly walked down the aisle with Junior and David on either side of her. She noticed how full the church was. Wouldn't Gordon be pleased that so many had come to pay their respects, she thought. She saw Louis and Ivy with Ella. She saw Rose and Charlie Wallace, and Bill and Patsy Barfield. She noticed Diana, Gordon's secretary, with some of the bank employees. She caught a glimpse of Gordon's golf buddies from the club. And of course, Glenda and Lillian sat in the second row next to her parents. Glenda made a show of dabbing her eyes with a white handkerchief.

Claire noticed that a number of the tobacco buyers had made the trip. Even some of Gordon's former customers from as far away as Yanceyville came to pay their respects. After all, hadn't the bank helped grow their businesses when they needed capital? There were also a few members of the local press, although Randy Grant, who had been given a tongue lashing by Gordon—which he deserved— was not among them.

It was not lost on Claire that many of the attendees had barely spoken to Gordon in the last two years and had not bothered to visit him in the final months of his life. She guessed they showed up today to demonstrate their place and position in the community. Despite everything that had happened, the Talmadge name still carried weight in Hobbsfield.

Reaching the first pew, Claire took her seat followed by David, Mary Grace, Junior, and Olivia. The organist played a Bach prelude that she had requested, and when the last note was struck, the minister took the podium, looking down directly over the open casket of Gordon Talmadge.

"Our scripture reading comes from Psalm 130, the Song of Ascent: If you, Lord, Kept a record of sins, Lord, who could stand? But with you there is forgiveness, so that we can, with reverence, serve you . . ."

Claire tried to focus on the minister's words, but her eyes kept returning to the heavy mahogany casket and the lifeless body inside. She had picked out Gordon's linen suit and his favorite red tie, and he wore the cufflinks she gave him three years ago for his fiftieth birthday. Before he was buried, she planned to remove them and save them for little Billy as a treasure once belonging to his grandfather.

Despite her sorrow, she was grateful Gordon was finally at peace. Their marriage had faced its share of challenges, but watching him fight a relentless disease until he could no longer take another breath seemed an especially cruel way for it all to end.

Claire was startled to realize the minister had finished and her son was walking up to take his place at the pulpit. She forced herself to concentrate. She was relieved David had agreed to speak at the service. The two had had their differences through the years, but the way Gordon had eventually welcomed Mary Grace into the family and doted on Billy had shown David that his father had a tender side after all.

David cleared his throat. "For those who may not know me, I am Gordon Talmadge's younger son, David. I didn't follow in my father's footsteps; I chose the field of education in which to make my mark on the world. Perhaps some of you have students in my English and history classes at Jefferson High School. On the first day, I always tell them, "Those who do not know their history are doomed to repeat it." David looked out onto the crowd with a commanding stare.

"We have a lot to learn from the history of the Talmadge family, who came to this country during the potato famine in Ireland. My great-grandfather extracted resin from the loblolly pines and then amassed property on which he grew bright leaf tobacco; and then my grandfather opened Farmers and Merchants Bank, which my father proudly ran for more than twenty-five years before a confluence of events wrenched the farm and the bank out of his control. It was his downfall. I truly believe that his illness was at least in part related to these cataclysmic events. I marveled at my father's courage as he fought the disease that ultimately took him." David took a long breath before speaking again.

"Although he wasn't a perfect man, Gordon Talmadge was a devoted husband, a loving father, and an over-the-moon grandfather to my son, Billy." David looked at Mary Grace and tears came to his eyes. "Junior, I'm sorry he won't get a chance to meet his second grandchild, who will be arriving in a few months.

"He was one of the luckiest men in the world to have met and married my mother, Claire, who stood by him through the years with grace and kindness. Her devoted care during his illness was an inspiration to us all.

"There's a quote by Daniel Webster that has always reminded me of my father, who thought a field full of tobacco leaves was the most beautiful site in the world. 'Let us not forget that the cultivation of the earth is the most important labor of man. When tillage begins, other arts will follow. The farmers, therefore, are the founders of civilization.' I think it would please my dad to be considered one of the 'founders of civilization.'" The congregation murmured their agreement.

"Rest in peace, my dear father. May the earth cradle and comfort you."

EPILOGUE

November 1970

The opening of the Hobbsfield Business Park marked the end of one era and the beginning of another. Claire endured the traffic passing the house as long as she could. When the Arboretum—a planned cul de sac community—was completed, her parents helped her buy a three-bedroom clapboard on Dogwood Lane. She left behind whatever pieces of furniture wouldn't fit in her new home.

The Talmadge mansion was designated to become the conference center of the business park, and Claire was asked to design the rooms for their new purposes. She hired a muralist to paint an exact rendering of Talmadge Farm to grace the dining room, which would now serve as both a conference room and a space for banquets. The old dining table still held pride of place, but she took down the crystal chandelier and installed more modern, recessed lighting that would show off the mural to its best advantage. She turned Gordon's office into a comfortable lounge and card room—painted a dark green—with copper-clad cocktail tables and a large bar stocked with a variety of excellent wines and hard liquor. She often thought how much Gordon would have loved it.

The upstairs bedrooms were stripped of wallpaper and rugs, and in their place, Claire put down wood floors and painted each room a soothing beige that would appeal to the guests. As a nod to the history of the farm, every room had a plaque bearing the name of a member of the Talmadge family: The Gordon Room; the Stephen Room; the Proctor Room; and so forth.

The house's exterior also received a makeover. Claire removed the two black-faced jockeys that flanked the front door and installed dwarf English boxwoods in their place. All the windows were given navy and white shades to cut down on the sun coming into the house, which would only fade the new fabrics Claire had picked out. And just as she was about to finish the commission, the Board asked her to install a swimming pool next to the dogwood grove and design a pool house and bar that would serve as a destination for parties and meetings in warmer months.

The entire project became Claire's calling card and gave her a satisfying outlet for her artistic and horticultural talents while keeping her mind off her grief. She called her business Dogwood Lane Interior Design, turning one of her bedrooms into a studio with racks of fabric samples, drawers filled with wood planks for flooring, and an armoire brimming with knickknacks for sale. She had a busy clientele even before she had an opportunity to print business cards or register her new venture at the courthouse. In a few months, she'd need to hire an assistant to help her with the mounting paperwork that her business generated.

Passing the other houses on Dogwood Lane, Claire waved to her neighbor, Pansy Dunlop, who was sweeping leaves from her front porch. Claire had recently installed a pair of curtains for Pansy that complemented the house's light blue façade—what the builder called Biarritz blue. She wondered whose job it was to come up with these names.

Traffic into the center of Hobbsfield was moving at a snail's pace. The traffic light that had been installed seemed to make things worse rather than better. So much for "progress," she thought.

She noticed that a few of the lawns on the houses she passed still had "David Talmadge for County Commissioner" signs displayed. Two weeks ago, David had been elected in a landslide. Claire wasn't sure how her son was going to manage his duties as a commissioner while still teaching full-time, but she was proud of him for wanting to serve his community. Hobbsfield needed smart people to lead the town into the next decade. He couldn't have done it without Mary Grace at his side. Her practical nature, combined with David's idealism, made them quite the winning pair. Plus, Claire had gotten to spend extra time with Billy and baby Charlotte during the campaign season.

As for Junior and Olivia, they were living in Greensboro. When they visited during holiday time, Claire's second bedroom was theirs, and Claire had installed a crib for their daughter, whom Olivia insisted on naming Tempest. Her daughter-in-law was full of surprises, but she provided a steady hand that had turned Junior into a family man and kept him out of trouble.

After a turn around the square, Claire finally found a parking spot. When she walked into the clerk's office, Ella was at her usual post, looking as much like a fashion model as ever.

"Have you got a minute, Ella?" Claire asked.

"For you, Miss Claire? Always."

"I need to file papers for my little business."

Ella laughed. "From what I hear, it's not so little." She gathered some forms and handed them to Claire. "Here's what you'll need to fill out."

Claire frowned. The forms were more extensive than she'd anticipated.

"Why don't you take them home with you and bring them back next time you're in town?" Ella suggested.

Claire looked relieved. "Thanks. As much as I love decorating, paperwork is not my strong suit. You should see my desk. I can barely keep up with it all. I've got to find an assistant."

Ella looked at Claire and then lowered her voice. "You know, I might be interested in helping you out. I'm pregnant with my second child—due in March—and I think it's about time I had a more flexible schedule. Pauline won't start school until next fall, and she's a sweet terror. I'm not sure Mama can handle her and a newborn."

Claire considered this. "I can't think of anyone I'd rather have helping me. And you could work part-time and bring the baby with you. Why don't I figure out what I can pay you and if it's satisfactory, we have a deal."

The two women didn't want to make a fuss, but they both thought this might just be the best arrangement they could possibly imagine.

"I'll be calling you soon, Ella."

"Have a nice day, Miss Claire."

"Don't you think it's time you dropped the 'Miss?'"

"I do, Miss Claire. But old habits die hard."

After a visit to the pharmacy to say hello to her father, Claire ducked into Hudson Belk. She'd received her annual invitation to the Barfields' Christmas party last week. But instead of calling Patsy to offer her usual excuse as to why she couldn't make it, she decided that this year she'd attend. She needed to go to Raleigh anyway; she was on a quest to find the perfect corner cabinet for a client.

Claire looked back through the racks of dresses one last time before taking the three she'd chosen to the fitting room. She remembered the red crepe de chine she'd worn to the Barfields' party all those years ago. She could still picture the look in Arthur Evans's eyes when they'd said goodnight. That had been quite an evening.

She slipped the black satin over her head and studied her reflection. She quickly pulled it off again. It reminded her too much of the dress she'd worn to Gordon's funeral.

The burgundy was a little tight around her hips. She must have gained some weight since she'd given up smoking.

She shimmied into the dark green silk and pulled it down into place. Looking in the mirror, she noticed how the nipped waist showed off her curves and the neckline would work nicely with her pearls. Yes, this was the one.

As she took the dress off and carefully placed it on the hanger, she made a mental note to schedule a hair appointment before the party. And to look for a new lipstick. After all, you never knew who you might bump into at the buffet table.

ACKNOWLEDGMENTS

A big thank you to Loren Stephens of Write Wisdom, and to JJ. Holshouser. Your words brought to life the story I've been thinking about for many years. Your creative genius and tireless dedication made my novel a reality. Thanks also to Josh Stephens of Write Wisdom, who organized us and served as a sharp editorial eye. Shannon Roberts gave us valuable tips to get us across the finish line.

Thank you to early readers Jewel Warlick, Harriett Richie, Reese Harvey, Gene Hoots, Joey Jones, Wingate Lassiter and Ella Ann Holding, who offered valuable feedback and encouragement. The sensitivity editors at moukies editing offered thoughtful comments and guidance.

A special note of appreciation to my publishing team at Story Merchant, in particular Ken Atchity, Sam Skelton, Charlotte Drummond and Amit Dey. And to Kevin Spark for designing a cover that perfectly captures the atmosphere of Talmadge Farm and the treasured landscape of eastern North Carolina.

I'd also like to thank Marissa DeCuir and her publicity team at Books Forward. I'm so fortunate to have you in my corner.

To Dana Riley and Kelly Daughtry, my daughters, thank you for your unwavering encouragement. I hope this book serves as a testament to the strength of family bonds.

To my wife, Helen, you are the love of my life and my best friend. You and my daughters were honest readers when this writer went off the rails.

And to Katherine, Christopher and Hannah, the stars that make my life full. I am immensely proud of you.

TO MY READERS

You're the reason for the effort that went into these pages; if you enjoyed *Talmadge Farm*, it will all have been worth it. Book reviews are often overlooked, but they are critical to helping authors gain visibility. Your feedback is important to me. Please take a moment to write an honest review on the e-tailer site of your choice.

—Leo Daughtry

Printed in the USA
CPSIA information can be obtained
at www.ICGtesting.com
LVHW041032081124
796075LV00008B/122